Will You Wait For Me?

BOOK THREE

The Courtship of Lizzie Andrews

Published by PJ Watters Books LLC
ISBN: 978-0-9908644-4-8

Book design by Barbara Ries with cover design by Teri Mathis
Cover design watercolor by Michaela Slattery
Cover image of woman source Victorian Picture Library

Image credits:

The Astor Hotel IMAGE ID 805 249 NYPL DIGITAL COLLECTION

The Metropolitan Hotel IMAGE ID 1659134 NYPL DIGITAL COLECTION

Niblo's IMAGE ID 11616 NYPL DIGITAL COLLECTION

State prison at Sing Sing, New York, 1855

Mother Carey and her chickens by J. G. Keulemans, 1877

"The San Francisco Floundering at Sea" The wreck of the steamship "San Francisco": disabled on her voyage from New York to San Francisco [California], Dec[ember] 24th, 1853 and in a sinking condition. c1854, UC Berkeley, Bancroft Library, Collection: Honeyman (Robert B., Jr.) - Collection of Early Californian and Western American Pictorial Material

The San Francisco life-saving medal WORTHOPEDIA

Rockwood Estate on the Hudson River - An exhaustive effort was made to locate the rights holder for the photograph of Edwin Bartlett's residence (Rockwood Estate) and to clear reprint permission. If the required acknowledgments have been omitted, or any right overlooked, it is unintentional and understanding is requested. The image of Rockwood was found in Gervase Wheeler, A British Architect in America 1847-1860, Tribert and O'Gorman, Wesleyan University Press, Middletown, Connecticut 2012

Map rendered by Elisabeth Johnson based on historic resources.

All other illustrations were procured from Victorian Picture Library

Will You Wait For Me?

The Courtship of Lizzie Andrews

PJ Watters

with Elisabeth Johnson

Prologue — iii

I. Preparing to Ship Out

Chapter 1: Wenham — 3

Chapter 2: Dear Little Gipsy — 11

Chapter 3: Hamilton Hall Soiree — 27

Chapter 4: Four Pets — 33

Chapter 5: Keep Our Hearts Within Our Breasts — 47

Chapter 6: Writing the Whole Time — 51

Chapter 7: The Last Thanksgiving — 59

Chapter 8: Visiting Sing Sing Prison — 65

Chapter 9: Edwin Bartlett — 73

Chapter 10: On Board the Steamer — 81

II. Waiting in New York

Chapter 11: Relieved of My Overcoat — 89

Chapter 12: Daguerreotype — 107

Chapter 13: Captain Watkins — 115

Chapter 14: Ring on My Finger — 123

Chapter 15: By Excuse of Umbrella — 131

Chapter 16: Steamer's Delay — 135

Chapter 17: Worthy of Your Respect — 141

Chapter 18: A Most Beautiful Reverie — 149

Chapter 19: Tarrytown — 155

Chapter 20: A Sister's Love — 161

Chapter 21: A Very Dear Friend to Leave Behind — 165

Chapter 22: With the Help of God — 175

Chapter 23: My Own Darling, May God Bless You 187

III. Weathering Changes

Chapter 24: Ships at Sea 195

Chapter 25: Startling Marine Disasters 197

Chapter 26: Conduct of the Government 203

Chapter 27: Description of the Steamer as She Appeared
   on Christmas 207

Chapter 28: Vessels Ordered to Sea 213

Chapter 29: 100 Soldiers Swept Overboard by a Single Wave 215

Chapter 30: Statement of Lieutenant Winder Aboard
   The Three Bells at Sea 217

Chapter 31: Fate of *The San Francisco* - News from the Wreck 223

Chapter 32: Statement by One of the Passengers 229

   Interesting Statement of a Passenger 241

   Statement of Colonel William Gates 243

Chapter 33: Obituaries - Messages of Consolation - Tributes 245

Chapter 34: Ever After 249

Epilogue 257

Appendices

Who's Who in the Courtship of Lizzie Andrews 259

Family Relationship Charts

  Andrews 335

  Sprague 337

  Bartlett 339

  Tenney 341

List of Illustrations

Family Relationship Charts

How Edward J. Tenney and Lizzie Andrews are Related   viii

Daguerreotypes

Edward Jarvis Tenney   1

Lizzie Andrews   10

Lizzie Oliver   258

Colonel Samuel Cook-Oliver   260

Illustrations

Map of New England states and railroads in 1853   2

Dancers in a large hall   29

Rockwood Estate on the Hudson River   45

Interior of Niblo's Opera House, New York City   57

Postal workers in a travelling sorting office on train   63

Astor House   85

The Metropolitan Hotel   105

State prison at Sing Sing, New York, 1855   113

Mother Carey and her chickens by J. G. Keulemans, 1877   121

Lizzie reading Edward's letter   129

Aunt Laur comforting Lizzie   147

Lizzie teaching at Miss Ward's   153

Waiting at the seashore   159

Laura and Lizzie singing Christmas carols   185

The San Francisco Floundering at Sea   191

The San Francisco life-saving medal   254

Prologue

"**S**o, you are to become Mrs. Edward Jarvis Tenney," my Aunt Eliza declares as she presses my cheeks with congratulatory kisses, as if I have won a prize.

Indeed, I have. I have won my dear Ned's heart and he has mine. I will become Mary Elizabeth Andrews Tenney, but not until my betrothed returns from his journey to Valparaiso, Chile. He will sail around the cape of South America, though sailing the entire way may not be necessary for his ship is steam powered. Thank God he will not be at the mercy of the winds. This certainly settles my heart, as Edward is not a rugged sailor. Sailing is not a subject he studied at Harvard, and I fear his scholarly lessons may not be to his great advantage on the open sea. Oh dear, I believe I am worrying about nothing! Father says I am a master of worry. At least I have something mastered, I tell him.

Edward will be away for two or possibly three years. He is 20 years old now, so when he returns to me in Salem, he will be 22 or 23 and we will be ever so much closer to an appropriate age for marriage. By that time, I will have reached the ripe old age of 20, or possibly even 21. He has asked me to wait for him. Oh dear, however am I to be so patient?

My Ned was just sixteen when he wrote me for the first time from Harvard in 1850. Now, four years later, I could be waiting another three years. Well, I fancy I would wait a decade for our future together, as husband and wife, with a gaggle of little ones. Edward reminds me that "The patient waiter is no loser." He has written me 39 letters as, of this day, and promises to continue writing every possible moment that we are apart.

How *Edward J. Tenney* & *Lizzie Andrews* are related

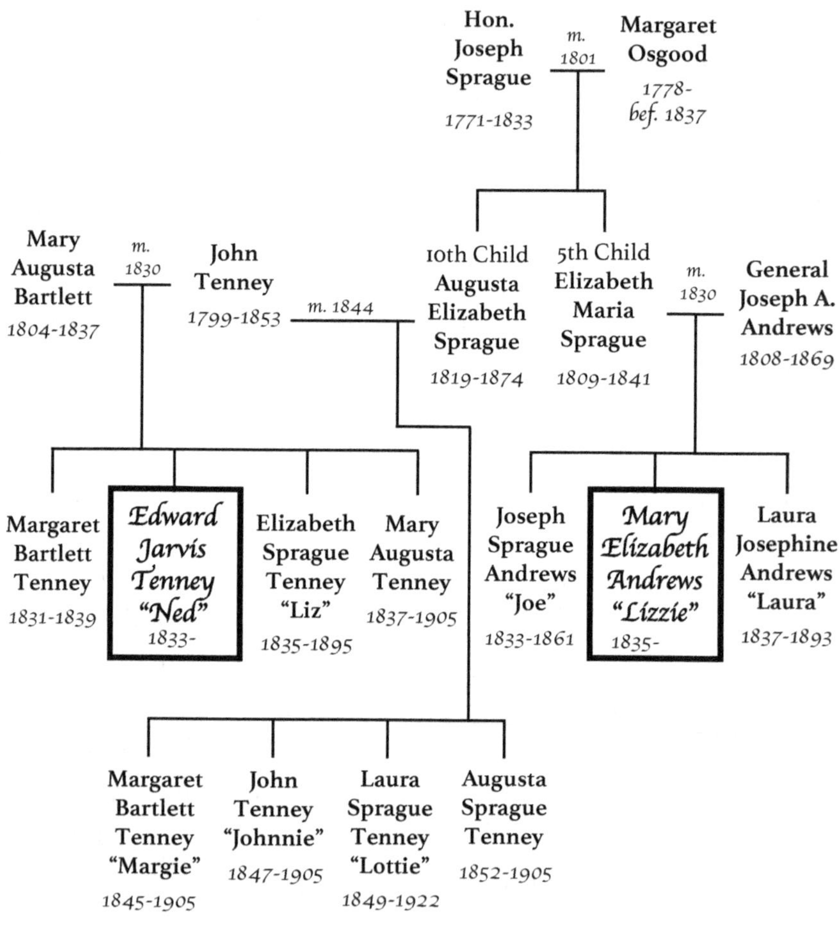

I. Preparing to Ship Out

Edward Jarvis Tenney is exploring his options for his future with the astute guidance of his uncle Edwin Bartlett, as well as other accomplished gentlemen who have filled the role for his late father. One intriguing option requires leaving Lizzie and going to sea. Edward is aware of the dangers an ocean journey can entail.

Edward Jarvis Tenney 1851

Vermont
Weathersfield
New Hampshire
Maine
Portsmouth
Methuen
Lowell
Salem
Boston
Massachusetts
Massachusetts
Hudson River
Connecticut River
Connecticut River
Connecticut
Hartford
Rhode Island
New York
Hudson River
Tarrytown
New York
N
S
Massachusetts and Nearby States
With Major Rail Roads of 1853

CHAPTER 1

Wenham

Miss M. E. Andrews
Care Gen. Andrews
Salem
Mass.
Miss Andrews
at Miss Ward's School
Salem
Mass.

Wednesday, 2d Nov. 1853

Dear L.

I am going to dine with my sister Liz at Lynn today and in the afternoon will ride out to Wenham and pass the night, if convenient to you.

I shall probably take the train which leaves Boston at 4 P.M. but possibly earlier -
G.B.
E.

Edward's curt note assures me to climb aboard the two o'clock train to Wenham so as to arrive at just past three. As we pull into the station, I clutch his note, the ink barely dry, thinking how miraculous the mail delivery is that allows one to post a letter at dawn and be assured of its arrival miles away within mere hours.

I prepare to disembark when I spot a familiar white hat in the distance on the platform. Could Edward have arrived earlier than anticipated? My bulky parcel at my side is filled with millinery pieces I plan to deliver to Mrs. Horton, one of my father's customers. I move toward the white hat, which is beginning to surface from a sea of black. I am swept along with waves of passengers. Someone is pulling me swiftly along, buffering me from the bumping and pushing of so many rushing to exit the depot. I recognize this 'someone' as Edward, my Ned, when he pulls me charmingly close to his side and says, "Come, my darling Lizzie. My beautiful and elegant cousin." He grabs my parcel and we move together from the station as he chatters on.

"Aunt Dolly is my favorite," he says, as he tucks my bag under his arm.

My father's sister, Dolly, is a milliner well-known for designing fashionable ladies' hats. Her hats are considered a "favorite" among her customers, so it is no surprise to hear she is one of Edward's favorite….favorite what, I wonder. Favorite Aunt? Favorite hatmaker? Perhaps he recognizes that I am wearing a hat she has designed and his greeting is a compliment.

"Thank you," I say, "I think." His quizzical look tells me I am mistaken.

Just outside the station, clear of the crowds, Ned places his hands on my shoulders and guides me to have a seat on a bench. Placing my parcel at his side, he presses his own self closely next to my skirts.

"There," he says and takes a deep breath. "I want to look at you, Lizzie. I want to flood my eyes with your likeness until my head is full." A woman approaches us and stops in front of us, but turns away as if she is looking for someone.

Edward falls silent, and then ventures into conversation fitting for public consumption.

"What have you brought for Mrs. Horton?" he asks, placing the bag on my lap.

"Mrs. Horton is my favorite," I say, acknowledging her as the reason for our meeting. I open my parcel and begin to nervously display its contents, knowing the show is a diversion we must continue until the stranger in front of us departs.

"What do you think of this veil for a hat?" I ask and hold it in front of my face. Edward places a hand on each of mine and I think he is going to plant a kiss on my face, just now, in public, in front of the stranger, or at least behind her back. He looks past me to assure the woman overhearing is turned away. He caressed the veil across my face. I drop my hands to my lap but he continues to hold the veil gently against my cheeks with his palms. His face comes within inches of mine and his breath is warm and sweet as he pretends to examine the veil. I drop my eyes and dig into my parcel, producing a miniature hat sample.

"Aunt Dolly said this would be perfect for a doll," I explain nervously, holding the doll hat in front of my own hat, as if Edward has an interest in dolls. Certainly he does have such an interest—any interest of Mrs. Horton's is now suddenly an authentic interest of Edward's. He says nothing, but continues to gaze at the veil pressed against my face.

"Aunt Dolly no longer uses this, so she provided it for our project," I continue, realizing he is not hearing a word.

A man approaches the woman bystander, remarks about finding someone to fetch their luggage and they hurry off, paying us no attention.

Ned leans forward, still seeming to examine the veil, and whispers closely in my ear, "You look like a gypsy, my Pet."

"A gypsy?" I implore a bit too loudly. "I only see one gypsy on this bench." I rise abruptly and proceed to walk away. Edward scrambles to replace the items in my parcel and is swiftly at my side, laughing.

"You cannot escape my affections as easily as that!" he scolds me and presents the crook of his arm to escort me.

"Thank God," I respond and thread my hand through the opening, which he quickly presses close to his side. "You are a goose, my dear Ned, an absolute goose!" I whisper.

We meander toward the Clafton-Horton House on Main Street languishing in each other's company. Knowing it would be unfashionable to arrive early, we pause to look at shoes in the shop windows. I prod Edward to describe for me what he might select for his fiancé and he describes an utterly absurd high-heeled, high-buttoned boots with brocade inlays. "Brocade inlays?" I question. "Why yes, and embroidered laces," he says with a pompous air of confidence.

"Embroidered laces?" My cheeks are beginning to hurt from smiling as we enjoy our silly conversation.

Coming to a small patch of garden between two shops, I ask "May we rest a moment?"

The bench is small, much to our liking for we must sit close and tight against each other. I lean toward Ned and find my head resting comfortably against his shoulder, wishing we could linger here unseen and unheard. Such is not to be as the clomping of heels along the wooden sidewalks foretells the arrival of shoppers.

We continue toward Mrs. Horton's, arranging plans for our next rendezvous—Edward will arrive in Salem by train on Saturday in time to meet Nellie Abbot, my companion for tea. I am to act surprised, as if this were an accidental meeting, and then casually invite my cousin Edward to join us.

"Shall I say, 'oh my, what a surprise, my beloved secret fiancé has miraculously arrived at this very moment! I do hope he is available to join us for a cup of tea.'?"

"Now, Lizzie," Edward scolds. "You know I am thinking only of your reputation, my darling. We must avert any scandal that could arise. You know many are easily tempted to gossip. Now, can you act as if you did not expect me?"

"Can I act? Of course I can. I am a supreme actress, for I just now convinced you that I might be fool enough to expose our tryst."

"You are a naughty gypsy, my pet, but you are my own and I would like to take you in my arms this very moment and taste a bite of that salty lie that just left your tongue." He says this in a low, matter-of-fact tone so passersby cannot ascertain the spicy words his own mouth has emitted.

"Ned! You are making it very difficult for me to maintain the very reputation you so promise to protect." A stern-looking woman of 40 years or so walks toward us escorted by a young man who I assume to be her son. He tips his hat and she lowers her eyes as they approach. Edward responds with a cordial smile that does not reveal the mischief that lurks inside him.

Once they are past us, he lays out our plans, conversing with complete disregard for my plight to fend off his enticement. "After tea, we will take the late afternoon car to Methuen for a visit with the family. We can arrive by evening, stay for the Sabbath and return to Salem after church in the morning. Hopefully, the day will be fit for a carriage ride—just the two of us."

We arrive at the door of our Wenham hostess and are greeted by Mrs. Horton herself. Her servant places a tray on the table and scurries to reach us at the door, but Mrs. Horton brushes her away with a flip of her hand saying, "Sally, I have this, thank you just the same. And, please slow down, my dear."

"Yes, Mrs. Horton," Sally complies, though she does not seem to slow a bit as she departs.

"The dear can be a bit like a bull in a china shop, poor darling. She means well but is simply too eager to do everything at top speed." Mrs. Horton begins her monologue and we soon learn all about her household, her hobbies, her challenges finding just the right satins to hold the shape of a dressing table skirt and the quest for the perfect silks to drape softly on a miniature scale for a small porcelain doll. She could not have guessed that Edward knows nothing and cares even less about such quandaries, for he is as charming as a dandy visiting a tailor shop for a new waistcoat. Mrs. Horton tells Edward he certainly is a good talker and assures him his Harvard education is sure to send him far and wide, to which he responds, "High ho! Indeed, it will for I am to ship offshore before you know."

Our time together flies by and too soon we depart to be, once again, consumed by the daily tasks of homemaking, grooming, dressing, reading and tending to the needs of others. All the while, I look forward to a visit over tea with my classmate Nellie Abbott, for that will be the next time I expect to see my Ned. Oh, how I await the clever plans Edward and I have made for this upcoming visit. I am eager to hear what Nellie thinks of my dear, dear cousin for I have told her nothing of our true fondness for each other. Surely, she will speak in a most candid manner. Until then, a week must pass, and patience will once again be my great challenge and constant companion.

———⚭———

I sit down at my writing desk, a bit too late on Friday to write Edward, my light too soon faded. Reaching a long stick into the fireplace, I bring its flaming tip carefully to my candle wick and light what is left of my candle. Returning the stick to the fire, I let my fingers linger by the flames for a moment to feel the warmth. The November days are short and cold. I can feel the chill of the wooden chair seeping through my skirts. My fingers feel stiff and awkward gripping the pen. Even my pen seems reluctant to drink the ink swiftly enough to fill the nib before my thoughts wander off. By the time I touch the nib to my page, my mind has wandered off so terribly that the words flowing from my pen are no longer suitable for the sentence in which I was hoping to profess my love. So, I begin by apologizing for my lapse in writing. My words dance around my feelings, reluctant to expose how much I long for the sight, the touch, the smell of my dear Ned. I want to hear his voice, to feel my own laughter well up in me without restraint or resistance prompted by his oft ridiculous antics. Dare I admit, my imagination allows me to almost feel the warmth of his hand caressing my waist?

Wiping my pen clean, as if I might wipe clean my disreputable thoughts, I cork my ink bottle and push aside my page with its lonely incomplete phrase. Surely, the page and I both needed to compose our thoughts. I carry my candle downstairs to join my family for the evening by the fire. I will continue my letter by daylight and prepare a long missive to send Monday morning, hoping to receive one from my Ned that same day.

Indeed, Edward's next letter arrives Monday.

Each time we meet in person, we fill ourselves with pieces of each other we cannot possibly transmit through words on a simple flat sheet—words that are vulnerable to fall into the wrong hands, words that become eternal as the ink stains the page. As much as I long for his words, my heart throbs louder when he is near. I hope my excitability does not show, for such emotionality would certainly precipitate my revealing more than would be fitting to share, even with my own Ned! I am nearly beyond myself already with his provocations!

M. Lizzie Andrews.
of all the fair, the fairest.

CHAPTER 2

Dear Little Gipsy

Miss M. Lizzie Andrews
Salem
Mass.
Per E. J. Tenney

Methuen, [Friday] 4th Novr. 1853

My dear little gipsy,

Now don't be awful provoked because I called you "gipsy." I only meant dear little darling pet. It seems so funny to think I am writing to you, when I shall carry my letter myself and perhaps be looking over your shoulder while you read it. What can I say? News I musn't tell till I see you, and as for "talking good" I don't feel a bit like it. "High-ho." If you were only here by my side, resting on my shoulder. I don't think I should find much trouble in saying something. What a funny world this is, isn't it?

"Now, Ned, you are a provoking fellow: why don't you write as you always do?" Why darling, I can't. I want you here with me. But think, dearest, if anything should happen, by which I could not bring this letter myself. Supposing there should be some accident. I ought not to write thus, Lizzie, I know. But at that moment the thought occurred to me "here am I writing as if it were certain I should see my pet tomorrow: yet who can tell what may happen?" And I have sometimes thought too how dreadful it would be if on my voyage to Valparaiso, nothing should be known for a long time of the fate of the steamers' passengers. Those we had left behind, wavering between hopes of safety and fear of death, it must be horrible to them. I ought not to talk so and raise in your mind such needless fears, but it often makes me feel very sad when I think of parting from you.

If it were not best that a distance so great should separate us, how happy we should both feel. I wish that I were well established in business and a little older; then our engagement might be public and I should take so much pride in having you go with me to Jullien's, the Germanians' the opera etc. &c.

But patience, patience. I hope some time to be a little more worthy of you than I now am, and the thought that I have something here to strive for will be so pleasant when I am far away from you. This is almost the last letter I shall write to you from my first home. As the time for my departure draws nigh, I long to add a few days to the limit for the steamer's sailing; although I have thought I should feel a great relief when some definite time were fixed. I have only one week left and I am so selfish that I want to spend every moment of it with you. Don't you wish I could?

I hope it will be pleasant and warm Saturday afternoon, for I want to drive you out. Shall we go to church half a day on Sunday?

Won't Nellie Abbot laugh when she sees me jump out of the car on Saturday? Won't you? And be real glad? In a very short time I shall see you.

Good bye-

Goosie Ned

———⊶⊷———

That appointed Saturday, I awake with a start, hearing the clock chime and believing I hear one more strike than is needed for the hour. Bridget lit the fire in my chamber without a peep before I awoke and the warmth is as welcomed as the light of this short winter's day. Edward has most certainly risen long ago and Nellie Abbot is likely still wiping a long night's slumber from her eyes, for I know her to be more a city girl than one to rise with the rooster.

There is no time to write before breaking my fast so I rally to the table just as others are settling in. The warmth of porridge on a frosty morning is comforting. Following a bevy of wishes for a good morning, our breakfast table is unusually quiet. Father seems to have much on his mind. Laura seems to have nothing on hers—she follows the servants with her eyes, studies the wallpaper and glances only sideways at Father and Joe. Our brother Joe seems transfixed with piling his oats as high as possible against the side of his bowl.

Everyone is well aware that Joe leaves tomorrow for London on *The Josephine*. He has been home from McLean Hospital for the Insane for a full 10 months now. During the year and a half he was in the asylum he was isolated from family, so we would not interfere with his treatment for melancholy. Such distance from family would easily have been the cause of melancholy if it were me! However, for Joe, the treatment seems to have helped. His presence at home is much improved. He is eager to rise in the morning and has not had a single angry outburst. At times, he is even able to relax with family; however, I still find myself walking on tip toe around him lest I step wrong on a floorboard and let loose a creak that might set him off. One never knows what to expect from him. Some days he seems to be everywhere and it is nearly impossible to avoid disturbing him. Other days, he disappears and emerges as the most affectionate, remorseful sort one could imagine. And it can change by the moment from kind and affable to harsh and critical—though usually the worst of it is directed at his own self. That is Joe's world, and the world of all who live with him. Some days, I am not sure anyone can do right by him; his thoughts can be so dark that shining a light seems to bring him more pain. So, we learn to tread carefully and steer clear of his looming shadows.

The morning meal ends with more wishes for a pleasant day and brief disclosures of each other's engagements. I think Joe does not want the women in the family to see him off for fear that, should we shed a tear, he too might cry. So, Father and Uncle Daniel will accompany him to the ship in the morrow. As for today, no one plans to venture out until near tea time so we part only briefly to fulfill our duties and plan to reunite four hours later for dinner.

I excuse myself to complete my handiwork, raising no suspicion that my handiwork is to fashion a ring from a lock of my hair, sheared from a spot just above the nape of my neck. The morning affords me time to complete the intricate work, carefully following a pattern I ordered from Godey's Lady's Book. The instructions insist the hair be dampened to form a manageable thread. I carefully weave six long strands of hair through and around two other thin locks into a perfect ring. Of course, I intertwine several shorter strands from my dear Ned's head. Then, I circle my hairs several more times like a net until I capture all the wayward curls. Thus, the ring becomes as wide as my smallest finger is thick.

I tuck the finished piece into a silk handkerchief embroidered with the letters EJT with the letter T quite large in the center and E and J diminished on either side. I simultaneously prepare another handkerchief with MEA in a similar style, which I can display should anyone care to call on me to examine my stitchery.

With the few locks of hair remaining, I fashion a simple, less intricate ring for my brother. I do not think the ring is something he will necessarily appreciate but I offer it as a gesture of kindness and good fortune. As I work, Edward's warning echoes through me 'how dreadful it would be if on his voyage, nothing should be known of the fate of the steamers' passengers.' Such a fate could face my brother as well. As I tuck the final loose strands into the ring, I repeat a simple prayer, as if I might weave it into the pattern, 'Please God, surround my brother with kindness and understanding. Protect him from any harm. And, please protect everyone around him from his own impertinence, for he truly means no harm.'

Just before dinner, I hand Joe the ring.

"For your journey," I tell him. "It carries my prayer that my love will keep you safe," I say quietly.

"Thank you, Lizzie," is all he says, but I can tell he likes it.

Just as we are completing dinner, Father attempts to engage his only son in conversation; however, today, Joe does not wish to converse. That matters not to Father who turns to Laura and me with queries of our studies. I speak most readily about the popular American literature to which I am being introduced at school in Hamilton and the intrigue still being caused, even three years after its publication, by the book Uncle Tom's Cabin.

"Are young ladies much interested in the social issues and political sciences?" Father asks. He watches me for my response with the same intensity he once watched me respond to a woman orator. I had never seen a lady speaking in public before that time. I was fascinated with her and what she had to say. Her topic was abolitionism, but she also commented on the fact that women have no right to vote, no right to own property. She claimed that their— 'their'? Well, I should say 'our'—our plight is not too different from that of the slave. Shocking! Women have no more rights than slaves? I was appalled, and honestly did not believe it, but since that time I have not viewed my role in the same manner, so was eager to engage Father in dialog.

I stumbled to begin my response to his question. "The girls… ladies…women with whom I study speak boldly about our concerns that women have no right to vote. Not only are we interested in so- cial issues as an intellectual topic, but also as a political anomaly." Laura teases me when I use words that are not familiar to her, but Father seems to delight in banter of this type. "Father, we learned that Massachusetts was the first colony to authorize legal ways someone could own a slave, but that was nearly 200 years ago! Women and Negroes did not make this law.

He nodded and said, "True, my dear, the law does not recognize women or slaves as voting citizens. So, tell me what you have learned about slavery in Massachusetts since that time?"

I paused to recollect my facts, and offered what I could recall, "I think slavery grew in Massachusetts for a hundred years but most slaves who came into a Massachusetts port were moved to other states, mostly southern states."

"That is true," Father confirmed. "in the mid-1700s, in Boston, ten percent of the population was free blacks. At that time, over two percent or more than 4000 of the colony's population were slaves."

"That is shocking, Father. There are no slaves in Massachusetts today, are there?"

"No. Legal actions in 1780 ruled that all men in our Commonwealth are born free and equal and entitled to liberty. That makes Massachusetts attractive to slaves who escape slavery in the south. Today, the black population in Salem is just over sixty persons in a population of nearly 5000. That does not mean this injustice has been resolved, however. The Fugitive Slave Act of 1850 has angered abolitionists in our state because black men can be arrested and questioned for simply walking in public. With such small numbers and no vote, their situation is difficult here, but still better than many other states."

"What about women? Who has the right to vote?

"When our laws say 'men' they are thought to refer to all people, but you are right that there are no laws specifically prohibiting or guaranteeing rights and freedom for either free blacks or women.

I dare say the reactions to this topic seem to be as varied as the girls in my school. Some never express an opinion and others base their responses on their interpretation of the word 'people' in the Constitution of the United States. Are slaves and women not people, Father?"

I had to ask.

"Yes, Father, aren't slaves and girls people?" Laura echoes.

"Indeed they—you—are.'

"Father, when we see that a 'right' is missing, why then do we not simply add an amendment to the Bill of Rights? Do not the legislative branches of government have the authority to add amendments?" This seemed to be a simple oversight and surely once realized, could be easily corrected.

"Not only does the legislature have the authority, but I dare say they have the responsibility." Father says, raising one eyebrow at me. "Lizzie, since free black men and women do not have the right to vote, there are few in the legislature representing the issues faced by them, by you."

"Why don't you represent these issues, Father?" At that, he laughs. "Well, I am not currently in a position with any legislative authority. Edward's father, as an attorney and state legislator, was well-suited to do something like that, and likely would have, had his life not ended too soon. Beginning as a Commissioner of Essex County, he became a Representative and then served as Senator in the Massachusetts State legislature. He did not run for Congress, however. Perhaps he would have if he had lived longer. As for me, that work requires specific education and quite a commitment of time. I believe I am better suited for business and, as a widower, it is important for me to have time with my family. My service to my community and country comes through my involvement with the Massachusetts Volunteer Infantry." He pauses, and challenges me, "You seem to have interest, Lizzie. Why don't you pursue work in politics?"

"Oh no, not me. Politics is not a matter to which I hold any particular interest," I look away to demonstrate my disinterest and explain, "I simply find it important to be knowledgeable about matters that affect the society into which I plan to rear my children." With this, Laura begins to giggle.

"Your children, Lizzie?" he asks in jest, glancing slyly at Laura.

"I will have children someday, in the future, I am sure," I speak with exaggerated confidence, such as I have seen postured by women orators. I dare admit Father's interest and amusement is fueling my fire and I continue.

"However, I do not expect to apply the fruits of my scholarly labors exclusively to the rearing of my own children. I intend to influence many more than I could possibly bear myself."

"You do?" said Laura, looking confused. I nod confidently.

"You do!?" Father seems surprised at my declaration.

"She does," whispered Laura after completely missing the rhetorical tone of Father's question.

"Why yes," how might I continue now? I wonder, only briefly. "Children whose mothers are working in factories do not have anyone to truly tend to their education. You know many of those children could be duly inclined toward academic pursuits, if only given a chance."

"If only given a chance," Father says. I think he mocks me now.

"Do you not think we should hold our expectations high so as to challenge their intellectual curiosity and encourage their ability to achieve beyond what their parents have accomplished?" I challenge him directly.

"Ah, but I do. Indeed I do," he replies in earnest.

"I do too, Father," Laura adds meekly, too obviously seeking approval.

Joe has been listening silently but now speaks under his breath, "Lizzie, you are such a smart-aleck," Joe blurts. Laura falls into a fit of nervous laughter with an occasional unladylike snort. Joe gives her a disapproving look and asks, "May I be excused?" He pushes his chair away from the table causing the chair legs to scrape noisily against the floor. He stands, waiting for Father's response.

"Yes, you may as well." Father never seems ruffled by Joe, whereas I struggle to know how to respond to my brother. I must remind myself not to take his attack personally. He means no harm.

Father says, "'Tis a shame you cannot study at the Latin School."

"He did study there!" Laura offers.

"I was not referring to Joe."

"Oh," piped Laura.

Believing my work here was done, I beg for my dismissal, feigning the inappropriateness of being the subject of a conversation in which I am referenced in the third person while my person is very much present. I depart, leaving Laura to continue conversing, or at least listening to Father. I do not get far, however, before I think I hear mention of Edward's name and stop to savor the exchange.

"Laura, Oliver Carlton may not be averse to extending admission to girls to attend the Latin School at Salem, if society would only bear it. Do you know who Oliver Carlton is?"

"No, Father."

"He was married to Edward's aunt, Louisa Amelia Bartlett." Father explains, and continues, "Louisa bore five children in less than ten years, and sadly childbirth took her life."

"Did the children become orphans?" Laura asked.

"No. Mr. Carlton married again and had a son with his third wife. That son was lost at sea a few years ago."

I must have gasped at the suggestion of being lost at sea because Laura leaned back and peered out the door inquiringly. Spotting me, I shushed her. Father had not heard me. He has reprimanded me before for listening in without proclaiming my presence, but surely he would not mind, I rationalized, since Laura had been in the room just a moment ago. Laura nodded and returned to the table. Father continued.

"I fear we will lose the best of such teaching when Mr. Carlton retires," Father says. "Beyond his excellent mastery of the classics, his students enter college as well prepared as those from the best schools. But what is far better than the academic preparation, they go forth into the world with a high sense of honor that clearly distinguishes them as scholars."

"Does Joe have a high sense of honor, Father?" Laura asked.

"That is an excellent question, Laura. Joe has challenges that interfered with him completing his education at the Latin School, but I think he formed good, solid values about human rights. Mr. Oliver's values, or at least his political convictions, led him to often say 'Christians should think more and say less,' perhaps speaking less of that in which they differ and more often—and more highly—of those things in which they are agreed," Father paused as if to savor this thought.

Father's valet appeared in the doorway, "Your carriage is ready, General."

Father's mind never seemed to stop. He followed James and as the door closed behind them, Laura and I looked at each other curiously.

"Laura, I have never heard you speak with Father about matters of society."

"I wish I could speak with him like you do, Lizzie. Where did you learn to speak like a man? Will you teach me how to do that?"

"Well, you are the silliest girl of all! Come on, I'll show you my handiwork before I meet my friend Nellie for tea."

———◦✕◦———

The conversation over tea is strikingly different from the stimulating discourse in the dining room. Nellie Abbott arrives for tea at three o'clock and I am glad for the early start to our visit, as Edward will not need to endure our talking about beaus who we might allow to escort us dancing on Tuesday evening.

My dear cousin Ned arrives right on schedule at half past three. Imagine listening to the one you love speaking of dancing with someone else! Edward knows we must not expose our secret engagement, so he endures a bit of frivolous conversation.

Nellie repeatedly gazes at Edward, her head tipped modestly downward but her eyes raised to see his face. Oh, I cannot blame her! His is a most handsome face. My eyes are also drawn in his direction. Edward listens respectfully, nodding on occasion and allows us our teatime travails. Though her conversation is to me, Nellie seems all the while to speak in Edward's direction. I decide I must demand her attention.

"Have you seen the divine manner in which Charlie Peirson dances? He stands so tall and erect and holds his dance partner so secure, yet his frame allows one great freedom to move easily by his lead. Do you not think him handsome?" Success is mine as she turns toward me with a most curious expression, yet she does not say a word.

"Have you not had occasion to dance with him, Nellie?" I ask innocently, for truly I do not know, but I sense I have sparked something in her.

"He has not once signed my dance card!" she says with dismay.

"I am sure he would if you were to cozy up to him just a bit more, Nellie." Edward suggests to her, eager to find a way into the conversation.

"Edward, she is a lady, not a gad-about. Now you stop that!" I shake my finger at him.

I doubt Nellie realizes the many levels of conversation at play. It is delightfully stimulating, albeit an unusual sort of discourse for two ladies and a gentleman over tea.

We finish our tea and bid Nellie good-bye. Her carriage arrives to pick her up just a few minutes before Father returns. Those moments allow me time to run upstairs and fetch my scissors, for Edward said I may cut a lock or two of his hair to make myself a ring. He sits very still as if I might slip and cut too much or harm him with my tiny little shears. My task is quickly accomplished without any permanent damage and we are off in the carriage to spend the evening and Sabbath with his family. I am somewhat surprised that Father allows us to take the carriage knowing we will have it over-night. That he trusts Edward with his horse, his carriage and eldest daughter speaks volumes of his respect for my secret fiancé.

The spirits are lively at the Tenney home. Even after the young children are tucked in bed, the rest of the family seems eager to continue to play games on our own. Thus begins a somewhat rau-cous round of charades. Edward has always excelled at dramatic feats such as this; and, for once, I feel as if I might hold my own, much to his delight. Aunt Augusta says we certainly have devel-oped an understanding of each other, almost as if we have our own unspoken language. If she only knew how often we speak through our letters.

Aunt Augusta retires first, followed shortly by Liz and Mary. Everyone seems to expect Edward and I to talk late into the night. I welcome the chance to be alone with him, just the two of us. I curl up by his side, while he picks up a book of poetry by Alexander Smith and begins reciting. He cannot resist interrupting his own reading to comment on this, that or the other. It matters not what he says or reads. I am content to be close to him, listening, soothed by the resonance of his voice.

"Shall we read the Bible before we go to bed, Lizzie?" He opens randomly to Proverbs Chapter 22 and reads, "A good name is to be more desired than riches." That is as far as he gets before beginning his heartfelt commentary.

"A good name is all I am seeking, my darling, not riches, only a good name, one in which you can be proud, Mrs. Mary Elizabeth Andrews Tenney! Mrs. Lizzie Tenney, the most beloved wife of any man." I reach to kiss his cheek and he surprises me by turning his face toward mine fully covering my lips with his, which forces me to open my mouth and fully receive his kiss. Of course, I never intended we should enter such a deep kiss, or to embrace as we do, though that is such a natural position for such a kiss. He pulls me very close and I think I could live forever in his arms, his hands reach all the way around my waist and he pulls me toward him, nearly lifting me from my seat. "This way I can whisper and you will be able to hear the verses," he explains.

He opens the Bible randomly to Luke 1 and reads, "And after three days Elizabeth his wife became pregnant; and she kept herself in seclusion for five months…"

Surprising himself, he interrupts the reading and beseeches me, "Oh, my darling, you must not seclude yourself from society with my child."

"Edward, I must not be pregnant with your child, for I am not yet your wife," I retort.

He laughs heartily at that. "Not yet, my darling, not yet," he says with a twinkle in his eye. "Not yet my wife, and not yet pregnant with my child."

"Let me make a selection," I quickly divert his imaginings, and my own. With eyes closed, I open to Jeremiah 51 paragraph 42.

"I shan't read this," says Edward, suddenly serious. "Choose again."

"What is it?" I ask. He places the Bible across my skirts and I lift it to read, "'The sea has come up over Babylon. She has been engulfed with its tumultuous waves...' I shall not read it either," I close the Great Book, but it is of no use for we speak somberly of death at sea, of Willie Carlton's brother, of a fate that could await my own brother. The thought of Edward venturing into something so dangerous is not a topic I want to discuss, but it hangs in the air like a dark storm cloud.

"No more reading." I suggest, "Let us simply talk." But, that proves to be just as challenging. Each time he begins to muse over 'what might happen if,' I turn the conversation to our love, our future, our home where we will live, our children. What will they be like? Will we have a boy who follows Edward's path through the Latin School to Harvard?

Mention of the Latin School leads to mention of Mr. Carlton and too soon comes full circle to the subject of Willie Carlton's brother going to sea and never returning. I am grateful to know of so many, many sailors, employed by my father, whose families wait patiently and welcome their loved ones' return time and again. I recall witnessing a seaman's return to the anticipation of a newborn child one Christmas. Each tender moment on shore is a celebration of love. I know we can create such a life for each other. I ask Edward to pray with me and we join hands with that happy vision between us.

"I am going to kiss you each time you do that!" Edward proclaims.

"Do what?" I ask. He kisses me.

"Each time I say black and you say white." He kisses me again.

"But I did not say 'white.'" He kisses me.

"Yes, you did." He kisses me.

"I said, 'do what?'" He kisses me.

"Each time you turn my black thoughts of being lost at sea to white thoughts of your love, I will kiss you."

"Oh." He kisses me again. "Oh, my." I say, and laugh as he seals my mouth with another kiss.

"This is easy." He kisses me. "I must fill you with kisses to last a lifetime," he says.

At that, I feel the tears well in my eyes, and I say, "Kisses to last two years, three at the most. I cannot bear to be away from you any longer than that." He kisses me.

"Two years," he says and kisses me. "Three years," he says and kisses me. "And a lifetime!" He kisses me once more and holds me as I am completely overcome with my tears. Try as I might, the thought of loss was spoken. We must continue to believe we can and will be the exception to all the loss we see around us.

In the morning, I am hardly ready for the vigorous greeting of small bodies flinging themselves on my bed while I remain deep in my slumber. Yet who can chastise such vibrant faces as Johnnie's,

Maggie's and Lottie's? Maggie even runs to fetch baby Augusta to give me sloppy kisses. I am not sure if it is Liz or Edward who puts them up to this antic, but it matters not. I welcome the tender rocking of their little hands and the wet kisses that cover my face. Johnnie soon declares himself my boyfriend and thus begins his clinging to me through the whole Sabbath, until it is time for Edward to drive me back to Salem.

Throughout the drive back to Salem, I am eager to present Edward with my gifts, but I decide to wait until my departure, knowing I will need something to sweeten the bitter moment of our parting. We arrive at Chestnut Street and James takes over driving for Edward to take him to the train station.

When the time comes for us to say good-bye, James stands down by our horse while I speak to my Ned, "Close your eyes, my noble Ned." I take his hand, turning his palm up, then over again and I slip the ring, braided from my own hair, onto his finger. "Now a part of me will always be touching you."

James presence limits the good-bye to a simple cousinly kiss on each cheek. Edward climbs out of the carriage. I wave.

"I will see you soon," he calls out to me. "Will you write to me?"

"Of course, I will write." I respond. "I will see you soon." And I will wait for you, I think to myself.

Monday, I have time to craft only one page before the train leaves with the mail to Methuen. I want to be certain my letter arrives on Wednesday to greet my Ned upon his return. Too soon we will be separated, making each of our contacts as precious as possible. To be so loved is so much more than I ever imagined.

Tuesday Charlie Peirson will escort me dancing at Hamilton Hall. We generally have a truly enjoyable time and I agree he may call on me again. I do not find good reason to say no without raising suspicion, but I am very careful to protect him from any misunderstanding of my interest. My interest is in dancing only, still I am careful to guard my betrothed heart.

The New York Times
January 16, 1854
Interesting Statement of a Passenger

...At 12 o'clock on December 24, the engine stopped and the vessel was left to the mercy of the waves. During the whole of that night, such of the cabin passengers as could be gathered together, assembled in the lower cabin, where with Mr. Cooper, an Episcopal clergyman, they united in prayer to God for their preservation from the impending danger. The sea ran high all night and great fears were entertained that the vessel would be unable to hold together much longer...

...At about 8 o'clock in the morning on December 25, the ship was struck amidships by a violent sea carrying the entire saloon, the paddle-boxes and smoke-stacks overboard, which caused the hurricane deck to break in half and fall upon the cabin floor. When the sea struck the vessel, it precipitated itself into the lower cabin, where passengers were still engaged in prayer, and instantly there were three feet of water in that part of the vessel. The horror of the moment cannot be described...

CHAPTER 3

Hamilton Hall Soiree

Genl. Joseph Andrews
Salem
Mass.
Miss M. E. Andrews,

Methuen, [Thursday] 10th Nov. 1853

Dear pet.

This is the first opportunity I have had of writing to you today, though it is now half past ten; for in the morning I went to Boston, dined at Chelsea and on reaching home tonight found Aunt & Willie Carlton here. Every one has now retired and I am pretty sure of passing an hour quietly with you. Willie and I are to chum for tonight; therefore I took occasion to go to my room a few moments before he went up (can you guess what for?) and bid somebody "good night." Aunt Carlton occasionally makes a very gentle allusion to you, but she always does it in that quiet way, which pleases rather than disturbs me. I showed her your slippers & watch-case. You can't imagine how happy that gift of your hair has made me. I try it on every day, though I dare not wear it about the house.

I have shown it only to Liz, for I thought Mother might let it escape her lips when talking with Aunts Mary or Laur, and I knew Mary would tell it everywhere. I can't think of anything I should have prized higher; and then it was so unexpected. I had often wished that I could have your hair in some form, but when I spoke of it, you had told me there was not enough to do anything with, so I had entirely given up the idea till I saw this "sweet pretty" ring. I am very much afraid that if I wear it upon extraordinary occasions it will break or that some accident will happen to it. But I ought not to talk so much of one thing. I am very very much obliged to you, my precious darling.

Did you go to the Hamilton Soiree Tuesday evening, and enjoy yourself? Did you dance? Who escorted you home? "Ah! You jealous Ned, I shan't tell you."

When I came home last Tuesday, Mary gave me a silver-fruit knife and Liz a gold tooth-pick. On Thursday I went to Bradford Haverhill; I did not see my cousin Caroline Longley; for she was in bed during my stay. Today I have been in Boston and Chelsea; tomorrow I shall probably go to Lawrence & Andover with Willie Carlton and on Saturday I am to dine at Mr. Storrow's in Lawrence. So you see "there is no place like home."

I have not yet heard from Uncle Edwin, but when I do I will write you about the Steamer's sailing. You may expect a letter at any time after Monday morning. I will try and send it so that it will reach Salem in the Lawrence mail about nine A.M. (perhaps 9½)

Major Stearns asked Liz if you were going to New York with me. He said that was the common report. Don't you wish we could go on to N. York together? If we could, I reckon I should not be very anxious to postpone my departure very long. Of course it is foolish to imagine such a thing, but think how pleasant it would be. You could see the Steamer & my room and then we could go about together to the opera etc. etc. But I can only see you once more.

I bought today a large quantity of thin letter paper to write on my voyage and during my exile. I do not mean that you shall lack news from me when I am so far away, and I shall expect such a long journal from you. It seems very sad now, my darling, to think of our parting so soon, but I can only see you once more and then farewell for I know not how long. We will love each other absent or present just as well however.

I have thought it would be very pleasant to have some appointed time each day when we would think of each other and so hold converse together. We will talk of that next week. Be sure and put your letter in the Post-Office early Monday morning; that is, when you usually do.

Good night, dear Lizzie,
Ned.

Willie C. thought I was coming up soon, and said he should be awake.

Dancers in a large hall

Edward's letter arrived Saturday. My thoughts linger on five painful words that burn in my heart—the words "only see you once more."

That just cannot be. I must reprimand Edward for that statement. He must say to me "once more before I go or once more until I return."

The trains are so fast at delivering mail that I wonder why they do not run passenger trains more often from Methuen. If they did, we could catch a car any time we wished.

Oh, that we could rendezvous in New York! If only I were older, and could control such things, I would go now and marry Edward secretly. I would give him all my love and never refuse him a moment of time together, never deny myself a minute of his love. I am in the deepest anguish for I know this can be neither as I desire; nor as he wishes.

I must stop acting as if I were a foolish school girl and have faith that the time will pass quickly and uneventfully. Patience is the true test of character and I pray mine will be rewarded by years of happiness. I try to convince myself of that which I want so fervently.

I read and re-read Edward's letters; then begin composing my response, point by point, as this seems the only way to keep my desperate fears from taking hold. If I write on Saturday and continue on Sunday, I can succeed in producing a nice long letter in preparation for our final visit. I will fill the pages with encouragement for Edward to indulge in his good-byes to everyone so as to alleviate any regrets while he is at sea.

Glancing at my hands, I notice that my fingernails have grown quite long. I pause to trim them with the very same scissors I used to cut my hair for Edward's ring. From my thumb I cut a perfect crescent moon and fold it into one corner of the letter in hopes that it might be one more piece of me that brings a smile across Edward's face. I describe my silly romanticism in the letter I will post on Monday, just before I board the train to Hamilton.

This is the last week before our Thanksgiving holiday. Edward could surprise me with a visit any day. If he does not, I will revert to hoping for another letter to greet me at home upon the week's end.

Indeed, a letter from my Ned has arrived on Saturday. I was not disappointed, especially as I read his news.

The New York Times
January 16, 1854
Interesting Statement of a Passenger

...Families had been gathered together, clinging to each other. Fathers, mothers, brothers and sisters – from the gray-haired veterans of the Army, to the child which nestled at the mother's breast – all were seen groping their way through the water to the upper deck. Several, in the excitement of the moment sprang overboard, and many of the first who reached the deck were under the impression that the steamer was floundering, and that it would be useless to go below again. I was of the number who entertained this opinion.

We remained many hours upon the deck, the sea washing over us at every lurch of the vessel, and the cold northwest wind chilling us to the heart. I never experienced such intense cold. It had been truly said by one of the oldest sailors on board, who had braved many a storm, and had saved many a life under perilous circumstances, that persons had never met so untimely a grave in such a glorious conflict of the elements; for while the sea was running – to use a cant phrase, but a true one – "mountains high," the sky was clear as on a Summer's day, and the sun was shining as brightly as I ever remember to have seen it...

CHAPTER 4

Four Pets

Miss M. E. Andrews
Care of Gen. Joseph Andrews
Salem
Mass.

Methuen, [Thursday] 17th Nov. /53

Dear Lizzie,

You didn't think my pet was forgotten, did you? When I left you in Salem, I expected that before this time I should have to say 'Good-bye' for so long a time; and I was to write to you when I could pass the last hours at Hamilton.

I have been waiting all the week for some decided news from New York, but I have heard nothing. Only last Saturday, Uncle Edwin wrote "The San Francisco will probably not sail for 8 or 10 days;" I will write again the exact day. I suppose we may sail next week, tho' perhaps not till after Thanksgiving. I wanted to pass this next Sunday with you, but I hardly dare to. If I stay more than one week longer, won't it do for me to spend Sunday the 27th in Salem? Still, if I leave home before Thanksgiving, which is possible, you may receive a letter the first of the week; but be sure and write to me on Sunday just such a letter as the last one, won't you, petta mia? I wish we could correspond daily for the little time I have to stay. If there was any way by which my letters would be sure to reach you safely, that is unbeknown to any one else, I would write every day. I wish the post-office might be changed and I, instead of you, have the exposure on my side. For in Methuen no one but the Postmaster knows when I receive a letter. I am going to send this through the Lawrence office. It will reach Salem about 9½ Friday morning.

I wrote to Martha Bird last Monday, and I felt so much gooder for it, that I immediately wrote to Coz. Mary Tenney, to whom I have not written before for a year. This morning I received a letter from Martha B. She forgives everything but thinks I ought not to go to South America: there is no chance for me to be good there. I am going to call there on my way to New York.

Haven't you some friends in Hartford you can visit during Thanksgiving week? Why can't you go and see Carrie Pollard? Perhaps by some curious coincidence, we might go in the same train. Mrs. Carlton said to me last Friday in the cars, "of course I don't believe any of the stories about you in Salem; o-f c-o-u-r-s-e n-o-t." Then she laughed so funny, but finally said, "no matter, it is no one's business but your own." Mrs. C. is very good about this, I think. Willie C. staid with me to go to Mr. Phillips' in the evening, where we had a very pleasant time, though there was a dreadful scarcity of young gentlemen. Mr. Briggs was there.

On Saturday I was to dine at Mr. Storrow's in Lawrence, so I made parting calls at Mrs. Cabot's, close by, and at Mrs. Perry's (Anne P's mother). Tonight I am to take tea at Mr. Abial Steven's, in Lawrence. I have been to Mr. Smith's in Andover (Harriet Sprague preached) and to Dr. Longley's (Caroline was in bed, so I didn't see her, but left a farewell with her mother).

I dined at Aunt Mary's in Chelsea. Saw Aunt Laur & Caddie F. who occasionally made me laugh by alluding to my frequent visits to Salem. Mrs. Sargent of Chelsea appears to know what is going on, too. Isn't it funny?

I suppose news has been received from Joe. I saw *The Jose-phine*'s arrival at Liverpool. I do hope Joe will prove a real good brother for you, my darling, while I am gone; and afterwards too, of course, but particularly then.

I wanted to go to Boston this week and see your father after the English Steamer's arrival, but I could not leave home. I may go tomorrow or Saturday. It seems too bad for me to wait so long here at home and yet see so little of you. I am expecting in every mail to find decisive news from New York. I now hope I can stay more than a week longer, so as to pass one Sunday more with you.

I look at your hair every day. I have four pets now, viz. one in Salem, two in square cases and one in a little white box with red cotton. You won't be jealous? It would be real cunning if you could send me a little note every day and a real long letter on Mondays, wouldn't it? You have a vacation next week—can't you attend the Germania Rehearsal on Wednesday afternoon? Do, please, dearest—I have had you in my pocket all the time I was writing. Don't tell any one.

Good bye Little gipsy-
Ned.

———⟨∞⟩———

I received Edward's letter yesterday morning, as he knew I would, and devoured it in the privacy of my bedroom. I must man-age to see him again. Somehow! But how?

Father has just returned from Boston to inform me he had a visit from Edward Tenney this morning. He said his whole name, as if there could possibly be any other Edward on my mind!

"We had a most enjoyable conversation," he concludes with a smile and says no more. I dare not press him for information, as I do not wish to raise any suspicions, from him or Aunt Eliza, whose eyes dart between mine and Father's as if she were engaged in listening to a good story and some salacious action is about to occur. The warmth of redness begins to creep up my throat as Aunt Eliza peers at me. Just keep breathing, Lizzie, I tell myself. This too will pass. Father says no more, and I do not ask, so the contents of his conversation with Edward remain a mystery. I suspect Edward may have spoken about his intentions upon his return from his journey.

Monday morning, I ride with Father to town; he will meet with an important customer, Mrs. Brownell, and I will post a letter. I hurry into the post office to speak with the Postmaster while Father waits with the carriage. Upon my return from the post office, we pull away and approach Mrs. Brownell's only to hear someone calling my name. The voice comes from the direction of the train depot. It sounds like Edward. Am I now imagining him everywhere?

"Did you hear that, Father?" I ask suspiciously, as I peer out the carriage door. Searching about furiously, Edward truly does appear, running toward the carriage. "General Andrews!" "Lizzie." His shouts are propelled by great urgency. James hears his cries and pulls the carriage to a stop.

"I came to say good-bye in person and to wish you a pleasant Thanksgiving. I am so happy to find you here." He pants as he opens the door and reaches his hand toward me, as if to fetch me from the carriage, right in front of Father! Oh, shocking!

"Good morning, General!" He is not the least bit intimidated, as some might be, by such a powerful man as my father.

After peering in the carriage to assure all greetings are complete, Ned reaches in and lifts me down. Once I am safely on my feet, Edward steps back to compose himself and speaks to both me and my father, saying "I am expecting to meet my train to Boston in less than an hour. I arrived early hoping to run to your house and bid you a proper good-bye, but here you are! I am a fortunate man, indeed." His excitement is palpable.

"I fear there will not be time to see you again before I leave," he exclaims.

"When does your ship leave?" I ask.

"The exact date is not yet determined, but I do not expect to see you again before I go," he says emphasizing the last three words.

"Will you not be home for even a moment at Thanksgiving?" I ask.

"I am to spend Thanksgiving in Tarrytown at Rockwood and possibly go from there to board the ship and depart," he says in an unsettled way.I offer an unnecessary temptation, "I plan to visit Methuen for Thanksgiving and stay through Monday morning before returning to Hamilton."

Edward's face turns pale. "I cannot see you there as I am committed to be with Uncle Edwin and his family, at least until I know the exact day I ship out."

We speak quickly, knowing Father is waiting patiently for me to climb back into the carriage. "How can I send a letter to you at your Uncle Edwin's?" I ask. Edward pulls a calling card from his pocket with Edwin Bartlett's address in Tarrytown, New York and hands it to me, pressing my hand and the card between both of his.

"Have you time to join us for a short while?" I inquire. "Father must see Mrs. Brownell, but we can sit in the carriage." I peer longingly at Father for his approval. With Father's assenting nod, Ned lifts me back into the carriage and squeezes in after me.

We arrive at Mrs. Brownell's and Father exits the carriage while James sets the wheel brake and ties the horse to the fence railing. There is no snow on the ground yet this winter but the temperature is dropping and carries a damp chill. James crosses the street where he can walk about yet keep an eye on the horse. My Ned and I are alone.

Inside the hooded carriage, Edward tells me of his visit to Father on Saturday. "I made it known that I had indeed asked you to marry me and that you had consented."

"You did what? Oh my. Edward!"

"I spoke with your father about marrying you, at a future date, of course, and I beseeched him to keep our secret from all others, including family, until my return so as to not tarnish your reputation in any way. I have told no one else besides my own step mother. Your father assured me he would not say a word. Lizzie, he went so far as to express his confidence that neither of us would defy our families' honor. Then, he shook my hand. And, then…he embraced me!" Edward explained. "I felt he knew I was looking to him as I would to a father. Indeed, I did at that moment think of him as a father to me, as I can no longer confide in my own father, except through prayer," Edward drops his eyes and I could feel his loss. He was so close with his father.

"Your father would be so proud of you, if he could see you today, Edward. I think my father is proud of you, too. I think he loves you as a son already."

"I hope so," he said. "But let us not waste another moment thinking of our imminent departure. Rather let us enjoy this time we have together."

After a brief silence, we fill the air with senseless murmurings about this, that and nothing in particular before falling silent again. Snuggling under the heavy wool blanket, absorbing its warmth and our closeness, Edward sinks down in the narrow carriage seat and pulls me toward him pressing his soft lips on mine, over and over. We breathe the same air and our hearts seem to beat as one. I pledge to remember every detail of this moment, the cool crisp air, Edward's warm touch upon my shoulder, my waist, my skirt, and the rhythm of his breathing so close to my own. No matter how far away he is from me and how long we are parted, I will never forget this vivid moment.

Too soon, James is upon the carriage, clearing his throat a bit too loudly as he approaches. It makes us laugh and my pure joy causes me to giggle incessantly, emitting a little snort like Laura does, which causes us both to laugh even more. I can no longer contain such utter happiness.

"Master Tenney, I believe that train, just arriving yonder, may be for you," James said as he points across the square. At that very moment Father approaches our carriage from Mrs. Brownell's house.

It all seems so abrupt and rude to me, but Edward reacts swiftly while maintaining his composure.

"Lizzie, it is best for you to bid me good-bye now." Edward kisses me quickly and climbs out of our carriage to whispers of 'good-bye, my pet.' He leans into the carriage window for one last brush of kisses on my cheeks, the kind I might give my own father. He runs toward the awaiting train as Father climbs aboard and calls out, "Godspeed, my son." The ring of it was music to my ears. Father called Edward 'my son.'

"I will write," he calls.

"I will write, also," I echo. "I will wait for you." I say aloud, but softly.

James unties our horse and, as we pull away, I cannot contain my tears. They pour forth the moment we clear the depot. Father puts his arm around my shoulder and pulls me to lean into him. He does not say a word.

———◦∞◦———

Arriving home, I want to do nothing but write the rest of the day, feeling soothed one moment by my thoughts of loving Ned and tortured the next by my fears of how we might change after being away from each other for so long. I plan to post a letter to him this afternoon so it will arrive on Wednesday. A letter only—it will have no hair, no fingernails, nothing more than a kiss on the page and all my love. I am uncertain I should share all my love, as we both struggle so much already to do the right thing. We long to be strong for each other. Yet, I must not hesitate to let him know the very depths of my love for him.

My musings are interrupted when Ruth Foster—now Mrs. Edwin O. Tufts—comes to Chestnut Street for a visit. Her brother-in-law George escorts her. He helps her off with her coat as she introduces us, "George is my husband's younger brother," she emphasizes younger. "He is much younger than my husband… and two years

39

older than Edward," she whispers discreetly to me as I take her hat and muff.

"Ruth has told me so much about you, Lizzie," George says and makes a slight bow. I do not think to offer my hand. "She says you are a scholar, as well as a design expert," he says.

"I would not call myself a design expert at all, but I do have my opinions about fashion!"

"I hear you work for your father in his business," he persists.

"I would not say I work for him," I try to diffuse any illusions he may have about me, as well as diffuse his attention, "although I have, on occasion, had the good fortune of assisting him in selecting silks to sell."

"He imports silk from the Far East?" he states in such a manner as to leave me unsure about whether he was stating a fact or asking a question. Despite my uncertainty, I respond 'Yes' to confirm. My response seems to end the conversation by its abruptness. Truth be told, I want to converse with my friend Ruth alone. I want to converse about how she fares in her marriage. I want to converse about things that are not appropriate for George's ears. He has very skillfully interjected himself into our visit and I am resigned to the change in my visit with Ruth. Oh, George appears pleasant enough, and he is a guest in my home.

I look up, realizing my manners have gone completely awry, for he has been a proper gentleman and has not said anything untoward. I realize, as if for the first time, that he is not unattractive in any way. Not at all. He has a straight modest nose and his teeth are remarkably straight and even. His jaw is strong and his eyes appear to sparkle due to their light blue color. But, unknown to Ruth, I am now an engaged woman and as such I am simply not interested. Not at all interested.

Ruth saves the conversation with a somewhat benign description of her final trousseau, which is a delightful continuation from the point at which she and I last departed.

I do not wish to encourage George in any manner, however, or mislead him to believe I have any interest in him, so I barely pay attention as he speaks, tuning all my focus to Ruth. George seems not to mind. In fact, he seems not to notice my disinterest and chats on comfortably about whatever crosses his mind. He speaks of completing his education and beginning his career in Boston having obtained a good position as a dry goods clerk. He shares his plans to advance his career in his field, so perhaps, I conjecture, his interest is more in silks and Father's business than in me personally. Upon later reflection, I realized he may have been trying very hard to impress me.

Upon their departure, I returned to my writing. I write Edward about Ruth and George visiting, again not so much because of any interest in George, but truly as a way to communicate to Edward the strength of my feelings for him.

I am home from school for the week and will remain on Chestnut Street two more days to prepare for Thanksgiving, only to miss the Thanksgiving festivities in the Andrews home. Following the death of Senator Tenney, it is my duty this year to join the Tenneys in Methuen to help care for the youngest Tenney children; yet I am doomed to miss my dear Ned. Of course, I will enjoy the visit with my cousins Liz and Mary.

Until I leave, my time is filled with helping Bridget with preparations for an exquisite Thanksgiving feast. There will be six at table with Father, Grandmother, Aunts Eliza and Dolly, Uncle Daniel and Laura. Laura leaves Monday to board in Hamilton and continue her studies over the winter. Both Joe and I will be away, this being the first year I have not been present with my family at Thanksgiving. It is the second year away for Joe, but he is in a much more favorable situation this year compared to last. By Thanksgiving, he will be nearly three weeks at sea on *The Josephine* and undoubtedly thankful to be well employed. Though clever beyond most people's imagination, he never cared for scholarly pursuits and his work as a seaman appears to suit him appreciably better. I pray daily for his safety.

———◇✕◇———

Soon all is prepared and positioned for a Thanksgiving feast. The mincemeat pie and pumpkin pies are ready to bake. The spices and breads to be stuffed into the bird are set out as if to say, 'we are ready when you are.' Tomorrow begins a full day of cooking, and eating, so this evening, I escape the kitchen to remain in my chamber and read my Ned's letter again.

I toss my clothing carelessly into my travel bag, taking care only with my ample letter-writing supplies. I finish my day with a prayer for one last visit with my Ned, just in case anyone is listening, and sit down at my writing desk to craft one last letter before my departure.

My missive cannot help but expose my joy, as I am filled with so much happiness I can almost taste my future with Edward. Someday I will hold him close to my heart. Someday I will bear his children. Someday Edward will be the most attentive, kind father one could ever want. He will look at his son and his daughter and beam with pride. Dare I share such sentiments with my dear Ned? The answer needs no reply and little consideration. It is done as my pen dances across the page.

My letter folded, I seal it with extra wax so it might travel safely and securely to New York. After pressing the stamp with my initial 'E' into the hot gooey mass, I hold the letter to my face and kiss my 'E' one last time, nearly burning my lips. I grab for a washing cloth, splash cool water from my dressing table pitcher onto it and quickly sooth my throbbing lip. Oh dear me. I really must be more careful; I reprimand myself. What good is all my praying for Edward's safety if I am to destroy myself with careless romantic enthusiasm?

The next morning, letter in hand, very discreetly in hand, I bid good-bye to my family, offer the servants my best wishes for a wonderful Thanksgiving, thankful no one notices my red lip, and depart with James by carriage to catch the train to Lawrence and onward to Methuen. James is kind enough to take my confidential letter to be posted. He is a trusted and obedient servant. As I head to Methuen knowing my Ned will be nowhere near, I think, 'What a great pity!' I turn my face heavenward, not to reprimand God, but as if His merciful intervention could make Edward miraculously appear.

⸺⸺◦✕◦⸺⸺

The next day in Methuen, a letter arrives from Edward to his family. After his mother reads it to his siblings, Liz and I take the treasure to his room. I sit at his writing desk and read it again, this time aloud to Liz. I sit with all Edward's belongings surrounding me as Liz lounges on his bed with a book. She begs me to repeat selected excerpts to her. I add a few pet terms he calls me, substituting his love for his family with references to my person alone. Liz shares stories of her brother as a child, some I had never heard. She says he has always been eager to please and win the favor of his father and Augusta, but he was alternately a rascal and a caretaker for his siblings. He would play schoolmaster to Liz and Mary and insist that Liz act out so he could pretend to be a stern disciplinarian, but they would end up laughing. Being here, it brings me much joy to speak so freely of him as no one would question a cousin's love when our two families are so close. Although I am dutifully attentive to the children, I have the leisure to write and relax and I cherish every moment.

Before I head home on Sunday, I join the family for church. I am certain Ned is thinking of me as I sit in his family's pew. I feel he is with me every moment.

⸺⸺◦✕◦⸺⸺

Upon my return to Salem, I am greeted with a fat envelope containing two letters. As James stables our horse, I meet briefly with Father to let him know I have returned. Then, I join Laura in her room to spend a few minutes helping her pack for Hamilton.

"Have you seen the big letter you received, Lizzie?!" Laura asks excitedly as we fold her day dresses and lay them neatly into her travel valise.

"Yes, I saw it," I respond calmly.

"It is from Edward, is it not?" she persists.

"Yes, it is, Laura. Do you want to bring these hair ribbons?" I ask.

"Yes, those would be lovely," she responds before turning back to her main interest. "Well, what does he say?"

"I do not know, Laura. I have been home but an hour and have not yet read it. I will be sure to let you know if he has a message for you." Her lower lip juts slightly and she returns silently to the task at hand.

Once alone in my chambers, I carefully break the seal on the fat envelope, unfold six sheets of Ned's true love and settle in to read.

Rockwood Estate on the Hudson River

The New York Times
January 16, 1854
Interesting Statement of a Passenger

...One of the most heart-rending sights that I ever witnessed occurred upon the deck. It was that of Dr. Satterlee, a veteran surgeon of the Army, whose hair had grown white in the service, and who, in answer to the orders of his Government, had left his family and home, although verging upon his 60th year, to join the regiment on their way back to California. He was lying on the deck but with his night garment upon him, and perfectly drenched with water. His limbs had been severely bruised in the general crash, and I could not help feeling, even in the imminent hour of danger, that it was improper that the government should allow an officer who had served his country so faithfully and so long to be sent, at his age, to so distant a station. He was, however, carried below; and I am glad to say, is among the number who were rescued...

CHAPTER 5

Keep Our Hearts Within Our Breasts

Miss M. E. Andrews
Rockwood, [Tuesday] 22 Nov. 11 P.M. [1853]

My darling Lizzie,

I could but think it would be pleasant for you to see me part from you full of hope and confident in our future happiness. But I regretted that we had no opportunity to say some parting words that would be so delightful to recollect now that we are parted.

I did leave you, my precious one, in perfect confidence; for I knew that I could leave you in the charge of One whose "watchfulness" would never fail and who would be to you the truest friend you could have. Yet I thought if I could have seen you once more after I departed the carriage I should never have let you go away from me. The closing of the door seemed such a barrier! Then we were separated - God only knows how soon I may again clasp you in my arms and receive such pledges of your love as only the truest love can give. Oh! Lizzie! I ought not to write so. I should try to make you feel as happy as I can, and I will, my darling, I was very happy to think that you were going to Methuen; for I knew you would love to talk with Liz of me, but oh how I wished that I could join you there.

During my ride to Hartford there would often come to my mind you and Liz together this week; and I could see my loved pet weeping for me. But I can talk to no one of you. I can sit and watch your face alone, but I can not have any one to sympathize with who I know loves you. That dear little face seems to be weeping now, as I look at it. Come we will join our tears together. Oh! my dear Lizzie. God grant I may some day be worthy of your truest love. I do love you and the aim of my life shall be to promote your happiness. It is so pleasant for me to think of you now, though when I am alone I can't help crying. But I shed tears, that do my heart good, and every time I look at you, I know that you love me as well as I love you. May God bless you, my precious one.

What if I had gone away uncertain of your love? How much should I have lost! It seems now as if I have not loved you half enough while we have been together. And think, darling, (I love to write that word) darling, when we shall meet again; oh can we then keep our hearts within our breasts? It seems to me now as if I had you in my arms, not to say "Good-bye" (I don't like that word now), but to whisper to "my love" and to feel your head press upon me as if you really were leaning upon Ned, your own Ned.

Your daguerreotype does actually kiss me of its own accord and it seems to say, "I wish I were in your arms Ned." I am thinking of you the whole time. I don't want to enjoy anything else.

During the evening at Hartford I wanted to go to my own room where I should be alone with you and talk with you, without interruption, but I did not leave the family till after one o'clock. In Mother's letter which you can read if you like, I will give an account of how my time has been spent. But, I don't want to write to you anything but to say over and over again how much I love you. I will write every day before I sail and send you a letter enclosed to Mother by Saturday. And will you write to me as often as you can? I expect to sail on Saturday and a letter put in the office by Thursday night would be sure to reach me. Uncle E. I have hardly seen, but about that I will write Mother.

I so love to put my cheek against what seems to be yours, my darling pet. I wish I only had some one who knew you. Then we might talk of you all day long, and perhaps I might be continually finding something new to love in you. It doesn't seem to me, yet that we are surely separated, for something may happen to the steamer that I might go home and spend a few more days with you. I wish something would happen yet I know it would not be for the best. I shall feel differently when I am fairly launched and there is no chance for a return. God bless you tonight, my pet. I read with you every night, and I hope, for your sake that I may be much better than I am.

Good night my own precious darling –
Your own Ned.

If you have to go home before my last letter comes, Mother will send it to you.

———⸺✕⸺———

Turning the page, I find an entirely new letter, written the very next day. I imagine my Ned writing the whole time and not even venturing out to post the letters. I expect the weather is not conducive to spending any time outside in the gardens. He probably would if he were engaged in conversation as he is not one to walk alone anyway, except to get somewhere. He would enjoy a pleasure walk with me despite the cold, I am sure; or a brisk walk with his Uncle Edwin, whom he loves dearly. It is funny how Edward enjoys visiting his uncle's magnificent estate—the local residents call it Rockwood Castle—yet spends so much time alone in his room writing. I am forever grateful he does, however, for I can continue to read the great package he has sent, alone, inside, by the fireplace. Perhaps we are two of a kind.

The New York Times

January 16, 1854
Interesting Statement of a Passenger

...It was a fearful sight to look upon the water immediately after the accident. I saw not less than 100 human beings clinging to spars, doors, and such other fragments as they could obtain for the preservation of their lives, but the next wave sealed their fate, and they were hurried without a moment's notice into eternity.

Then rose from the sea to the sky the wild farewell
Then shrieked the timid, and stood still the brave
Then some leaped overboard with dreadful yell,
   As eager to anticipate their grave;
And the sea yawn'd around her like a hell.

CHAPTER 6

Writing the Whole Time

Miss M. E. Andrews
Care of Gen. Joseph Andrews
Salem
Massachusetts

Wednesday morning 23d. Nov. [Rockwood] [1853]

My dear Lizzie,

I have this morning sent you one letter but I want to be writing the whole time, so we will talk till dinner time, and I can have room to add more tomorrow. I am going to try, my darling, and be as happy as I can while I am in New York, but it seems so bad that while I am delayed from sailing, I must be so near you and yet unable to see you. I do miss you very much.

Every little trifle calls to my mind something connected with you, and strive against it as hard as I can, can't help being sad. This morning I had to cut my nails and all the time I was engaged in this I could see before me my little pet with her scissors. Oh how I wished I could be with you a few moments more, before I leave New York. I would go home again tomorrow, but of course it would not do.

All the way from Boston to Hartford and from Hartford to New York and from New York to Tarrytown I tried to picture you by my side. Whenever I have a moment by myself, it is the same darling that always comes to me so willingly. It would be such a pleasure to have some dear friend here with whom I could talk of my pet, so far away, and who would sympathize with me. Till I come home again (in a short time, I hope) my happiest hours shall be those I pass in thinking of you, and of what you are doing.

Now you are at Lawrence waiting for the Methuen cars and wishing you could find Ned in the depot.

I shuddered this morning as I read an account of a terrible accident which befell "the train of cars which left Boston for New York at 4 P.M. on Monday." So said the paper. But it was on the Fall River line and not the New Haven line. It made me think what would be your feelings, if it should meet your eye, and I thought too, by what a slender thread our meeting again did hang. But we must not think of that. If God sees fit to ordain that we shall not meet again—oh, my precious one it would seem as if all the object of my life would be ended. But we shall meet soon, darling, and our joy will be increased by our separation. How happy will this hope make me feel.

Today, I have been by myself a good deal and walking with Mrs. Bartlett's father. We went to see the men employed in laying out grounds for a garden. While we stood there, how I wished you had been leaning on my arm. We took a walk together. If Lizzie had only been my companion.

I was reading from Alexander Smith's poems, and every line seemed so applicable to me. He introduced the figure of the sun leaving the Eastern sky every morning. Isn't that Ned, said I. Each day he says farewell to his darling in the East, and he journeys toward the West as I do. But he is sure to come back again; he is received so gladly and his beloved's face is made as bright and joyous by his presence as will be my pet's when her sun comes and clasps her in his arms. He is sure to return; and I can see you now so happy and joyful.

We are walking down Essex Street together and you are leaning on my arm, as if you really loved me. I knew she would be engaged to Edward Tenney says everybody.

We are at some party together and my eyes can't help publicly expressing their owner's admiration for you. Everyone says then "He ought to be proud of her," and so he is, my darling, and he will picture to himself while he is away from you, his precious pet as she appears to everyone.

It made me feel very happy on Monday and last Saturday too, to see that your father knew how much we loved each other, and that he was evidently pleased to see it. And when he told me that Laura was going to school, I could but think it would add to your happiness, for it must seem sad to you now to have anyone near you who is likely at any time to say something of your own Ned that would grieve you.

I feel so happy here, my dear pet, writing to you, with no one near me but that little face, that I don't want to leave you again today. Uncle Edwin will probably return from New York this afternoon and I shall know more certainly, about sailing. The Steamer was to make her trial trip yesterday and to sail on Saturday. A Mr. Boyd who is staying here is acquainted with some of the army officers who are to go in her to California, and he tells me they will be very pleasant companions. I am glad of that because it will add so much to my comfort. I shall have a very pleasant companion all to myself, though she will be at the same time absent bodily. I think it would be very pleasant if at some hour of each day we would always think of each other at the same time. Then we can talk together like little children, and each know as well what the other is saying, as if there was no distance between us.

It seems to me now as if I had begun a new life. I am going to work, and I mean to try very hard for success. For I shall know that some one will be waiting for me, and that she will consider my success as hers and my failure—no, we won't have any such word to think of. I must leave some room till I have seen Uncle Edwin, so I will stop now, though I have not yet been summoned to dinner.

Last night while I was writing to you, I could not help crying all the time. But today I have felt very happy almost all the time to think so quietly and pleasantly of you. When I was cutting my nails, a tear would drop, for then my loss was called to mind by such a little thing.

But au revoir, darling, till Uncle E. comes home

"Dear noble Ned" - Who could help loving you my own darling?

Uncle Edwin has just returned from New York - and brought me your letter. I must thank you very much for it.

My dear Lizzie. It seems such a God-send to me here. I had to go to my own room after reading it. For I could not sit quietly in a room full of company and imagine you by me. It forces the tears from my eyes, dearest, but they are pleasant tears and I can only weep alone. But I must go down as soon as possible, for the house is full of guests waiting tea and I could not be excused. God bless you always my darling, and may He make me worthy of your truest love. I have had time only to shake hands with uncle, so I know nothing of the future. It is so pleasant to weep now, precious darling.

11 P.M. I know a letter must be acceptable, or I should not persist in writing so much, Lizzie mine. And it is very pleasant for me to come to you after I can leave everyone else, and see your face and read what you have written and think what you are doing. I felt very glad to read what you wrote about George Tufts, for it seemed so good, so like yourself, to tell me everything. I could not help shedding a few tears when I received your letter this evening. For I was carried back to those "last few happy months," we have passed together. We shall meet again soon, and I will be better than I am now, and

our engagement will be public and then we can be together when we choose, no matter what the world says.

Every little event that has taken place between us is now so pleasant to remember, and thousands of little things are called to mind that might have been forgotten but for our separation.

It seems to me now as if I should be almost satisfied if I could spend a few hours more with you before I leave for South America; and all this evening I have felt troubled to decide whether or not I ought to go home once more. For, though I have had no talk with Uncle Edwin yet he mentioned that he feared the Steamer might not leave before Wednesday next. Yet even if she does wait till then I know I ought not to go back again, but I feel as if I might disobey duty only for this once. How much surprised you would be to see me walk in on Saturday morning, wouldn't you?

Do you think I could possibly be content with a simple shake of the hands from you even if every one was in the room?

But if I came back to you, for a few hours, my pet, I should have to say 'Good-bye' again all the same and open anew the wounds of Monday. Now I must not go home again unless I find there is a certainty of the steamer's being delayed. If I can see Uncle Edwin before breakfast tomorrow so as to write to Mother I will send this long letter; but if not I will wait till Friday's mail. I wish I could be reading your letters and writing to you the whole time. It is very pleasant to me to leave those below on some excuse and pass my time with one whose heart is mine, and who loves me. (How I love to say that!)

Dearest Lizzie. There were fourteen at the tea-table tonight, and with these must I pass Thanksgiving. How much pleasanter it would be if I had some one to talk with of you. I do enjoy myself a good deal here but it is only when I am thinking of you. I could never have imagined before this week what separation was. I wish that the next mail from New York might bring your next letter, for one each day while I am waiting here, would be such treasures. I mean to write something every day while I am gone; for I can find enough to say all the time. I will write a larger and plainer hand for this must be very difficult to read.

Good night! My precious darling. We will read the bible together. I shall kiss you ever so many times and I want to dream of you. I will write again tomorrow.

Good night - dear pet –
Your own Ned.

————⌒∝⌒————

What a delight to know my Ned has arrived safely in Tarrytown and to hear how he is faring! I must not worry for I know he is as cautious as can be, and God would surely do nothing to harm him or deprive me of his love. We both know anything can happen at any time, but it is not our place to control such things. It is His place to create and ours to trust that whatever He creates will help us better understand our own place. Still, we must not lose focus on the things we can change, those very things we must change to make our place in society and to infuse compassion into our society.

Oh how I wish my whole self, rather than my daguerreotype, could be a stowaway in his luggage. If my eyes could only see through my dag., Edward could set me up and I could view every bit of his life.

With so many at the table for tea, I cannot imagine what a feast the Bartletts might have at Thanksgiving.

Thanksgiving at the Tenney's was a sheer delight with all the children gathered around one large table. We were seven people at table, with only one male, the little ones offset by older siblings to encourage their best manners. Aunt Augusta sat at the head of the table with Lottie at her side, next to me, and Johnny to my other side (the six-year old insisting he must sit by his Aunt "Libbie"). Maggie sat between Liz and Mary on the other side of Aunt Augusta.

Aunt Augusta said the blessing. Halfway through the meal she asked Johnnie, as the only "man" at the table, if he would like to make a toast. He nodded his consent and with a serious expression, rose slowly, raised his glass filled with milk and said, "A toast to all the ladies! And the food."

Interior of Niblo's Opera House, New York City

The New York Times
January 16, 1854

Interesting Statement of a Passenger

...Two of the passengers remained upon the deck for five hours after the accident, under the supposition that nothing but the deck itself was left, and that it was floating at the mercy of the waves. One of those passengers was brought down stairs with his hands and feet frozen, but owing to the kindness and prompt attention of Lieut. F.R. Murray, of the U.S. Navy, and Dr. Wirtz, of the medical staff, the torpid circulation of his limbs was restored by stimulating applications...

CHAPTER 7

The Last Thanksgiving

Rockwood, Thursday, Nov. 24, 1853 - 3 P.M.
The last Thanksgiving I shall spend near you for a long time

My own darling Lizzie –

I must be away from you and yet be tantalized by the thought that I might be so much happier and make you much happier by going to Methuen again, if even for one day only. I will complain no more, my darling, for it must be right or Providence would not have so ordained.

It is such a joy to be loved, dearest, that if I were away from the possibility of a return to you, I think I should be perfectly happy in the hope of our meeting when I could bring some real token of my love for you. But now I confess I feel impatient to waiting quietly here for the steamer's departure, and the only happy moments I have are spent alone with you. I should be content for Uncle tries to make every guest as happy as he can, and he is such a kind man one can't help loving him.

Aunt Carrie is confined to her room by a sudden attack of sickness, but there are enough in the house beside. There are Commodore & Mrs. McKeever with two daughters and a niece, Mr. & Mrs. Boyd of Portland, one son, a daughter & niece, Miss Adams of Quincy and Mrs. Bartlett's father Mr. Harrod.

Yet I try to stay as little time with these as I can, though they are very pleasant people, and I am wishing the whole time to escape to my own room. As yet dinner is not announced, but I should go down for it is very near the hour I suppose.

It was proposed to go to the opera tomorrow evening but I shall not go, for I should feel very sad to think I was there and you thinking of me at home. I could not send your letter this morning, for the mail had gone before I saw Uncle Edwin, so I will enclose this with it.

I know you will not think it too much of a task to read so much, shall you? Tomorrow I think I shall go to New York, and perhaps see the steamer though she may be at sea till Saturday or Sunday.

Perhaps I shall find there a letter from my darling pet to make me feel happy.

When I read in my bible it makes me think so much of you and I am always carried back to the week you spent in Methuen when you used to stand by my side for a few moments every night, darling. How pleasant was that week and how much joy does the remembrance of it give me now! How different to you must this week at Methuen seem!

I hope you will be very happy there, dearest, but it must seem so very different from last summer especially when you go into my room. I have thought you would love to think of me then and love to write to me sitting at my desk.

Did you attend church today and who sat in my place, where I sat last summer as proud to think the congregation would suppose you were my betrothed? It makes me gloomy, love, to leave you now, perhaps for two hours but Uncle will think it very strange if I am absent just at dinner time. I may kiss you before I go down, my own pet?

11 P.M. – "For two hours" I said and it has been nearly eight since I left you. But we did not finish dinner till about seven, and since then there have been games, fireworks etc. etc. and it would

have been very rude for me to have left. The Steamer will not be in New York tomorrow so I shall stay here and write some of the time to you. Uncle E. carries this sheet to New York tomorrow and I am in hopes you will receive it before you leave Methuen.

It makes me feel very happy here, my precious Lizzie, to read what you have written to me, and I think what you wrote of George Tufts was so good and so kind of you. I have thought that he must love you from what I have heard you say and it was very kind of you to tell me what you thought about it. I have imagined myself pressing you to me time and again for saying that you must try to discourage anything but the best of friendship for you. I used sometimes, when I was with you, to wish that I were like George Tufts, for I thought he must possess many accomplishments which I lacked.

What if Uncle Edwin should know to whom I had been writing so much since I came here? Wouldn't he think it was funny?

How different has seemed this Thanksgiving from what it would if I had been with you at Methuen. I have enjoyed myself to be sure sometimes today but it has been in thinking of one who is absent from me, and not as I usually would have done, in games and sports with others.

Last evening they gave me some wedding cake, with some ladies names, to dream of and then draw a name in the morning. I put the parcel under the bed so that I might say I slept with it under my pillow. The only name I ever heard of before was "Your best friend," and that I knew was meant for you though the writer knew it not.

I want very much to see the *Steamer San Francisco* a day or two before I leave New York for I know you will feel interested to hear how I am to be situated during my long voyage. How pleasant it would be, dearest, if we could go to San Francisco together. Or if I were expecting to meet you there, my feelings about sailing would be very different from what they now are.

I know, my precious little pet, that it will seem very different to me from what our separation now does when I am fairly under way and I see my native shores—your dwelling place—receding from my view. Now I sometimes have a notion that something may happen which would permit us to meet again, but then all hope will be cut off. I shall read in my bible with you tonight, my dearest love, and I shall go to sleep with my face resting against yours.

Good night, darling; may God bless you. I wish you would come into my room tonight as you did in Methuen to say Good night.

Take the best care of your health for the sake of
Your own dear Ned.

These last pages must be written very badly for I have been writing by the light of one flickering candle.

———◦✕◦———

Letters from New York do not arrive as quickly as from Methuen and are, therefore, even more precious to me. As I closed the last sheet of the final letter, I began to hope for his next letter, which I will not deserve until I have responded. That thought prompted me to set up my writing implements and begin to earn my Ned's love. Is love something that can be earned? I actually do not think so. I think it is discovered, but it can certainly be unearned. All that would take is bad behavior. I have seen as much due to neglect or abuse, but not due to absence.

I wondered, what have I done to deserve such adoration? Can I truly be worthy of his devotion? I am inspired to be and do all I can to make him proud of me.

Postal workers in a traveling sorting office on a train

The New York Times
January 16, 1854

Interesting Statement of a Passenger

...Capt. Gardiner, an officer of the First Dragoons, was sleeping in one of the state rooms on the main deck, when the accident occurred. His servant-man had entered his state-room to tell him that they were in great danger; and had hardly uttered the words when the wave which had hurried so many into eternity swept the servant overboard, while Captain Gardiner, by a special Providence, was the only man on that deck who was saved. When I came down, I found my friend completely covered and surrounded by the debris of the hurricane deck which had fallen upon him. He was slightly injured and very enfeebled, but owing to the kindness of several officers, he was restored to comparative health, and when rescued by another ship, afforded much valuable assistance to the other passengers, and was most justly esteemed by them as one of the most efficient of the officers of the Army who were rescued by that rescue vessel...

CHAPTER 8

Visiting Sing Sing Prison

General Joseph Andrews

Salem

Essex County

Mass.

For Miss M. E. Andrews

Friday - 25th November, 1853.

My dear Lizzie-

Today I have been to the state prison at Sing-Sing, but you must know how little pleasure I could even at any time take in visiting such a scene. 1000 convicts shut out from all intercourse with the world, not allowed to speak even with one another, and deprived of all their liberty can not be seen by any one, without exciting a feeling of compassion. We saw the males (900 in number) at dinner; each man receiving his portion in silence and eating with so little evidence of enjoyment. As we walked about the prison-yard and saw these poor men so gloomy and unhappy, I could not but think what would be our feelings should there be some impossible barrier between us. Though we are now separated, yet we expect we can in a very short time be with each other, and this hope makes us so very happy that our lot is paradise compared to some separations. But, darling mine, if I had gone from you last Monday with no hope of seeing you again, what would life have been worth? Could you love me without any hope?

Since I have been at Rockwood I can think of no one but you, Lizzie pet. I love Mother and sisters, but I am yours and yours only. When I sit by myself building castles in the air, it is for Lizzie, my own Lizzie, and for her only that I am dreaming all this splendor. How I wish some of my castles would only be real castles and we could have in them just such times as I imagine ourselves having.

Do you think I should go to San Francisco next Wednesday? At least I should wait for the next steamer, unless somebody else were going to the same place as a passenger.

I have been tempted to call and ask your friend Mrs. French to send for you to come on to New York immediately. Will you come, dearest-dear, if I will? Uncle Edwin will probably return from New York in a few moments and I may receive a letter by him from Methuen. If I do I shall feel as happy as possible all the evening, but even if I do not I shall try and not feel very unhappy, for I know you would write to me if you could. And you will write very long letters, when I am far, far away, won't you my darling? There will be enough to say, I know, my dear pet, if you can only find time; for it will be much harder for you to write alone by yourself often, than it will be for me, for you will have very many continually wanting to come into your room, while I am sure to be alone. Don't you think I shall have something to say every Sunday?

What should I have done if you had not acknowledged I was your dear dear Ned? If I had gone to South America, loving you as I have done and some time have received from you "Dear Cousin - I am engaged to Mr. __________" do you think I should have been in a very great hurry to return home? What would have been my feeling to have received an invitation to attend your wedding? But all that is settled now, and I am satisfied with my hope in the future. I hope to attend your wedding and yet I shan't expect a special written invitation except those long invitations I shall look for every fortnight. Won't you please send me, darling an invitation before I go away: do darling—a real bona fide invitation, because I shall love to read it over sometimes. Be sure and have Ned's own name with it.

10½ P.M. Uncle Edwin did not return from New York tonight but will be here tomorrow. Still I have imagined what you would have said in a letter and I have imagined you were sitting by me this evening and once in a while looking up in my face as if you thought—well, I won't say what, but it means as if you thought I was your "dear Ned."

Every once in a while I put my hand to my head and that always carries me back to that last afternoon I spent in Salem. For I can feel two places where the hair is very short; how happy I was while you were cutting off my hair! And I was very, very glad, darling, to have that beautiful ring from your hair.

Since Monday I have not seen it and I almost feel as if it were lost. But I put it (in my writing desk) in my trunk with the large daguerreotype supposing I should stop at a Hotel in New York. But I brought only a valise to Tarrytown and I can not see my writing desk till I go to the city. The little pet, with my bible I put in my valise that I might be sure of them at Hartford. Neither of the pets in my desk are forgotten, however, and I think I should be aware of their removal when I saw my trunk should any one rob me.

How curious it must seem, darling Lizzie, to be visiting at a house and yet see none of the family. Yet it is so here now. For Mrs. Bartlett has been unable to leave her bed since yesterday and Uncle Edwin has been in New York all day and will be detained till tomorrow evening.

Still there are eleven guests tonight, and everything goes on as well as if Mrs. Bartlett were below to superintend. Tomorrow a portion will leave and on Monday nearly all of the rest. I must leave a little room for tomorrow, so I will say Good night, my love. Good night, my beautiful pet.

Saturday A.M. Darling - The above was written with a pencil last evening, as others were writing in the library and I could not have the inkstand. I have just copied it as you see. I have just thought, dear Lizzie, that I ought not to write in such a small hand, for it must be very difficult for you to read my letters. But I do so love to come here and talk with you; and if I write a large hand I can not spend half as much time with you for fear of making too large (in size) a letter to send. But I will do better when I am on board the Steamer, if you will allow this a few days longer. I think I shall stay here till Monday morning, and then, if Uncle Edwin goes to the city I will go down and stay Monday and Tuesday night at the Astor House, and on Wednesday begin my voyage.

When I am in New York I shall have my daguerreotype taken to send home in place of that Crystallotype they now have.

There is one thoughtful thing Uncle Edwin has done for me, which I should not have thought of. He says some accident may happen to the Steamer by which I would be left at Rio; or I might be sick or unfortunate at Valparaiso or San Francisco. Therefore he has given me power to draw $500 from any merchant there in his name. Unless something unforeseen should happen I shall not use this letter of credit, but it was very kind of Uncle to give it to me. I would rather, darling, that you would not mention this, for I feel very much afraid of anyone's supposing Uncle Edwin provides me with money.

You know that this pride is one of my great failings. Yet I can not nor do I want to overcome it, that is unless you wish me to. Uncle Edwin has not and will not, as far as I know, give me one cent of money. He procures me a free passage to San Francisco from Aspinwall & Co. and gives me such letters to Alsop & Co. as will probably place me in that house. But beyond that I am not aware of any obligation I am under to him in anything. He is very kind to me and I think would do anything for me that was necessary, but I should try to avoid the necessity of his doing anything for me. If it is possible that I can work my own way in the world unaided except by advice, would you not prefer, my guardian angel, that I should do so?

It may be wrong pride but I can not convince myself of it. But I would not act contrary to your wishes my darling love, in anything.

I think it would be better not to mention Uncle's letter of credit, don't you?

It is very pleasant to have some dear friend whom I can call my love, and to whom I can tell everything without restraint; for I mean that nothing shall be kept secret from you while I am gone. Dear - dear, Lizzie. If I can only some time be as rich and as much respected as is Uncle Edwin, I know you will be happy. Riches are not happiness by any means, but they certainly can add to one's comfort.

Uncle E. must think I use a good deal of paper writing to someone—but no matter so long as we are happy. I am going to put something for you just here. May I? I received what you sent me.

———◇———

I trust by now my own Ned receives my letter, and my kiss, as I have just received his. Surely, he receives other greetings as well being sent by post from his family near and far. We all anticipate his departure any day.

Until two days ago, the warm, humid weather seemed to be posturing a defense against winter's arrival. Then, the winds whipped in from the northwest and rapidly pulled the mercury down ten degrees and freezing the ground solid overnight. We awoke to frosted windows, the first of the season. At port, a schooner limped in from the north weighed down with a heavy sheet of ice covering her decks. Father tells me the temperature dropped from nearly 60 degrees Thursday morning to 20 degrees by nine o'clock in the evening and reached 10 degrees Friday morning, falling 50 degrees in 24 hours.

That is not the only news Father brings that gives me reason for concern. A ship from Liverpool arrived in New York with reports of having lost 76 of its 754 passengers from deaths caused by cholera.

My dear Ned makes such a funny request for an invitation to our wedding. I shall enjoy preparing just such an invitation and send it to him when he is at sea, but he must have no fear as to whose name will stand beside my own!

I sleep with Edward's letter under my pillow hoping he will visit me in my dreams. Indeed, I do dream about Edward, but am disturbed by my dream - we are walking arm in arm, and to my horror, when Edward turns to kiss me, I see not him, to whom I am betrothed, but George Tufts! Shocking! In my dream, I wonder if it was Edward all along. I feel I love this man still, but am very confused at the deception. I ask Edward, or George, or whoever this man is that has my arm, how he can change so much while I am not looking. He says, 'we all must change, Lizzie,' and that is when I wake, feeling very glad it is only a silly dream. I pull my dear Ned's letter from under my pillow and spank it, "You must not tease me so!"

I begin filling perfectly clean pages with everyday happenings at the Tenney household, hoping to instill in Ned all our love and assure him of his place in my heart and home. I will not share my dreadful dream, however. I will not talk to the icy weather and deaths from cholera. I will simply expand to include the happenings of his family and other bits of information regarding those he knows and loves. My intent is to reassure him of his family's ability to carry on in his absence, though the truth is that any household with small children and no adult man faces many struggles and must depend on neighbors and the church for so many kindnesses. Preparing for winter requires supplies of firewood for heat, a sufficient store of water from the pump for drinking and bathing and blocks of ice that can be melted in the winter when the pump freezes. Winter preparation requires warm clothing each year for growing children, a supply of wax candles and kerosene for lamps, which must be kept out of reach of little hands. On top of this, there are many fresh foods to can and meats to salt. Keeping the root cellar accessible when there is snow can be a difficult job. I do not know how Aunt Augusta manages, but she does. She must.

Whenever possible, I will flock to relatives and social circles in which Edward is often the topic of conversation, as so many depend on his success, and long for his eventual return. Johnny, Lottie and Margie will seem so much older two or three years hence. Try as we might to remain unchanged, none can predict how things might change.

With only a short letter to my credit, posted on Tuesday, my next bundle of treasures arrive in the mail on Monday, the 5th of December. I promised myself to savor them slowly so they might last the whole week, not knowing when I might hear next. I also vow not to ever tuck them under my pillow at night.

The New York Times
January 16, 1854

Interesting Statement of a Passenger

...In the lower cabin, the consternation cannot be depicted. It baffles description. I noticed one family particularly when I went below. The affection which seemed to exist among its members, even in that hour of peril, was truly a beautiful sight. The mother, the father, the daughters and the grandchildren were all clinging together, and seemed each one more interested in the fate of the other, than in their individual safety. I allude to Major Merchant and his family. They are all saved - God be thanked!...

CHAPTER 9

Edwin Bartlett

At Rockwood - Sunday the 27th of Nov. [1853]

Dear Lizzie,

Today I have attended church twice, seen Washington Irving, and taken a good long walk through "Sleepy Hollow," famous for Rip Van Winkle's adventures. I attended the Episcopal Church and made all the responses so clearly and readily that Mr. Boyd and the others were surprised to find I was not an Episcopalian. This is a pretty good beginning, I think, for I shall probably have to attend either that church or the Catholic at Valparaiso. (This ink is so very thin and colorless that I can't see what I write; but I suppose it will become black by tomorrow.)

Yesterday morning when Uncle Edwin returned from New York, he brought me a letter postmarked Methuen, but it was not from my darling. It was written on Tuesday night, before she reached Methuen. Perhaps I shall find one from her tomorrow in the city, for I am going down in the first train. I intend to call on Mrs. Col. Sprague either Monday or Tuesday, and then with the exception of a few purchases I have to make I have nothing in view till I sail. I have two or three classmates there and I may call on them. But this is probably the last Sunday I shall pass so near you for a long time.

How pleasant have been those Sabbaths that I have lately passed at Hamilton; how very pleasant they will seem to me in Valparaiso and on my long voyage. I shall devote each Sunday while I am gone to you, my darling, and if I am not writing all day long, I shall be thinking of you, and be calling to mind my dear pet as I see those beautiful talismans she has given me. I had no idea, before we were engaged, what power there was in such tokens of love, but now it seems as if I could not be without them.

Do you remember how proud I was of that large daguerreotype, when we rode from Boston to Roxbury last Summer? Do you remember when I visited Charles Paine and wanted to show you the daguerreotype as I rode out from Salem? Since I have had that I have not passed a day without seeing and bidding good morning to you; and there have been only three nights when I have not taken a look at you the last thing before retiring for the night. Those three nights were passed on board the Steam boat between New York and Boston. I thought of you then, my darling, and if I could not see your face I imagined myself quite near to it.

The only fear I have had in regard to my quarters on board the steamer to California is that I might be so situated that I can not be sure of being alone with you every night (so as to see your face) just before going to bed. But now I am satisfied that there will be no trouble about that, for Uncle Edwin says there will only be 15 or 25 to occupy a cabin capable of carrying and accommodating 300 passengers.

I have not yet seen my quarters or even the steamer itself, but I shall of course go on board the first opportunity I have. She is probably at sea today, and possibly may not leave New York till Thursday. It will require about two days to get the troops on board and they may be unable to begin that before Tuesday. Every one hurries as fast as they can for completion, as the builders have to pay $100 per day for every day till she is delivered to the owners, Messrs. Aspinwall & Co.

It is very, very pleasant darling, to rattle on as I do now, and be writing to you as I am, yet without saying anything either of interest in itself or value any way. But I shall have too large a pile to send and when I began tonight I restricted myself to one half a sheet, yet see how much I have trespassed. So against my will, dearest, I must say "Good-night." That dear little face looks as if it didn't object; so _____________ (Thank you, dear pet.)

Monday - at Rockwood still - Mrs. Bartlett is so sick that Uncle Edwin could not go to New York today and so I have postponed my departure. I fear he will be unable to go down tomorrow, but I shall not wait myself any longer. Uncle showed me today the letters he had written to Alsop & Co. at Valparaiso and California, and also a letter for myself, besides the letter of credit of which I have spoken. The letters to Alsop & Co. are more than I could have expected; for he pledges himself for my fidelity, and "unexceptionable morality," although he has seen but very little of me.

He wished to introduce me to Mr. Chauncey, Senator of New York, who would probably give me a letter to their partners on the West coast. Mr. Riley, another New York partner, has promised me a letter when I call. All this makes me feel so happy, darling, and so indicative of success that I want you here to share my own feeling; for I know that you will feel glad to see so favorable a beginning to my plans. Uncle will probably be in New York before I sail; but Aunt Carrie is so sick that I may not be able to leave home.

There are now here Mrs. Boyd, of Portland with a child and niece, Miss Adams and Mr. Harrod. All but Mr. Harrod will stay some time, even if Mrs. Bartlett should have a long attack of sickness. What a waste of time has been this last week. How much pleasanter would each day have been could we have been together; and had I or had Uncle Edwin even only known how long the steamer was to be delayed, we could have passed so many happy hours together.

It is just one week this afternoon, dearest, since I took that last precious look as I left Mrs. Brownell's door. I left you then full of sadness yet joyous at the thought that now at last I am going to do something for you. I know what your feelings were and oh - how I longed to turn back again and fold you in my arms for one last moment more! What a change may come over either or both of us before we meet again! Something tells me that we shall soon be together again, and be happy as a pair of young doves; yet with all this even, we may be greatly changed.

My darling may be even fairer than she is now, and perhaps Ned may be more manly-looking than he is. You will try, precious one, and not change, won't you? I will try as hard as I can to grow no worse but become better and better every day.

Uncle says in his letter to Valparaiso that he thinks it will be better for me to stay one or two years at that city before I go to San Francisco. I think this is very good indeed, my pet, I think: for probably on leaving Valparaiso for San Francisco, I could spend a few weeks at home without injury to my business prospects. But you won't tell anybody, darling, that I expect to come home so soon will you? For I always say I have no idea when I may return, and it may be a year longer than this. Shall you be glad to see me in two years? Oh! My dearest love, I ought not to have asked that question, for I know you will be glad to see me. But you didn't think I meant to ask "for information," did you?

Today I have been wondering whether you are in Methuen or in Salem. I know you expected to return home by today at least but I have thought something might detain you.

Did you think at four o'clock where you were last Monday at that time? I shall want to come back again some Monday at that hour, and perhaps we can persuade ourselves that no time has elapsed since our parting. But won't we have a deal to say to each other; for all the paper in the United States couldn't contain half of what we shall think for each other while we are separated. But I am called to tea – Adieu-

11 P.M. Did I ever tell you darling that I have sometimes fancied a resemblance to you in Mrs. Bartlett; about some things? And tonight my attention was called particularly to the same thing, by hearing what caused her sickness. When she was young, she used very often to be troubled with a sore throat caused by swelling of the tonsils, and she was never relieved till her tonsils were cut. Since then she has had no attack till this last week and now her throat is in such a state that she can swallow nothing.

You know this has been a great trouble of yours often making you ill. Do you remember when I was in Salem one winter; you had an ill-turn of this sort, which was very bad? I shan't forget how happy I was when you consented to have the doctor, at my request; how I ran to his house, then to Dr. Farrington's for prescriptions;- how I sat for a time with you in "father's room;" how Aunt Eliza came to see you and I saw her weeping over you. I felt so glad to see her love you. Then what perfect joy I was in when you came down stairs from your room, and we sat side by side on the sofa in the upper entry, till Mary Thompson came in to interrupt us. (Something else happened just before, we sat down together on the sofa - oh! I was very happy.) Then, when I went home to Methuen I wrote in my journal that I thought Lizzie at least liked me. It is very pleasant to call up reminiscences like these, dearest once in a while; and I do very very often – now. They comfort me very much.

The ink on this first page is so light that I fear you can not read what I have written; when I wrote I supposed it would turn darker in a few hours. Will you excuse me, dear Lizzie! It does seem so pleasant, my darling to come and talk with you every night after being with those in whom I feel no particular interest, that I can't help telling you of it time and again.

My thoughts this evening have been very pleasant; for I have been tracing over the progress of our loves; and every little incident that would recur to mind always brought so many others with it and suggested so much besides that I have been thinking of them ever since tea. By request of Mrs. Boyd I read aloud Eliza Cook's

"Melaia" but I was all that time thinking of my visit in Salem when you were sick. Since I have been at Rockwood, I have read a part of Dr. Rushenberger's Life in So. America, and so far I like the place very much, but of course I know nothing of it yet.

Don't be afraid, darling, that I am going always to give you such crowded sheets to read. I have too much regard for those eyes of mine you are using till I come back. This is only to last till I sail; for now I want to say all I can in little space. But now there is no more room - I must say Good night - I guess you have seen me too some time this evening, so you know how I look. I do love you my darling little pet. If I was only going to see you in New York tomorrow how happy I should be. I mean see the real live you for I shall see you.

Good night - dear Lizzie - Pleasant dreams. It's here.

———◇✕◇———

Ned's letter fills me with a cacophony of emotions—joy and hope, mingled with fears and regret. Yes, fear that I may disappoint him, and regret I have not found time to write more. I regret not writing a complete letter each day and posting one as often as he does, which must be terribly disappointing to him. I fear my negligence will be seen as something other than a reflection of how I truly feel. How I truly feel is utterly joyful about our love and hopeful about the future I know we will have upon Edward's return.

My mind sifts through possibilities of foregoing other undertakings, perhaps diminishing some volume of the literature I enjoy reading in the evenings, though now, upon reading Edward's letter, I wish to pick up Washington Irving's Sleepy Hollow and read it again as a way to be closer to my Ned. I read most evenings to be near Father, without disturbing him as he works on papers.

I write daily, albeit not so prolifically as my own true darling. My Ned is not yet bearing the demands of routine household responsibilities and, once he sets sail, his leisure time will lessen. Perhaps as Father is writing, so might I, though I dare not do so in a space shared so openly by others. After all, I have not even revealed our engagement to Aunt Eliza and I would be cruel to tempt her to keep our secret. Oh how I wish I might speak to her in confidence about my feelings. She is the closest person I have to a mother. Surely my mother would wish to hear what is in my heart and on my mind. Could I possible spare time away from my studies? Could I possibly be by Edward's side in Chile or San Francisco? In a year?

All these rambling thoughts somehow find their way onto my page as I share a moment with my darling. I want to tell my dear Ned all that is on my mind. I vow to steal any moment possible to visit him, to gaze upon his likeness, and I begin now musing at his modest demeanor, his fine strong jaw and most delicious lips. In his dag., he appears to study some document, intently. I am sure it is my letter. I squint. Do I recognize the paper? Do I see my own script upon the page? Lifting the frame close to my face and then up, I tilt it as if I might peek over his shoulder. How I wish his daguerreotype allowed me to look into his cunning eyes. Oh, that our waiting could be past and a new life with my true love begun. Good night, my darling dear. As I undress for bed, I turn his head, certainly not to tease, only to preserve my modesty, I insist to myself. I think I hear him moan.

"Patience, my dear," I say to comfort us both.

The New York Times
January 16, 1854

Interesting Statement of a Passenger

...Mr. Aspinwall, who had left New York for the benefit of his health, was in the cabin at the time of the accident, and on hearing that the ship was leaking immediately went below, and taking off his coat, assisted the men in bailing the ship. For several hours he continued there cheering the people on until his strength gave way, and he was at length borne on a litter into the cabin in which the ladies were assembled. His conduct from the time of the catastrophe until our arrival in New York, has proved him to be a man of determined courage and energy, and perfectly resigned to his fate. Without a murmur he partook with the sailors the rations which were served out, while the soldiers and others around were grumbling...

CHAPTER 10

On Board the Steamer

[Nov. 29, 1853] Astor House, N.Y. Tuesday evening

Dear Lizzie-

I am writing this in a public room with strangers continually passing and repassing, and stopping behind my chair as if to see what I am writing. I met tonight in the Hotel, Frank Holyoke bound home from Jamaica. He looks very sick, and says he left Jamaica solely on account of his health. He inquired for all Salem people.

Today I came from Tarrytown with Uncle Edwin, expecting to sail by tomorrow or the next day. But I found that the Steamer will not leave before Saturday, owing to some little imperfection in her machinery. I went on board of her for a short time, but I could only stay a few moments as the sea was getting too high to permit me to land in safety. She is anchored in the harbor about a mile from the shore and I had to go out to her in a small row-boat. I found the Captain to be on first appearance a very pleasant man indeed. He showed me about the cabin &c, which was very splendid. If I can enjoy any sea voyage I ought certainly to enjoy a voyage in this vessel.

On going to Mr. Riley's office with Uncle, I found the long expected letter from you. I couldn't do just what I wanted in Mr. Riley's counting room, but I seized the first opportunity I had to read your letter as I wished. Oh my darling Lizzie I was so happy while reading my treasure that I wanted you here to share my joy with me. But my dear pet, you must not think you are very bad. For you are not, and it always makes me feel sad to have you say you are. Ned wants to love you always just as you are now: he does not want you to try and change. And you will always keep this in mind for me, won't you, darling? When I come home to you from Valparaiso I expect to see you just as I left you; not altered in the least.

Tomorrow I think I shall return to Tarrytown and stay till Friday; for it is too expensive for me to remain here a whole week, if I can help it. I shall probably not have my daguerreotype taken till Friday.

I have received today also a letter from Mother written last Thursday and Friday. Among other things she says "I was repeatedly asked yesterday before the mail came in, 'Aunt Augusta, don't you think we shall get letters today.'" I wonder if I don't know who asked such a funny question! I suppose you have received my letter of Friday before now: and tomorrow's mail may bring me one from you. I shall ask Mr. Riley if he doesn't think we shall receive letters.

The third letter I received today was from Martha Bird. It was written Nov. 23d and M. said she was coming to New York to make a Christmas visit this week and she wants me to call and see her. And she says, too, that if I have to leave New York before her arrival, I must have my daguerreotype taken and left at Mr. Riley's office till she sends for it. What can I do, my darling counsellor? I don't want to give any one my daguerreotype but you and sisters but if I see Martha Bird she will insist upon my sitting for her. I am determined that she shall not have a copy, and yet I don't want to do anything to hurt her feelings: and I think she would feel hurt if I should refuse such a request without some very good reason. Now if you were only here, or if I were only there, you would advise me what to do.

I have felt very ill-natured all this evening till I sat down to write to you: for though it is very pleasant to feel that I can correspond with you every day, yet every delay in the ship's sailing, now that I have said Good bye to you, seems such a waste of time. I have no idea of going before Saturday and it may be Monday before we are able to leave.

It seems so different in writing to you tonight, my darling Lizzie from my last letters; for usually I have been so quiet and alone that I had nothing to disturb me. But now I have smoking, and chatting, and laughing and swearing all going on at once. But I can't write in my own room: for the house is so full that I could only find an upper story room, with two occupied beds in it besides mine. I knew I should not be alone any time after nine o'clock; so about seven, I went up and bade you good-night and read with you a little while. This alone would make me want to go back to Rockwood if nothing else influenced me.

I am going to send this in tomorrow's mail and I hope you will receive it in season to write me before Saturday, that is if you are able to finish reading what I have written, before that time. I will write every day, and send another bundle before I sail. Please direct as before.

Good night my dear love – from
Your own Ned.

P.S. I can't help adding a few lines, my darling, though I fear if you read what I have already written, you must either stay away from school or be doing something else than studying in school.

I have been thinking, my dear, betrothed Lizzie, since I wrote the first three pages of this sheet, how very happy we shall be, when we are publicly engaged to talk of each other to third persons. For then they will of course sometimes mention you to me and me to you and we can very easily persuade them to converse of one another, while we are enjoying what they say.

How I wish this last fortnight might have been spent with you instead of whiled away here in New York. I know I have said the same thing time and again in writing to you, but it seems such a waste of time to be doing nothing here.

The porters have been walking up and down the hall and putting out every light but the one by which I am writing ever since I began this last page; poor fellows; they must have but little sleep.

You will write to me if you can, darling, won't you after you receive this letter. If you put your letter in the Post Office by Friday morning I shall be sure to receive it, before I sail.

Good night again, darling mine.

———◦✕◦———

Rev. Phillips and Margie came to Salem this Saturday afternoon and stopped by for a tea. Not long ago, before Edward asked me to marry him, I feared he had given his heart to Margie for I know she has been steadfastly fond, even smitten, with him. While our fathers sat in the dining room, Margie and I took our tea in the parlor to have a private conversation. Margie still seems to think of Edward as often as I do, and moreover, she speaks of him as if they have an intimate relationship! Fiddle-sticks! This is none too true. All they have in common is horse-back outings! Perhaps that is more meaningful than I imagine. Oh, how absurd to picture the two of them riding into the horizon as lovers so often do. She knows not of our engagement. I cannot reveal a thing!

Horse-back riding is not a pleasure Edward and I share. I feel suddenly desperate to arrange a horse-back outing with my dear, darling Ned. Speaking of Ned nearly always brings me so much

84

pleasure, but on this occasion with Margie, it leaves me feeling fearful and at a loss.

Oh, that I could have thrown all my letters upon her to show her how my Ned loves me, how he lavishes me with attention and affection. Now, as I sit at my writing desk recalling the events of the day in a letter to my true love, I laugh aloud at the vision of such a spectacle. If this is how I behave now, I dare not even imagine how short-tempered I will be in a year or two! Surely I should not have to refuse tea with Margie until Edward returns, just to appease my vicious insecurity!

Astor House

II. Waiting in New York

Edward seeks the convenience of being in New York City, initally with a stay at the Astor House, but is quickly discouraged and ventures to the comfort of his Uncle Bartlett's estate, known as Rockwood Castle, in Tarrytown 30 miles up the Hudson River. When in New York, he discovers the Metropolitan Hotel is quite agreeable, but Massachusetts pulls heavily on his heart.

The New York Times
January 16, 1854

Interesting Statement of a Passenger

...On Sunday, December 25, service was read to the passengers by Rev. Mr. Cooper, and prayers for speedy deliverance were offered up by Mr. Aspinwall and others. The storm continued to rage upon that day, and towards evening Lieutenant Murray, who had been the life and support, as it were, of others whose spirits had given way, reported a sail in sight. Soon after we found, as she approached, that she was the brig Napoleon, of Portland, and, in reply to a hail from Captain Watkins, her Captain promised to lay alongside until the passengers could be taken on board; but unfortunately that night a severe gale sprang up, and in the morning the Napoleon was invisible...

CHAPTER 11

Relieved of My Overcoat

Genl. Joseph Andrews
Salem
Mass.
For Miss M. E. Andrews

Thursday A.M. 1st December-1853

My dear Lizzie-

If ever in my life I have felt cross, real, bona-fide cross, it was during the time I was staying in New York. I wasn't very well when I reached the city, and I found after writing your letter last Tuesday evening that I not only had a room in the upper story of the Astor house, but a room with four beds in it, two of which were occupied. Of course I wasn't very well satisfied with that, but I grumbled to bed the best way I could.

To cap the climax; having left my overcoat on a chair in the public sitting room for about a minute, I found on returning that some kind friend had relieved me of that. I complained at the office but they said (to console me) you should be more careful; the same thing happens here daily. That was comforting, and I determined to leave New York as quick as I could.

On reaching Tarrytown, I thought I would walk to Uncle Edwin's; so I trudged alone till I was safe and sound at Rockwood. It was a delightful walk from the depot; only four miles by the way I came; very pleasant to walk four miles without an overcoat in a cold, blowing night, with a heavy valise in one hand and a bundle of books in another! That was the end when I reached Uncle's house: all seemed glad to see me: Uncle said he knew I wouldn't stay in New York till the Steamer sailed.

You mustn't think, dear Lizzie, that I am cross now, because I write so dolefully. On the contrary I feel just as I always do and always want to feel when I am writing to you.

Last night when I came up to my room, quite late, I found there was no ink here and I had no paper, so I had to go to bed without writing a word. But I sat and talked a long time with you; I read with you as you asked me to every night. And I went to sleep, darling, thinking of my best friend on earth. This morning, too, I woke some time before sunrise and it was so delightful to indulge in such reveries as I then did.

When I found my overcoat was stolen, the first thing that troubled me was lest your last letter might be in the pocket, but I found I had it in my other coat. The letter Aunt Laur gave me for Mrs. Col. Sprague was taken with the coat and I yesterday sent word to Uncle John, so that another might be sent, if Aunt Laur wished.

Oh! Lizzie, I am so discontented to be kept here waiting for the Steamer's departure a whole fortnight and yet be unable to go to Massachusetts. For when I reached New York, Tuesday I was told the Steamer would go Friday or Saturday; when Saturday night came; "she will go Wednesday morning," now Wednesday has passed and she is still in New York. I asked the Captain if I should have time to go to Boston; he said "not with safety, for she may go at any time, though I think not before Saturday." I think she may be delayed till Monday or Tuesday, but it would not do for me to venture to go home this week for I might find her gone when I reached New York.

I wish something would call you to New York; can't you think of any excuse. Then I should be satisfied to wait quietly till the steamer is ready, and then too, I want very much that you should go on board and see how I am going out.

I had no time, when I was on board to more than glance over the Steamer and I did not even see what is to be my own room. There will be several ladies as passengers, as many of the Army officers will take their wives and families. But I know no one except the Captain.

11¼ P.M. I had only a small bit of candle given me to retire by tonight, so I must write fast or I shall be left in total darkness. Mrs. Bartlett seems worse and worse every day, so that Uncle Edwin will be unable to go down to the city with me tomorrow as I had hoped, for I wanted him to introduce me to another of the partners in Alsop & Co. who had expressed a desire to know his protégé, and who will probably give me a letter to the firm in Valparaiso, if I can judge from Uncle's letter to Alsop & Co.

I think there is not much doubt but that I shall remain at Valparaiso; at any rate, if I do not stay there, they will forward to me at San Francisco any letters received for me; and so darling, I shall not have to wait as long as I feared for your letters. But I will inquire tomorrow of Mr. Riley particularly in regard to direction etc. so that we may be sure of receiving every letter that is sent. This makes me feel very happy, dearest, to think that I shall find such a package from you almost as soon as I reach Valparaiso.

Tomorrow morning I shall go to the city and I really hope we may sail before Monday, for I have been disappointed so many times that I am now really chafing to be away. I should be content if I could only go out of call of New York, but here I must wait as quietly as I can till everything is ready.

But I must unwillingly say "Good night," my pet, for my candle is almost gone and I have to fold & seal a letter for Liz Tenney before I go to bed. Good night my dearest; may God bless you - darling,

Good-night –

Shall I find another letter from you tomorrow?

One kiss - dear Lizzie - my own Lizzie - Good night, from

Your true Ned.

Friday 2d Dec. At Metropolitan Hotel - Oh, my darling, I was so glad to find your letter at Mr. Riley's office this noon when I came from Tarrytown. To be sure I thought I should see it there, but still I had just as much real comfort in it as if it had been unexpected. I say "comfort" instead of pleasure because it seems much more expressive. I thank you very very much, my dear pet; and I am very glad you enjoyed your visit in Methuen as well as you did, but how I wish I could have been there with you. I ought not to complain, dearest, for everything is of course ordered for the best, and I will find no more fault. Yet one piece of news I received today does not tend to make me feel much happier.

When I reached New York this noon, Mr. Aspinwall said he "feared we should not be off before Tuesday next but it would not be safe to depend upon that." I shall probably stay here till the Steamer does sail, and try to wait as patiently as I can.

I met one of my classmates this afternoon, who sent for a second and then by chance we met a third in Broadway with whom I spent the afternoon and a part of the evening quite pleasantly.

Then, too, in Broadway I met a cousin of the Birds, who in-formed me that Martha and Carrie would be here tomorrow. So I must call and see them. I should like to do so very much, yet I know Martha will insist upon having my daguerreotype and I am determined she shall not have it. I have had one taken for Mother, but it is quite a sober one. I tried three times before I succeeded even as I have done.

I met my old college chum Dorsheimer, this evening of whom you have probably heard me speak, but I had only time to exchange greetings with him. I am to see him again tomorrow.

My accommodations are so much better here than they were at the Astor house that I hope not to be quite as cross as I was when I reached Tarrytown last Wednesday evening.

The opera of "Il Profeta" has been given tonight at Niblo's by Maretzek's troupe. Niblo's is next door to the Metropolitan and I can now hear the audience coming out. How much we should have enjoyed witnessing this opera here if you could only have been in New York. It is spoken of as the finest opera ever produced in America, now for the first time presented. I am usually very fond of attending the opera, but now I care nothing for it. It is so much pleasanter to sit in my own room with you, then I am free from others company. Besides, my darling, (and you won't box my ears for telling you of it will you?) I don't feel as if it would be right for me to run round after places of amusement, when I have just been torn away from one who is dearer to me than life itself. Even if I wanted to go to theatre, opera etc. now, I don't think I should allow myself to do so: but I don't want to go, and if I should be obliged during my stay here to accompany any one there, I should feel uncomfortable all the evening. For I should be wishing the whole time that you were sitting by me instead of Ward or Dorsheimer or Sargent or Kimball or any others like them; good enough companions in their places, but dreadful companions in your place, dear pet.

Your letter which I have just received probably reached New York on Wednesday Evening after I had left for Tarrytown. I suppose you received my letter on Wednesday evening or Thursday morning. If "Aunt Augusta" laughed at eight pages what would she say to twelve?

You will excuse (won't you darling?) the dissimilarity between the first and second leaf of this sheet. For the first was written with lines at Rockwood and the second without lines in New York.

Dearest pet, I must tell you one thing which your letter of yesterday suggested. I used to think Margaret Phillips was quite a pleasant girl, but now I feel almost like berating her for making you jealous. Do try and not feel so dearest, for there is no reason at all for it. I love you with all my heart, and no one but you; it is wrong for me to feel so strongly about this, dear Lizzie, but nothing would, of course, trouble me more than to suppose you thought me not true. But I won't say any more about it. You can trust your own Ned, can't you? And you do I know.

Probably before you read this I shall be on the water, without knowing what would have been your answer to this long letter, but I can imagine.

Good night my dearest darling – (tho I say dear-est, nobody else is dear). We will sit together a little while and read a little and talk a little and ____________,

Good night, little gipsy - Ned-ward.

—◦✕◦—

Sitting at my writing table Wednesday night, I read the final letter in the package I received Monday and vow to have my letters ready to mail Thursday, or Friday morning at the very latest. I resisted the temptation to read all three letters from my darling's most recent bundle in one day and was successful at savoring them for three nights. As a result, I looked forward each day to my evening with Ned.

At evening's end, while Ned waits cross, cold and coatless in New York, I carefully fold my three daily letters and press my initial stamp into hot, gooey sealing wax, making an extra seal. L for Lizzie. L for love. L for longing to be near my Ned.

The mail travels so fast these days! I am immensely grateful, since Edward and I are writing at a furious pace to secure our love with as many memories as we can. To our good fortune, a letter he writes one day arrives to me the next! Such expeditious delivery will not be possible once he is at sea for then we will wait weeks and months with no word. Our patience will be tested, indeed, but our faith and strength will grow from that.

One can never know what God has in store for us. When we first began to write I never expected my best friend would one day become my fiancé, and someday my husband! I only knew my country cousin's charm never ceased to spin me around and leave me blushing. In my wildest imagination I dared not think as much as to become his dearest darling wife. Soon, it will be so.

There is so much one cannot know until the day presents itself in bold truth, staring you in the eyes and demanding attention. None could have seen that Joe would be in and out—thank God!—of the hospital, then shipping miles away for an extended stay at sea. And who could have predicted, Edward—oh conscience!—would have been in and out of Harvard, have lost his father and be starting a profession completely other than the one everyone initially expected of him.

Ned knows how Father, Joe and even Uncle Edwin have all profited from international commerce. This should fill him with hope that he too can be a successful merchant. I am filled with hope. I can see perfectly how we will shape a comfortable future together. Though I must say, I hope Edward would one day find importing something like fine silks from China, as Father has, to be preferable over importing bat guana fertilizer from South America, as his Uncle Edwin has. Yet, I know of no one who has made such a fortune from nothing. That is not to say, guana is nothing. It is worse than nothing! Mr. Bartlett is an immensely clever man to take something no one wanted, something available in abundance, and at no cost, something others wanted to be rid of, and find a way to use it as fertilizer and profit from its sale! How could he have even known how beneficial it would be for growing just about everything—foliage, flowers, vegetable gardens and fruit trees? His gardens are enormously admired.

Perhaps, one day, Edward will be so clever as his uncle to make something from nothing! I am as filled with hope as he is with promise. So, I must forgive him if, upon his travels, he does not write me often, provided he is working hard, as his uncle has warned he must.

During his voyage, his reprieve will come from the news I bring him of his family and chums; yet I must be mindful of the pains it could cause to hear of life continuing as normal so far from his reach. Surely his own adventures will fill him with lively and exotic stories to tell. Oh dear, I must not think of the temptations he will face.

Having filled my page with my musings, I pulled myself from my writing desk and readied to be off to post his letter. If I post it before Friday's mail is loaded in the train, Edward should receive it on Saturday.

My hurried efforts to reach the post office today were not rewarded, for there is nothing for me today. No letter for Ned's dear one. I tuck my handbag into my coat pocket and bury my hands in my muff for the brisk walk home. As I hurry down Chestnut Street, I do not mind the chill in the air for the sooner winter comes, the sooner goes. I have only two, or maybe three, winters to bear before I can begin my life with Ned as my own betrothed. The heat from my brisk pace is all I need to feel warm.

No letter on Saturday.

No letter on Monday.

When I finish re-reading Edward's letters in my room, I stand at the looking glass on my dresser. Holding it up to examine my likeness, I think, 'Oh no! Already, I no longer look like my daguerreotype and it has been only weeks since it was captured.' I turn and try to see myself at an angle, as my Ned might see me. What does he see? 'How in heaven's name am I to remain unchanged until his return?' Then, I reason, I must not have changed all that much, but I am changing constantly, I argued with myself. What if Edward does not recognize me? What if, in three years, as I turn twenty-one, he is looking for a girl of eighteen years old? He will expect to return to the exact girl he keeps in a box to whom he has been writing. Oh, dread!

I place the glass face down and pick up a brush. Uncoiling my hair I tip my head and begin to brush. One, two, three. I will never reach one hundred strokes. Fiddle-sticks! I am as I am and this, I say, looking once more in the glass, is as I am.

I prefer to engage him with my words and my mind anyway, I justify, as I place the glass face-down again. Throwing my hair back into a knot at the nape of my neck, I take out my inkwell, pen and paper and begin to speak my mind, about daguerreotypes, that the outside appearance does not matter as much as what is inside. Outside appearance does not matter as much as the intent of the viewer. Now, I do not want to frighten my Ned to thinking I have already changed, and that the change is dreadful, but I do tell him there is no reason to withhold sharing his likeness. It is only that—a likeness. It is not his heart and soul. Those must not be given so freely. If a daguerreotype helps someone feel close to you, that is a gift that should not be withheld. Then I proceed to enumerate the many reasons to look beyond the physical likeness of one in order to truly know them.

———◦✕◦———

Midday Tuesday, 6 December 1853, there is a knock on the front door.

James comes running up the front steps to the house calling inside, "Special delivery for Miss Lizzie Andrews!" I bound down the stairs to see James bumbling on, "'Tis for you, Miss Lizzie, on the door, a special personal delivery, from New York," he concludes.

My heart leaps out of my chest! A special delivery from Edward? A letter he could not wait to post, or perhaps something else!

"Mr. Tenney," James announces as if he were a butler, though his strong Irish accent made the announcement both laughable and especially joyous.

There is my Ned, holding an intricate reticule. He reaches it out to me as a gift. "Forgive me for surprising you," he says. Without taking the bag from his hand, I hold and kiss my Ned, truly my darling Edward. James backs quickly away. I truly kiss my darling Ned and he kisses me right there inside the front door of my own home. Then I laugh at the thought of him carrying a lady's handbag. Now I accept it, "Thank you. This is so beautiful. From New York?"

I kiss him again and do not care who sees, until I hear a voice.

"Oh, Lizzie," he sighs, then holds his breath and stiffens slightly, which tells me Laura is approaching. I do not care, but then I remember how Laura caught Edward kissing me once before and she has never let him forget it. Laura emerges from the dining room where she has been setting the silver and linens around the table to see what all the excitement is. I pull back and begin to take Edward's coat, a very nice new coat, having lost his last coat due to dreadful circumstances at the Astor House in New York.

"Edward!?" Laura squeals, her voice blasting into the kitchen where Bridget is readying to carry a plate of steaming food to the table. Thank goodness Bridget has barely lifted the dishes, for Laura's exclamation startles her and she runs into the front room, nearly knocking James aside with her urgency. Seeing that everything is all right, she rolls her eyes at Laura and, laughs as she turns to James, "Perhaps this calls for another setting at the table?"

"Yes, do set another place at the table." I shoo Laura away like a pesky moth and welcome Edward in.

"Oh, Edward! What brings you here today? Are you still going to ship out? Tell me everything."

Edward is excited to share and, over dinner, he tells us all that has transpired in New York and his anxiousness about the prolonged wait. He speaks openly to Father about feeling distraught at what he faces with so much being new and unknown. In the middle of his story, he interrupts himself.

"What is this delicious meat?"

"Chicken," I respond, surprised at his inquiry. "It is a recipe Bridget acquired from a Charley Morris, a cook at the Pickman's."

"Surely, it is not simply chicken!"

Laura pipes in, "It has pecans and pork sausage inside. I helped prepare the pecans. Charley has them brought in from the southern states. Georgia, I think. Aren't they simply delectable?"

"You helped prepare this, Laura? Well, you did a masterful job." Edward's compliment delights Laura and prompts her to explain. "Yes, you crack the pecan shells and remove every tiny bit of meat, then chop the nutmeats very finely and mix them with the ground pork sausage. I also helped pound the chicken very thin and rolled the pork and pecan mixture inside. Then dust it with flour and dip it in egg mixture and brown it..."

"Laura," Father interrupts and continues quietly toward her, "Edward did not ask for a cooking lesson. Simply accepting the compliment is sufficient."

"Yes, Father."

Edward breaks the brief silence, "Well, it is truly delicious, and I am happy to know how to prepare it, should I ever have the opportunity." Edward smiles so kindly at Laura. "In fact, as I have been dining in New York, I have found many dining establishments are serving unique dishes, but none as delicious as this." Laura beams.

After dinner, Edward comments again on the chicken and looks at me as if I might have something to say, so I offer, "This is a southern dish, from Charlie Morris' mother, called Chicken Pietro." I describe to Ned what Bridget has told me. Bridget thinks Charlie Morris is quite handsome, and presumed he was dark Irish with his deep brown eyes and hair, until she heard his accent. Only then did she realize he wasn't Irish at all. His skin is light, but his mother comes from the South, from a slave family. He is part Negro, a free black man, though. Charlie told Bridget he thinks his grandfather was probably white and was likely his mother's owner. Although she may have been someone's property, she somehow managed to get an education and share that with her children. The idea of one person owning another is despicable to us in New England. Still, this unimaginable circumstance remains very real for so many people today in the southern states.

Edward shared some shocking news, "A woman name Margaret Douglass was fined and imprisoned this week for teaching Negro children to read and write. Her daughter was also charged but while Mrs. Douglass pleaded her case in court, her daughter simply fled to New York."

"Do you know the Douglasses?"

"No, I read about their story in the Christian Watchman from Boston. I have heard Christians in the south, mostly women, are taking such actions in an effort to make amends for their family's perpetuation of slavery. Of course, they do so at great risk, as this report shows."

"I cannot imagine anything like that happening in Massachusetts. The behavior and laws seem so foreign. How could any state find fault with teaching children to read and write?"

"I expect I will experience much that will be foreign to me on my trip. For one thing, I must get acclimated to being outside more often, despite the cold air. In fact, I think I should take in some of this night air in preparation for my journey," Ned explains as he grabs his coat and my wrap. He leads me out the front door around to the frozen garden. We find the garden bench and sit down to talk.

"It is necessary to adjust to the cold by sitting very close to stay warm," he explains earnestly. This is bone-chilling air, even with a blanket over our laps. He holds me so close that I can lay my head on his shoulder and we remain for what seems like hours. He needs to talk, and I need to be held as much as he seems to want to hold me.

Edward explains, "When I did not receive a telegraph at noon last Monday, I inquired of Mr. Riley as to the ship's expected departure.

He told me they would not ship out before Wednesday at the earliest. So…" he pauses, looks at me and shrugs his shoulders.

I finish his sentence, "So, that rascal, who I love more than the sun and the moon and the stars in the heavens, took the next train to Salem to the Andrews' home just in time for supper."

———⚮———

As evening sets in, the family begins to gather in the parlor. Ned and I long for more time alone so venture outdoors. As the lights in the house are extinguished, we come into the house and continue to talk late into the night. Edward wants to hear about my schooling and my work as an assistant teacher at Miss Ward's finishing school for girls, which is conveniently located next door. He wants to hear about my work helping Father with his business.

Then, he asks about George Tufts.

"You are certain George does not misunderstand your natural kindness as something more, Lizzie? If you need to hint at our engagement, you should do that." I assure him my interest is only in my fiancé Ned.

He asks about dancing with Charlie Pierson.

"You are certain Charlie does not mistake your love of dancing to be a love of him? Is he someone you need to tell of our engagement?" I admit to loving dancing, but assure him my only other love is for my dear darling Ned.

He asks about Charlie Morris. "In Chile, I expect to meet many people unlike any I have ever seen. Perhaps I can meet Charlie Morris some time, so that no one will surprise me?"

"Perhaps, although I am not sure how. Since the 1850 Fugitive Slave Act was put into law requiring all citizens to report escaped slaves, Bridget says he rarely leaves Salem anymore. Although he has been to New York in the past, now he fears someone who does not know him could mistake him for an escaped slave."

Although neither of us felt tired, once the yawning began, we both knew we needed to get some sleep. Edward staid in Joe's room, merely a wall away from where I slept. I feared we would not rise easily in the morning, but we were up with the crow of the rooster and the moment Ned opened Joe's bedroom door, we met in the hall. "Good morning, my dear Lizzie. Did you sleep well? I woke once thinking I heard you turning in the bed."

"Good morning, my darling cousin. I slept soundly and feel completely rested. I am sorry if you were wakened though. If I had known you were awake, I would have greeted you earlier and we could have talked all night." He smiles and steals a kiss, at risk of someone seeing us in the upstairs hallway.

After breakfast, Edward escorts me early to explain to Miss Ward about his unexpected visit. She graciously allows me to assist her a different day this week. She says Friday will be best since that is the last day before the girls' winter break and she can use the most assistance then.

Edward and I spend most of the day by a cozy fire in the parlor. We speak of music, of nature and of the unknown. We speak of literature and the power of words to sooth and heal a wounded soul or to destroy one. We speak of our special words for each other, our pet names. We talk, laugh and cry together as we read from the bible, from Tennyson, Emerson, Lewis Carroll and Charles Dickens.

It really matters not what we read for we instill each passage with our own meaning and we explore the similarities and differences in how we understand what we read. Never before had we delighted so purely in the unpressured verbal intercourse derived from being in each other's presence. Periodically, we remove to the garden. As the sun breaks through early in the afternoon, Edward suggests a walk to fill ourselves with fresh cold air.

"Where shall we go?" I ask.

"Does it matter?" He replies and begins walking down the street.

"If we don't know where we are going, I suppose any road will get us there." I quote Lewis Carroll, which earns me a tender kiss before we leave the garden. We walk vigorously until one o'clock. Our teeth nearly frozen from smiling so.

I tell Edward of a new dress I have just received from the dressmaker late last week. It is for the upcoming holyday and I am excited to wear it as it is new style being fashioned after one I have seen in Godey's Lady's Book.

"What makes the style new?" he asks. I wondered if this is true interest or simply courteous conversation. As if he could hear my thoughts, he adds, "I really want to know."

"Well then, I will tell you that you have not seen the likes of it for it is a tiered plaid silk taffeta with flounced sleeves, lace under-sleeves and a lace collar that lays across my shoulders just so," I explain and touch my shoulders to show the width of the lace.

"Just so?" He traces my shoulders, sending shivers up my spine.

"Uh huh," I lose my train of thought. "What was I saying?"

"Just so," he retraces his fingers steps across my shoulders.

"Oh, dear. This will never do." I compose myself, "Aunt Dolly fashioned the lace. The same handiwork is used on the ruffle around the brim of a matching bonnet." I trace the front of my forehead where the brim will be. He reaches over and traces his fingers along my forehead, slowly and gently. "Like so?"

"Mmmmm. Uh huh."

"I really cannot imagine it," he admits. "I regret that I will not be here to see its debut."

"Shall I show it to you?"

"Oh yes. I think we should go back to your house. Very soon. Can you wear it for me?" He asks with a grin.

"I suppose I can," I say. "Yes, I certainly will," I conclude and resolve to do so before the day is out. I can hardly bear the thought of George Tufts or some other seeing it before Edward does, so now that will never occur.

After dinner, I excuse myself to my room as Edward sits a few moments with Father in the parlor. Father sees me first as I emerge from the hallway, "It is handsome, indeed, Lizzie. I think you feature that silk admirably. It is no wonder I am beginning to receive dressmaker requests for bolts of it."

"Oh yes," said Edward, almost whimsically. "It is no wonder." He stares with his mouth slightly agape.

"Well, I will excuse myself and let you continue your visit," Father says and leaves the room, smiling.

Edward exclaimed, "You are so beautiful and you look nothing like an ascot."

"What? An ascot?" I laugh.

"That is the only time I have seen a plaid dress, and never imagined it could look so feminine." He explains. "May I feel it?"

"Of course," I reply as he carefully caresses my shoulder and then my back, stroking toward my waist.

"Very nice."

"Yes, it is, isn't it?" I gasp.

"How does it twirl?" He proceeds to lift me clear off my feet and turn me in a circle, thereby causing me to twirl around the room. "It moves so freely, Lizzie." He sets my feet on the floor, still holding me, "May I kiss you, my pet?"

"Just once, my own pet darling," I reply, but of course, once is only the beginning for Edward. One kiss warrants another spin and each spin leads to yet one more kiss, though I truly do not object.

This does not continue until tea time, but nearly so. By the time he puts me down on the fainting couch I am truly breathless and so is he. He says he must fill me with enough kisses and embraces to last three years until his return.

———◇◇———

After tea, James takes Edward to the train station to catch the five o'clock car to Methuen. I ride along, savoring a few more minutes together before he reunites with his family. As he departs the carriage, and before James pulls away, I remove my glove and reach out to touch him once more. "I love you," I whisper. He kisses my hand with the tenderest of all kisses. I savor the touch of his warm lips, so soft against my skin. He promises to write from Methuen although he explains he will stay there only two nights as he is obligated to return to New York Thursday.

As I watch him walk away toward the train station, I reach back to settle onto the bench and feel something behind me. It is his umbrella. I tap the carriage ceiling and James pulls over, whereby I run toward the station, but Edward does not look back. That requires me to scurry as quickly as I can to reach him.

"Your umbrella!" I say breathlessly.

"My umbrella!" he repeats, grinning broadly. "Those have just become the most beautiful words I have ever heard uttered from someone's lips."

With that I could only smile as I backed away, "Go now, no more excuses! You mustn't miss the car's departure."

The Metropolitan Hotel

The New York Times
January 16, 1854

Interesting Statement of a Passenger

...On Monday, December 26, Lieutenant Murray still encouraged us with the fond hope that we were in the track of vessels, and we need not despair. Towards evening the welcome words, "A sail in sight!" were again passed from mouth to mouth. On her approaching us we found her to be the Maria Freeman (bound to Liverpool, Nova Scotia). When she came within hailing distance we spoke to her, and she promised to remain near. The night gale continued still from the northwest, and the next morning, the Maria Freeman had also disappeared...

CHAPTER 12

Daguerreotype

New York, [Saturday] 3d December, 1853 A. M.

Dear Lizzie,

I am uncommonly happy now, even more happy than I usually am when writing to you: for when I went to Mr. Riley's office this morning, he handed me your letter of yesterday morning which of course made me a little bit glad. I thought Mr. R. smiled a little when he gave me the envelope, but I laughed very loud ("in my sleeve") when I saw the hand writing. This was the beginning of my joy, but it was not half begun. I left directions to have my two trunks sent to the hotel from 42 South St. and when I reached here, I found them in my room. I had to wait a few moments, for the servant was sweeping &c. but when my room was ready, I locked the door, opened my large trunk, and took out my writing desk. You know what I keep there? Don't be jealous, if I tell you it is somebody's daguerreotype in a large case, and the same somebody's hair in a beautiful little ring. It seemed such an age since I had seen either of them: to be sure they didn't look like strangers, but I was so very glad to see them again. Only think, it is almost a fortnight since I had seen either of them. I am writing this with the ring on and my darling's face is looking up at me so beautifully.

A servant has just called to say I have a caller below.

Adieu – pet - till he goes –

Later - my friend was Marsh a young lawyer of New York, who was an old school-mate of mine. He has staid some time and it is half past four now, so that I can spend barely half an hour with you now; for I am expecting Ward, a Cambridge class-mate, to dine with me and we dine at five. This is rather late for one who is accustomed to one o'clock as a dining hour. But I have become gradually accustomed to this, for Uncle dines at three and the Astor at 4 P.M. I was going down to see Mr. Marsh with your ring on my finger, but I thought he might think it funny, so I locked it safely up in my desk.

It looks very much like a snow storm here today and I may have a sleigh ride before I leave New York. But that is hardly possible even if there should be three feet of snow.

Though I have written to you every day, Lizzie, yet I have sent two or three letters in one envelope, for I thought gossip in Salem would say some things that you would not like if it were known every mail brought you a letter from New York. But with me of course it is different for no one here can suppose I have a letter every day from the same pen. So, darling, please send to me as often as you can. Mr. Riley thinks I always look as if I expect something, when I enter his office.

I feel much happier in this room than I have any time since I left you, for now I can have my writing-desk, with both daguerreotypes and the ring, and I am sure of being alone. When I was at Rockwood I was sure of being uninterrupted but I was afraid my absence so much would be thought strange by those below stairs.

I think I will call on Mrs. Sprague on Monday.

Wm. Kimball told me this morning (he promised last night to call) that Martha Bird would reach New York today and he told me where I should find her. But should I not call till Monday she would think I did right to pass over Sunday.

Tomorrow I mean to devote exclusively to you, unless some one should send to my room for me. I may attend church, though I don't know where to go. But you shall be told tomorrow everything

I do. It is nearly five o'clock and I must go down to meet Mr. Ward. Au revoir dearest.

10¼ A.M. Dear Lizzie. I had hardly put this sheet in my writing desk at five o'clock, when 'rap' at the door and Mr. Ward's card was handed to me. I hastened down and found not only Ward, but two other classmates, Sargent and Cary. We made a quartette at dinner and after dinner Ward said he had arranged for an evening at Wallack's Theatre; and as I could not plead an engagement (for I had promised yesterday to pass the evening with Ward) why to Wallack's I went, though I had told you only last evening that I could not go to a theatre with any pleasure. What a jewel is consistency! But I guess you won't feel very bad, shall you, for I have done nothing very wrong.

To go on - At Wallack's we saw the old comedy of "A cure for the heart-ache." The acting (they all said) was very fine, but I did not enjoy it quite as much as I should at any other time. During the evening I thought of that afternoon we went together at the Boston Museum. Do you remember it? Caddie Fellows was with us. I met you in Cambridge Street as you passed the Revere house, and after-wards at the Museum and left you in the Chelsea omnibus. When I reached home (Cambridge) I remember I wrote in my Journal I know I am very fond of Lizzie, and I think she at least likes my attention. Sometimes now I feel very sorry that I destroyed my Journal, for it used to be very pleasant to read over what I had written; for the sight of a passage like the above would always call to mind some very pleasant scenes that had passed. Still I think it is for the best that I did burn it up; for had any accident happened to me; had our house caught on fire and my books been thrown into the street, I should then have felt much more sorry than I now do, if any one had had an opportunity of reading what I had written. How I ramble from one thing to another! Just as if we were sitting side by side and talking with each other.

When I reached my room this evening I found a card at my door with a name on it, which I can't for the life of me make out. It begins with S. W. but the name is perfectly, unintelligible to me. Can you imagine any S. W. &c whom I know? I hardly suppose you can, but it is barely possible. However he will probably call again.

It seems very pleasant, dear pet, to be alone with you now, & I am much happier since I have had the contents of my writing desk. I inquired of Mr. Riley today about letters between here and Valparaiso. He said merely direct to "E. J. Tenney, care of Alsop & Co. Valparaiso – Chile," in all cases prepaying postage. The postage is he thinks about 50-cents for half an ounce, so in all cases use thin letter paper like this if you can. Perhaps you had better have your father direct some envelopes for you; but I will tell you more decidedly about this before I go and perhaps I can obtain a copy of the Post-office regulations, and see by what mail you can write so that I may have some letters from you soon after I reach Valp.

I shan't go to Mr. Riley's office tomorrow and so, I shall not find my pet's letter, but I shall know you will be writing to me, perhaps at the same time I am writing to you. I hope I shall not have many callers tomorrow, for I want to be alone with you, as much as I can. Our Steamer was to make her trial trip (the second one) this afternoon and if she finds her machinery perfect she will start on Tuesday. The Captain is at this hotel but I have not seen him yet, except a moment on board the Steamer.

I want to go on board once more before I leave so that I may write you a full description of my state room. Mr. Chancy told me yesterday it was a very fine room. I hope it may be.

Should anyone be looking over your shoulder while you are reading this letter they will think you have some friend who likes to write very well. So he does to you. I have only room to say Good night - I shan't forget my bible - nor something else - darling pet. I love you very much darling and you may tell everyone of it if you choose.

Good night - my love – can't you dream tonight – Just for once –
do - Goodnight --E

————◁✕▷————

My life with Edward becomes very real when it is lifted from his
pages by his words. I truly feel as if I am at his side listening to him
rattle on, as I was so fortunate to be during his surprise visit! A sigh
escapes my lips as I settle in once again to wait for my true love's
next visit, knowing this time the wait may be very, very long.

When I am not in the world of Ned's letters, I move restlessly
through the motions of my routine life. Chores and tasks, reading
and conversing—all of this is as if it were a vivid dream. My true
life lies hidden between the lines of these little sheets of paper. As
long as I have this, I am content to wait.

The Nor-Easter winds have been whipping the Massachusetts
shores and City of Boston. The walls seem to struggle to keep
out the cold and I hear them groan in the wind as their backsides
are whipped by sleet. I do hope New York's weather fares more
favorably in the days to come and does not become the reason for
additional delays of the steamer, unless, of course, such a delay is
sufficient time to bring my Ned back into my arms.

Joe and Laura have both moved on, it seems, and, without Ed-
ward, I find myself waiting, waiting, waiting for a sign as to what
I am to do next. Am I to fill in the roles left by any of these three?
I think not, but what?

I wonder how Joe fares on *The Josephine* this winter. He enjoys
being out of doors. He used to help keep the snow from the front
door of our home. Surely, that is not a task for me.

Laura was fond of grinding the herbs for teas and spices—of
cinnamon, clove and nutmeg. Yet, that is not a task for me.

James splits and Bridget stacks wood by each fireplace daily.
Thanks to them, we are ready to keep the house warm. That is not
a task for me.

111

Aunt Eliza fills the house with the smell of yeast breads twice a week. I join her to bake blueberry muffins and lemon-cake for tea. But, there must be more for me. Why is it I feel I am simply an observer? A patient observer. Waiting. Waiting. Waiting.

As I spread a fresh sheet of paper on my writing desk, preparing to record my thoughts, I ask myself, 'Is my purpose to bring the life I observe in Salem off the pages, so Edward can feel it and taste it and be comforted by it?' That thought brings a smile to my face.

I am faithful to my promise to read no more than a letter a day and write a response of my own ramblings and observations from the streets to the skies, from my heart to my eyes. I resist the temptation to read the next day's pages of this letter bundle, and place the envelope seal down to keep it from flapping open and teasing me. I can almost hear Ned's voice calling from the envelope. 'I am in here bursting with love,' it says … 'come get me, Lizzie. Release me from the prison of duty that binds me to New York and the steamer *San Francisco*!' I imagine Edward is singing. The envelope sings to me, 'Do not wait to read me!' It sings. It truly sings. The image of Sing Sing prison comes to mind. I am sure the devil is attempting to corrupt my resolve. I pat the envelope with a sharp flick of my wrist, like I would pat the nose of a puppy needing to learn not to nip at me. I place the letter under my bible, 'You wait!' I speak aloud and leave the desperate letter alone in my room, certain that my Bible will keep it company until morning.

I ready for bed and sleep fitfully among dreams of prisoners reaching through the bars of their cells, calling out to me, as they wave letters pleading, 'Lizzie, read this. Lizzie, please read this.' I walk by the desperate men but do not look, keeping my face pointed forward. The next morning, I awake early, relieved to be awake and in my own bed. Sitting up, I drop my feet to greet the cold floor, snatch the envelope off my bureau and hop back into bed to read guiltlessly. I have kept my promise to wait to devour my reward.

State prison at Sing Sing, New York, 1855

The New York Times
January 16, 1854

Interesting Statement of a Passenger

...A strange fate seemed to be hanging over us, and despair was more clearly depicted upon every countenance. All hopes seemed now to have vanished, and had it not been for Lieutenant Murray – the Good Samaritan of our little flock – many, I fear, would have lost their reason. The suffering and privations of the ladies can only be imagined. Most of them had lost all their baggage, and every article of raiment excepting a few which they themselves had saved about their persons. Such of them as had retained any extra clothing, generously distributed it to the needy. Several hours in each day were passed in substituting dry for wet clothes. The sea, which had been continually breaking over the vessel, came rushing in at intervals from the portholes and skylights above, so that the floor of the cabin was always wet, and the mattresses upon which we laid were perfectly saturated...

CHAPTER 13

Captain Watkins

Sunday Morning - 4th Dec. 1853
[Metropolitan Hotel]

My dear Lizzie,

You won't scold me very hard for staying away from church this morning, will you? For in the first place, being a stranger in the city, I knew not where to go, secondly it is very cold out of doors and I am so weak and delicate, you know, that I feared I might catch cold if I ventured out. These are two nominal reasons why I have remained at home; the real reason is that I wanted to spend the day with you. (Perhaps you will say I did right now you have the true cause.)

My room is so cold now, that I have brought my paper down to the parlor and I am writing in a large room with a dozen or so occupants, writing, reading, talking, looking out of the window &c. &c. But everything is done so much more quietly and politely in this hotel than at the Astor House that I am not half as much disturbed as I was last Tuesday. I am so much better satisfied here than I was there. For at the Astor, I could not write in my own room, and if I attempted to write in the public room, I was suffocated with tobacco-smoke, crazed by the din of noisy talkers, swearing & laughing the whole time. Many of the hotel guests are away, at church I suppose, and therefore more quiet than usual even pervades the house.

This morning I met Captain Watkins (of the *San Francisco*). He told me his steamer would not, he feared, be able to leave till after Tuesday, though he could not say decidedly till tomorrow. I am going on board of her tomorrow, and if possible I will try to obtain a bird's-eye view of her state-rooms etc. and write you an account of it. She has made a second trial trip and is now lying at her wharf. If she is to be delayed the greater part of the week, I may possibly go back to Boston again. I am almost tempted to go home just once more, but even if I should go to Methuen, I fear I might be more restless there than I am here, for then I could not spend all my time with you, and it would perhaps seem as if I had purposely postponed my departure and waited for another ship.

I am going to send my daguerreotype home tomorrow, and I think it will be more satisfactory than the one they now have. Won't you tell me what you think of it, darling, when you see it one of these days? I am glad that I know what you would advise me in regard to giving Martha Bird a copy. Still I should very much prefer not giving it to her, and if I can help it (that is without offence) I shall certainly not give her one. I never thought there would be anything improper in it of course, for I have been so much in the family that they always say I am as their own brother.

I have not found out yet who my caller of last evening is, but I am expecting to see his face any time today.

Dorsheimer said that he would call on me about three o'clock this afternoon if he could, but he was going away last evening and might not return in season. I spent an hour with him at the "St. Nicholas" yesterday morning.

There is one of my classmates in Wall Street (Howland) whom I am going to see before I leave New York.

I have not yet seen any one in New York whom I thought looked enough like Charlie Morris to permit of a self-introduction; and what is more, I am afraid I shall not. But don't be alarmed; pet; that is only a joke: of course I have no idea of introducing myself to Charlie Morris. But I have nevertheless some curiosity to see him, for _______ for _______ oh "I shan't tell you, you old goosie Ned."

Such fierce mustaches as there are at the Metropolitan! In some cases all one can see of the face is a pair of very small eyes and the tip end of a nose. Then other poor fellows have only a few miserable stray hairs hanging loosely about, evidently pulled to their utmost tension in hopes that others would follow their example.

Frank Holyoke had just the same face he always had except that it was much thinner and very pale. He said that he tho't he might go back to the Cambridge Scientific School as an Assistant to Professor Horsford.

I have been interested this morning by watching the carriages passing up and down Broadway. They are so different from those in Boston, and I like very much to see a fine looking carriage drawn by a large handsome span with a colored coachman and footman in livery. Sometimes the livery and harness is too gaudy, and that looks so much like display, that it seems to savor of vulgarity. But in most cases, where the coach & foot men are dressed neatly with heavy claret colored (isn't that the color) coats and perhaps a simple band round their hats, I think the appearance is very fine. The distances between the upper and lower parts of the city are so great that almost every lady who can afford it, keeps a carriage, and therefore we see many more private carriages in proportion to the citizens than in Boston.

What a funny letter this is to write to you, darling! But it seems so different to be writing to you in company with so many others, and writing alone with no one to look at except a pleasant little face that seems to be saying "Dear Ned."

I had just written that last word when somebody tapped me on the shoulder and I saw - Cary, who said he had been waiting for me half an hour down stairs. So I ran up here to my room to put this away and I must go down. Adieu, darling, I am going to see your face before I go. – "Dear pet"

2¼ P.M. I have just returned from a walk with Cary (no relation to "Mother Carey's Chickens"). If I write any more after dinner, what a letter you will have. If I go on in the same geometrical progression I have begun, by the time I come back again you will have a ship-load of stationery. First I sent you four pages, then eight, then twelve and now it may be sixteen.

But it is such a pleasure to me, dearest, to sit and chat with you that though I say nothing of any use or profit, yet I want to be writing all the time. If I try to write slowly, I forget what I am saying so I have to rattle on as if I were really talking.

We have said nothing about Mr. & Mrs. Edwin Tufts, as we usually do when alone together, and I was thinking of that this morning. We have talked of George Tufts, though, my own darling, and perhaps that will do instead.

In our walk today; we found everything as different from week days. All the streets but Broadway seemed deserted. We went down to the wharf where lay the *San Francisco*, but of course only passed by the vessel, as no one would be admitted, I suppose, on Sunday. I do hope she will be able to go by the middle of the week, for it seems very provoking to have them add one day at a time to her remaining. Don't think, darling, I am very impatient, for I try to wait as contentedly as possible. Still I think I should like to sail right away unless they would give me a fortnight, so that I might see you.

I won't begin another sheet till after dinner, darling and perhaps before that time I may have some visitors.

I have been writing the last page in my room, and am quite cold, so that I can't hold my pen very steadily.

If I go on at this rate your desk won't hold my letters much longer. I shall expect such a Journal from you at Valpo. as will make me perfectly happy for a month when I shall look for another.

Adieu, darling -

The Ned of his own pet ---

I glance at the next page and notice my Ned continues to write on the fourth of December, so justify that I may continue to read with no violation of my pledge to myself. Then I hear a loud squawk outside my bedroom window and look over to see a bird on my window sill. A bird? It is winter, I complain. How did this bird come to be at my window when the weather has already turned cold?

"Are you lost from your flock?" I ask, as if this bird has come to see me. As if the bird can hear me through the window. As if the bird understands my words.

"Go now. You must find your flock and join them for the journey to warmer climes." He simply looks at me as if to say, 'let me in. I am cold.'

"Go now. It is time. Go!" I say. "Go!" I brush my hands as if to shoo him away and he takes off with a wide wing span and disappears so quickly I am haunted by images of Mother Carey's chickens. Was this a lost soul come to visit me? Was this a drowned seaman whose lost soul is transformed into a storm petrel? I have heard all the old seamen tales about Mother Nature, or Mother Carey, as she is more often described in mixed company. She takes the seamen she wants, the bravest, the most handsome, those with the brightest wit and plucks them from the sea in a storm or a wave. They simply disappear, only to be replaced with petrels that scavenge the surface of the sea looking for food.

Is this my brother? Could he be lost at sea unbeknownst to anyone? No. No. No, I quickly reprimand myself. This cannot be him. This is all old tales made up by lonely men at sea, bored old lonely men, men who have had too much drink, men who have too much time, men with too vivid of imaginations.

I peer out and there is no bird in sight. No other bird, anywhere in sight. Perhaps I am the one with too vivid an imagination, an absurd imagination. Joe is fine, I know in my heart.

Perhaps, I shan't read one more letter today, with respect to my pledge, even though it is written the same day. Just in case. I do not want to anger Mother Carey.

Instead, I begin the next morning with a paper visit from my Ned.

"Good morning, darling!" I say as I grab the pages and crawl back into my bed to read.

Mother Carey and her chickens by J. G. Keulemans, 1877

The New York Times
January 16, 1854

Interesting Statement of a Passenger

...On December 28, owing to the imprudence of the waiters in eating some pickled cabbage and such articles as they could procure, the diarrhea broke out in the fore cabin of the vessel. Johnson, the head waiter, was the first victim, and the corpses of several others, dying from the same cause, were committed to the deep. This melancholy circumstance was only known to a few on board...

CHAPTER 14

Ring on My Finger

Sunday evening – 9½ o'clock. [Dec. 4, 1853]

Dear pet.

I should have exhausted my cabinet of writing material for to-day, you will think; and so to conjure up something to say, I have before beginning to write, taken every means of forcing that was in my power.

My ring, my only ring is on my finger while I write and in front of me are both daguerreotypes looking me full in the face. Shall I tell you what I think they seem to be saying? The large one says "Now, Ned, you know I am h_nd_ _ _e: and you couldn't deny it if you wanted to: I really love you, Ned, but I love to plague you a little just to see you cry once in a while." This is what the mouth says; the eyes tell me "dear Ned, I won't plague you for I do love you very, very much; do you love me a little bit - so much?" Oh, I know that face loves me very much and I am very much charmed by the face: I am very proud of it. Sometimes I think it is going to say "Fiddle-stick;" I can almost see the lips parting to speak and then I can't help snatching it right up in my hands and - and - a dozen times. Then again it seems as if the head were on my shoulder perfectly contented, and then I am very happy and I resolve that

I will try as hard as I can to make you always happy and always perfectly contented.

Oh, Lizzie, I do love that large daguerreotype and I love to gaze at it all the time. You will forgive me, darling just this once, for I must say what I think. I think that daguerreotype is very, very beautiful. There, it seemed to smile when I looked up after writing that, as if to say "Well, dear! Ned, I love you so much that I will forgive you, but I think you are a silly fellow." Dearest, that picture is such a treasure to me that I do not think I could possibly be without it. Should it be destroyed by any accident you may depend upon my sending immediately home for another. I have taken up almost a whole page in talking about this, but every time I look at it, there is something else to say. Please rest your head on my shoulder a little while, darling, and then we will talk about the little pet. Won't you turn your face up towards mine? There, darling, (thank you) I will be quiet now. I did not think what I was doing till I felt a tear on my cheek.

You are very dear to me, Lizzie, and as I was looking in your face then, I thought of our last afternoon in Boston, and I felt one tear on my cheek. It is the first time I have shed a tear for a good many days. Why, pet, you are crying too! "Dear Lizzie." I mean, darling, to do nothing which I think you would disapprove. I did something today for your sake which I think would please you a little, but I must not tell you "for self praise &c."

Dearest I must shut up the large picture, while I write about the little pet, for I can't help stopping to look at it very often and very long: and when I do, it always lays its head on my shoulder and then I can think of nothing else, when it turns up its face and looks in my face so confidingly. How happy we should be if fate never separated us, my precious darling. It is very pleasant, now that we are absent from each other, that we can write so freely and unreservedly. You don't think I write too sillily do you, darling, or with too little modesty? Because when I am writing to you, I put down almost everything that comes into my head; I try to write just as I would talk and of course a third person would think I wanted a little more reserve and delicacy. You don't think so, do you? You know I don't want you to resemble Mrs. Bradstreet in everything.

And now I'll tell you what little pet says to me. "Dear Ned, I am your own, yours alone; I am going to try to be as good as I can while you are gone and I want you to try and be good too, Ned; won't you read a chapter in the bible every day, Ned?" Often when I am looking at your face in this daguerreotype, darling, I think of your mother. I don't know why, but it very often calls her to mind, and I always love to think of you and your mother together. I think it used to be very pleasant to talk of her. Do you remember those long talks we had about your mother that Winter I was in Salem? I thought then, each night when I left you and retired to my own room, that you had a great deal of confidence in me, and I used to indulge a hope that you loved me better than you could love a cousin or even, a brother. It was very hard sometimes, as we sat alone for an hour or more and talked so affectionately to each other and so kindly, to restrain my tongue from telling you that I loved you, really "true-loved" you. And now "I have a charge to keep." I hope God may aid me to keep that precious carefully and faithfully.

Why, darling mine, what a nice long talk we have had together this evening. When I first began to write, I had no idea that my brain would furnish more than four pages in one day. My brain has not furnished this sheet; I trusted entirely to my three talismen, and you see what they have done.

I had not written three lines on the first page when a servant came to tell me a gentleman was waiting in the parlor to see me. I left my sentence unfinished, went down and found Dorsheimer who dropped in to explain why he had been unable to call this afternoon. But he said he could only remain a few moments now, for he had promised to meet some gentlemen at the "St. Nicholas."

I called at Commodore McKeever's just after dinner this evening, but he was away with Mrs. McKeever. The Captain is a very fine, modest, man.

This week the New Yorkers will have the opera at Niblo's and Jullien at Metropolitan Hall. I wish you were here: for we could go to Niblo's tomorrow, evening and hear Jullien's orchestra on Tuesday. But it is cruel for me to tell you what comfort we might have together (under some circumstances) when I know it is almost impossible, under the present circumstances.

I had a fire made in my room this evening so that I might write to you, or I should have frozen otherwise. I am going to leave a little space to bid you Good-morning in before breakfast, if it is not too cold in my room when I get up, so I say "Good-night" now darling. Good night.

<hr>

"Goodnight, my darling Ned," I say, "and a good morning as well." I roll out of bed to dress by the warmth from the fireplace. How fortunate am I! Bridget came early to light the logs, for although it is December, winter feels mild to me now. I pull on my day dress, again filled with gratitude that I am to work with Father today, not travel to Hamilton for school. I make entries in his ledgers to assure nothing is amiss. I tell him I am tidying his books. I do like to see that his business is as neat and tidy as a General's business should be. At the end of these short winter days, I fall into bed and sleep soundly. Tonight, I have saved a page from my Ned. The page crackles as I unfold it in the cool air to read.

5th Dec. – 'Good morning,' little pet! You will chide me for being lazy this morning, for you have been dressed more than an hour. It is just nine o'clock and I have only this moment finished dressing myself, not having breakfasted yet. But I did not go to bed till it was very late last night & the breakfast hour is from 5 to 12; so I am rather early than late. I am going on board the *San Francisco* after breakfast and by the time the Eastern mail is distributed I shall be at Mr. Riley's office. Shall I find a letter?

If you could leave Salem for a day or two this week, darling, and come part way to New York to visit any friends you have perhaps our Steamer may be delayed long enough to permit me to see you. I really think an hour or two in each other's society would be very valuable to both of us, though the parting again would be as hard as it was before. Oh, dearest, if you only lived in New York city, how very pleasant would the past fortnight have seemed to both of us.

I think I never knew till lately how much I loved my little treasure. I was always certain that you were very, very dear to me, but I think of so many things now that never occurred to me before.

But we shall see each other in a few years, and then, oh, darling, who can have greater joy?

I shall probably see Martha Bird today and I think I may be occupied all day till late in the evening.

I shall bid your lips good morning and then go down stairs -

Adieu my own loved one,

Ned.

P.S. Monday noon - I have just resolved to do something- can you guess it!   Ned.

———◦✕◦———

The final line of this letter brings back the full thrill of seeing my darling Ned at my door last week, on December 5th, that was the very day he wrote this letter and teased me about how he had to hand-delivered a package of letters too large to mail. Though I begged him, much like a young child, to give me the package immediately or read the letters aloud to me, I am now grateful we did not. Edward waited until the moment he left me to give me his envelope, nearly a full week since he had written the first page.

Waiting allowed me another week with him, one that would have been missed if either he or I had read the letters in the short time we had together. Had I rushed through them without patience this week, I would use up our extra days of visits. Instead, I savored each one as if it were the last. This is my practice for becoming patient.

He fills me with such immense joy there is no room left for sorrow to emerge about his departure. His parting is not as scorching on my heart this time, for I had just experienced the elation of his unexpected return, and the pleasure of my release from fear that each time he leaves could be the last. I now know he will always return to me.

I settle into my writing desk this Sunday the 11th of December to gaze at his handsome face, framed just before me. I can almost see him talking. During his last visit I paid special attention to the manner in which he relaxes his jaw when preparing to speak. He tilts his head slightly forward to emphasize the conclusion of a statement. I posture now as if I were Edward and treasure the comfort of knowing him so intimately. These are not gestures I can see in his writing, but when I gaze at his daguerreotype, which I love so dearly, they appear. He is convincingly brilliant, masterfully charming and dreadfully handsome to me—someone Mother Carey would love, I think, and then chastise myself immediately for having had that thought and cover it quickly with thoughts of Edward's strength of courage. His courage is matched only by his tenderness, a balance so rare and beautiful he could choose any lady he wanted. In fact, many ladies have dreamed of being his, but I know he is my true love and I am his only pet. Well, one of four pets, to hear him speak. But I am not in the least bit jealous for they are all me! I snicker to myself. That will never change, not in two years or twenty years. What great fortune has been bestowed upon me!

I looked up with a revelation and shock that I am becoming just like Edward, musing on ad infinitum, staring dreamily at a framed likeness. Now I laugh at my own blushing self!

Lizzie reading Edward's letter

The New York Times
January 16, 1854

Interesting Statement of a Passenger

...During the morning on December 28, the *Bark Kilby* from New Orleans and bound to Boston, hove in sight, and reported herself short of provisions and water, and promised to remain alongside of us, which promise we had reason to hope would be fulfilled, from the fact of her being short of provisions. All hearts were cheered, and as the weather moderated our brave Captain was enabled on the following morning to ask the Captain of the *Kilby* to send his boats to the steamer, (our boats having of course been lost). On the next morning when Captain Watkins boarded the *Kilby*, he, on behalf of the United States Government, contracted to pay the owners $15,000 to take as many of the passengers off the steamer on board his vessel as was possible. He further agreed to give the Captain $200 a day, on behalf of the Pacific Mail Steamship Company, to lay alongside in case he should be obliged to do so for any great length of time. The Captain was also to receive $1,000 for his noble conduct in launching his boats, when his crew had refused the duty, and the sea threatened to swallow him up with his frail craft, as well as five percent primage on the amount contracted to be paid by the Government...

CHAPTER 15

⸺◦✕◦⸺

By Excuse of Umbrella

Miss M. E. Andrews
Salem
Mass.

Methuen, Wednesday evening. [Dec. 7th, 1853]

My own darling Lizzie,

I am certain that I shall see you again before I go to New York. I can't feel that I have said "good-bye," and that the last touch of your hand from the window was the last I shall have for a long time. I don't know what makes me so positive of this, but something tells me we shall yet pass a few happy hours together very soon. Though I received no telegraphic despatch tonight, I know I shall find one tomorrow. But if I should not, darling! Oh then; how much I shall think of the last ten hours we spent together and the evening before: how pleasant they will seem in the remembrance of them!

Why, my dear pet, I feel as different as possible from what I did on Monday night, a fortnight since. And it is this which makes me so positive of being told to stay a few days longer. When I look at your little face, I tell it "I am coming soon": then it seems to smile, tho' sadly as if it feared not. But I can't have any doubt about it - Do you remember, darling, what I said to you about my wishing to sit alone with you or talking of you all this evening?

I felt so unhappy then, when I reached home, to find Margaret Phillips and Jacob Emerson sitting here. But what could I do, dearest? I could almost cry, for I knew you would be at home because Ned had asked you to, and I was to think of you all the evening. And I did darling, but not as happily as I wanted to, for I had to say something once in a while. But I took particular pains to show Margaret Phillips, by my conversation that I loved Lizzie Andrews. Wasn't that right dear pet? But they had heard of my arrival and so Mary had invited Johnny & M. to tea, expecting I would be at home by six o'clock. But you are glad, darling, that I have told you all about it are you not, Dearest? I want to tell you everything, though I know anything like this makes you feel unhappy.

Do tell me when you send your letter on Friday morning, what I should have done. I must say Good-night, dear pet, for I could only find this half sheet of paper, after all have retired, and I want to say something tomorrow morning.

Thursday A.M.-ll½ - Dear - dear Lizzie - I write now with fear & trembling, for I have rec'd no despatch yet, and I am almost afraid to ask at the office this noon - If I have said "Good bye," darling! Oh, dear pet, how I shall enjoy yesterday.

Good bye dear, my own, dear Lizzie.

I will write from New York - dear pet - Good bye - My own darling.

If you could buy that for Lizzie and have it charged at Miss Shillaber's, she would be glad she says.

I send this by excuse of umbrella; please give it to Mr. Stevens?

———◦✕◦———

"Lizzie?" Laura called from behind my closed door. "Are you awake?"

132

"Mmm. Yes? What time is it?"

"It is eight o'clock and already light. Are you not going to Miss Ward's today?

"Oh, dear! Come in Laura. Did Father inquire as to my where-abouts?" Laura pushed open the door and appeared fully dressed.

"Not exactly. He asked Bridget if she had lit your fire this morning and she assured him she had."

"Oh my, I did not even hear her enter. Can you help me ready? I am still in my dishabille."

"Your dishabille? Lizzie, you are funny, waking up and speaking French. Do you dream in French?"

"Heavens, no. Dishabille is not French and there is simply no better word to describe my state of dress, or undress, and disarray."

"Laura laid my dress out on the bed. Bridget had indeed been there for my water pitcher had been filled. I splashed water on my face and sat on the bedside to slip my feet into my boots and lace them before I dress. It is much easier to reach my feet before I am clad with corset and crinoline as that makes such a maneuver trying. Stepping into my bloomers, Laura wrapped my corset around my midsection and gave a swift tug to tighten the laces. With my arms up she threw my crinoline over my head and I dove into my dress.

"There, have we set a race record for swiftness of dress, Laura?" I asked and twisted my hair into a knot pinning it securely.

"I believe we have."

I wondered how a poor woman without a servant or a sister, or a pioneer woman, would dress with no assistance.

Tea and a scone in hand, I wrapped my cape around my shoulders, grabbed my hat and muff and was out the door. The image of the umbrellas in the stand by the door harkened me back to Edward. He certainly was not rushed as he left the carriage, rather was distracted. I opened the door and grabbed the umbrella. I will only be a few minutes late, I thought, and can simply explain my tardiness to Miss Ward's by excuse of umbrella.

The New York Times
January 16, 1854

Interesting Statement of a Passenger

...At 3 o'clock P.M. the hawser was run to the bow of the *Kilby*, and soon after, the disembarkation of the passengers commenced. Great fears were entertained by many that the boats would be swamped, owing to the rush to get into them. Several of the officers had provided themselves with weapons to keep back the crowd, and Colonel Gates addressed the troops, declaring that he would be the last to desert the ship, and that he hoped the officers and soldiers on board would follow his example, and wait with patience until their names were called. The first boat which left carried Col. Gates and family...

CHAPTER 16

Steamer's Delay

Miss M. E. Andrews
Care of Gen. Joseph Andrews
Salem
Masstts.

Friday Decr. 9th/ 53
New York - 2 o'clock in the morning.

Dear Lizzie-

I have just reached my room after a very long ride from Boston, and though it is so late and I am very tired, I could not sleep, dear pet, without saying a few words to my darling. I hardly could control my actions at Lawrence this noon. I found the telegraph office closed and I was uncertain whether I was allowed to stay a few days more or not. I had but a moment in which to decide what to do; but I thought duty bade me wait no longer. I was so bewildered that I can't tell whether your letter was sealed or not, when I put it in the express box. I was very anxious to send that note today that you might have no doubt of what I had decided upon.

Oh, dear, good Lizzie, I can hardly guide my pen now. That sweet, darling face smiles so pleasantly, as if to persuade me that all was for the best, and yet I think perhaps I might have staid a few days longer. But perhaps it is as well, dearest, that our parting was so uncertain. When I left you last night I was sure of seeing you again, and so when I wrote to you; but this morning I began to doubt and now, dear Lizzie - I shall not see you again for a long time. I can't help crying darling, even when I think of the happy day we have just spent together. May God preserve us both faithful to each other for ever? I can write more calmly tomorrow, but now it seems as if I felt far more badly than I did when we parted a fortnight ago. May God bless you, my own darling! Good night: those dear faces, and that cherished ring, good night. Good night - my dear love: Ned.

Friday 9th Dec'r - 1 P.M. Dear Lizzie. I went on board our Steamer this forenoon and Capt. Watkins told me we shall not sail before the middle of next week, probably not before the last of the week. Why he did not telegraph to me, I know not: but he may have been uncertain himself of the time he should have to wait. I try hard to think it is for the best, and I will wait as patiently as I can. But I do feel unhappy this morning; for I can't help thinking how much better it would have been, could I have staid at home a week longer.

I have not seen Uncle Edwin this morning: he was engaged at a Director's meeting and I did not wish to interrupt him. I may see him before he leaves New York. It seems as if I could not be contented here another week. Oh Lizzie I can hardly write to you. If I could only see you now. I know I should put my head on your shoulder and burst out crying. I could not help it. This forenoon I have been imagining everything that I was almost killed by an omnibus and that yours was the first face I saw when I came to myself, that I was struck by a falling stone in Broadway and confined to my room till the Steamer sailed, while you came on to see me and thus made our engagement public. I have been as nervous as possible since I heard of the Steamer's delay: and I have felt as if I had no strength left. Do forgive me, darling, for writing so complainingly: but I can't help it. I never was in such a state before in all my life. It seems as if I could drop from my chair, lifeless. I must be more manly, dearest, I will not allow myself to feel so. I think when I find your letter tomorrow noon, I shall feel much happier.

Dear, dear Lizzie! Perhaps the day we have just spent together was too pleasant for me. How I love to think of that morning and afternoon, my own darling. I felt such pride. Lizzie, when you came down after dinner, dressed in the plaid silk. But I must not tell you what I thought, for you don't love to have even Ned tell you some things. How I love to say over to myself, "My own darling!" I think I have such a treasure all to myself, and I hope I may prove worthy of my trust. And I want you to try and feel, dearest, as much confidence in me as you can; and tell me everything. We do love each other now and I know we always shall if we tell everything that passes through our minds of any interest to each other. I am sure, my darling, I love you too well to wish that you should see me in any other light than that of nature.

My dear love, I think I feel much better than I did when I began to write to you, this noon. I was so nervous, I could hardly sit in my chair: and for me, darling, you know that is very strange. I have hardly time to finish this letter, for I want to send it tonight, so that you may receive it on Saturday. The boat leaves at four and probably the mail at the Metropolitan closes at three. I must send a line home, by the same mail, telling mother of the delay. I have a letter from Liz in my pocket, written a week ago, but I have not had time to read it as I hurried up from Mr. Riley's office to write to you.

Oh my own pet, I was very happy to think I saw you at the window on Wednesday night. I dared not look back again after I kissed your hand for the last time. And I thought you would not forget that last touch for a long while. Shall you darling? All that evening at home, I could not help thinking of that; it was so pleasant, and then it was so unexpected. When I looked back for my umbrella, I thought I could not see you again, and I was looking as quietly as possible, when you came out. But I am so glad it was left, for I could send to you on Thursday. Dear pet, Heaven bless you. I am much happier than I was an hour ago.

Your own true
Ned.

I shall go on writing when this mail goes.

———◇———

"I received a visit from Mr. Stevens today, Lizzie," Father said as we sat at the supper table. I thought, what a peculiar thing to tell me, and with no explanation, indeed.

"Was it a pleasant visit?" I asked, now quite curious as to why I was being so informed. Uncle Daniel and Aunt Dolly were at table, as was Grandmother and Laura, but he seemed to speak only to me.

"He came to apologize for he said he had been charged to bring me a note scribed by a young accountant from Methuen," he replied.

"Was it an important note?" I inquired, not yet registering that my Edward was indeed an accountant. Father was certainly teasing me, as he was not readily forthcoming with information.

"I cannot tell you that, and I hope not, for he confessed that he had misplaced the note." Father continued, "Mr. Stevens mentioned something about Edward leaving his umbrella in the carriage and seemed to insinuate some level of urgency that you know this."

"Thank you, Father. That is most curious indeed." I responded, knowing there was no true urgency, for I had returned his umbrella, and this was merely one more bit of Edward's delightful silliness to remind me of his excuse by way of umbrella. Touché, I thought as I planned my next move to tickle him back.

"Then, this afternoon, I also received this," he said and handed me an unsealed envelope. It was postmarked Boston. I looked it over and recognized the author as my own pet, so did not open it at the dining table.

"I paid the postmaster since it arrived with postage due," he continued. Certainly, this looked to be Edward's hand. So curious, I thought, to come in such a manner.

"From Boston? Unsealed and unpaid?" I looked at it curiously, and as an afterthought, disapprovingly.

"My sentiments, exactly," said Father.

"Thank you, Father. I will read it immediately after supper," was all I could say as I finished dinner and retreated to my room, leaving Father shaking his head, Aunt Dolly beaming ear to ear, and Grandmother with a warm pleasant expression that made me the most nervous of all.

The New York Times
January 16, 1854

Interesting Statement of a Passenger

...The provisions that were to have been sent on board the *Kilby* were not received, and we retired that night fully confident that on the morrow the necessities of life, as well as the remainder of the passengers would be transferred to her. At about 10 o'clock that night the hawser which had been run from the steamer was parted, and fears were entertained among the gentlemen passengers that we should lose sight of the steamer, which only proved too true, for the northwester which had threatened us returned with renewed force, and drifted us off...

CHAPTER 17

Worthy of Your Respect

Miss M. E. Andrews
Care of Gen. Joseph Andrews
Salem
Mass.

Metropolitan [Hotel] [New York] 9th December, 1853.

Dear pet,

I have just returned from Brooklyn, where I went to see Martha Bird. It is only half past eight, and perhaps you may wonder at my returning so early. But neither she nor Carrie Bird were at home, so I came right back again. I was really glad when I knew they were out, for I thought if I saw Martha this evening she would expect me to go to Brooklyn every day I was in New York, and I should have to spend some time with her, which I should prefer passing with you alone. Do you think I do wrong dearest, to thus want to avoid society when I can't talk of you? Perhaps it would not be right to do so if we had just parted for only a few days. But now, darling, I can't take half as much pleasure in the company of others that I otherwise should, for I am so much happier when I am thinking of you, dear pet, that I always want to be in my own room alone with you. Then I am almost always happy. I shall call again to see Martha Bird next week.

I met Uncle Edwin this afternoon with Mr. Harrod, Miss Adams & Mrs. Boyd and all urged me to go to Tarrytown again. Uncle said - do just as you please, but I should be happy to have you come, if you can't find a better place. I may go up tomorrow afternoon & stay a few days longer, but that depends upon the *San Francisco.*

Will you forgive, darling, the impropriety of my sending your letter today unpaid? When I carried it to the Hotel office, the Boston mail had been gone some time, but the landlord asked a gentleman who was going to Boston if he would drop it in the Post-office there. The gentleman was on the point of leaving: I had no stamp and your letter must either have been delayed a day or sent unpaid. I know you overlook it, darling, and say, "too many words about nothing" but I ought to have explained.

Tomorrow I think I shall call on Mrs. Sprague; also on Mrs. Nevins who has sent specially for me.

I shall expect your letter tomorrow but if I don't find it I shall know you could not send in season. I always want to read your letters, darling by myself: for sometimes I am so happy that I want to shed a few tears as proof that I am glad; and then I always can imagine you when you are writing to me. Every sentence brings up some new thought, which had never occurred before.

Dear Lizzie, I have been thinking of you this evening as you rested on my shoulder that happy Wednesday we have just dreamed of together; for it does seem too happy and too unexpected to be reality, does it not, dear pet? It was very short, but very sweet, dearest, and I shall love to think of it when I am gone: for I can't feel now that I am irrevocably gone from you.

Possibly I may go back to you once more before we sail.

No, my own true darling, I must not say so; for I know it is not possible Dear Lizzie.

I must say 'Good-night.' We will read together shall we not darling; and you will rest a while on the shoulder of your own Ned, will you not?

_______________ Dear pet - my own darling -

Good night _______________

Saturday morning 10th December – My "own pet darling." Dearest Lizzie - Your letter was just handed me, precious one, as I was going in to breakfast, and I can't help saying one word now, though my room is occupied and I must write in the public room. Dear Lizzie, I was made very happy by your letter, and I thank you for it, my own "pet darling" (so you say). Oh, I know you do love me very much and my hope is that sometime I may be more worthy of your respect and confidence than I am now. I feel certain that God will prosper our love, while we are separated, and very soon restore us to each other.

How happy we shall be then, darling! And I think we shall both be very happy in this hope till we do meet, dearest, shall we not? I am so happy now, my own precious pet, because I have received your letter that I don't know what to do. Dear Lizzie, you did not receive my note on Thursday as I intended and I suppose it must have been lost. For I was so much bewildered at Lawrence that noon, when I found the telegraph office closed, that I hardly knew what I was doing; for I had indulged a hope till that moment, that I might be allowed to see you again, and it was terrible to have it so suddenly crushed. I thought I dropped your note in Mr. Stevens' box as the cars were starting (I can't tell whether I sealed it or not) and then as I jumped on board, I knew I had said "Good-bye." I know I have never felt so in all my life before. I would have given everything I had to have sobbed a few moments on your shoulder at that time. Dear pet, I do love you very much. I must write no more now. Darling, "Good-bye," for I can't help saying that now.

At Tarrytown Saturday 11 P.M. Dear pet. I am writing now in my room, with one darling face on each side of my paper and your precious letter open in front of me. The ring is on my finger (and I may kiss that too, dearest?) and those beautiful slippers you worked for me are on my feet. I value everything you have given me very much, and I love to think it came from you. I am going to sleep tonight with your ring on, may I not, darling? I don't think you will object very much. Your face doesn't seem to.

Today I called at Mrs. Col. Sprague and saw Mrs. S. and Lucretia. They asked particularly for you, and of course I was very glad to find someone to whom I could at least mention your name. I promised to go again to Mrs. Sprague's if I was in town next week. From Mrs. Sprague's I went to see a Mrs. Nevins whose husband, a New York merchant is from Methuen. Mrs. Nevins is a very pleasant lady and I promised to dine there next week if I have time. On reaching Tarrytown I found Uncle's carriage at the depot, with Mrs. Boyd & Miss Adams waiting for me. Mrs. Bartlett is still confined to her room and of course I have not seen her. My hands are so cold now I ought to write no more, so I will say Good-night, precious one. I shall kiss you "just once", my own "pet darling" - by your leave and _________ times without special leave, may I not, dear pet? and I shall put your own hair next to my face tonight Lizzie, and perhaps dream about you. "Good night," darling.

Dear pet, I shan't forget your request.

Your own (To-what-you-choose-with-him)
Ned

Saturday, Laura and I dined at Grandmother Sprague's house and spent the afternoon visiting. J.W. and Harriet. Aunt Laur and Mamie were there, along with Edward's Aunt Sarah Bartlett and Uncle Joseph Sprague. With so many knowing Edward I longed for news of him. Though I enjoy my evenings at home writing, it was good to be with family and stay well occupied. Father joined us later that evening for cookies and hot cider. That is when I had an opportunity to speak with Aunt Laur in a manner that was both delightful and disturbing, so much so that it touched me deeply for days.

"Lizzie, what have you heard from your cousin, Edward?" she asked, speaking softly as she settled next to me in the front room.

"He has been writing about the endless delays in his scheduled departure."

"It is best that they test everything on a new ship before they are out to sea for at that time, they would be unable to easily order supplies for repairs."

"I had not thought of that. Is such a delay common?" I asked, knowing her husband, my Uncle George had been a mariner. Once the words left my mouth I regretted the question. George Allen had been lost at sea just last November from a ship that had left New York on her way to California, less than three years after he and Aunt Laur had been married. I thought the question insensitive of me to ask.

To make matters worse, shortly thereafter, she lost her only son. Her grief must have been immense and I feared I had just opened a wound.

"Yes. Quite common," she responded, matter of factly. "A life at sea can be lonely and men must seek solace in each other's honest company to avoid the pitfalls of idleness since idleness leads to boredom and boredom only leads to too much drink and too much drink leads to despair." She seemed concerned, "I hope someone has prepared Edward for what is ahead."

"I hope so as well."

We sat in silence and I felt compelled to say something more.

"Aunt Laur, I am so sorry for all you have lost. I think Uncle George loved you very much." I reached over to hug her and said,

"Little Frankie also loved you very much." I am not sure I was making anything better, but she embraced me and thanked me.

"I appreciate that, Lizzie. I will be alright. Life is a mystery but somehow everything always works out. We learn to manage to carry on by loving the living. Life may be short so we mustn't miss a moment of loving and caring. None of us ever knows when a moment or a day might be our last." After a slight pause, she asked, "May I ask you something?"

"Of course."

"Do you love him very much?"

I hesitated before responding, feeling a rush of heat rise to my face. It seemed she knew Edward and I were closer than cousins, and she did not seem to judge. "Yes, I do."

"That is precious and you need not ever lose that. No matter what life brings."

Aunt Laur and Lizzie

The New York Times
January 16, 1854

Interesting Statement of a Passenger

...The following morning, finding the *Kilby* out of sight of the steamer and exceedingly short on provisions, council was held in the cabin as to the most judicious course which should be persuaded. I regret to say, as an impartial narrator, that several of the superior officers suggested the propriety of our giving up all hopes of the steamer, and steering for the nearest land. Lieutenant Murray, however, and some of the junior officers came forward promptly and appealed to the sympathies of those on board, calling upon them in the names of those who were left behind to stand on her course toward the latitude where the steamer was supposed to be, which noble suggestion was finally determined upon...

CHAPTER 18

A Most Beautiful Reverie

Rockwood, 11th December, 1853.

Dear Lizzie,

I have attended church this morning at the Reformed Dutch Church in "Sleepy Hollow," and heard a dreadful tiresome sermon. The minister preached about love, and I was thinking about the same thing and yet not of his sermon. Wasn't it funny? I was thinking of someone from whom I shall receive a letter next Tuesday, and who says she is my own pet darling (of her own accord, too). Perhaps she is writing to me now. This morning in church I had a most beautiful reverie, for it was just at the time I returned from South America. I reached New York unexpectedly, hurried on to Boston, but didn't go to Methuen first that time. You were living in Chestnut Street and I rang the bell, expecting the servant to open the door. But as chance would have it you opened the door looking just as you now do. You knew your own Ned in a second, though he was altered, but the unexpected shock was too great and you had fainted before I could speak. I was very much frightened, but you recovered very soon in Ned's arms and then, oh, darling, we did love each other as well as we do now: for God had kept us both faithful. But I won't come home, without warning, dearest, for if you are exposed to such danger, even in a happy reverie, I would not for the world do anything dangerous. I do feel very different since we were engaged,

Lizzie, and I think I have more energy and manliness than I had. For now I feel that there are two of us, and that I have some one else beside myself not merely to love but to take care of.

Don't you want me to have this feeling, dearest, and to make it my motive for action? But I sometimes can't help thinking that if I should not succeed as I hope to, what should I have to answer for. I will not think of that, darling, for it can do no good. You will trust me, (Will you not?) for what I can do. May God assist me and make me all that you can wish, precious one!

11 P.M. I have been wanting to leave the others and come up to you dear Lizzie, all the evening, but I could not excuse myself till now. I shall send this in tomorrow morning's mail, hoping that you will receive it on Tuesday. On Tuesday evening I shall expect to know decidedly when I am to leave New York and I will send word to you by the next mail after that. I shall expect a letter from you the first of the week; for if one is received at either the Metropolitan or Mr. Riley's it will be sent to me here. I feel a little bit anxious about the note I sent by express; for it may have fallen into some strange hands, and perhaps I did not seal it. I left it open purposely, intending to seal it in Lawrence, after adding something more if I found a telegraphic despatch. But I knew not what I did at Lawrence. I felt as if I was being driven on blindfolded. I knew not whither.

When I wrote to you Wednesday evening, on the only half sheet of paper I could find, I was almost certain of seeing you soon again: on Thursday morning I still had hopes, strong hopes of being allowed to stay; but all doubt was ended on Thursday noon. I could not tell whether there was any message or not for the office was closed, but I dared not stay. And now I can't help feeling sorry that I had not remained a few days longer, though I try to be content. But you say, darling, that perhaps it is best that I did come on, for another parting would have been still more trying. Yet it must have been very pleasant to have passed a few more hours together, before we separate for so long a time.

I feel very happy now to think of the last day we spent together. I think it will be the pleasantest day I shall have to look back upon, though there are a great many that I call my happy days. When I reached home I told all how surprised Lizzie was to see my head above the stairs. Liz Tenney says "she won't tell anyone," nor have I any fears that she will. I think, darling, that you must be much happier now than you have been: for there is no one at home to trouble you about everything.

Probably Joe will be at home before you hear from me at Valparaiso but I hope he will be a different brother to you. Before Joe sailed in the *Josephine*, I used to sometimes feel very unhappy to think I must leave you with him and I often imagined you situated very differently. How pleasant it would be now, if your father only lived in New York! Do you think I should spend all my time at Tarrytown. Then I shouldn't be in such a hurry for the *San Francisco* to leave.

Mrs. Boyd has asked me if I would go down to New York with herself and Miss Adams to attend Jullien's concert or the opera. Of course I said yes, as they could not go without some escort. How different it will seem from our intended going to Jullien's in Boston. But you will hear his band this winter and perhaps I may be with you then (in spirit).

This afternoon I did not go to church for no one went but Mr. Harrod. While I was sitting in the library; I heard Mrs. Boyd whisper to Miss A. "What beautiful slippers Mr. Tenney has," and pretty soon Miss Adams asked if she might look at them. Of course I was delighted; and so would you have been, dear pet; they were very anxious to know who made them for me and I told them "a pet cousin of mine, Miss Andrews from Salem." You don't care do you 'pet cousin of mine'? Mrs. Sprague and Harriet are coming on to New York quite soon I believe. Mrs. S. was at Methuen last Wednesday; so that probably the Stearnses know I came home don't they?

Good night, dear pet; I am going to wear your ring all night, and I shall expect a letter from you as often as you find time to write.

Dear pet darling – good night "______________"

Your own Ned.

Direct to me at Metropolitan as before.

Reading that Edward has seen his Aunt Sarah Sprague and Cousin Harriet made me wish I had sought them out for conversation the other day when I visited their home. I guess that home will always be 'Grandmother Sprague's home' as now there is a next generation of grandchildren who visit there with Edwards's Aunt, who is Mrs. Sprague to me and Grandmother Sprague to already six grandchildren! I was struck with how swiftly time marches on. It now seems so long ago that Edward and I were the 'grandchildren.' I began to count in my head how many of our cousins had so far survived to adulthood. Grandmother Sprague and Dr. Stearns had ten children and nine became adults, with five marrying and bearing thirty children who were our cousins, of whom eighteen lived. My Grandfather Sprague had eleven children and seven lived to be adults with four still living today. Their thirteen living children, of course I must count Edward and his sisters Liz and Mary as they are family, though they are not the birth children of my Aunt Augusta. What a great joy it must be to live long enough to see your children's offspring who are the heirs to your family's legacy.

I wrote on Friday after working at Miss Ward's, again on Saturday after visiting at the Sprague's and Sunday after church, so I managed a nice long letter to post on Monday.

Lizzie teaching at Miss Ward's

The New York Times
January 16, 1854

Interesting Statement of a Passenger

...Two days were spent by the *Kilby* in a fruitless search for the steamer. Meanwhile the provisions on board were fast diminishing. A rigid system of economy was immediately adopted, and an officer of that day was appointed in turn to deal out the rations to the passengers, as well as to the soldiers and crew. Biscuit on the second day was denied to the officers and the other male passengers throughout the vessel, and we were obliged to break out and make use of the corn which constituted part of the cargo, and which seems to have been most graciously provided, as if by a kind Providence, for our subsistence. The corn was used by roasting it like coffee and then dealt out by the handful...

CHAPTER 19

Tarrytown

Rockwood, [Monday] 12th December, 1853

Dear Lizzie,

This morning I rode to Tarrytown to drop your letter in the post-office to be sure of its going; and since then I have been reading, walking, chatting, playing billiards, etc., &c. It has been a most beautiful day and I have wished you and I were riding out together, well wrapped up in robes. I have been reading an account of manners and customs on the West Coast of South America, by a Surgeon in the US navy. According to his idea, life in Valparaiso will not be much like life at home, but I think I shall not be discontented. This afternoon uncle, with Mr. Harrod and Miss Adams have ridden over to Gen'l Webb's and I was invited to accompany them but did not go. Had I not stayed at home, I should have seen Washington Irving who happened to call at Gen'l W.'s at the same time.

Mrs. Bartlett is still confirmed to her room; and today has been worried by the agonies of her dying dog, who will probably not live but a few hours. It was really laughable this morning to see the old housekeeper, crying like a baby and telling everyone she met "Me and Lulu has passed many a day together."

This morning when I woke, I missed my ring which was on my finger when I went to sleep at night. I was frightened for a moment and jumped up to see what had become of my little pet: but I soon found it, it having slipped off my finger during the night and I saw it was much looser than when you first put it on. I am very sorry about its stretching, darling, for I am afraid I may hurt it by wearing it much, and I want to keep the ring and slippers just as when my pet darling gave them to me. I have seen work boxes (reticules?) much prettier than the one I gave you, since I left home. Will you excuse me, darling? But I meant you should have the best one I could find and I saw none better then.

I keep wishing and hoping every hour now that you could come to New York this week. Why didn't the *San Francisco* start from Salem? I think, dear pet, it would have been much better for us to have remained together till I was obliged to go, and not have parted thus, to remain near each other so many days. But I have done only what I could not very well avoid, and I try to be as content as I can. Tomorrow Mr. Bartlett goes to New York and on his return I shall expect to know decidedly about the steamer's departure. Oh, I wish, darling, that I was not at Valparaiso, ready to come home, after having fairly started in business. I know I shall be very much changed when I do return, even if I am less than a year away; for thus far I have never done anything in my life and it seems as if active life must make some alteration in my appearance.

Uncle Edwin said to me last night – "You will find that you will have to work out there, Edward: there will be no place for idleness." This is just what I want: I know I shall be much the happiest if I am busy the whole time. But I guess I shall find an opportunity to write to you once in awhile, however busy I may be. To be sure, darling pet, I don't intend to inflict upon you as much as I have done lately, for then I shall not have the excuse for writing that I now have. But I hope you won't chide me for sending you so many pages of nothing as I have the last two weeks, will you darling? for you know I am so much alone that when I am thinking of you, I want to be talking too, and I can't help writing a great deal more than I mean to. When I am ready to send a letter, I don't think you would like to have me tear up a part and so off it goes.

Today I meant to have made one of these great sheets answer for two days, but I have already covered three fourths in one day and left no room to say "Good night" in. After tea I must add one word more and then I have no space for tomorrow. I am going to buy in New York some thinner paper for Valparaiso. This is too heavy though I bought a large quantity of it expressly to take out with me. I must go down stairs now darling, but I shall see you again in a few hours -- Dear pet darling.

Monday night - 12 o'clock. We have been talking this evening till I have no idea how late it was, when I rose to come up stairs. Mrs. Bartlett's dog died during the evening, and Aunt is not as well in consequence. It does seem funny for a lady's house to be filled with company for a whole week while she is unable to be out of her room. Tomorrow night darling, I shall be reading the second letter from you written since Wednesday, unless the Metropolitan hotel-keepers delay sending beyond Tuesday's mail.

Wednesday shall be my "Saints-day"; for it was on Wednesday you first told me "Yes" when I asked you if you could love me, and Wednesday of last week was my last "happy day" in New England. Perhaps I shall return on Wednesday and perhaps on Wednesday; "oh, Ned, Ned - - Ned." My precious darling, I don't want you to tell any one what I am going to say, unless you think best, bend down your ear to my lips - Lizzie Andrews has told me she is my own pet darling! What would you give to be in my place? She is very lovely, I assure you and I do love her very very much and I never will and I never can love any body else. I hope that someday I may be somebody for her sake, and I mean to try and do my best. I always think of her when I am going to do any thing, and every night she sits a while, with her head resting fondly on my shoulder. She is very good. My own precious darling - I must say 'Good night' for it is very late. Good night dear pet

Your own exclusive Ned.

⸺◦⊰⊱◦⸺

Each day my Ned's love arrives in an envelope and unfolds another glimpse into my future, into my glorious life with my true darling love. It is clear we are and can remain in good society. Even a simple visit, like that to General Webb, can expose one to so great an author as Washington Irving. For now, I live secretly and joyfully, albeit vicariously, through my Ned and his letters.

Waiting at the seashore

The New York Times
January 16, 1854

Interesting Statement of a Passenger

...Water was also a scarce commodity on the *Kilby* and it was served out to us twice a day - our rations being a tumblerfull to every four men. To complete our frugal fare, each person received a piece of bacon, varying from the size of a fifty cent piece to a dollar piece. During the fortnight which we passed on board the *Kilby* we were in constant fear of the water giving entirely out. On several occasions we were favored with rains, from which we were able to add to our little store, and a snow storm also fell, when we gathered a small supply of the refreshing element...

CHAPTER 20

A Sister's Love

Rockwood, Tuesday morning – 13th [December 1853]

Dear Pet,

Just now when I went into the library, after a game of billiards with Miss Adams, I found Mr. Harrod weeping alone. Miss A. was in her room and soon he told me they had received news of her brother's death. She did not know of it but Mrs. Boyd was to inform her. I can't tell you, my dear Lizzie the thought suggested by this. He was a lieutenant in the Navy, now stationed at China. On Saturday she had received a long letter from him and last evening only, I directed for her the envelope containing her answer. As we came down stairs, she had been speaking of her brother Joe and saying she wished I knew him. I could not help feeling very sad when Mr. Harrod spoke to me, for I thought - - oh, darling, I must not tell you.

Only two years ago he had sailed from home with the expectation of returning soon; perhaps the thought of death had never rested on his mind. Oh, my own darling Lizzie, what if he were engaged? A sister's love can be nothing compared to a darling betrothed one's love. My dear, dear love, I have never thought I might not return. What a subject for reflection! But I will not write of this. I will not make you unnecessarily sad, for it can do no good. Your own true

Ned does love you and he hopes nothing may ever separate us. I hope God will preserve us both, darling. I feel restless now, because you are not with me: I want to be sure of your safety. Dear pet, I must not write so; I shall imagine you were resting on my shoulder. Do come to me Darling. Will you kiss me, my own darling?

9 o'clock P.M. Uncle Edwin returned from New York this evening but brought no letter from me as he had only time to go in Mr. Riley's counting room. I shall watch the mail from New York tomorrow morning.

Mr. Aspinwall told Mr. Bartlett that the *San Francisco* would make another trip this afternoon and if they found her machinery all right she would sail immediately. But I do not think we shall leave before Saturday, though to be sure I shall go to New York on Thursday, and perhaps come back to Tarrytown the same day. I think you had better direct your letters this week to the care of Theo. W. Riley Esq. so that he will forward to me at Valparaiso if I leave before they reach New York.

This afternoon I have been copying letters for the friends of Mr. Adams announcing his death. I was so nervous when I was writing to you this morning that I knew I ought to stop at once, for I was making you feel very unhappy. Now I do not feel as I did then, but I should soon be in the same state if I begin to think as I then did. I have promised to write one or two more letters tonight, but I came up to my room because the table in the library was occupied and I would not be missed.

I have felt sad sometimes today, darling, when thinking that it will not be very long before I leave New York. For though I have been wishing each day that we only could sail (& I do wish so now), yet it seems to me that a greater barrier will then be between us than has ever before separated us. Oh, darling, I wish that I could succeed as well without going far away from you. Perhaps I should not be any happier there, but I think I should feel safer if I saw you often. While I am absent, the expectation of our meeting again will make me very happy, I know, and I must make an answer. And when I do come home, dear pet, what can we do to contain our joy!

10 ½ P.M. Everyone in the house seems very sad today on account of their cousin's death; they can talk of nothing but "poor Joe." I have copied another letter since I went down and my fingers are so stiff from holding the pen that I can hardly write. I have not heard from home since Thursday, but I expect a letter at any time. I must write them tomorrow about the ship's continued delay. Think how much too soon I came on from Methuen. It is more than three weeks; three weeks today since I reached Tarrytown and I dare say it will be four before we go. The mail is sent so early to Tarrytown that I can't expect to have any time for writing tomorrow morning and my hand aches now, so I will stop here. You will write to me, darling, as often as you can till I sail, won't you? I will send word when a day is decided upon. I shall expect you will receive this Thursday noon. Good night - - pet – darling '-----' I wish I could watch over you while you sleep.

Ned.

Poor Edward! Imagine readying to ship out and having to write death notices about someone who has died at sea! Oh, conscience! My poor pet! Poor Miss Adams! Poor Mr. Adams! He was only away two years. When I read this news, I drop to my knees in my room to pray. A half hour passes before I can contain the tears. They flow so strongly I throw myself prostrate across my bed all the time knowing my behavior is self-indulgent and unacceptable. Before a full hour has passed I pull myself upright into some semblance of sensibility. Aunt Laur's advice echoes through me, remembering that love is precious and we need not ever lose it. She also tells me not to pine over it. Her words echo in my memory, 'Treasure love and be grateful, Lizzie, but beware pining is not becoming.'

The New York Times
January 16, 1854

Interesting Statement of a Passenger

...The effect of our diet on the *Kilby* became quite apparent after the first two or three days, and all on board, were, more or less, affected with violent attacks of diarrhea. We were constantly alternating between hope and fear. The *Kilby*, when we boarded her, was not only short of provisions but was deficient in the supply of sails and rigging, and had left New Orleans on her way to Boston to be refitted there, as the Captain stated, because it could be done cheaper than in New Orleans...

CHAPTER 21

A Very Dear Friend To Leave Behind

Rockwood, [Thursday] 15th. December, 1853

My dear Lizzie,

I had no-letter today, but I have been reading over your last letter instead. Tomorrow morning I am going to New York in the first train. So if any letter should be sent to me from New York after today I shall not receive it till Mr. Bartlett goes down on Friday. I could not wait for the second train for Mrs. Boyd and Mr. Harrod are going, and it would seem strange for me to be driven alone to the depot, without giving some excuse. Possibly the *San Francisco* will sail tomorrow, though I don't think she can before Friday or Saturday at least. But, enough of that tomorrow, when I have seen the Captain.

My letter almost missed being sent this morning, for I wanted to give it to the coachman myself, and not let it lie with the others for public inspection, and he went so much earlier than usual, that if I had not chanced to meet him driving out from the farm, I should have had to wait another day. I could not help feeling a little disturbed, my darling, this morning, at not finding your letter, for it suggested the possibility of danger happening to you. But I sat quietly by myself some time, not daring to touch my pen, lest I might write as I did yesterday morning, when the news of Mr.

Adams' death startled me so much. I couldn't bear saying anything more suggestive of such thoughts, dearest pet. But now, my own darling, I feel very differently, and I am uncertain of finding your letter tomorrow or next day.

I have been reading, walking and so forth, today. Neither Mrs. Bartlett nor Miss Adams have been able to come down stairs today, and I can not expect to see them before I go. Poor Miss Adams; I can but pity her, for she was very fond of her brother and he of her. She has another brother in the navy who sailed from New York only a few hours before the news of his brother's death was received; consequently he will learn of it through the public/newspapers.

Perhaps you will be at Sontag's concert tonight, darling. I hope you are there, (for I think she gives a concert in Salem Wednesday eve.) and enjoying yourself, too, dear pet. Don't forget to tell me everything about it when you write, what you were dressed with, &c. &c. will you? I shall expect very particular accounts of everything, darling, all the time I am gone, unless you don't want to tell me sometimes. And, I in turn, will give you a chronicle of what I do; though my life will be unvaried after the first few weeks.

Shan't you take the 'Cambridge Chronicle,' of which, Mr. Nichols says I am to be a contributor?

I have been expecting to see Mrs. Sprague or Harriet here this week, but they have not come yet. I was ready to be quizzed about you by them. Mrs. Boyd and Miss Adams one evening were talking with me and tried hard to find out if I had any "very dear friend to leave behind." I showed them the slippers and said you worked them for me, but even then they wouldn't take. Uncle Edwin never asked me anything about you, though I think he must have heard from Mrs. Longley &c. that I "was rather attentive" (to say the least) to you. I asked him once if he knew Mr. Joseph Andrews; he said "very little he thought." I expected he would then make some inquiries about his family, but nothing was said.

I must say "Good-night" now, "pet darling." Haven't I been real good today only to write two pages? Won't you give me credit for it; tomorrow I will be just as good too, darling. If I could only meet you in New York tomorrow, how happy I should be to hurry down. To be sure I shall see you there but I can see you here just as well, without having a hotel bill to pay. I shall go to see Martha Bird if the *San Francisco* doesn't sail immediately. Goodnight - my own pet darling. We will read one chapter together and then I shall go to bed. "-------" Dearest I hope to have your letter tomorrow.

Good night, my own,

Ned

Dear pet,

I have just read your letter, which was not sent to me at Tarrytown as I had expected, I want to send to you today, because I am delayed longer than I expected (Dear me, I have to say that in every letter) and I fear you may not write for fear that I have sailed. But perhaps I had better wait till morning: and in the meantime I may know more decisively. I am sorry about the express note, for fear that it may be in someone else's hands, but I could do nothing now about it. I made the umbrella an excuse for sending it so soon after seeing you.

Liz said she would like to have you make that purchase for her and have it charged to Mother at Miss Shillaber's.

It made me feel very badly, darling, to read the first page of your letter today, for I longed so much to have been with you last Saturday morning. And you too, wished Ned were by you, I know, dear pet, that you might confide everything to him and look to him for love. Ned was with you then, darling, and thinking of you as happily as possible.

Our Steamer is to be delayed at least till Monday and, I fear, she will not go to sea till later even than that. I shall stay at the Metropolitan till she does sail, unless her machinery proves too much in need of change.

I shall call at Mrs. Sprague's and perhaps dine there; dine also with Mrs. Nevins, who invited me last week. Tomorrow I am to meet Uncle Edwin in the city, and perhaps he will have time to go on board the *San Francisco*. I shall expect one more letter, this week, dear pet, though perhaps you may not write for fear that I have sailed. But I shall hope to find one Friday or Saturday. I will leave the last page till evening darling, so till then, adieu. My own precious -- Trust me,

Ned.

Thursday evening, 11½ o'clock. Ned Howland, a Cambridge classmate and club companion, came in about five o'clock and dined with me. After tea we went to Wallack's Theatre and saw a fine, laughable comedy. Since then Howland and I have been sitting together, talking over old (?) college times. E. H. is a very pleasant companion and perhaps you may have heard me speak of him before. He has just gone home, promising to call again.

I have been reading over your letter again Dear pet, and it makes me feel very very happy. I shall send this tomorrow so that you will (probably) receive it on Saturday. I had some of that thin paper you used and it is dreadful to write upon, as you say; my pen kept going right through the page: this is almost as thin but very easy to write upon, and if you can find some like it in Salem you will like it much better. I will cut out a corner (with the stamp) and if you give it to Mr. Ives he will get some just like it. Tell him you want a million sheets of it. How funny it seems to be writing of anything so like business, darling; we don't usually talk of such things, but I thought my experience (oh, dear me) might be of some service in this matter; won't it, darling?

I wonder what has become of the note I wrote last Thursday. Possibly Mr. Stevens forgot to go to his box for a day or two. I hope it is so, but that hope is very faint. I won't feel worried about it, dear pet, for if some stranger should find it, he could only laugh and wonder who the parties were; and if some one whom I know should see it-why-then, they may all have the benefit of its perusal. I do hope our steamer will go by Monday, for I am tired waiting in and about New York. Oh, what wouldn't I give, dear pet, for one look at you before I go. Even if I couldn't touch you, that I might only peek at you through some hole in the wall. Now if I only "had wings like a dove!" Dear, dear little pet darling, do come to sit by me a little while tonight, won't you? Now look up in my face '----' Dear little pet, I do love you very, very much. Good night, for it 'tis very late -- Good night, darling,

Your own

Ned

------⚭------

I spilled a large spot of ink on my letter to Edward so I had to write it out again. I saved the soiled copy, and will keep it until my darling Ned's return, simply as a reminder of what I said, or forgot to say. Nothing must be left unsaid before his departure.

Mr. Edward Jarvis Tenney
c/o Theo. W. Riley Esq.
New York City, N. York

Salem, [Friday] 16th Dec. 1853

My dearest darling Ned,
    You have asked that I send a chronicle of particular accounts of everything I do, what I think and what I wear. As you wish: I am writing a letter, thinking of you, wearing a dress. Oh, heavens! I am not thinking of you wearing a dress. Absurd! It is I who wear the dress. Although I must admit you looked lovely carrying a lady's handbag to my home. Sincerely, I am touched and grateful

for not only that kindness and generosity, but for the care you took to select a reticule that I find perfect. I do not believe any could be more fitting for me.

I am laughing, missing you and loving you so much, my dear darling Ned.

Do you also wish to know what I eat? I think about how much you enjoyed Charlie Morris' chicken recipe. Perhaps you do—and will—want to know every detail of life in Salem as you venture into foreign lands with foreign foods being enjoyed by foreign peoples speaking foreign languages. I think you are a sentimental sort, my darling pet, but it is that very tender soul that binds me to you.

As for who I am with, I do want to tell you about one day this past week that troubled me, but please do not fear that I was in any danger. On Saturday, I was invited by George Tufts to join him for a sleigh ride and a dance. I was prepared to reply by saying, 'I am sorry I cannot accompany you for I am Ned's own little darling gypsy pet;' but as our engagement is not public, I had no way to refuse him without raising suspicion, so I accepted. I must confess, my dear Ned, I did not go with a sour face of obligation. That would have been as useless as declining his invitation for no good reason. I so wanted to see if I could display a modicum of grace while my heart is being torn from my breast. The conversations were light and cordial and Mr. Tufts did not impose any inappropriate intimacy. Rather he was polite and charming and protective of my self with only a few too many glances at my waist. I did once catch his eye upon your pet and gave him the look that a mother might when seeing her child with a hand in the cookie jar, all the time thinking I am saving all the cookies for my darling Ned. So you see you have nothing to fear for I am and will always be your own true and faithful pet.

With Christmas less than two weeks away, we are beginning to see well-wishers drop by and invitations are being received for various gatherings at which Father and all of us will be present. I want you to know that you can trust me to be courteous and kind, but no more. I will not stand anywhere near the mistletoe and trust you in the same. Oh, but you will be on a ship filled with mariners, so please forgive that I even suggested the thought of mistletoe! I will wipe that image from my mind as well, along with the image of you carrying the reticule on board the ship during your shopping expedition. I truly do not know if you did such a thing, but the image popped into my head.

I will also wipe from my mind the sour feeling that your uncle Edwin has taken you away from me and does not care to know about my family. I know he intends the best for you, but must you go so long, so far, so soon? Forgive me, I wish to be so much more supportive and trusting!

I have been reading my bible nightly and saying a special prayer for your safe travels, as I have done for my brother Joe since he set sail.

We went to church on Sunday, which was much as you might expect. I tried to find some assurance in the sermon but there was only a sober warning of the need for temperance or at least prudence throughout the upcoming holyday celebrations with mindfulness to the reason for this being a holy time in celebration of the birth of our Lord Jesus Christ. I thought how much you would enjoy knowing your temperance is a virtue in which I feel immensely proud. You emit a purer joy than ever could come from lips that had kissed a bottle. I long to be the only source of intoxicating sweetness that touches your lips, every day for the rest of our lives.

Have you not been to Jullien's concert?

Have you heard from Mr. Aspinwall as to your departure date?

Monday I accompanied Father to town for tea with a gentleman widow whose daughter was seeking a companion to help her select silks for a Christmas dress. He was too grateful to me for doing something which I am sure I found as pleasurable as did his daughter. Just 16 days until Christmas, so it seems everyone is busily preparing for the holyday.

I did ask Father if he might acquire copies of the 'Cambridge Chronicle.' He assented. I will be so proud to read your writing.

I do hope you can be forgiven any further obligation to write out death notices. Oh the torture that must have inflicted on your heart to share such sad news over and over, seeing the faces in your mind of those who might read it.

Although I promise to focus my letter on topics that best represent our love and hopeful future, I cannot free my thoughts from a tragedy of which I have become aware. Three days ago, a fire in Boston destroyed the Harper and Brothers Building in Boston. You may recall that this is where Harper Collins Publishers employed many workers. The fire trapped many workers in the building, which was several stories in height. The building is completely destroyed and the loss of life is tragic. I am painfully reminded that we are here today by the grace of God and with His grace we shall endure to live happily ever after.

Today, it is with a lifted heart and a heavy pen that I begin this letter to my one and only true love, to the wise and kind man with whom I dream of many many days, not days only, but nights (Oh my!), years and decades, as his wife and mother to his children. My heart is so filled with his love that it seems to float as light and happily as a cloud has ever soared. My pen stops for I want to tell him more than words can say. He looks upon me from his perch on my writing table with such a concentrated look as if to say, "What would you tell me if you could see me, my darling pet? Write it thus and I shall savour your words. No," he says, "I cannot savour them, I will devour them with my lips, the very lips that long to kiss you and speak to you with such softness as you have never heard."

I lift your likeness to my face and whisper simply, "I love you, my dear darling Ned. I am yours now and I will remain yours until the end of time, no matter how far and wide you travel for I know you journey for me and for the future of our children."

I hear your reply as if you were in this very room, "Then why such heaviness in your pen?" you ask? You speak to me, "Write those words and send them forth on the wings of angels to the man who longs to hear them more than any words ever uttered in the name of love."

You issue that command and I am obliged —oh, I am grateful for the chance—to obey. My ink well is filled with all I want to say and my pen cannot move as quickly as the words flow.

I want to wish you strength to forebear the silence of the seas, confidence to know my heart is with you—and only you—every moment of every day you are at sea, and until your return to me. I send you laughter to grace the table at which you dine, and a tender smile to fill your heart with grace, so others in your presence will shower you with kindness.

With that I must send a prayer that you do not let the temptations of others lead you astray for it will take every bit of resolve to remain your good, true self while you are away. Never doubt for a moment that you can do it. I know you can.

I pray for your protection from the elements that your journey will be calm and that the winds will carry you to a destiny as bright and promising as you are to me.

Ever faithfully yours in love,

Your pet Lizzie

The New York Times
January 16, 1854

Interesting Statement of a Passenger

...Several times we approached ports in the United States, when by adverse winds we were driven back into the Gulf Stream. We were at one time in sight of Nantucket Shoals, and had to stand out to sea to avoid running ashore. At another time, by soundings, we supposed ourselves to be within ten miles of Sandy Hook, and three lights being in sight, the Captain became quite sure that they were the Sandy Hook lights, (probably these lights proceeded from the relief steamer *Alabama*, as she took out a reflecting light). The greatest state of uncertainty prevailed as to our whereabouts, the weather being so thick that for several days the Captain was unable to take his observation. During all this time, the greater part of us has been stowed away in the hold, where one hundred bales of cotton had been taken out to make the necessary room – the Government officer having contracted to pay the highest market value for the cargo that was thrown overboard...

CHAPTER 22

With the Help of God

Gen. Joseph Andrews
Salem
Mass.
Miss M. E. Andrews

New York. [Friday] 16th Dec. 1853

Dear Lizzie,

I have just read your letter over again and I feel just as if your little face was close by me, looking towards Ned once in a while, as if you thought you might trust everything with him without fear. Isn't it so, darling? Oh, I love very much to think I am so truly confided in: and I sometimes puff myself out very grandly and say "I'll protect her against all the world and she shall never have trouble, if I can prevent it. Whenever I begin to doubt my ability, I always drive such doubt away, for I know that with the help of God, I may be to you all that you can wish. I mean to try and do the best I can, my own darling Lizzie, to make you always happy.

I have not been to Jullien's concert yet; for Lieut. Adams' death of course broke up the intended party from Rockwood. Possibly I may hear his band before I leave New York, but who knows. I am to meet Uncle Edwin this afternoon at 4 o'clock to learn what Mr.

Aspinwall says about our sailing and after that I may go again to
Mrs. Sprague's.

This morning I found a note in my room from Martha Bird,
when I returned from South Street. She and Carrie called for me at
the hotel, when I was in Salem last week; and they called again this
morning, but I was absent. I must go over to Brooklyn tomorrow
forenoon to see them without fail. Today Martha and Carrie were
going to pass the day in the city with a friend of the family, and M.
asked me to call and see her there; but I don't think that would be
proper, do you (?) unless under pressing circumstances. So I will
see her tomorrow. It is quarter after three now, and, I must hurry to
meet Uncle Edwin. I will see you again this evening - til then,
dear pet - -

adieu - - Ned.

6½ P. M. Just after dinner, little gipsy darling. I did not go to Mrs.
Sprague's, perhaps I may go tomorrow some time. Uncle Edwin
told me I must go again to Tarrytown if the ship's delay allowed.
Tonight I don't know what I shall do; I am going out to walk and I
may go to Burton's or Christy's or I may come back very soon to
the hotel. But an evening here is not very pleasant, for I like to sit
up late and I can't write all the evening, for my hand becomes tired.
I would have gone to Jullien's, but I fear 'tis too late now to obtain
a good seat. Now if Somebody was only in the city this evening,
I shouldn't hesitate where to go. I shall imagine my pet walking
down Broadway with me this eve - - "Dear pet" - -

Ned

11½ o'clock. Dear pet. I went into Burton's, and staid through the
first piece, then walked quietly back to the hotel, ate some oysters,
met Howland and have been talking a while with him. Howland
proposed calling for me Sunday morning and going to Trinity

Church with me, and I am very glad indeed of the arrangement. I wished I had gone to Jullien's concert this evening and yet I felt some disinclination to go; for whenever I have thought of it, I have also thought of our plan for going to Jullien's together and were I to go alone now, I should miss you very, very much, even more than any where else. Tonight is the last of the opera season, I believe, and Jullien remains here only a few days longer.

Today I spent nearly an hour, trying to find some letter paper like that I sent you; for that was some I brought from Uncle Edwin's, and at last I succeeded, after inquiring at almost every store in New York (not quite so bad as that, Ned). I was going to send you a ream of it, for fear you might not find any in Salem to suit you, but then I thought perhaps you would not like it. But send me word, won't you, darling, if you don't find it.

I have just received your letter, and must add one line before sending this—Now you must not deny that you are "my own little darling gipsy pet Lizzie", for you are every bit of it (and ten times as much more beside). The mail is nearly ready and I don't dare to wait any longer. I will write to you today, of course.

Dear, dear, dear, dearest, little good pet gipsy, darling angel of mine. I shall kiss you now and then seal one up here for you - - Look out sharp for it. "＿＿＿＿＿＿＿＿＿＿" Goodbye pet Lizzie - - Be sure and write as soon as you can.

Your own Ned.

Dear Lizzie, won't you come and sit with me a little while before I go away? Can't you possibly come to New York. I may be here till New Year's, and you would not allow me to pass both New Years and Christmas in this country and yet away from you, would you, dear pet! But I mustn't wish that. If you could only change places with Martha Bird for a little while, darling; then I think we shouldn't have so much trouble in meeting. What if I should ring your door-bell again very soon, dear Lizzie? Wouldn't you jump almost as much as before?

My daguerreotype does speak the truth about my wanting to go to Salem; and you may always rely upon that when Ned himself is not near. Sometimes when I hesitate whether or not to do some particular thing and I am in doubt whether Lizzie would say yes or no, I look first at the little face for aid and then go to the large one for a decision. Don't you like to have me always consult you, darling? I don't mean ever to do anything to displease you, but I may through ignorance sometimes; and won't you tell me then, my own little pet?

I have been writing this evening with the ring on my finger, which I love so much. I am going to keep that always for my best ring. Not that I expect another, but I mean to keep, this one very choice. I must say 'Good-night!' -- dear little pet -- Ned loves you

New York [Saturday] 17th December, 1853

My dear Lizzie,

One day longer, we are told today we must wait in New York. Captain Watkins said he hoped to sail on Tuesday night or Wednesday morning but that depends upon the success or failure of another trial trip. I had my trunks carried on board this afternoon, keeping-at the hotel a valise and my writing desk. I was very careful this time to keep by me three things I use every day. Can you guess what I mean? I do hope we shall not be delayed beyond Tuesday.

This morning I called again to see Martha Bird; but she and Carrie were at the Crystal Palace; I left a note (on the back of my card) saying that if the steamer permitted, I would call next Monday. It has been raining quite hard all the afternoon, and tomorrow threatens to be like today. Still I hope to go to Trinity Church; perhaps to Grace Church half the day. Today I met one of the 3rd Artillery Officers who is going out in the *San Francisco*; but who is now in a most desperate condition for a long voyage. He was coming from

Fort Hamilton with all his baggage both for himself and his wife and child, to be put on board the Steamer, when a ferry-boat ran into them and every trunk, box and all freight went to the bottom. Fortunately the passengers were all saved, but I can't see what this gentleman and his family are to do on the voyage to California. He says that neither himself nor his wife have a single piece of clothing, but what is in their trunks in the East River.

I received a letter from Liz Tenney today and I watched the arrival of the Eastern Mail very closely to see if another Lizzie entrusted a letter to the mail. But there was none for me from Salem and I must wait till Monday for my letter. And I shall wait very patiently, dear pet, and I shall see you very often between now and then. Be sure and write to me, darling Lizzie, at New York until I send you definite word about our sailing, won't you, please?

This afternoon after I had packed my trunks to go away, I opened your daguerreotype, intending to just take a peep and then go out. But the little gipsy face was so cunning and smiled so sweetly that I couldn't get away for a long time. We stood by the window talking with each other and very, very happy. It was the longest "interview" we have had since I left Salem. You told me a great many new things I never knew before. Why, my precious pet-darling, every time I see you I find something new to admire, though I have loved you from the first as well as I could by the time I come back, I shall have a barrel full of beautiful things I have discovered in my absent treasure. I hope that I may improve in my absence and that I may not only seem but be all that you deserve. If I can't succeed in doing something, with such a motive for exertion, I may as well give up at once. My reward shall be the satisfaction of seeing you happy. If you are happy, I am happy and if I am happy you are happy; is it not so, darling mine? And will it not always be so, dearest? I am as confident in the future, as possible; and though I sometimes see there is a possibility of failure in South America, yet I do not allow myself to dwell upon it. If I strive to do my best, I can not reproach-myself if success does not follow, though I may be very, very sorry.

Dear, dear Lizzie, I can't think that our heavenly father would have allowed you to give your heart to one, to whom he does not grant his favor. I will, by his aid, be almost worthy of you. But I must leave two pages for tomorrow though it is quite early yet. We will talk together silently(!) darling. Good night, dear pet.

Something here "________________"

Your own true Ned

Sunday, 18th. Dec. 1853

Dear pet. This morning, not meeting Howland at the time I understood we agreed upon, I walked up Broadway to Grace Church. It is really magnificent both inside and outside but I do not like it - as well as Trinity Church, which has more of a sacred look in my eyes. The music was fine indeed and well worth a long walk. I do not think I ever heard as good church music before. The sermon is still a perfect mystery to me, for Grace Church is so large, that from my seat I could only catch a word occasionally. But I enjoyed myself at church very much, for I was in one of those delightful reveries I sometimes have.

This morning I began by dreaming you and your father came to New York and without knowing I was here, engaged rooms at the Metropolitan. Then almost every imaginable pleasant thing followed; on Monday, Maretzek's benefit and last night the opera in the city, we went (you and Ned) to Niblo's, on Wednesday to Jullien's, where we heard the American Quadrille, "by particular request." Then somebody (I couldn't reverie who) placed their carriage at my disposal and we drove all about the city and vicinity together, day after day. To crown all, Uncle Edwin found out that we were engaged; he went to your father and insisted (without telling me beforehand) upon your spending a week at Rockwood. Before the week was over, Mr. Bartlett said to me, that if I didn't love Lizzie Andrews I was a rascal. (I tho't so too.) Then little pet said to me one evening, "Well Ned, after all, I do like your uncle very well." This was not half my reverie, but I would be content if only that half would prove true.

When I came back from church I found a note from Howland, wondering where I was this morning when he called. He said he waited half an hour for me, then "poked off home, mad as hops." I shall tell him tomorrow that he was not punctual, but I am sorry I did not see him.

There is a mail leaves for Boston this P. M. at 5 o'clock and I shall send this, hoping you will receive it tomorrow (Monday). Then I will send again Tuesday evening, so that you will know certainly whether we leave by Wednesday. Just one week from today is Christmas, and I don't want to pass that day here. It is four weeks that I have been waiting to sail, and now if the steamer's machinery does not prove well tomorrow, we may be delayed two weeks more. I shall send a note home today, also one to Mr. Bartlett, informing him of our delay.

This evening I shall call at Mrs. McKeever's, whom I found absent when I last called, but who met me in the street last week; and, she said she would give me a letter of introduction to a friend in Valparaiso; also one for Rio Janeiro where we shall stop some days.

It is a beautiful day today, just after yesterday's rain; and if you were only here I should be very happy. I wonder what you are doing today, perhaps writing to Ned. It is half past one: I think you are writing, darling mine. I am very glad that my note was not lost; and I can't help repeating it; but I should have felt a little happier, had you received it on Thursday, for then it would have been evidence that Ned was thinking of you. But did you need any proof of that, dear pet? I have felt very glad indeed, my own darling Lizzie, to find a letter from you so often lately. But what shall I do till I reach Valparaiso? I have a good large package already received, and I can read those over very often. I think it is very pleasant to read old letters (from one I love best) they call up very many pleasant things. I almost always say, after reading one of your letters, "I know she loves me," for they always remind me so forcibly of your love. How funnily we began our correspondence, didn't we! I shan't forget it, shall you, little gipsy love? Did you find something in my last letter? May I send another something? "Yes" --- Dear true good Lizzie -- pet, Goodbye -- Your own (I don't care who denies it) Ned My own darling

⸎

Mr. Edward Jarvis Tenney
c/o Theo. W. Riley Esq.
New York City, N. York

Salem, Saturday 17th Dec. 1853

My dear Gypsy Ned,

I have concluded it is you who are the gypsy, not I, for I remain here at home as you embark on an adventure of a lifetime. Oh my darling, please send many letters even if they might be a mere description of the exotic life you are seeing. This is a voyage you will remember for the rest of your life. I imagine you bouncing our grandchild on your lap one day, describing in words he is too young to understand all that you saw and experienced on your voyage.

Shall I tell you now about this past week so you might know you did not miss a moment of excitement for my life? Hearing no answer, I shall proceed, according to the principle that "Silence gives consent." (Of course, I remember your first letter and how sillily you used that very line after asking if I would write to you.)

Monday Bridget started my fire early so my room would be warm by the time the sun rose and heated water for my wash basin. I dressed by myself – though I shan't tell you how, you goosie Ned. I wore a deep green silk dress with an ivory lace bodice and a rabbit fur wrap, not an evening dress but a day dress appropriate to join Father at work. We breakfasted as typical at 8 o'clock and I accompanied him to work by half past nine. Oh dear, this is much too mundane to waste another drop of ink. I shall be brief. Father had me greeting merchants and arranging meetings. We met with one merchant seeking calico cottons for a shipment to Ohio by wagon and another who was preparing a shipment to San Francisco. We will provide him with both cottons and fine linens and he will receive for us a shipment from China upon his return to Salem.

Tuesday, I dressed in a simple day dress to bake breads with Aunt Eliza while Bridget washed laundry and Johnny cleaned and filled oil lamps. He has secured a fine load of wood for winter and is stocking the fireplaces and stoking the stove well into the night to ward off the increasing chill of morning. He also tends so lovingly to our horse Bobby. Father picked up the mail on his way home for dinner and brought a letter for me from my Ned. He was opening his mail so quickly that he popped the seal on your letter before realizing it was not for him. I do not think he read any of it. I sat by the fire in the parlor to read after dinner and no one suspected the book I held in front of your letter was simply a cover.

After reading your letter, I wanted to box your ears, for I was saddened to even imagine the possibility of failure in South America. You really must trust this journey will position you in such favorable association with your uncle Edwin and his partners that you will prove to be a trusted protégé. I am beginning to truly like your uncle. I have always admired him.

I worked some lace with Aunt Eliza in the afternoon until supper and read the rest of the evening by the fire. Yes, I have been enjoying Washington Irving, due to the company he is keeping of late!

Wednesday, I worked with Father again in the morning and after dinner I went to church with Laura to organize songbooks for caroling groups. We practiced a few songs on the pianoforte but of course we will not have the luxury of such an instrument this weekend. We will rely on only the instruments of our voices.

Thursday Laura and I joined Aunt Eliza after dinner to shop for gifts and decorations for Christmas. We stopped by Aunt Sarah's for tea and spent the evening decorating the house with garlands, poinsettias and lace angels. These simple touches bring out the hope, faith and joy of Christmas and then I think about you being at sea and I feel so sad. I re-read your letter and I see how you are simply waiting and fear you are pining and I want to send Aunt Laur to box your ears!

Please be strong for me, my darling Ned, for I could not bear to think of you as anything but happy and adventurous, and filled with promise. Now, darling, that is not to say I do not want you to tell me your deepest true feelings. I do, no matter how dark or worrisome they may appear to be. We can help each other see more clearly. I need to know all that is you and I offer true myself in return. I love you for all your light, despite any clouds that gather to block the light. Together we can whisk them away.

Yesterday Laura and I met at church to decorate for afternoon tea with the older youth and young adults. We formed caroling groups, some as large as 12, and wrapped up warmly to venture out with our songs to reach as many in the town as we could. We were out for more than two hours and came home tired and filled with sweets and sweet contentment.

This morning I woke up eager to write and thus I have spent my morning. I will put this in the mail today in hopes that it will reach you before you leave!

Ever faithfully yours in love,

Your own pet Lizzie

Laura and Lizzie singing Christmas carols

The New York Times
January 16, 1854

Interesting Statement of a Passenger

...The confusion that had existed on board for several days, in regard to cooking in the galley, had been so great that stringent regulations were enforced by the officers on board, and orders were given that none but two cooks, who were appointed, should enter the galley. Guards were stationed at the doors to prevent intrusion. On the 11th of January, Lieutenant Fremont, the officer of the day, having gone forward, found two sailors in the galley, and gave orders for them to retire, which they refused to do, and on his attempting to eject them, they drew their knives upon him. On this, Lieutenant Fremont called for the corporal, and ordered him to bring the guard up to use the necessary force to carry out his orders, and demanded of the Captain the immediate arrest of the two sailors. Captain Low, however, pacified him by stating that if these men were placed in irons, the crew would mutiny, and they would lose the necessary assistance to work the vessel. Upon these grounds, the Lieutenant allowed the matter to pass. Meanwhile, Lieutenant Fremont armed himself with a club, the only weapon which at the moment was within his reach – and was about to drive the sailors from the galley. Upon this, the crew collected together, and had the Lieutenant not desisted, there would undoubtedly have been a mutiny upon the spot...

CHAPTER 23

My Own Darling, May God Bless You

Miss M. E. Andrews
Care of General Andrews
Salem
Mass.

New York, [Monday] 19th Dec. 1853 - - P.M.

Dear Lizzie,

I have just returned from my first (and last, probably) visit to Jullien. Oh, why were you not there, darling? I want you to promise that 'Ned' you have in your writing desk that, if it is possible, you will hear Jullien this season. Won't you do that, dear pet, after reading this? I had no idea I should be so much pleased by this music before I went tonight. Though I know nothing about it (can hardly distinguish Yankee Doodle from Rory O'More), yet I have been taken by storm this evening. The great piece was "The great exhibition Quadrille," but I thought almost every piece incomparable. When you hear Jullien's band in Boston, won't you please write me what you think, dear pet? Oh, I thought tonight I would have given everything (but your love) to have been sitting by you this evening. I know you would have enjoyed it very much. I wish we had gone that evening we proposed going last fall.

I went to Mr. Riley's counting room this morning and found something. Can you guess what! "Here it is" I was watching for that when I opened your letter and I seized upon it the first thing. It is safe now, darling. Oh, my own dear Lizzie, I was very glad to find your letter today. It has made me very amiable (oh, Ned!) ever since. So you want to box my ears, little gipsy, do you? You may, if you are very anxious to. There, I have allowed your daguerreotype to do it for you. It didn't hurt very much, but I will be real good: only I won't wear your slippers out very fast, dear pet. I was afraid if I tried to buckle the ring I should hurt it so I didn't dare to try. (It is on my finger now.) I couldn't help laughing this morning, coming up from South St. to think your father had opened my last letter. Didn't he laugh a little?

Just before going to Mr. Riley's, I went to Brooklyn and saw Martha and Carrie Bird and Maria Kimball. Martha inquired particularly why I had not brought my daguerreotype, and I told her I had great repugnance to having it taken at all. They are going to Hartford Wednesday or Thursday, so I shall probably not see them again.

By tomorrow morning, I shall expect to know if we sail very soon or not. I do hope that everything will prove right, for I can't bear the idea of waiting here any longer. I was on board the Steamer this morning, when she expected to go out on a trial trip in a few moments, to return tonight or tomorrow morning. Last evening I called at Cap't McKeever's and spent half an hour. Mrs. Sprague I have not seen since the week I came from home. I was hesitating tonight whether to go to Jullien's or the opera, Maretzek's benefit; but the opera was announced postponed at a very late hour, on account of Salvi's indisposition.

I am very sorry, dear pet, that any part of my letter should make you sad, for I want you always to be very happy. But I won't do so any more, darling. I have been thinking of you very much today. Hasn't your cheek burned? For I have been talking about you; with whom, do you think? Why, with a little prisoner I keep in my writing desk. I wish there was somebody in New York with whom I might have real long talks about you. When I was at Mrs. Sprague's they asked about you, but I could not say very much. I love to have any one ask me what I think of you; for then I can go on and give a long list of praises without exciting suspicion.

It is very late, darling, and I ought not to sit up later. I may wake up to find sleighing tomorrow, for it was snowing quite fast when I came in. Now, if I was only in Salem on Christmas; wouldn't we do something? I wish I could be near you now, my own darling pet. Good night, dearest.

Your own Ned.

New York, Tuesday - 1 o'clock P. M. [December 20, 1853]

My dear Lizzie,

I have just returned from South St. Our steamer is to sail tomorrow morning, and I shall go on board quite early. I feel glad to know this, yet it seems almost like another parting from you. My own darling, may God bless you. This is the last time I shall write you from near home for a long, long time. Even now I can only say a few words for it is near the hour for closing the mail. I can not say Goodbye calmly, my own dear Lizzie, tho' I shall in reality be no farther distant from you than I have been. It does seem to me as if you were near me now and I was bidding you farewell.

Dear pet darling "Good-bye." We shall meet very soon, I hope.

If you will send a letter to me "Care of Alsop & Co. Valparaiso, Chile" in about four weeks, I shall receive it soon after my arrival. To insure safety, perhaps your father had better make inquiry at the Boston Post Office about the Chile mails, &c. If there is any letter now on the way to me at New York, Mr. Riley will probably forward it to Alsop & Co., Valpo.

Will you excuse my hurried writing, darling, my own true darling? And now, dear pet, "Good-Bye,"

When I come back I hope to be better in every respect than I
have been. I shall write after the mail closes if I can.

Farewell, my own Lizzie
Ned.

The San Francisco Floundering at Sea

The New York Times
January 16, 1854

Interesting Statement of a Passenger

...On the evening of January 12, while standing in the Sandy Hook in a state of uncertainty as to our positive proximity to the coast, the Captain concluded to put out to sea again. In fact it was his only alternative, as a violent northwester was then blowing, and he was fearful of being driven on the Long Island Coast. The crew, however, on ascertaining that the ship was again standing away from shore, went in body to the Captain, and refused any longer to perform their duties unless he would steer shoreward...

III. Weathering Changes

Once Edward has safely departed, Lizzie's focus turns to monitoring weather conditions and reports of ships at sea.

Father typically perused the New York Daily Herald to keep abreast of the comings and goings of mercantile ships in which he had a financial interest. He promised me he would also watch for any mention of *The Josephine* and *The San Francisco*. Many, many lives had been lost at sea in 1853. Father reasoned I had little cause for concern however, since improvements in shipbuilding were making vessels much safer. *The San Francisco* was a brand new ship. I will know for certain there is no need for worry once I receive my first letter, which can take weeks or months.

On Wednesday, December 21, 1853, the Herald reported names of ships cleared at the Port of New York. Among the steamships was *The San Francisco*. The ship was listed as new and owned by Howland and Aspinwall, with Captain Watkins bound for San Francisco. Carrying my future, I thought and said a quick silent prayer, which was a courtesy Father instilled in me as this was his custom when accounting for ships at sea.

The New York Times
January 16, 1854

Interesting Statement of a Passenger

...Lieutenant Murray, on ascertaining the facts, immediately went forward, and after stating his position as a naval officer to the crew to give weight to his remarks, convinced them that the Captain was acting judiciously in bearing away, although they had actually extorted a promise from the Captain that at 8 o'clock on the next morning he would make for the nearest shore, regardless of the consequences. But few of the passengers of the *Kilby* were informed of this circumstance, and it can readily be imagined in the complication of our miseries, how much additional anxiety was thereby created. All night long we laid upon our cotton bales, praying for the morning...

CHAPTER 24

Ships at Sea

On Friday, January 6, 1854, I arrived home at the dinner hour to find Father waiting at the front door.

"Greetings, Father. Good heavens, are you not frozen in the bitter wind? Why are you standing outside?"

"I wanted to be the first to greet you, Lizzie. I have some news to tell you. Let's go inside."

Father's behavior was very strange and rather somber, so I did not expect joyous news; however, he did not appear distressed. I followed him into his private office, of which I was not particularly fond, preferring to converse in the comfort of the parlor.

"Please sit." I did as I was told, positioning myself on one of his wooden library chairs.

"Lizzie, there has been an incident at sea; however not much is known yet." He did not wait for my response, but continued. "I will tell you what I know and you may read the rest for yourself in the **New York Herald**." He held the paper in one hand with the other positioned gently on top. He did not appear to try to hide the news, but seemed to hold and comfort it. His manner was matter-of-fact, not in any way alarmed. He was simply discharging his duty. My first thought was of *The San Francisco*; yet it had barely left port, so I was certain the next words he uttered would concern *The Josephine*. I was wrong.

"*The San Francisco* met a storm and has been disabled. The ship is seeking assistance," he began. "We do not know if any lives are lost; however, many are hopeful for a full rescue—despite what the news reports—for it is a new vessel and quite staunchly constructed." He took a slight breath and continued, "There are many U. S. Army troops on board. Ships are being ordered to locate the vessel and bring the passengers home."

"Thank God. Edward will be coming home!" I blurted.

"We hope," Father said softly. He handed me the newspaper, whereupon I unfolded it to read the headline. My feeling of great hope was quickly dashed with terror as I read the headlines. Then certain that my prayers were being answered, I felt a calm come over me. I simply knew Edward should not – could not – be away from me for so long a journey as three years! This changes everything. Surely now he will be home sooner and he can find a new, safer vocation.

"May I read it in my room?" I asked.

"Of course. You may keep it."

I began reading the **New York Herald** Morning Edition as I slowly climbed the stairs.

CHAPTER 25

Startling Marine Disasters

The New Steamship *San Francisco* Reported Disabled –
HER DECKS SWEPT AND BOATS GONE –
She Had Over Five Hundred Troops on Board,
Bound for California –
Disaster to the Steamship *San Francisco*.

TO THE STEAMER *SAN FRANCISCO*, &c.
EXCITEMENT IN WASHINGTON-
SPECIAL CORRESPONDENCE OF
THE NEW YORK HERALD.

Halifax, Jan. 5, 1854

A telegraphic dispatch from Liverpool, Nova Scotia dated yesterday, says the brig *Maria's* Capt. Freeman arrived there and reports that on 26th of December, in lat. 38 20, lon. 69, the *Maria* fell in with the new American steamship *San Francisco*, from New York to San Francisco, with her decks swept, boats gone, and completely disabled. Could not render her any assistance, as she drifted out of sight during the gale.

I absorbed the front page news by the time my bedroom door latched shut and settled in, filled with shock and disbelief, to scour the rest of paper for word of Edward.

PREPARATIONS OF THE WAR AND NAVY DEPARTMENTS TO SEND RELIEF TO *THE STEAMER SAN FRANCISCO,* &c. EXCITEMENT IN WASHINGTON-SPECIAL CORRESPONDENCE OF THE *NEW YORK HERALD.*

Washington, Jan. 5, 7½ P.M.

News has just arrived of the wreck of the new steamer *San Francisco*, which recently left New York for California with the Third Regiment of United States Artillery on board. She was seen in lat 38 20, with her decks swept, boats lost, and wholly disabled. Senator Gwin at once applied to the Secretary of the Navy for aid; but there is not a government vessel in any port fit for immediate service. The Secretary of War, on being applied to by the Senator from California, ordered a merchant steamer to be chartered at once to go in search of the wreck. The Secretary of the Treasury will order several revenue cutters on the same errand. The steamer had from seven to eight hundred men on board, with three months provisions for the crew, and twelve months provisions for the troops. The *San Francisco* was a new staunch built vessel and well officered – circumstances that would strengthen the hope that

I turned the pages until I came to The News Editorial, and read the startling announcement. How could a new steamship be completely disabled? Her decks swept and boats gone? Edward was in a cabin on her decks! How could there not be a single government steamer in any of the ports fit to be sent on such a voyage of mercy? Certainly one of the revenue cutters would come to the rescue. I could not pull myself away from scouring the news for a bit of hope.

...would eventually reach their homes safely. She was destined for San Francisco, via the straits of Magellan, touching at Rio Janeiro, Valparaiso and Acapulco. She had on board Companies A, B, D, G, H, I, K and L of the Third Regiment of United States Artillery. Those companies, with the commissioned staff and band of the regiment, constituted a force of about five hundred men.

Oh heavens! I scanned the list of passengers known to be aboard. It did not list civilians. There was no word of Edward. May I trust this is good news? More information will be forthcoming, but I have read no horrific news of my Ned.

Certainly this matter of the wreck is of the utmost urgency to the Government, there being so many military officials and families on board. I folded the newspaper using all the courage I could muster to stop my fearful imaginings. What was I to think? God will bring my Ned home safely.

On Saturday, I approached Father to see if there was any more news of *The San Francisco*. He simply handed me the Herald. On the Editorial page, I read The News:

January 7, 1854, Saturday

As yet, no additional particulars have been received relative to the reported disaster to the steamship *San Francisco*... her owners are somewhat inclined to discredit the report that she has met with any accident whatever. She was insured on Wall Street for three hundred thousand dollars...is gratifying to know that the Secretary of War immediately ordered a merchant steamer to be chartered and sent to the relief of *The San Francisco*...there was not a government steamer in any port fit to be sent out on a similar voyage of mercy. This is certainly a startling and humiliating illustration of the present imbecile condition of our navy.

My hope was eager to be restored and I was certain each day would bring better news.

The wreck of *The San Francisco* buzzed throughout the pews at church. Prayers for lives of all those on board permeated the minister's sermon, which gave me a much-needed sense of calm. Yet, the moment we left the church, I was desperate for more certain details. Father stopped on the way home from church to purchase the Sunday *Herald* and I found exactly what I was seeking. Certain details.

January 8, 1854

The Captain of the *Maria*, Freeman states that when he saw the *San Francisco*, her engines were not working, her smoke pipes were gone and her decks were swept of everything. The Captain of the steamer requested him to stay by him. The *Maria* laid to, but lost sight of the steamer overnight. He thinks she must have floundered during the gale, as he could not find her afterwards.

The brig *Napoleon*, Capt. Strout reports experiencing three tremendous gales, lost sails, a leak, and had to stave twenty one casks of molasses to ease the vessel. On December 25th, he fell in with the steamship *San Francisco*, dismantled, everything swept above deck, and the spray making a complete breach over her. Capt. Watkins stated that the steamer was leaking fast, and requested Capt. Strout lay by, which he did; but the next morning the steamer was not in sight, having drifted far to the eastward.

The first mate of the brig states that a part of the hurricane deck forward was standing and the crew was busily engaged cutting away and throwing it overboard. The steamer was on the southeast edge of the Gulf Stream, and was drifting out. Capt. Strout judged that they were safer on board the steamer than those on board his brig. There were about two hundred persons on deck, and when the brig hove in sight they loudly cheered her.

Captain Watkin said the ship was making water, but did not say fast. He wanted a boat sent, but at that time the sea was running high. The smoke pipe was gone but the galley saved. The mate says he saw heavy smoke from the galley, part of the house standing forward and the masts gone. When the brig last saw her, at 12 o'clock M., the ship was on the S.E. edge of the Gulf Stream, and would soon be out of it, in smooth water. The Captain says her hull was all right, and he felt as if he had rather, for safety, been on board of her than on his brig.

A revenue cutter was dispatched by Collector Redfield in search of *The San Francisco* immediately upon his reception of the dispatch from Washington. The steamer *Alabama*, of the Savannah line, has been chartered, and will sail this morning on the same errand, coaled and provisioned for a fortnight's cruise.

As *The San Francisco* was supplied with three independent pumps in addition to those attached to the engine, besides others that could be worked by hand, and as she was very strongly built, there is no doubt that, with the assistance of the large number of men on board, she would easily be kept free of what water she might make, until assistance arrived. This would most probably be immediately after the cessation of the gale, as she lay in the direct track of vessels trading to the Southern ports and West Indies.

Captain Watkins would most probably endeavor, by the aid of jury masts, to make for the Bermudas, where it is likely we shall next hear of her.

I devoured the news and even after church spent my days praying. There was nothing more I could do. Certain now Edward would be gone some days in Bermuda, I began composing a letter he could read upon his return.

I told him he was causing me such a fright and held his framed likeness to my lips, gently kissing his face. There, I thought. You felt that, didn't you? My love will keep you safe, I whispered to his ear.

Turning away from my pet so he could not see or hear me, I began to fiercely reprimand him for not sending word sooner of his safety. Then I sobbed. Can you not have a message delivered to me? Please, Edward, I pleaded. Realizing the magnitude of my request, I prayed to God to send me word on the wings of a dove. That is how Edward would reach me, I thought. I looked to the window and listened. Nothing. Only the horrid memory of Mother Carey's chicken smacking against the pane. I quickly suppressed the memory but could not suppress my fears and tears flooded my eyes. My Father's voice inside me reasoned, "Lizzie, now, you cannot blame Edward for any circumstance of weather." Then my mother's voice resounded in me, "You must let God have his way in this matter. You must trust Him. Pray to Him, but trust Him. Edward will be fine." Mother's voice was calm and loving and I could almost feel her holding me. The thought that my mother knew Edward would be fine sent a torrent of goose flesh up my arms.

I pledged to live and breathe nothing other than the recovery efforts until I am certain such efforts are underway. I will talk only of the News until my Ned is found to keep the rescue alive.

The next day, my despair was echoed in an editorial I read:

CHAPTER 26

Conduct of the Government

Monday, January 9, 1854

Editorial

We publish today a narrative of the incidents connected with the late disaster to the steamer *San Francisco*. While awaiting later intelligence it is well to ask what has the government done in the emergency, and what efforts have the proper authorities made for the relief of the sufferers on board? Among the passengers are over 500 soldiers belonging to the United States Army. These men are commanded by officers who have already rendered such services to their country as to obtain brevet ranks as rewards for their bravery. On this occasion many of them were accompanied by their wives and families. Suddenly the announcement comes that the lives of all are in jeopardy; and the only effort that the government makes to rescue these brave men is to dispatch a small revenue cutter in search of them - a vessel of dimensions scarcely sufficient to accommodate the officers with their families, and which could not take off one fourth of those on board *The San Francisco*. No effort was made to employ the steamship *Black Warrior*, now in our port - the revenue cutter was deemed sufficient. But we are happy to say that Messrs. Howland &

Aspinwall have chartered the *Alabama*, and sent her in search of *The San Francisco*, and it is very probably that aid will reach those on board the unfortunate steamer from this source before the government revenue cutter can make out the track of the missing vessel.

The ship was new, and constructed with a peculiar regard to the health and convenience of any troops she might carry; whilst the companies which sailed in her attracted additional attention from the fact that they only preceded General Webb to his new scene of service on the Pacific.

The San Francisco was built by Messrs. W. H. Aspinwall, for the Pacific Mail Steamship Company, and cost $340,000. Her constructor was Mr. William H. Webb, one of the most successful and accomplished shipbuilders in this city, under the immediate inspection of Commodore Kearney and Captain Bell, both officers of the U.S. Navy, who, from time to time, expressed their views and made their suggestions. Captain Skiddy, so long and so favorably known for his nautical skill and practical knowledge, was also employed by the government to superintend her build. Her model and outward appearance are very beautiful, although somewhat spoiled by guards, giving her too much the appearance of a sound or river steamer. This is the first time, we believe, a government vessel has been built in this manner, which adds so much to the comfort and convenience of passengers in a hot climate, at the same time serving all purposes for which she was originally intended.

Her spar or hurricane deck extends the entire length and breadth, giving a wider range for both deck and cabin passengers than any vessel, perhaps, ever built. She has a clipper bow, perfectly plain, without ornament or figurehead of any kind; on the stern is her name, in plain white letters. She is rigged with two masts, carrying foresail, foretopsail, and two jibs, with smokepipes forward and aft.

Her internal arrangements were planned entirely by Captain Watkins, who commands her, and who knows the size and strength of every piece of timber and metal in her.

The following are her dimensions: –
Length on deck..285 ft
Length of keel..250 ft
Breadth of beam..41 ft
Depth of hold....25 ft
She measures 3,000 tons, customs house register. She is double ironed, diagonally braced forward and aft, with plates let into the timbers inside, running from bilge to bottom. A large iron band rounds the ship upon the top of the timbers, directly under the waterways, to which the diagonal plates are riveted. The plates are all bolted to the timbers and riveted at each crossing, forming perfect truss work the whole length of the ship, keeping her from "hogging."

In order to give additional strength lengthwise, two bulkheads have been built fore and aft, on either side of the engines and boilers, from the bottom of the ship to the second deck, secured to the keelsons and to beams and stringers, and under beams in both decks above. She is further strengthened by letting into this bulkhead, double iron diagonal braces, bolted to stancheons and keelsons at the bottom, and stringers above under beams. This is an entirely new mode of fastening, never before introduced in any ship. She is planked with oak five inches thick, bolted edgewise and on face, copper fastened and coppered to deep level line. She has two powerful engines of 1,000 horse power each, both working upon the same crank, opposite each other. They are called the "Oscillating Engine," and have been adopted by the government, and will be used hereafter in preference to the side lever as combining greater strength, less complication, less liable to accident, and occupying less space. The wheels are twenty-eight feet in diameter, ten feet face, five feet dip and constructed upon a scientific principle lately discovered in England, but never before introduced in this country. It is called "Morgan's Eccentric" or the "feathering float" by which a difficulty has been overcome long considered impracticable, on account of being too complex for any practicable purpose. She has stateroom accommodations for 350 passengers, and steerage berths for 1,000, and may lawfully carry 1,500. The upper deck is occupied exclusively by the officers of the ship. On the deck below is the steerage quarters, water closets, store room, wash room, ice house, porter's room, cook's room, barber's shop, kitchen, bakery, officer's mess room, engine room, bath room, and ladies' cabin. The staterooms are very large, with two doors, one opening into the cabin, the other out upon a fine spacious walk on deck, where ladies and children may sit or promenade without being molested by passengers from other parts of the ship. Her ornamental work, finish, and decorations it is necessary to repeat as those now given will convey a good idea of the points which ensure strength and stability, the only qualities which *The San Francisco* would need during the existence of the late gales.

Never before had I cared about the construction of a ship. Now, I prayed the strength of the *San Francisco* would save my beloved's life.

The next day, I read much that had already been written – still, I devoured every word.

CHAPTER 27

Description of the Steamer as She Appeared on Christmas

January 10, 1854

Editorial

There is no later news from *The San Francisco*. Vessels daily arrive with accounts of wrecks at sea, swelling the disasters by the gale of December to an awful extent. Our ship news columns of this morning, and indeed of every morning, teem with these sad details. The loss of life, to say nothing of the loss of property, must have been very great - greater than we shall ever know.

But in the absence of any later intelligence from *The San Francisco*, we give all the information we can gather of the steamer and of the chances of her safety. We learn from Mr. William McCarty, the chief mate of the brig *Napoleon*, some exceedingly interesting facts in relation to the falling in with *The San Francisco* on Christmas day, the position of the vessels and the occurrences and conversations which took place between the two captains.

Mr. McCarty says:-

On Friday, the 24th of December 1853, at 8 P.M., land time, the brig was struck with a severe gale, which soon increased to a perfect hurricane from N.W. The *Napoleon* continued, without intermission, until Sunday, December 25, a dreadful sea running all the time. At 7 A.M. we discovered on our weather quarter, distant some seven or eight miles a dismasted vessel judged to be a bark. The mizzen mast and mizzen topmast were standing. We could not make out her flag.

The vessel in distress being to windward, it was impossible to render her any assistance; and the wind blew so fiercely, and the sea ran so high no boat could possibly have lived.

At 11:00 A.M., 26th of December, the disabled vessel had drifted to leeward of us distant some four miles. The weather was clear, and through the glass we discovered her, manageable, but lying in the trough of the sea, and rolling to and fro.

By this time, the wind having lulled some, though it still blew violently and the sea dreadfully high, Capt. Strout wore ship, set a reefed main staysail and foretopmastsail, and run for the wreck.

At 12:30 we approached her, and passed under her stern, which was a round one, and I read clearly and distinctly her name – it was "*San Francisco*, New York." She had side wheels and guards, and the hull was painted black. We sailed under her stern, within fifty or sixty yards, and ranged ahead of her, for we did not wish to be on her lee, as she was drifting faster than we were. I saw her bow; she had a very short bowsprit, painted black; sharp boas but I could not observe her model closely, as my attention was directed to her damaged condition, and mainly to the suffering people on board.

We passed to leeward abreast of her, when a man, whom we supposed to be the master, hailed us through a speaking trumpet. He was a stout man, and had on a dark coat and cap, either of cloth or leather.

His first salutation was – "Brig ahoy!" Capt. Strout answered;

The Captain of the steamer then said: "I want you to lie by and send a boat." Capt. Strout replied in effect that he could not send a boat, but added: "Put up a light at night."

Capt. Strout then said, that a boat could not live in so fearful a sea, he would lie by till morning, and then would, if more moderate, board the wreck. He then asked:-

"Where are you from?"

"From New York to California."

"When were you disabled?"

"On the night of the 23rd – my vessel is making water."

To which Capt. Strout replied, "I am in distress too, and short of provisions."

"I have plenty of provisions," answered the Captain of the steamer.

We passed by this time too far to hear anything more. As we came under her stern some twenty persons came from the cabin on deck, wearing dark clothes and caps.

On the forward deck I saw one hundred or one hundred and fifty men, dressed in caps and blue coats, and I took them at the time for soldiers. As we approached we heard them as they gave three hearty cheers.

We saw no females on deck.

Amidships I observed several men wearing oiled clothes and some caps and blue jackets. Some four or five of these men had axes in their hands, and were cutting away on some woodwork, and throwing pieces of it, perhaps chips, overboard. I could not see what they were cutting, but supposed at the time that they were making something for the security of the vessel – perhaps a drag. There seemed to be no fear among any of the people on deck, and those amidships continued their work, and appeared to pay little heed to the approach of the brig

Napoleon.

Also amidships observed smoke, or rather steam, issuing from a small pipe. I did not see any people working pumps.

She had no boats left.

The mizzen and mizzen topmast were standing, with a spanker gaff attached. On its end hung small remnants of a sail.

I saw also the stump of a foremast, which reached as high as the top of the pilothouse. That house was situated on the hurricane deck, just abaft of the foremast; its doors and windows were stove in, and no person in it.

The paddle boxes on both sides were gone; the wheels remained, and seemed uninjured; I did not observe any of the floats to be off. The bulwarks were gone on both sides, from abreast of the pilot house to ten or twelve feet forward of the Laizenmast. The hurricane deck, too, was gone an equal distance. The hull seemed uninjured.

These observations being at a distance of only some fifty or sixty yards, I think if she had been more seriously injured I would have observed it.

Captain Strout kept his vessel merely under steerage way, and continued to see the steamer until dark. She was then about three miles to the eastward of us. When night set in we lost sight of her.

The steamer was drifting much faster and next morning she was not in sight.

I think that, so far as personal safety is concerned, I would rather have been on board the unmanageable steamer than in the disabled brig.

When *The San Francisco* left this port she drew fifteen and a quarter feet of water on even keel, and when seen she was still lighter. She was abundantly supplied with staples and provisions, and was in the best condition to meet with such a disaster as has happened to her. And, if any additional evidence is necessary in regard to the strength of her hull, the following note will be sufficient.

And the following from Mr. Aspinwall also sets the matter right:-

Letter To The Editor
of the
NEW YORK HERALD

January 10, 1854

I must ask of you, as a matter of justice, to correct your editorial notice of the disaster to *The San Francisco*, wherein you allude to the steamer *Alabama* as having been chartered by Messrs. Howland & Aspinwall for the rescue of the unfortunate passengers.

The *Alabama* was chartered by the order of government, and went to sea yesterday, within twenty-six hours after coming into port with a full cargo of cotton.

On receiving the first telegraphic report of the disaster I deemed it my duty immediately to transmit the sad intelligence to Washington; and as soon thereafter as the wires could take and bring back a message, there came orders from the Secretary of War to charter the most available steamer, of sufficient power and size for the service, without restriction as to expense. All that was enjoined with efficiency and dispatch. My agency arose from the deep interest I felt in the result, and from my having been requested to aid Col. Swords in the selection of the steamer.

The Secretary of the Navy, by telegraph, also ordered Commodore Boarman to charter the North Star, and, failing to accomplish this, he has since, under fresh orders, chartered the steamer Union, and she leaves tomorrow.

The Secretary of the Treasury immediately

telegraphed orders to
this port, Wilmington,
and Charleston, to
dispatch the revenue
cutters, and he has
since ordered them from
Boston and New London to
join in the search.
You will thus see that
no action could have
been more prompt- the
pity is that government
has not in service more
available steamers for
such emergencies.

Very respectfully,
your obedient servant,

WM. H. ASPINWALL

The editorial delivered hope by way of the comments from the chief mate of the brig *Napoleon,* Mr. William McCarty and the letter to the editor from Mr. Aspinwall. In addition, the ***New York Herald*** prints an account from another newspaper the previous day. I could not miss a word until I found the words I longed to see: Edward Jarvis Tenney, survivor.

CHAPTER 28

Vessels Ordered to Sea

Sunday, January 9, 1854
The Washington Union

The Secretary of the Navy has directed two energetic officers of the navy - Lieutenant Gansevoort and Boggs - to proceed in the *Alabama*, (the vessel chartered by the War Department for the purpose of rendering assistance to *The San Francisco*,) to afford such aid and advice as their experience and judgment may suggest.

The Secretary has also directed the sloop of war *Decatur*, now fitting for sea at Boston, to proceed in the search, if, in the opinion of the commandant of the yard, she can be of any service.

The Secretary of the Navy has directed the steamer *North Star*, at New York, to be chartered, officered, and manned, and sent to the relief of *The San Francisco*.

In addition, we learn that Capt. Ludlow of the Savannah line volunteered his services and accompanied Capt. Schenck in the search for *The San Francisco*. The steamship *Union* will leave this morning completely coaled and provisioned. We learn that Messrs. Howland and Aspinwall have thoughtfully placed on board the steamer supplies of blankets and clothing for those on board of *The San Francisco*, in case they should be in need of such comforts. If not required by them, they are to be distributed to those vessels in distress that may be fallen in with.

The following vessels compose the list ordered to sea in search of *The San Francisco*: -

```
Vessel                    Captain          From
Steamship Alabama  -  Schenck  -    New York
Steamship Union    -  Adams    -    New York
Revenue cutter Washington - - - - New York
Revenue cutter Forward - - - - -  Philadelphia
Pilotboat - - - - - - - - - - - - Philadelphia
Sloop-of-war Decatur - - - - - -  Boston
Revenue cutter - - - - - - - - -  Boston
Revenue cutter - - - - - - - - -  Charleston
Revenue cutter - - - - - - - - -  Wilmington
```

All but the *Decatur* will be at sea today. They will take different directions to reach one point - Bermuda; and unsuccessful on arriving at that place, they will take different directions homeward, and by this arrangement they can scarcely fail in falling in with the disabled steamer.

Now, twenty-five days since Edward wrote his last letter, the news is pouring in at a furious pace and completely consuming me. I still have not found the news I long for. The distress of not knowing the fate of my dear Edward is destroying me. I cannot eat. I rarely sleep.

CHAPTER 29

One Hundred Soldiers Swept Overboard by a Single Wave

**TOTAL LOSS OF *THE STEAMSHIP SAN FRANCISCO*
WITH NEARLY TWO HUNDRED LIVES –
Over Five Hundred Lives Saved –
Awful Scenes on Board *The San Francisco* –
ABANDONMENT OF THE WRECK –
Noble Conduct of a British and Two American Captains –
Arrival at this Port of Two Hundred and Thirty of the
Survivors
in the British Ship *Three Bells* –
AUTHENTIC AND FULL ACCOUNTS OF THE DISASTER
- &c, &c. &c.**

Saturday, January 14, 1854

After a painful suspense of several days, we have received news of the fate of the steamship *San Francisco*, and those who left this port in her for California. The British ship *Three Bells*, Capt. Creighton, arrived last night, with the sad intelligence of the total loss of *The San Francisco*, with about two hundred lives, and the joyful news of the saving of over five hundred - officers of the army, their wives, passengers, soldiers, and officers and crew of the steamer.

The details of the disaster are given in a Statement of Lieutenant Winder, U.S. ARMY. I could not turn away from its contents, which were a collection of news and reports from the past two weeks, including the following reports from among the 500 rescued survivors!

CHAPTER 30

Statement of Lieutenant Winder Aboard the *Three Bells* at Sea

Friday Jan. 6, 1854.

The steamer *San Francisco*, as you are aware, sailed from New York on the 22nd of December, with United States troops, bound for California. The day was beautiful and everything promised a pleasant and prosperous voyage. The ship was well provided with everything which could render us comfortable, and every luxury that could be procured was placed on board. All these things, together with the gentlemanly and efficient officers of the ship, and pleasant company in the cabin, served to render us happy and contented. But, alas for all human calculations; about nine o'clock the second day out a gale sprang up, and continued to increase all night. At daylight it was perfectly frightful. During the night our engine gave out, and soon after our foremast was carried away, which left us entirely at the mercy of the wind and waves. The scene in the cabin during this time was truly distressing. Nearly all had turned out of the staterooms, despair depicted on the countenances of all. A few of us who occupied the upper cabin left it and went below; and well it was for us, for soon after day, a sea broke over our starboard wheelhouse, and with frightful force dashed against the after cabin, carrying away all of the cabin, and about one hundred and fifty people.

I studied the list of the one hundred and fifty people and was satisfied Edward's name was not among them. Lt. Winder continued most articulately as I read with rapt attention:

Mr. Rankin, our sutler, the other names I have not learned, were swept off, but the return wave brought them back. I had gone below but a few moments before this terrible crash, and was lying at the foot of the steps at the time. I never experienced such a sensation as when the water came pouring into the cabin, together with the debris of the upper cabin, down upon my head and breast. I was swept across the cabin with terrible force, but after three attempts succeeded in regaining my feet. I supposed that the ship had broken in half, and that we were fast sinking. I followed after some I saw going on deck, and on reaching it my blood ran cold at the sight of the poor fellows struggling among the fragments in the sea. The waves were, to my eyes, frightful. We could render no assistance whatever, and, in fact, expected ourselves that we should go down every minute. With great difficulty, we clung to the deck, the sea making a perfect breach over us, and the cold so great that an hour longer must have finished us. Close by me was Major Wyse, his young wife and babe. It was truly a heartrending sight. The poor child must have been nearly frozen.

About this time, Mr. Mellus, the first officer of the ship, than whom no braver seaman lives, came aft with his axe; this not only surprised me, but greatly raised my hopes. I watched him closely as he approached the only remaining mast. He attempted to cut it away, but the sea ran so high that he was unable to do it. This was the first time that I was aware that the ship was not full of water. Soon after this our gallant

Commodore Watkins came along. I asked him what our chances were; he replied, "Good." I then determined to get into the cabin.

The sea was running very high at the time, and the wreck was strewn on each side with pieces of wreck scattered here and there, with men and women clinging to the pieces in order to save themselves. In a few moments it was still, none of them appearing. Not a sound was heard except the dismal moan of the wind. On looking around, I saw Lt. Murray standing at the mizzenmast. I went aft to him, and held on there for awhile, until the first mate came to cut it away, which he failed in doing owing to the roughness of the sea. I then went forward where I was first, and saw Major Wyse, his wife and child, Lieuts. Chandler, Van Voast, and Dr. Satterlee. We talked over our chances for escape. And all came to the conclusion that we could not survive twenty minutes. At that time two Negroes came along with life preservers, and one of the soldiers handed me one, but it was so cold that we thought it would be only prolonging our misery, and thinking that the vessel would go down any minute, we did not use them. The sea was making a breach over us at every roll. About this time we discovered that there were many persons in the lower cabin under us, principally ladies.

An incident occurred at this time. Corporal Smith came to me and said his child was sick, and in about an hour after that he sent word to me and said he was very sick himself and would like to see me. I went to him and found he was dying; soon after his wife came in and told me that he and the child were dead. I had her put into a stateroom, and during the night she was found dead in bed, her only child, then living, lying asleep beside her. She was followed to the other world soon after by her other child.

I sat in shock at the horrific scene portrayed by the Lieutenant. My hands tremble, I cannot stop reading, though stop I must to wipe from my eyes the welling of tears that pour forth. I have to find Edward's name among the survivors! He must be tending to the sick and injured. Edward, you must stop and let someone know who you are, I beg him. With every death, I hold the newspaper to my breast and let forth prayers to our Heavenly Father for the souls of the dearly departed.

Just as my cogitations turn to prayers, Aunt Eliza appears at my chamber door and sees me embracing the newspaper.

"Lizzie, I am in need of baking assistance today. I refreshed the dough starter last night once I learned Bridget is delaying her return. James received word that she will stay away a fortnight if necessary to minister to her father as the poor man is not recovering well."

"Of course," I consent, proceeding slowly to my basin where I revive my tired eyes with a splash of water before obliging her.

"Is the starter ready?" I ask, strangely relived to have a task demanding my attention. I follow her downstairs to the kitchen, passing Laura reading in the parlor. Nearby, Grandmother has come over and is busily working her lace and, rather oddly, Aunt Dolly has also brought her handiwork and is tacking a veil to a hat brim.

"It should be," Aunt Eliza replies to my question. I do not seem to notice that any one of these three women could have tended to the dough.

"I have yet to grind the flour," she says, as she hands me an apron, which I donned over my day dress. Together we lift a burlap bag of wheat berries and she slices the top open to pour an amount into the hopper. I stoke the stove and put the kettle on to boil. She proceeds to turn the crank, as she engages me in conversation. She rattles on about seemingly anything, as well as nothing, of consequence, in a manner unaccustomed to her person. Once she has ground three cups of flour, I separate the starter and gently feed one cup of flour to the starter along with a cup of warm water. She folds in the remaining cups of flour and begins to mix the dough, while I take my turn at the mill. I heartily cranking several more cups of wheat while Aunt Eliza works the flour into the dough and sets it to rise. Then she begins to speak in earnest.

"Joe must be getting on well or he would have written your father by now," she muses.

"I suppose so. At least there is no word of disaster upon *The Josephine*," I say, wishing I had bitten my tongue a moment sooner, but I could think of nothing but loss at sea.

"No word of that, indeed," she kindly replies and refrains from engaging my wretched ruminations.

"She has been under way for nearly two months now," she comments on the ship. "I understand she is to transport nearly two hundred Irish immigrants as well as British goods on the return voyage."

"So be it now." My reply could not muffle my concern. How could she ignore the situation with *The San Francisco*? I had to ask,

"Do you not wonder as to the dilatory nature of *The San Francisco's* departure and the news about its disposition at sea?"

"Delays are commonplace. This can be a sign of careful preparation for all we know. She was well stocked for her exceedingly long journey. Stocked to the gills, I hear. One could live well for some time at sea with her provisions."

"Do you surmise the delayed departure may have been a sign of trouble to come?" I inquire.

"Whether 'tis or not, the storm could not have been foreseen, my dear girl. You must not torture yourself by thinking so, Lizzie. We can only know what we hear and must wait for word," she says.

"You can and must continue to live as you wait for word."
Wait for word. I selfishly contemplate how my situation might be otherwise, should Edward have taken the opportunity to disembark from such a journey. Yet, my situation was not as grave as that of his step-mother who must be worried sick. Her well-being and that of her children lay at the mercy of the ship's fate. Yet, he would never have retreated from the journey, despite any potential danger at sea, despite his fears and premonitions. That would be seen as cowardice, pusillanimous, and looked on unfavorably. Certainly, it would reflect poorly on the legacy of his father. The thought harrowed up my melancholic feelings. Just as my tears began to well, Aunt Eliza spoke.

"Now is the time for a stiff upper lip, dear child. Believe only in the facts you know and your own prayers, for that alone will carry you forward," she advises.

Laura begins tinkering on the keys of the melodeon and soon her humming emerges as song. Aunt Eliza smiles at me as she begins to cut vegetables for a pot of stew. How can she even think about singing? I wonder.

"Join me in this, Lizzie," she pleads and hands me a paring knife. "You prepare the carrots and potatoes and I will cube the meat." The warmth of the stove fills the kitchen by now and Laura's sweet song creates an ambiance contrary to the sour mood I have been indulging. Grateful for my home and safety, after a while I am able to return a smile.

With the stew in the pot and the bread dough rising, we begin preparing non-yeast cakes allowing sufficient time for the starter to awake. It is a blessing to be busy and productive.

Once the bread is in the oven I excuse myself and join the family burying my nose in Laura's book until dinner. This book is the first literature I've read since the disaster.

Father brought home the newspaper and, after a leisurely meal, I ventured upstairs to read the evening news:

CHAPTER 31

Fate of *The San Francisco*
News From the Wreck

January 14, 1854

The copious details which will be found on the first page of our paper this morning, concerning the wreck of the steamer *San Francisco*, will be read with painful interest, far and wide. The loss of nearly two hundred souls, washed overboard, or killed, or dying from the exposure, sickness and hardships of the wreck is the melancholy feature of the story; but the saving of from four to five hundred lives by the *Kilby*, the *Three Bells*, and the *Antarctic*, is a matter for sincere congratulations. There was a chance that all might have been lost - the ship, and every soul on board - leaving, as in the case of the ill-starred *President*, no vestige afloat to tell the tale. While we lament, therefore, the loss of life from this last fatal disaster, we rejoice that so large a proportion of her passengers, soldiers and crew, were snatched from the angry waves.

It will be seen that the fatal storm struck the ship on the 24th December, two days out from this port; that on the 25th (Christmas Day), she was rendered wholly unmanageable from the dislocation of her machinery and her rigging; that on the same day, her decks were swept clean by a heavy sea, carrying away all the upper saloon, and the mass of people who were lost. On that day the ship, but for the extraordinary strength of her hull, must have gone down, yet she continued drifting in the Gulf Stream, and under a succession of heavy gales, almost unparalleled on our Atlantic coast, still inhabitable though unmanageable, till finally relieved, and abandoned on the 6th of January. Perhaps there is not another steamer afloat that could have withstood, in her dismantled condition, the buffeting of a fortnight's such wintry storms in the trough of the sea.

When first struck by the gale, on the night of the 24th, *The San Francisco*, was but one hundred and fifty miles out from Sandy Hook; when abandoned, on the 6th inst., she was some seven hundred miles off, having floundered away to that distance, at the mercy of the winds, the waves and the Gulf Stream.

On the 28th of December, after having previously spoke two vessels, which were lost sight of upon heavy sea in the night, the bark *Kilby*, of and for Boston, hove to, and took off a hundred passengers, including the women and children on board. On the 31st, the British ship *Three Bells*, of Glasgow, came up; and on the 3d of January she was joined, while lying by the wreck, by the ship *Antarctic*, of this port, bound for Liverpool; and on the 6th, between the two relieving vessels the wreck was relieved of every remaining soul on board, and left in a sinking condition to her fate.

Late evening the *Three Bells* arrived off the Battery, and the following modest report is found from the log of her Captain:-

British Ship *Three Bells*,

(of Glasgow) [Captain] Creighton, Glasgow, 45 days, with merchandise and 16 passengers, to McDonald & Co. Dec. 31, lat. 40 12. Lon. 59 30. spoke the steamship *San Francisco*, of New York, Capt. Watkins, hence for San Francisco, having on board United States troops. The S.F. being in a disabled condition, having decks swept, &c., and wanting assistance, concluded to lay by her, which he did for six days, and succeeded in getting on board two hundred and thirty of her passengers, and brought them to this port.

This is, we repeat, a modest report; but Capt. Creighton has not told all. Those from the lost ship say that the *Three Bells* was leaking all the time, had to keep her pumps going constantly; that the ship had lost her sails, and was short of water and provisions. But in this last item, the *Kilby*, the *Three Bells* and the *Antarctic* were plentifully supplied from the abundant stores of the wreck, or they could not have carried off so many passengers with any other prospect than immediate starvation.

To the captains and crews of the three relieving ships, though they simply discharged their duty in the premises, something more than ordinary credit is due, for the case was an extraordinary one in the labors and hazards of the rescue. Our government, as an act of reciprocity and of sound policy, should approve the gallant conduct of the relieving parties, and especially the Jack-tar and his crew of the British ship *Three Bells*.

It is estimated that the *Antarctic* carried off for Liverpool some two hundred passengers, soldiers and crew- that one hundred were taken to Boston or Bermuda- as she had a leading wind for that island- by the *Kilby*, (Capt. Low), and two hundred and thirty were brought to this port by the *Three Bells*- making a total of five hundred and thirty saved.

Three weeks since the disaster occurred and still no word of Edward's well being. My heart grows heavier each day. I have cancelled all my social obligations and am declining visitors. I can no longer talk about the news; no longer talk about anything. I write and pray and then begin such routine again, pleading with God for some word of Edward.

After managing to maintain a most appropriate demeanor at dinner, I become filled with rage and self-pity at my ill fortune. Father attempts to engage me before supper. I beg him to excuse me to my room and make my apologies to family feigning I cannot join them due to my monthly period of indisposition. Father gently points out that such a period could not last a full month and insists I speak with him.

Our conversation is hardly civil. When my anger turns to guilt and morphs into true remorse, Father holds me and allows me to sob, but for only a short time before declaring, "That is enough. You can overcome this, Lizzie." He leaves me to my own devices.

I awake early and ready for church dressing myself, tugging only slightly on my corset strings so as to allow myself a chance to breathe. I struggle angrily with my hair-comb as I gaze in the mirror at my weary and defeated demeanor. I pinch my cheeks hard and bite my lips in a vain attempt to bring some color to my face while turning up the corners of my mouth to mock a smile. Averting my gaze today might dissuade anyone from engaging me at church, I conclude. I do not want their pitiful looks at my haggard ways for I have enough self-pity of my own making. I pack an extra handkerchief in my satchel and head downstairs.

It is Sunday, January 15, 1854. The sermon is on the valley of death. I sink in the pew seeking to shrink from the words as they ring out from the pulpit. 'You cannot flee this enemy! We must march on toward death. Each step of life one pace closer to our end. Focus not on that end but on each step, on each moment. Your life is a blessing, a celebration of love and glory for having lived.' The sermon seems to never end.

After dinner, Father retreats to his study. When I appear at his door requesting the newspaper, he refuses.

"Let us speak first." He, once again, asks me to sit.

"Lizzie, there is news today of Edward."

I reach desperately for the paper but he holds it tight and will not release his grip.

"Wait, Lizzie," he says and secures my arms at my sides. Then he holds me gently and says softly, "There are names of those who were taken off *The San Francisco* and saved. Edward is not listed there. He is listed among those lost."

I feel my heart racing and I struggle to catch my breath. I can hear my heart pounding in my ears. Father continues to talk but I hear nothing. Nothing but my own whimpering cry. I realize I am crying as I begin to slide to his feet. He catches me before I collapse and carries me to the fainting couch in the parlor. I curl into myself. Nothing can console me.

I know not whether minutes or hours pass before I fall asleep. I seem to wake from a nap, still in the parlor. My corset is unlaced in back and Aunt Eliza is looking over me. I feel vulnerable and in full display of the family. I am confused.

"Was I sleeping?" I ask with great hope.

"Just momentarily, my dear," she replies. "You have had a shock."

"Oh no. No, no, no. It cannot be. Please don't tell me," I beg and turn my head away.

"It is true," she says very softly.

I struggle to sit up and want to pull away. I want to run from the parlor but Father is in the doorway, blocking me. He is too big and there is no escape.

"I am so sorry, my dear, dear Lizzie. My dear, dear daughter," he says. "Edward loved you so much. If it had been in his power to come back to you, he would be here now. He did not want to leave you."

"Oh, Father. If he is missing, they did not find him dead. If they did not find him at all, there is still uncertainty. Will they not keep looking?"

"Shhh. Listen," he looks at me directly and says, "They are certain he did not survive. He was seen just before he went missing in the wave that swept her decks clean. He was swept to sea on that wave. He is not coming back, Lizzie. He is gone."

"Others were swept back on board!" I argue. I bargain for Edward's life. "We cannot give up on him this easily, Father!" If they did not save him, he must have been injured and could not come to the rescue boats."

"Edward was not on the ship when they left it." He hands me the newspaper then and sit nearby.

"I do not believe this." I agonize and begin to read. I need to see his name.

CHAPTER 32

Statement by One of the Passengers

On Monday, December 21, the troops, consisting of eight companies of the Third Regiment of Artillery, were embarked from steamtugs on board the steamer, then anchored in the North River. They numbered, rank and file, some five hundred men. The officers with their families, together with the soldiers' wives and females- a certain portion of whom were allowed to each company- brought the number up to about six hundred. There were twenty or thirty other passengers. The crew numbered from one hundred to one hundred fifty; so that all told, we were between seven hundred and fifty and eight hundred souls on board.

On Wednesday morning the steamer dropped down to the Quarantine, and anchored for the night. On Thursday, the 22d, after having been detained for two or three hours, waiting for a dilatory officer, she weighed anchor about 10 o'clock and stood out to sea. At 12 discharged our pilot.

Our voyage was now fairly commenced. A succession of constantly recurring and oft-repeated delays had delayed our departure week after week, and month after month. At last every obstacle had been overcome, and the gallant ship, with her head pointed to the southwest, moved steadily, though not swiftly, on her course. She was deeply laden - far too deeply, as the results proved. Her engines were new and untried, and the strain upon them great. Thursday was a lovely morning, the sea calm and smooth, with gentle breezes from the northwest. Whatever gloomy foreboding might have existed seemed quieted by so fair a presage.

Friday morning, the 23d, rose brightly on our course. We had entered the Gulf Stream, and the weather, which yesterday had been chilly, and caused the ladies and children to gather about the stove, had become mild. The winds still from the northwest stirred the sea enough to cause the dinner table to be comparatively deserted. The day passed without incident of any kind, and gave no presage of the awful disaster so soon to follow.

Immediately after tea, I retired to my room, and after reading two hours as quietly as if on shore, undressed and retired. There was more roll to the ship than I had previously experienced, and the wind seemed unrelenting, but I thought nothing of it. Soon there was no sleeping. It soon blew a gale. The ship rolled and pitched to a degree that it was difficult to keep my berth. All the books and loose articles upon the table were thrown to the floor. Every article in the room, though confined, was thrown about in an alarming manner.

At 11 o'clock I could bear it no longer. I rose, dressed hurriedly, and went out upon the deck. My room was on the hurricane deck, on the forward part of the ship. The scene, as I stepped back, was terrific. The sea was a complete mass of foam, boiling and swelling like a cauldron. The gale was terrific. The steamer had broached to twice, and had become unmanageable. Her head was towards the wind. The whole crew was engaged in strenuous but vain efforts to take in the sails. They were blown to ribbons. The foremast- we carried no mainmast- was wreathing and twisting like a young sapling. It was large enough for the mainmast of a 1,000 ton ship. The fury of the tempest was such that I could not stand before it a moment; but I seized the iron brace connecting the kingbolts, and surveyed the scene for a moment. Then I threw myself on my hands and knees, and made for the nearest hatch, to get below. This happened to be over the forward galley. Swinging myself down by the cabin, I reached the main deck. Here a scene of confusion and confounding presented itself. Four hundred soldiers were berthed on this deck, in double rows of standee berths, three tiers each. They had been broken and thrown down. The live stock, of which there was considerable, had escaped their pens on the same deck, and soldiers, calves, pigs, sheep and poultry, were all mingled together amid the broken standees. The steamer's guards had been carried away some time previously, and the sea washed over the deck with every roll of the ship. The lanterns were extinguished, and the darkness was almost total. I made an effort to reach the after cabin, but found it impossible. With my penknife I cut a leather belt from one of the soldier's knapsacks hanging around, and fastening it to a carline, made a secure place to hold on. I remained there towards an hour, the storm all the while increasing.

About one o'clock the foremast came down almost over my head, crushing in the hurricane deck. I feared now that the deck would be swept clean of everything, and determined to seek refuge below. I went first into the steerage, but as they commenced battening down the hatch, with perhaps two hundred soldiers in it, I left and went to the second cabin, occupied by the noncommissioned officers and their families. I was wet to the skin and chilled through. After waiting here for two hours, with no abatement to the fury of the gale, I crept into one of the soldier's berths, pulled a blanket over me, and after a while fell asleep. The first ray of dawn awoke me. I arose, and through the store room and pantry succeeded in gaining the main saloon. Saturday morning, the 24th, had at last dawned upon us, and this awful night had an end.

While passing between the second and after cabin, I felt a tremendous sea strike the ship, but I had no idea of the awful consequences. It was the denouement - the finale of the awful tragedy, which had been going on through the night. An overwhelming sea had struck the ship on her starboard quarter, carried away the starboard paddle box, both smoke stacks, the whole promenade deck abaft the paddle boxes, two rows of state rooms, of twelve each on the main deck, and stove in the main deck hatch. This was the smallest part of the havoc.

At one fell swoop nearly one hundred and fifty human beings were swept into eternity. The majority were private soldiers of the different companies of the Third Artillery. One company lost all but ten of its members. Four officers went with them:- Lieut. Col. Washington, distinguished at Buena Vista and other hard fought fields; Maj. Taylor and wife; Capt. Field and Lieut. Smith. The sea was covered with drowning men. The roar of the tempest smothered the "bubbling cry of strong swimmers in their agony." In a few moments, they sank to rise no more till the sea gives up her dead. Two of all the crowd succeeded in regaining the ship- Mr. Rankin, an army sutler, and a merchant of Rio Janeiro.

A few moments had elapsed when I reached the saloon. It was filled with water to the depth of nearly two feet. The females and children, mostly in their nightclothes and wet to the skin, were scattered on the planks; some wailing and sobbing; some apparently stupefied; and some calmly awaiting what seemed their inevitable fate. All supposed the last hour had arrived, and in a few moments they would meet their Maker face to face.

"Then rose from sea to sky the wild farewell-Happily those who, in this awful moment, felt that their peace was made, and nothing left but calm resignation to their Maker's hand. But death is the King of Terrors, and when he meets us in the midst of life, with our bones full of marrow and our limbs full of sap, human nature clings to life, and even the instinct of the animal shrinks from death.

The officers of the ship went from man to man, inspiring all with hope, and cheering them with the promise of safety.

Some of the officers of the troops showed themselves as daring in this trying hour, amid creaking cordage and falling spars, as they could have been amid clashing sabres and gleaming arms. Major F.O. Wyse, Lieut. W.A. Winder, Lieut. C.S. Winder, Lieut. Van Voast. Lieut. Chandler, and Sergeant Brown of Company G were among those most conspicuous in their efforts to revive the drooping spirits of the passengers.

Another sea like that which struck us and our fate had been that of the President- not a soul would have survived to tell the tale. But it pleased a merciful and all wise Providence to say to the sea, "Hitherto shall thou come, and no further, and here shall thy proud waves be stayed." It is proverbial that drowning men catch at straws, and instinctively did many of us lash ourselves to life preservers, though in the raging billows of that angry sea, five hundred miles from the nearest shore, one would have been but little better dependence than the other.

After the first burst of dismay was over, hope began to revive our bosoms. The hull was still staunch and strong and some passing vessel might rescue us from the wreck. Something whispered, "You are safe," and after committing myself and those most dear to me to the Father of Mercies, I too felt at peace.

Ascending the companion-way, from the saloon to the main deck, I seated myself at the head of the staircase, and surveyed the scene. The steamer was, in all her upper works, a perfect wreck. Foremast, smokestack, the greater part of the promenade deck, the saloon, and all the staterooms on the main deck - all were gone. The main deck was stove, and the water rushing in at every sea we shipped. On the opposite side of the companionway lay the mangled and bleeding corpse of a soldier, who was killed instantly by the falling of the deck. A few feet further lay a man groaning and near death from injuries received at the same time. The sea was running mountains high, and every billow that came with its curling crest towards us, seemed about to pour into our shattered deck and sink us.

It was not so to be. We were in imminent danger of floundering; but our gallant and undaunted commander, Captain Watkins, whose exertions during all that fearful night had been almost superhuman, directed all his energies to save us. To lighten the ship and stop the leaks were the first objects. To break up the hatches and commence discharging cargo was the work of the moment. Soldiers and sailors all lent a helping hand, as each man knew he worked for his life, all worked with a will. Stanchions were placed under the broken deck, and it was partially forced back in place. It was found that the water gained upon us rapidly.

The steam pump had become obstructed. Fifty soldiers were detailed to commence bailing.

All day and all night the work went on without intermission. Still, with every roll the ship took in large quantities of water, and we gained little upon the leak.

Sunday morning, the 25th, the day of nativity of our blessed Saviour, at last dawned upon us. The sky lighted up a little; there was a short gleam of sunshine, and the sea calmed a little. A sail or two were seen in the distance, but none approached us. It was a gloomy Christmas for us. The work of bailing and pumping went on, and we had gained on the leak.

Monday, the 26th, the gale continued with little abatement. All night Sunday the tempest roared round our devoted ship. The waves thundered against our sides and stern like cannon at the gates of a beleaguered city. Sleep was out of the question. For three nights we had had none. We discovered a sail not far off. On approaching us she proved to be a brig; we spoke her. She reported herself short of provisions and after supplying herself with barrels of beef and pork we had thrown overboard she went on her way.

On Tuesday, the 27th discovered another sail bearing down upon us. She proved to be the bark *Kilby*, of and for Boston, from New Orleans, loaded with cotton, thirty-five days out. By authority of Col. Gates, commanding the detachment, she was chartered for government to convey the troops to the nearest accessible port.

Tuesday was too rough to disembark any part of the detachment, but Wednesday, the 28th, Col. Gates and family, Maj. Merchant and family, Col. Burke, Captains Fremont and Judd, with their families, Drs. Satterlee and Wirts, with some others whose names are not recollected, were safely embarked on board the *Kilby*. Some forty or fifty soldiers, and some soldier's wives, also embarked- in all nearly one hundred persons. Night came on and put a stop to any further operations. It had been agreed that the bark should lie by us till all on board the steamer were disembarked, but it came to blow heavily in the night, and in the morning she had disappeared, and we saw her no more. Thus all hopes of escape we based upon the *Kilby* were doomed to disappointment; and when, in the morning, we could trace no vestige of her on the remotest verge of the horizon, we experienced the sickness of heart from hope deferred.

Once more we were alone on the boundless expanse of waters. Our ship lay as helpless as a log upon the waves. She was completely crippled. Her engine, as should have been mentioned, broke down the first night of the storm; it was never of use afterwards, except to work the pumps. With infinite exertion, a small sail was rigged to the mizzenmast, which assisted a little in steadying her; but she rolled and tumbled about at a fearful rate. We had succeeded in stopping some of the leaks, and in lightening the vessel to a considerable extent, by throwing over provisions and coal. The ship was also very much relieved by cutting off the timber of her guards, upon which the sea broke heavily, lifting her decks every time it broke.

We had now (Thursday, the 29th) reached the sixth day since the storm commenced. We were about to encounter death in a new form. A very large portion of the ship's steerage had been filled with cargo, provisions, military stores, &c. The consequence was that the portion left for the soldiers was much crowded. It had been expected we should soon be in fine weather, and that they could sleep comfortably in standee berths on deck. When the storm came, that was impossible, and they were consequently driven below. Crowded in narrow quarters, exposed to wet and cold, obliged to be fed on an insufficient diet, in consequence of the loss of the galleys and the impossibility of cooking for such numbers, it is no matter of surprise that disease soon made its appearance. Add to this the influence of depressing passions, anxiety of mind, fright, and despondency, and it is no wonder that they sickened and died. The disease more nearly than anything assumed the form of Asiatic Cholera-commencing with diarrhea and terminating in a few hours.

Both the army surgeons having left, the charge of the sick fell upon the surgeons of the ship. To add to our distress, nearly all the medicine in the ship had been either washed overboard or destroyed. The mortality was necessarily great. For several days it averaged ten deaths a day. Men, women and children fell indiscriminately before it, and whole families perished within twenty-four hours. It was a scene of awful suffering over which I should rather wish to draw a veil, and the like of which I trust a merciful God will spare me ever witnessing again.

During Thursday and Friday our eyes were not gladdened by a single sail. The hours dragged on most heavily. We had abundance of provisions on board, but it was almost impossible to get them cooked. The roll of the ship was so heavy that the provisions were thrown from the galley. When we could get a cup of hot tea with our hard biscuit it was a treat; and when a roasted potato and piece of fried pork was added to our bill of fare it was a sumptuous repast. We attempted to issue the soldiers once a day, but a sufficient quantity of hot water could not be procured, and we were compelled to abandon it. On their miserable fare of hard biscuit and cold water it was not to be wondered that the poor soldiers sickened and died.

During the night of Friday or the morning of Saturday the 31st, the cheering sound rang through the vessel that a ship was at hand. A light was discovered off the bow. We immediately commenced firing signal shots. They were answered by blue lights from the strange vessel.

When the morning dawned we discovered a vessel with English colors. She came near enough to speak to us, but the wind was so light as to render it quite impossible. We reverted to a kind of telegraphic communication, by writing on boards in chalk with large letters. We succeeded in making her understand our situation, which later was sufficiently obvious. She promised to lay by us. This intelligence cheered every heart. The weather during Saturday and Sunday was too rough to attempt to lower a boat. There was too,

another dilemma. The English ship had but one reliable boat, the longboat. We had none at all. Of the nine splendid boats with which we left New York not one remained. Captain Watkins, not to be overcome by any difficulty, commenced the construction of rafts. They seemed but a frail dependence, and providentially they were not needed. Other means of relief were at hand.

On Monday, the 2d of January, the sea calmed so much towards evening the English ship lowered her yawl boat, and our second mate, Mr. Grattan, went on board of her.

On Tuesday, the 3d January, our hearts were gladdened by another sail, under American colors. She came near enough to speak to her, and we learned that she was the *Antarctic*, three days out from New York, bound for Liverpool. She had five fine boats. And after enduring the agony of suspense for so many days it seemed that the hour of our deliverance had at last arrived. With the aid of the *Antarctic's* boats we could all be conveyed on board the English ship, now ascertained to be the *Three Bells*, Captain Creighton, of Glasgow, bound for New York. The *Bells* had experienced much rough weather, and was leaky.

On Tuesday we succeeded in putting a sergeant and file of soldiers on board to work the pumps. On Wednesday morning, the 4th of January, the work of disembarking commenced in earnest. The sick, of whom there was a large number and some in a dying condition, were wrapped in blankets, brought on deck, and lowered carefully into the boats. Casks of water were lowered down and towed on board the *Bells*. Bread and bacon and other provisions were sent off. By evening much of the work had been accomplished. It was found necessary, however, in consequence of the shortness of provisions on board the *Bells*, to divide our numbers between the two ships. Lieutenants Winder and Chandler, with about 110 soldiers, embarked on the *Antarctic* for Liverpool. Captain Watkins also determined to accompany that portion of our number.

Thursday morning, the 5th, rose bright and beautiful. The sea was calm, the wind gentle. It is a day which will ever live in my memory. By noon the work of disembarking and re-embarking was complete. Every man, woman and child had left the ship. Our Captain was the last on board. He saw every officer, every sailor, every fireman, and every Negro waiter, of whom there were forty or fifty, safely in the boats, then lowered himself down, and the boat pulled away. He was rowed alongside the *Three Bells*, where he was greeted with nine hearty cheers and then pulled away for the *Antarctic*. The *San Francisco* had, by his orders, been scuttled, and we could see her settling gradually deeper into the water.

About 2 P.M. the *Three Bells* hauled sail, and moved away from the wreck. I stood on the deck and gazed at the ill-fated vessel with mingled emotions. She had been our prison for fourteen anxious, agonizing days and nights. She was near being our grave. Yet she was a gallant ship, and a stauncher hull was never launched, else she would have been our grave. Now she lay stretched in all her vast length upon the deep, one hundred fathoms long, battered and mutilated, like some huge monster of the deep which, in a contest with a deadly foe, had been conquered and slain. Farewell to you, ill starred vessel. Receive your doom and sink down like lead into the mighty waters. The blackest chapter in my experience is comprised in those fourteen days I passed within your bosom. We found the *Three Bells* a snug, staunch vessel. Her cargo consisted in part of chloride of lime, which had to be thrown overboard, mostly to make room for the sailors between decks. The atmosphere of the ship was strongly impregnated with chlorine gas, and its qualities as a disinfecting agent were strongly tested. It caused a good deal of irritation about the lungs and incessant coughing for the first day or two. The sickness began to abate almost immediately, owing, in part to moral causes. The diet of the soldiers was mostly biscuit and water, as there was a scarcity of provisions. They had occasionally a slice of fried bacon, and a ration of brandy was issued to them daily.

When the *Three Bells* left the wreck she was in latitude 39 and longitude 59 60, about 600 miles from New York. We encountered a great deal of northeasterly wind, and our progress was slow until Wednesday, the 11th of January, when we were favored with a stiff breeze from the southeast, which drove us rapidly on, and on Thursday afternoon we were off soundings. Towards the evening it grew thick, and the captain, fearing to venture too far in, stood off and on till morning.

Friday dawned bright and fair. We signaled for a pilot and after a steamtug and at 5 P.M. we were at anchor in the harbor at New York.

Interesting Statement of a Passenger
The New York Times
January 16, 1854

...On January 13, at about 4 o'clock I was on deck of the *Kilby* with many other passengers, when a cry was heard that a ship was lying close by us, which we had not observed in consequence of the dense fog which prevailed at the time, but immediately upon our attention being directed to the quarters in which she lay, a vessel was plainly visibly looming up through the mist. The Captain immediately hailed her, and to the joy of all on deck, a light was seen passing along her deck. The hail was soon answered. Capt. Low stated that we were short of provisions, and the cheering answer, delivered in a stentorian voice, was "Send your boats alongside."

The passengers now tumbled out of their berths and from the hold, in every style of garment, anxious to hear anything which might be communicated. The greatest state of anxiety prevailed as to her destination, and this was continued for some time. Owing to the officers being unable to determine who should man the small boat to go on board, Lieut. Murray promptly offered his services; but as it was necessary to effect a contract on behalf of the government, it was the duty of Lieut. Fremont, the Quartermaster of the regiment; and he was obliged, at the solicitation of all the officers, to go on board. On the return of the boat which carried

Lieut. Fremont on board, word came to send all the passengers over; and, to our joy, we noticed, as the fog cleared away, that the *Lucy Thompson* was lowering two of her boats, which soon came alongside.

The second disembarkation of the passengers then commenced from the *Kilby* to the *Lucy Thompson*, and continued for about six hours. All were at length transferred, with the exception of four passengers and twelve of the United States troops, who volunteered to remain behind to assist the Captain in bringing his vessel into port. On reaching the ship, Capt. Pendleton immediately sent provisions and sails to the *Kilby*, sufficient to last them for several weeks.

I cannot describe the joy which followed, when the passengers, one by one, entered the cabin of the *Lucy Thompson*. Upon the table we found a most delicious meal of bread and butter, together with an abundance of porter. The treatment we received from Capt. Pendleton was the most kind, generous and warm-hearted that one human being could show another.

The ship was soon underway, and in a few hours, a pilot-boat came in sight, and furnished us with a pilot.

The bark *Kilby* was then almost out of sight. About five hours after the pilot had boarded us we approached in sight of the light ship off Sandy Hook, where we remained until Saturday night, when the steam tug *Titan* arrived laden with every essential of clothing and provision for our comfort. She had been dispatched by Wm. H. Aspinwall, Esq. The passengers stepped on board and were conveyed to this city. On our way up Mr. Lloyd Aspinwall read a letter from his father tendering the hospitalities of his house to the officers and passengers on board; and my brother, who had also come in the Titan to receive us, read to a crowd of eager listeners the papers containing the particulars related to the fate of our fellow passengers who we had left on board the wreck.

I have thus endeavored to give the particulars of our shipwreck in the simplest matter-of-fact language, without attempting to describe the sufferings of those on board, or to do justice to the noble conduct of the various officers and sailors, or to the Christian resignation and heroism of many of the passengers. No language can adequately describe the scenes of danger and terror through which we have passed; and words of gratitude and thankfulness are fittest to close my hurried narrative of the disaster of the ill-fated *San Francisco*.

James Lorimer Graham, Jr.

Statement of Colonel William Gates, commander of the Third Regiment of Artillery January 15, 1854

The narrative of events in relation to the disaster on board the steamer *San Francisco*, I perceive, has been given by different persons who have preceded me. They are mainly correct. The whole number of persons under my command was about 520. This includes women and children. Of these, 106 were transferred on board the *Kilby*, and brought to this port. I estimate that the whole number which embarked for California from 200 to 220 were swept overboard by raging sea. The names of the officers and citizens who were lost, including my own son, Charles, have been given... the good ship *Kilby* appeared...the commodore requested me to embark those under my command on that vessel...we cruised about, endeavoring to find *The San Francisco*, for three days without meeting any success...

My eyes begin to jump around the page searching for Edward's name. It was there. On this day, January 15, 1854, there were four names added to the official list of those swept overboard with that first furious wave.

Mr. Tenney, Miss Belton, Mr. Gates, D.C. Stockwell.

I did not read another word of News.

Thus began my descent into a world that was fast slipping from my fingertips. I read Edward's last letter. Over and over again. I read the penultimate letter; and the one previous. I read until there were no more letters to read. Then I read them from the beginning.

I managed that week truly as if in a fog. Father called us to begin packing our belongings for we were to join the Tenney family in Methuen by week's end. Bridget had returned and foodstuffs were being gathered over the next two days. Laura and I attended to any matter that aided in the preparation. I could not think, let alone carry on a civil conversation, but no one expected as much of me. Laura often walked up behind me and simply stroked my back saying nothing. Nothing could be said that would make any difference in this dreadful loss for any and all who had loved Edward and been loved by him.

On Friday, the carriage was fully loaded. Father, Laura and I joined Aunt Eliza to journey to Methuen to offer our condolences and assistance to Aunt Augusta in any way we might. We arrived to learn that Aunt Augusta had been preparing a move to Andover, now since news arrived last Sunday, she had stopped everything. Liz and Mary took charge of caring for their siblings Margie, Lottie and Johnny to allow Aunt Augusta to seek counsel. The family seemed to bear up as well as could be expected, thanks be to the innocence of the youngest among them. The family's prayers took my breath away. We began to read the obituaries. There were several.

CHAPTER 33

Obituaries

I.

Cambridge Chronicle. EDWARD J. TENNEY - We perceive among the lost of the ill-fated ship *San Francisco*, the name of Edward Jarvis Tenney, of Methuen, who, on the 26th of December, was swept by a heavy sea from the deck of that vessel, and drowned. Young Tenney was a graduate of Harvard University of the class of 1853. He possessed natural abilities that gave promise of future usefulness and distinction. A few months previous to graduation he had the great misfortune to lose his father, which circumstance entirely changed his plans of life, and instead of adopting a professional course, he decided to engage in mercantile pursuits, and was on his way to Valparaiso for that purpose, with high hopes and cheering prospects. This sudden and afflictive event has cast a deep gloom over a very large circle of affectionate relatives, as well as a large number of personal friends. The age of Mr. Tenney was about 20.

II.

SAN FRANCISCO. - Among the passengers who were washed overboard from this ill-fated steamer, on the first day of the gale, Dec. 24, was Edward J. Tenney, son of the late Hon. John Tenney, of Methuen, aged about 20. He had recently graduated at Harvard College, and was on his way to Valparaiso, to engage in mercantile pursuits, with the future all bright and glowing before him; but his career has been suddenly cut short, just as he was about entering upon the active duties of life. He was a young man of fine promise, and his loss will be long and deeply lamented.

III.

Among those who were lost on board *The San Francisco* there was one who, as a resident in this vicinity, deserves notice in the public records. He bore no title to attract public regard, but he was well known and deeply loved by a large circle of acquaintances. There is always a tender and melancholy interest attending "the early dead" and his removal at the age of 20, and under such peculiar circumstances has cast a deep shadow over many hearts. He was possessed of an active and well cultivated mind, his manners were at once pleasing and manly and his kindness of disposition will never be forgotten by those who enjoyed his friendship. His prospects were bright. The prompt and active and practical talents with which he was endowed, united to his generous temper, would have earned to him a full measure of earthly prosperity in the new field of enterprise to which he was repairing. His loss is great and falls with peculiar heaviness on surviving relatives.

IV.

EDWARD J. TENNEY. - We perceive, among the lost from the ill-fated ship, San Francisco, the name of Edward Jarvis Tenney, oldest son of the late Hon. John Tenney, of Methuen, who on the 25th of December was swept, by a heavy sea, from the deck of that vessel and drowned. Young Tenney was a graduate of Harvard University, of the class of 1853, and no doubt is well remembered by many in this city. In addition to a good education, he possessed natural abilities that gave promise of future usefulness and distinction. A few months previous to graduation, he had the great misfortune to lose his father; which circumstances entirely changed his plans of life, and, instead of adopting a professional course, he decided to engage in mercantile pursuits, and was on his way to Valparaiso for that purpose, with high hopes and cheering prospects. This sudden and afflictive event has cast a deep gloom over a very large circle of affectionate relatives, as well as a large number of personal friends who loved and honored him for the amiability of his character, his modest deportment, and his many prepossessing and social qualities. They feel that a vacuum has been made in their social circle that will not easily be filled. The age of Mr. Tenney was about 20 years.

———◦∞◦———

The following tributes were sent through family members, including one that came for me by way of Emily Oliver.

Tell Lizzie love is stronger after death has destroyed all earthly feelings. In Heaven we will be reunited, each joy shall be brighter for these sorrows of youth.

An Attaché of the Lewiston, ME. Advocate - probably John Abbott, late of Lowell, says of Edward:

"He had but recently graduated at Harvard College, and … young as he was, in point of ability had very few superiors of his age. He possessed a clear mind, and energy of character, rarely surpassed. In his deportment he was extremely kind and gentlemanly, and unwavering in his attachment to friends.

"When forced to part from those we love,
Though sure to meet tomorrow,
We yet a kind of censer prove,
And feel a sense of sorrow;
But Oh! what art can paint the grief
Of those who are forced to sever
To meet no more - to meet no more forever."

Mrs. Boyd made a long visit at Mr. Bartlett's at Tarrytown & young Tenney was there all the time till he left on his ill fated voyage. She became well acquainted with him & speaks in the highest terms of his intelligence & amiable, affectionate disposition. He was leaving with splendid prospects such as few young men have the good fortune to start in life with.

Class of 1853 Harvard College

Resolved; -that the melancholy death of our classmate, Edward Jarvis Tenney, occurring just as he had honorably completed his college labors, and was about to enter on the more exciting duties of active life with so many well-rounded hopes of success, has filled us with the deepest sorrow. - By his scholarly abilities and his integrity of purpose - and action, he had won our respect, while he had endeared himself to each of us by his manly frankness and independence, his cheerful disposition, his mild and conciliatory temper and his many and eminent social virtues. He was more than a classmate to us; he was a much loved companion; and in him not only does the class mourn the loss of one of its brightest ornaments, but each member of it, the loss of a true hearted friend.

Resolved; - that we sincerely sympathize with the relatives and friends of the deceased in this sad event; by which their happiness has been marred, and their bright hopes of the future extinguished.

Resolved: That these resolutions, be enrolled in the class records; and that a copy of them be transmitted to the mother of the deceased.

CHAPTER 34

Ever After

On December 24, 1854, I re-read Edward's obituaries and the tributes. Each year from that day forward, I would steal time away from our Christmas Eve celebration to spend a few moments alone to pray that Edward's soul was resting in peace. Oh, I kept a pleasant enough face and lived as if I were not a damaged soul, for few knew the despair that had set into my heart. Mine was a secret despair.

For the next eight years, I read each of his letters only on the day of the month it had been sent. Yet, Edward came to me many nights in my dreams. Time and again, he assured me he would see me again and praised me for my faithful and patient waiting.

On Christmas day 1861, my Ned came to me again in a dream. He stood before me just as he had so many times in life. I greeted him with great affection and relief to see his warm smile once again. He spoke most clearly to me this night.

"My beloved dear gipsy, do not be angry. It is over for now, my dear pet. You must let me go. I must go on. It is time. I will look over you always, but now you too must go on. Carry all my love forever. You must begin to share it. I love you eternally. Good bye."

That was all he said. Then he was gone.

I awoke in a cold sweat, my nightclothes clinging to me as if I had been under the sea with him. Yet I felt calm, even peaceful. For the first time in years, I felt I could carry on knowing his love would guide me.

I beckoned Laura and she came quickly, certain something was amiss.

"What is it, Lizzie?"

"Help me dress quickly please. I want to walk outside today."

"Lizzie, it is cold and snowy."

I peeked out the window. Yes, there is snow on the ground, but nothing falling from the sky. Look there, I see sunshine, Laura." She joined me at the window.

"Indeed!" she declared. Surely enough, the sun was glistening on a layer of snow that had fallen in the night.

"So, I will wear woolies under my dress," I concluded and pulled as much from my wardrobe.

Properly layered and laced, I popped downstairs as if walking on clouds and spoke briefly to Father and his wife Judith, while their two young sons climbed upon his knees for a story. Much had changed in the years since Edward was lost at sea. All of life had moved on and now, so must I.

In the years since Edward left, Father had served as the eighth Mayor of Salem in 1854 and been Adjutant General Commander at Fort Warren that same fateful year. He married Judith Walker the next year. They had two young sons, now just two and three years old. Laura and I had remained at home to help care for the dear little ones.

Laura was now being courted by a young man named Edward Crowell Mundy, who was studying to become a physician.

Edward's step-mother had moved to Andover after all. She established a boarding house, which allowed her sufficient income to feed her family. Even she had moved on, yet, where was I? Had I been sleeping away the years like Rip Van Winkle?

I wrapped myself in my cloak and covered my head with a fur hat. With my rabbit fur muff in hand, I walked briskly to the train. I did not plan to travel anywhere by train. I simply wanted to breathe the cold air into my lungs.

A train pulled into the station shortly after I arrived. I sat on a wooden bench and watched the passengers disembark. Life had certainly moved on. Union soldiers were being greeted by ladies with babes in arms. Children ran freely with not a woe in the world. Ladies cried while embracing their soldiers and the men allowed themselves to be smothered unashamedly by the wet little kisses of excited children.

Soon after Father left his post at Fort Warren, it began to hold Confederate prisoners.

A year and a half ago, the nation had elected a new President from the West -- a tall lanky statesman from Illinois. He vowed to abolish slavery and, in fierce reaction, the southern states declared their secession from the Union. President Lincoln exerted every effort to keep the states together as one nation but a war between the states had begun in the spring.

While life was continuing, much change had commenced and concluded. Somehow I had become so near-sighted that I could only live day by day in my own little world. The turmoil of the times seemed so far away that I paid little mind to it. Now I began to see all that had passed me by during my lost years of sorrow. Army troops and militia were being formed in Massachusetts. Less than two weeks ago a thousand men, mostly Irish, were mustered into the 28th Massachusetts Volunteer Infantry Regiment and into the Union Army at Cambridge and Somerville. Local sons of Massachusetts were called upon as their leaders.

My brother Joe did not live long enough to be called for duty. He fulfilled his dream of going to sea and became a clerk on the ship, a skill he later found useful back in Salem, before his life was cut short. In October of this year, he died from consumption, like mother had. He was only 28 years old. He had never married. I don't believe he was ever in love.

As I sat musing about all that had transpired, I felt a tap on my shoulder. It was Emily Oliver. She was waiting for her brother Samuel to arrive at the station. We spoke for some time about her husband, James Olcott Brown. Emily and I were both 26 years of age. I told her I had not married and watched her face draw long. I assured her I was finally at peace with my loss. Her face lit up as she said something ever so softly. When I begged her pardon, requesting she repeat herself, she said, "It is time, Lizzie."

I had just heard these words from Edward in my dream and must have given Emily a profoundly confused look, for she quickly went on to explain, "It is time I invited you to the Oliver home for a visit. You must come posthaste!" she urged. Of course, I accepted her invitation. Emily was one of the few people who knew about Edward and me. Though she was now married and living in Portland, Maine, she had returned to her family's home in Salem for the holyday to spend time with her brother. She talked excitedly, telling me he was a lieutenant colonel engaged in leading the 14th Massachusetts Infantry in the War Between the States. He was 35 years old and recently widowed. She thought I might enjoy his company and vice versa.

The next day, told Father I accepted an invitation to bring in the New Year with the Oliver household. He seemed pleased to learn I had ventured out at all and he encouraged me to have a pleasant visit.

I arrived at the Oliver home the next day, second Christmas Day, December 26, 1861, never imaging how fateful this visit would be.

Emily's brother, Samuel welcomed me under the mistletoe with a kiss that shocked me and sent shivers up my spine, until my whole body felt as if it were filled with light. Only Edward's lips had ever touched mine. I will forever remember that kiss as one that changed my life, perhaps saved my life.

Sam and I remained in each other's company every moment we were able and, just as Emily expected, I found great comfort in his company.

On December 30, 1861, Sam left his home abruptly in the morning and did not return until that evening.

On New Year's Eve, he privately revealed to me that he had gone to visit my father to tell him he was in love with me and to ask for my hand. Then, he bent down on one knee and proposed marriage. I do not know what came over me, but I said, 'of course.'

The Oliver family was quite prominent. Everyone knew Sam and Emily's father, Henry Oliver, for he had served as state treasurer. He was also known as the musician who composed the popular hymn "Federal Street." I needed little introduction to Emily's family and they seemed to know as much about mine.

Like my own brother, Emily's brother Sam had been well educated in private schools. He entered Harvard in 1845 at age 19, when I was but 10 years old. He left two and a half years later to pursue business endeavors with his father at Atlantic Mills, one of the booming textile mill towns of Lawrence, Massachusetts.

Like my own father, Emily's father Henry Oliver had been very successful in Salem as a businessman and philanthropist. He had also been Adjutant General of the Massachusetts militia.

While Henry left the military to pursue business, the times were different now and Sam felt called to a career in the military. At age 22, he associated himself with a military company, the Salem Light Infantry, New England Guards and for several years the Boston Independent Corps of Cadets. The summer before we met, Sam had joined the 14th Massachusetts Volunteer Regiment and became Lieutenant Colonel.

We married on January 23, 1862 in a quiet, simple ceremony at the North Church in Salem.

By mid-March, Sam had resigned his post. Within a few months, he obtained a new commission recruiting a company of volunteers for the newly organized Company F of the 35th Regiment Massachusetts Volunteers.

He was elected their Captain in August and the regiment fought a battle at South Mountain before marching into heavy action during the Battle of Antietam. He operated heavy artillery, positioned near the Stone Bridge, directly in the heat of the battle. That day, his regiment lost more than 200 men, including officers. Sixty-nine men were killed or mortally wounded, but not Samuel. After avoiding injury through the day, just as evening hit, my Sam was hit by the concussion of an exploding shell, thrown backwards against a wall of stones and rendered senseless. He had to be carried from the field for both legs were paralyzed.

By the grace of God, Samuel regained use of his legs. He returned to the regiment and served for another year as Major in the 2nd Massachusetts Heavy Artillery until the end of the war.

Our first child, Josephine Sprague Oliver, who we called 'Posie,' was born in Salem on December 2, 1863. Sam ended his career in May 1866. His paralysis returned and, although he could walk with the aid of canes, he was never again able to sit comfortably. We fashioned a mantle over the fireplace where he could stand to take his meals as the family sat nearby. When I was four months pregnant with our second child, Posie, at three years and eight months, died of cholera.

In July 1866, Congress awarded the *S.S. San Francisco* Congressional Life Saving medal to Captain George Stouffer, Captain Edwin Lowe and Captain Robert Creighton.

S.S. San Francisco Congressional Life Saving medal

Joseph Henry Oliver was born in Salem on January 10, 1868.

Two years later, I gave birth to our third child, a son we named James Edward Oliver, but everyone called him Tommy.

After graduating from Salem High School, Tommy officially changed his name to Thomas Edward Oliver.

Sam continued to attend to business in town where he was seen by the town's children as the officer with the white horse. He bore his pains gallantly and cheerfully. Soon after his trusty steed passed away, Sam too fell ill with what appeared to be a simple cold. He died soon after on March 25, 1888.

Tommy graduated Harvard. By 1899, he was teaching French at the University of Michigan. In 1900 he accepted a position as Assistant Professor of Romance Languages at the College for Women, Western Reserve University in Cleveland, where he met his bride to be. He married Elisabeth Reinhardt and moved to Champaign-Urbana, Illinois where he taught at the University of Illinois until his retirement, becoming the Chairman of the Department of Romance Languages.

Tommy was everything a mother could hope for in a son. He never disappointed me. He cared for me until my death and gave me three beautiful granddaughters.

I left Sam's sword from the Battle of Antietam to Tommy and left him my bundle of letters from Edward, something of which I had never spoken since my marriage to Sam. I hoped Tommy might learn the significance of his middle name and preserve them so my story would not be forgotten.

Lizzie at age 40

Epilogue

Following the Sword and the Story

Tommy passed Samuel's sword to his eldest daughter Elisabeth Oliver Martin. She passed the sword to her youngest son Thomas Oliver Martin to pass to one of his two sons.

As for Edward's letters, Tommy meticulously typed copies and stored them in his attic. Following his death in 1946, his wife Elizabeth Reinhardt Oliver sent the box to their eldest daughter Elisabeth Oliver, the wife of Dr. Webster Martin. The box of letters was once again relegated to an attic, most likely not realizing its contents. The letters sat undiscovered, along with many unanswered questions, for nearly 80 years. After both Dr. Webster Martin and his wife Elisabeth died, the box made its way to their eldest son Web, with the letters still undiscovered. His children knew that their father Web's sister Elisabeth, "Aunt Betty," had assumed the role of the family genealogist and was always asking her brothers for information about the family. When Web's son Andy found the box of 'stuff,' he asked his Aunt Betty if she wanted it. The idea of the book came to her after Lizzie appeared in her dream and beckoned her to "Tell my story."

Following Rockwood in Tarrytown

Edward's uncle Edwin sold Rockwood Estate to his business partner, William Henry Aspinwall, the well-known New York shipbuilder who built the ill-fated *San Francisco*. Aspinwall was one of Edwin Bartlett's partners in the Pacific Mail Steamship Company and the Panama Railroad. Aspinwall went on to sell Rockwood Estate to the Rockefeller family. The Rockefellers eventually tore it down and the property became, and remains, a state park.

Colonel Samuel Cook Oliver

Who's Who in
The Courtship of Lizzie Andrews

A

Abbot, Mary Elizabeth "Nellie" (1835-1916) Born Andover, MA to Joseph Thomson Abbot (1809-1865) and Betsey (Kershaw) (1810-1899). Joseph was a postmaster. South Church Burial Ground, Andover, Massachusetts also lists other family members in plot: John K. died Aug. 28, 1834 at 1 year old; William T. died Sept. 15, 1836 at 6 mos. old; Martha A. died Apr. 26, 1842 at 4 years old; and Mary Kershaw (1785-1872). Nellie joined Lizzie and Edward for tea.

Adams, Abigail Browne (Brooks) (1808-1881) Born to Hon. Peter Chardon Brooks (1767-1849) and Anna Nancy (Gorham) (1771-1830). Married Charles Francis Adams, son of President John Quincy Adams and had seven children. Lived in Boston. Her sister was Charlotte Gray (Brooks) Everett.

Adams, Charles Francis, Sr. (1807-1886) Son of sixth U.S. President John Quincy Adams and grandson of second U.S. President John Adams. Harvard Class of 1825. Served in the U.S. House of Representatives under President Abraham Lincoln. U.S. Ambassador to the U.K., 1861-1868. Married Abigail Browne (Brooks) (1808-1889). Unitarian, Diplomat, Republican.

Adams, Charles Francis, Jr. (1835-1915) Second son of Charles Francis Adams, Sr. and Abigail Browne (Brooks). "Chum" of Edward's at Harvard Class of 1856. Served on the Union side during the Civil War. Fought with distinction at Gettysburg, South Mountain and Antietam. Colonel Adams awarded the grade of brevet brigadier general for distinguished gallantry and for meritorious services during the war (1866). President of the Union Pacific Railroad 1884-1890. Married Mary Elizabeth (Ogden), daughter of Abram Ogden of New York City, New York in 1865. Had three daughters and twin sons: John Adams (1875-1964) and Henry Adams (1875-1951). Sons graduated Harvard Class of 1898.

Adams, John Quincy II (1833-1894) Eldest son of Charles Francis Adams and Abigail Browne Brooks. Graduated Harvard 1853 with Edward Tenney. Admitted to the Suffolk bar in 1855. 1861 married Fanny C. Crowninshield. Had five children: John Quincy (1861-1876); Fanny (1864-1876); George Caspar (Harvard Class of 1886); Arthur (Harvard Class of 1899) and Abigail (1862-1865). Military staff of Governor Andrew. Elected Massachusetts House of Representatives as Republican in 1865. Candidate for Governor as Democrat in 1867. State Director of Fitchberg Railroad in 1889. Trustee of the Boston Real Estate Trust. Trustee Sailors' Snug Harbor at Quincy. President of the Quincy and Boston Street Railway. Director American Loan and Trust Company, Director Security Safe Deposit Co., Director West Michigan Lumber Co. and others.

Adams, Elizabeth Coombs (1808-1903) Daughter of Thomas Boylston Adams (1772-1832) and Ann (Harrod) (1774-1846). Joined Edward at Rockwood for Thanksgiving in 1853 (Miss Adams") and received the tragic news of her brother's death (see Lt. Joseph Harrod Adams).

Adams, Lt. Joseph Harrod (1817-1853) Died while in the U.S. Navy on the ship *Powhattan* during the Perry expedition to Japan. Buried in the Protestant cemetery in Macao, China. Older brother Lt. John Quincy Adams (1815-1854) also lost at sea from the U.S. frigate *Albany*.

Alboni, Marietta (1826-1894) Born Citta di Castello Umbria, Italy. Renowned Italian contralto and pupil of Rossini sang throughout Europe before coming with Henrietta Sontag to New York in

September 1852. Walt Whitman was inspired to write about Alboni as "the lustrous orb, Venus contralto, the blooming mother, Sister of loftiest gods." Died in Paris, France.

Allen, "Ellen" may be Eveline Allen (1797-1879) Half-sister to George Allen. Married Thomas Saunders and lived in Manchester, Massachusetts. Edward wrote that "Ellen" came by train to Methuen after "Little Frankie Allen" died. Edward met her and Caddie Fellows (cousin Louisa Fellows) at the train.

Allen, Frank George (1852-1853) Born in Salem, New Hampshire. Died in 1853 of dysentery. Lizzie's cousin "Little Frankie," son of Laura White Sprague ("Aunt Laur") and George Allen.

Allen, George Frank (1813-1852) Son of Capt. William Allen (1766-) and Mary Hunt (1775-1842). Received award for good writing in August 1829 at Mr. James Gerrish's school at Franklin Hall. Listed in the Salem City Directory 1842 and 1846 as "mariner". Married Laura White (Sprague), Lizzie's "Aunt Laur," Jan. 2, 1850 in Providence, Rhode Island. Lost at sea on November 8, 1852. Last seen on board the extreme clipper ship *The Celestial*, built by Wm. H. Webb, Jr. *The Celestial* launched on June 10, 1852 in New York bound for California. [Daily Alto, California, August 18, 1850].

Allen, Laura White (Sprague) "Aunt Laur" (1816-after 1859) Lizzie's mother's sister. Listed in 1836 Salem City Directory as "milliner" and in 1856-59 Salem City Directory as "fancy goods." No record of death. Buried in Harmony Grove Cemetery, Salem, Massachusetts. Referred to in the book as "Laur" to avoid confusion with Lizzie's sister Laura.

Allen, Mary Osgood "Mamie" (1851-after 1920 Hartford, CT). Lizzie's cousin and sister to Frankie Allen. Name also given as "Minnie" in the letters, perhaps because the original letters were old and difficult to read and transcribe. Married at age 18 on March 9, 1870 in Salem to William Thorndike Howe (1849-after 1930 Hartford, CT). Had one son Edward Thorndike Howe, born Apr. 1, 1871.

Alsop, Joseph Wright (1804-1878) Third child of Joseph Wright Alsop, and Lucy Whittlesey. Grandchild of Richard Alsop. Entered the house of Alsop & Chauncey, of New York, at age fifteen. Made several voyages to St. Croix and other commercial ports. Returned to New York 1834 and established himself in business. Married Mary Caroline Alsop Oliver (1815-1893), daughter of Francis J. Oliver, of Boston on October 25, 1837. Had one child also named Joseph Wright Alsop (1838-1891). Established the house of Alsop & Co. at Valparaiso (1840) in connection with the firm of Alsop & Chauncey of South Street, New York. First president of the Ohio & Mississippi Railroad. Partner in the Pacific Mail Steamship Co. and Panama Railroad Co. Wealthy New York merchant and shipbuilder. Edward was given a position in his accounting firm in Valparaiso. Died February 26, 1878 and left his one-third interest in the house of Alsop & Co. to his son. For many years Alsop & Co. made a profit every five years of over a million dollars.

Andrews, Clement Walker (1858-1930) Lizzie's half-brother. Born in Salem, Massachusetts to General Joseph Andrews and his second wife Judith Walker. Attended the Boston Latin School and Harvard College. Harvard Class of 1879. Earned master's degree in 1880. Taught organic chemistry at the Massachusetts Institute of Technology 1883-1892 and became a librarian there 1889-1892. Moved to Chicago to establish the John Crerar Library, based on the system he had established at M.I.T. Never married. Died on November 20, 1930 in Chicago. Buried in the Andrews plot at Harmony Grove Cemetery, Salem, Massachusetts.

Andrews, Daniel (1798-1879) Lizzie's uncle, her father's brother. Never married. Lived in the Andrews family home at 24 Lynde St., Salem, Massachusetts with his mother and sister Dolly.

Andrews, Dolly Ann Watkins (1806-1877) Lizzie's aunt, her father's sister. Never married. Lived at 24 Lynde St., Salem, Massachusetts until 1874. Occupation: milliner.

Andrews, Edward Reynolds "Spooney" (1831-after 1903) Harvard Class of 1853 and AM (Master of Arts) degree in 1857. No relation to Mary Elizabeth Andrews. Son of William Turell Andrews and Fannie Mackey (Reynolds). William graduated Harvard Class of 1812 and was treasurer of the college from 1853-1857. "Spooney" roomed with Charles Edward Briggs at Harvard. Pursued the crockery business and ten years of farming in West Roxbury before he established Andrews & Co. in Paris 1866-1875. Married Sarah Addoms of New York, December 1855, whom he had met in the American Colony in Rome. Sarah died in 1893. In 1903, Spooney was living with two daughters.

Andrews, Eliza (1800-1876) Lizzie's aunt, her father's sister. Never married. Eliza lived with Lizzie's family after Lizzie's mother died and helped raise the children until Joseph married Judith Walker in 1857.

Andrews, George (1828-1920) George Lippitt Andrews married Alice Potter and had a son named George A. Andrews who graduated from West Point. After Alice died, he married Emily Kemble (Oliver). They did not have children. See Oliver, Emily Kemble for additional information.

Andrews, Horace Davis (1859-1910) Lizzie's half-brother. Born in Salem, Massachusetts to General Joseph Andrews and his second wife Judith Walker, their second child. Died in Colorado, 1910.

Andrews, James (1732-1820) Grandfather of Gen. Joseph Andrews, Lizzie's father. He was a housewright. Married Mary Glover in 1758. Bought land on Lynde Street in Salem in 1757. Remained the family home. Served in 1777 in the troops who guarded the prisoners from Burgoyne's Army at Winter Hill, Somerville.

Andrews, "Joe" see Andrews, Joseph Sprague (1833-1861) Lizzie's brother.

Andrews, Gen. Joseph A. (1808-1869) Lizzie's father, born in Salem, died in Boston. Married Elizabeth Maria Sprague on Oct. 10, 1832 and had three children: Joseph, Elizabeth and Laura. Brigadier General in the Massachusetts Volunteer Infantry. Ninth Mayor of Salem 1854-1856. Married second wife Judith Walker on Jan. 15, 1857 and had three more children: Clement Walker, Horace Davis and Joseph L. Served as Adjutant General Commander at Fort Warren on Georgia Island in Boston Harbor from May 1862 to August 21, 1862. The Fort was used to hold Confederate prisoners and political prisoners in the Civil War. Buried in the Andrews plot at Harmony Grove Cemetery in Salem.

Andrews, Joseph (1773-1824) Lizzies' grandfather who died before she was born. Merchant. Born in Salem. Son of James Andrew, housewright (1732-1820) and Mary Glover (1739-1821). Built Andrews family home at 24 Lynde. Owned a pew in the first Church in Salem. Married Mary Bell, May 14, 1797 in Salem and had seven children. Gen. Joseph A. Andrews was the youngest son and the only child to marry and have children.

Andrews, Joseph L. (1862-1937) Lizzie's half-brother. Third child and youngest son of General Joseph Andrews and his second wife Judith Walker. Executive with the Bank of New York. Married Theodosia Burr Bartow (1865-1949) in 1891 and had three children. Died in 1937 in Englewood, New Jersey.

Andrews, Joseph Sprague "Joe" (1833-1861) Lizzie's older brother. Son of General Joseph Andrews and his first wife Elizabeth Maria (Sprague). Never married. Struggled most of his life with his mental health. Died of consumption (i.e. tuberculosis) in October 1861 at age 28. He was a resident of the asylum in Somerville, August 1851 through January 1853. The Andrews family tombstone in Harmony Grove Cemetery lists General Joseph Andrews' children beginning with his eldest child, Joseph, born in October 1834, with no specific day noted. That tombstone lists his sister "Lizzie" as being born on April 19, 1835, just six months later and to the same mother. We believe Joe was actually born in 1833 and the tombstone is wrong. That would make Joseph nearer in age to Edward Tenney.

Andrews, Laura Josephine (1837-1893) Lizzie's sister. Married Dr. Edward Crowell Mundy on March 25, 1863 in Salem. He was a prominent physician from Staten Island, New York and a surgeon with the 12th New York Cavalry during the War of the Rebellion. He also served in the 175th infantry, New York. He was first married to Mary Miriam Barrett (1830-1855) and had two children. Married second wife Laura and had two more children. U.S. Federal Census in 1870 for Northfield, Richmond, New York lists E.C. Mundy age 39 physician, Laura J. Mundy age 32, Edward Mundy age 5, Elizabeth Mundy age 2, two female domestic servants born in Ireland and a 15-year-old stable boy.

Andrews, "Lizzie" (1834-) Edward mentions "Lizzie Andrews" was at Mr. Disbrow's riding school. She was a sister of Edward "Spooney" Reynolds Andrews, Harvard Class of 1853. No relation to Mary Elizabeth "Lizzie" Andrews.

Andrews, Mary (Bell) (1774-1856) Lizzie's paternal grandmother. Lived at 24 Lynde St., Salem in the Andrews family home. Born in Portsmouth, New Hampshire. Married Joseph Andrews (1773-1824) on May 14, 1797 in Salem. Had seven children. Six lived to adulthood and never married. Only youngest child Joseph married twice and had six children. Mary lived to age 81½.

Andrews, Mary Elizabeth "Lizzie" (1835-1922) Born on April 19, 1835, the second child to Joseph A. Andrews and his first wife Elizabeth Maria Sprague. Lizzie's mother died in 1841 when Lizzie was six. Between 1850 and 1853, she received 62 letters from her third cousin and fiancé Edward J. Tenney. She gave her second son the middle name of "Edward." A daguerreotype of Edward was found sandwiched behind her wedding photo and the photo frame backing. Refer to Afterword in this book for additional information.

Andrews Servants: 1850 U.S. Federal Census, Salem: Margaret Soley age 30 born in Ireland (referred to in the story as "Margo" to avoid confusion with the others named Margaret); James Ridley age 27 born in Ireland. 1855 Massachusetts State Census, Salem: Edward Clark age 30 born in Massachusetts; Bridget Haley age 23 born in Ireland; Matilda Hamilton age 20 born in Ireland. 1860 U.S. Federal Census, Salem: Elizabeth Carrigan age 27 born in Ireland; Frances Hulsey age 18 born in Ireland; Daniel Clark age 25 born in Ireland. 1865 Massachusetts State Census, Boston: Kate Gilmore age 30 born in Ireland, Mary Murphy age 24 born in Ireland; 1870 U.S. Federal Census, Boston: Household of Judith (Walker) Andrews; Kattie Delaney age 29 born in Nova Scotia; Sarah Delaney age 25 born in Nova Scotia.

Archer, Mary Beckford – see Osgood, Mary Beckford (Archer)

Aspinwall, William Henry (1807-1875) Son of John Aspinwall (1774-1847). Mother was Susan Howland (1779-1852). Well-known New York shipbuilder of the time. One of Edwin Bartlett's partners in the Pacific Mail Steamship Company and the Panama Railroad. Career began at the age of 25 in the family business, 'Howland and Aspinwall," specializing in trade in the Caribbean. Expanded into new markets: South America, China, Europe, the Mediterranean and the East and West Indies. Mr. Aspinwall owned *The San Fran-*

cisco. Edward was listed as "clerk" on the passenger list. William H. Aspinwall was brought up in the house of his uncles, Gardiner G. and Samuel S. Howland. They gave him an interest in the business, and he signed the name of the firm as early as 1830 or 1831. He received 20 percent of the commission account. He became an open partner, under the name of Howland & Aspinwall, about 1837. At that time the two old Howlands went out, leaving about $150,000 each in cash as special partners. William Edgar Howland, a son of Gardiner G., was one of the general partners.

Astor Place Riot occurred on May 10, 1849 at the now demolished Astor Opera House in Manhattan, New York and left at least 25 dead and more than 120 injured. It was the deadliest to date of a number of civic disturbances in New York City which generally pitted immigrants and nativists against each other, or together against the upper classes who controlled the city's police and the state militia. The riot marked the first time a state militia had been called out and had shot into a crowd of citizens, and it led to the creation of the first police force armed with deadly weapons, yet its genesis was a dispute between Edwin Forrest, one of the best-known American actors of that time, and William Charles Macready, a similarly notable English actor, which largely revolved around which of them was better than the other at acting the major roles of Shakespeare.

> **Aunt Anna** - see Bartlett, Anna Bailey
> **Aunt Augusta** – see Tenney, Augusta
> **Aunt Caroline**- see Bartlett, Carolyn Eliza (Harrod)
> **Aunt Dolly** - see Andrews, Dolly Ann Watkins
> **Aunt Eliza** - see Andrews, Eliza
> **Aunt Gray** – see Gray, Olive Bell
> **Aunt Laur** - see Allen, Laura White (Sprague)
> **Aunt Margaret** - see Nichols, Margaret (Sprague)
> **Aunt Margaret** – see Bartlett, Margaret "Peggy"

Aunt Mary Louisa - see Fellows, Mary Louisa

Aunt Sarah – see Sprague, Sarah Leonard (Bartlett)

B

Barrett, Henry (1807-1892) Married Lucy (Stearns) (1824-1914) daughter of Richard Stearns (1801-1840). Lucy was Henry's third wife and had five children. Lived in Malden, Massachusetts. Occupation: "Silk Dyer."

Barrett, Lucy (Stearns) (1824-1914) Lizzie's second cousin. Lucy's and Edward's great grandmothers were sisters. Lucy's father was Richard Stearns. Lucy married Henry Barrett in 1848 and lived in Malden, Massachusetts. They had five children.

Bartlett, Abigail Osgood – see Kimball, Abigail Osgood (Bartlett). Edward's mother's sister. She was the 10th of 15 children born in Haverhill, Massachusetts to the Honorable Bailey Bartlett and Peggy White.

Bartlett, Anna Bailey (1787-1869) – See Jarvis, Anna Bailey (Bartlett). Edward's mother's sister. She was the first of 15 children born in Haverhill, Massachusetts to the Honorable Bailey Bartlett and Peggy White. Married William Jarvis.

Bartlett, Bailey (1794-1886) Edward's mother's brother. Sixth child and first son born in Haverhill, Massachusetts to the Honorable Bailey Bartlett and Peggy White. In 1843, married Caroline Long (1803-1902). Had two children.

Bartlett, Honorable Bailey (1750-1830) Edward's grandfather and his wife Peggy White had 15 children, 11 of whom were daughters. Edward's mother was Mary Augusta Bartlett. Bailey was the High Sheriff of Essex County for 41 years. He was a friend of John and Samuel Adams, boarding with them in Philadelphia when the Declaration of Independence was made in 1776 and was present in the yard of Congress when it was proclaimed. Member of the State House of Representatives 1781-1784, member of the convention which adopted the Constitution of the United States in 1788 and member of Congress 1789-1784.

Bartlett, Carolyn (or Caroline) Eliza (Harrod) (1796-1893) Wife of Edwin Bartlett, Edward's uncle. Born in Portland, Maine to Joseph Harrod (1785-1875) and Elizabeth Cox (1788-). Resided for several years in South America with her husband and twice visited Europe; spending much time in England, Scotland, France and Switzerland. Then on an estate on the Hudson River at Tarrytown, called "Rockwood." Edward spent quite a bit of time with them while waiting for *The San Francisco* to sail in December 1853. No children. Died at Annadale, New York on July 8, 1893.

Bartlett, Charles Leonard (1802-1883) Edward's mother's brother. Eleventh child born in Haverhill, Massachusetts to the Honorable Bailey Bartlett and Peggy White. Married Harriet Plummer (1805-1901) and had six children: five daughters and one son, William Francis Bartlett.

Bartlett, Edwin (1796-1867) Edward's mother's brother. Eighth child born in Haverhill, Massachusetts to the Honorable Bailey Bartlett and Peggy White. Married Carolyn (Harrod). Built what was known to be the largest mansion in the United States in 1853 called "Rockwood" near Tarrytown, New York. It consisted of several hundred acres and employed 80 men to care for the grounds. Sold this estate to William Aspinwall in 1860, who later sold it to William Rockefeller (1841-1922), brother of John D. Rockefeller. Bought an estate at Annandale, New York named "Miramont." At one time, counsel at Lima, Peru. In 1844 he was involved in importing guano used in composts for agriculture and was a promoter of many enterprises in foreign countries. Mr. Bartlett became the sole agent of the company which imported the entire crop of Peruvian bark and quinine (obtained from guano). With five other business partners, he established the Pacific Mail Steamship Company and Panama Railroad Company. Uncle Edwin arranged for Edward's passage to Valparaiso and helped him secure a position in the Alsop accounting firm.

Bartlett, Elizabeth – See Sprague, Elizabeth "Eliza" (Bartlett) (1789-1817). Edward's mother's sister. She was the second of 15 children born in Haverhill, Massachusetts to the Honorable Bailey Bartlett and Peggy White.

Bartlett, Francis (1806-1848) Edward's mother's brother. He was the 14th of 15 children born in Haverhill, Massachusetts to the Honorable Bailey Bartlett and Peggy White

Bartlett, Fredrick Augustus (1805-1805) He was the 13th of 15 children born in Haverhill, Massachusetts to the Honorable Bailey Bartlett and Peggy White. Died at two weeks old of a sore throat.

Bartlett, Harriet (1792-1820). Edward's mother's sister. She was the fourth of 15 children born in Haverhill, Massachusetts to the Honorable Bailey Bartlett and Peggy White. Died of consumption at age 27. Never married.

Bartlett, Katherine (1795-1878) – See Felt, Katherine (Bartlett) Edward's mother's sister. She was the seventh of 15 children born in Haverhill, Massachusetts to the Honorable Bailey Bartlett and Peggy White.

Bartlett, Louisa Amelia - See Carlton, Louisa Amelia (Bartlett). Edward's mother's sister. She was the 15th of 15 children born in Haverhill, Massachusetts to the Honorable Bailey Bartlett and Peggy White.

Bartlett, Margaret– See Longley, Margaret "Peggy" (Bartlett) (1790-1880). Edward's mother's sister. She was the third of 15 children born in Haverhill, Massachusetts to the Honorable Bailey Bartlett and Peggy White.

Bartlett, Mary Augusta (1804-1837) – See Tenney, Mary Augusta (Bartlett). Edward's mother. Twelfth child born in Haverhill, Massachusetts to the Honorable Bailey Bartlett and Peggy White. Married John Tenney in 1830 and had four children: Margaret (1831-1839); Edward (1833-1853); Lizzie ("Liz" in the story, 1835-1895); and Mary (1837-1905). Lived in Methuen.

Bartlett, Mary (1799-1802) Edward's mother's sister. Ninth of 15 children born in Haverhill, Massachusetts to the Honorable Bailey Bartlett and Peggy White.

Bartlett, Sarah Leonard – See Sprague, Sarah Leonard (Bartlett) (1793-1864). Edward's mother's sister. She was the fifth of 15 children born in Haverhill, Massachusetts to the Honorable Bailey Bartlett and Peggy White.

Battles, Joseph Porter (1822-1900) Agent of the Atlantic Mills in Lawrence, MA. Married Sarah Elizabeth Oliver (1828-1883) in 1852, daughter of Henry Kemble Oliver (1800-1885) and Sarah Elizabeth Cook (1801-1866). They had five children: Ellen "Nellie" P. (1853-aft. 1923); Emily O. (1862-1945); Sarah E. (1863- aft. 1923); Josephine (1866-1932) and Joseph (1866-1937) twins.

Bell, Dr. Luther V. (1806-1862) Born Francestown, New Hampshire, son of state governor and two-term Senator Samuel Bell. Entered Bowdoin College at age 12. Graduated in 1823. Moved to New York. Studied medicine with older brother John. Earned a medical degree at Dartmouth in 1826. Superintendent of Mclean Asylum during "Joe" Andrews stay there. McLean was the first mental hospital in Massachusetts. During his tenure at McLean, three of his seven children died and his wife died in childbirth. Surgeon U.S. Army, Civil War, Eleventh Regiment of Massachusetts Volunteers.

Bell, Mary (about 1775-1856) "Grandmother Andrews" - See Andrews, Mary (Bell).

Beneventano, Francesco (1824-1880) Opera singer who toured with Maretzek from Italy to New York. Maretzek engaged artists with the best of his former company, which included Mme. Bertucca, Signora Truffi, and Beneventano to perform at Castle Garden in New York in 1850. Beneventano was a baritone. Born and died in Scicli, bei Ragusa, Yugoslavia.

Bird, Isaac, Rev. (1800-1881) Edward's teacher from approximately age nine in Hartford, Connecticut. The name of their family boarding school was "Pavillion School." A prominent worker in the field of foreign missions, Isaac married Anne (Parker), the daughter of William Parker (1773-1815) and Martha Tenney (1771-1842). Edward's father, John Tenney, was a nephew of Martha. Isaac and Anne had five children living with them in Hartford in 1850: William, graduated Dartmouth in 1844, Ann Emily, Martha Jane, James (Yale), Mary Elizabeth and Caroline. All the Bird children were born in Syria. The Birds celebrated their 50th wedding anniversary with a family reunion at their home "Sedgwick Institute," in Great Barrington, Massachusetts on November 28, 1872. They moved to Great Barrington from Hartford in 1868 or 1769. Isaac passed away January 5, 1881, at Morristown, New Jersey.

Bird, Martha (1829-1867) Daughter of Isaac Bird who ran the school Edward attended in Hartford was four years older than Edward and would have known him when he was between the ages of nine and fourteen. Married Henry Ephraim Robbins (1827-1907) in 1864 in Hartford, CT.

Bissell, Edwin (1807-1876) Business acquaintance of Edwin Bartlett. 1850 U.S. Federal Census lists his home in Johnstown, Fulton, NY, a Merchant with his wife Permelia, and six children. NY State Census 1855:Edwin age 48, Permelia age 42, Hiram age 20,

Martha age 19, Amanda age 14, Edwin age 9, May age 7, Welthen age 5, John H. age 2.

Bleak House. A novel by English writer Charles Dickens. Published in 20 monthly installments between March 1852 and September 1853. It is held to be one of Dickens's finest novels. See "Caroline Chisholm."

Bosio, Angiolina (Mrs. Xinda Velonis) (1830-1859) Italian soprano who came from a family of performance artists. Made her debut at age 16 in 1846 in Milan in Verdi's *I Due Foscari*. Sang in Verona, Copenhagen, Madrid and Paris. Made international stops in Havana, New York, Philadelphia, Boston, London and St. Petersbourg. Notably portrayed the role of Lady Macbeth in the United States premiere of Verdi's *Macbeth* at Niblo's Garden in New York in 1850.

Boyd, Mr. and Mrs. Guests of Edwin and Carolyn Bartlett for Thanksgiving 1853. Edward mentions they knew some of the Army officers going to San Francisco. This may be Samuel Boyd, who was born in 1802 in Winsted, Connecticut. He married Sylvia Coe and, in 1850, was a commission merchant in hardware in New York City. Later, he became a Customs House Appraiser in New York City. His daughter Sarah Jane Boyd, born 1831, married Thomas Howe Bird in Brooklyn. Thomas was listed as a stock broker in the 1880 U.S. Federal Census. Samuel and Sylvia lived with the Birds in New Jersey in 1880.

Bridges, Charles Moody (1833-1864) Son of Lt. Moody Bridges and Rebecca Osgood. Cousin of Edward Tenney. Brother to Joseph Edward. Lived in Andover. Died of disease in Mississippi during the Civil War serving in Co. D, 3rd Cavalry Regiment, Massachusetts.

Bridges, Joseph Edward (1836-1916) Son of Lt. Moody Bridges and Rebecca Osgood. Cousin of Edward Tenney. Brother to Charles Bridges. Resided in Worcester, MA in 1874, teamster.

Bridges, Lt. Moody (1784-1858) Deputy Sheriff of Essex County. In this capacity, he must have worked with Joseph E. (Stearns) Sprague who was the High Sheriff of Essex County. Married Rebecca Osgood (1796-1856) on July 12, 1819. Had eight children.

Bridges, Rebecca (Osgood) (1796-1856) Daughter of Dr. George Osgood (1758-1823) and Elizabeth Otis (1760-1802). Married Lt. Bridges on July 12, 1819. Had eight children. Lived in Andover, Massachusetts. Joe and Edward drove to Mrs. Bridges' in Andover with Aunts Mary (Fellows) and Margaret,

Bridget Servant in the household of Joseph Andrews. (See Healy, Bridget)

Briggs, Dr. Charles Edward (1833-1894) A friend or acquaintance of Emily Oliver. Graduated Harvard Class of 1853, MD in 1856, AM (Master of Arts) in 1860. Assistant Surgeon during the Civil War, 54th Colored Regiment Infantry Massachusetts. Married Rebekah Whittaker 1869. Prof. at St. Louis College of Physicians and Surgeons, Vice President of St. Louis Medical Society, Professor of Diseases of Children in Post Graduate School of Medicine of St. Louis. Practiced in St. Louis, Missouri. Left a widow and four children. Wife Rebekah died in Santa Barbara, California in 1912.

Brooks, Abigail Browne (1808-1881) – See Adams, Abigail Browne (Brooks)

Brooks, Hon. Peter Chardon (1767-1849) Married Anna Nancy (Gorham) (1771-1830). Had 12 children. Daughter Ann Gorham Brooks married Nathaniel Langdon Frothingham, and were parents of Octavius Frothingham who was the minister of the North Unitarian Church of Salem. Daughter Abigail Browne (Brooks) married Charles Francis Adams, son of President John Quincy Adams. Daughter Charlotte Gray (Brooks) married the Honorable Edward Everett.

Brooks, Ann Gorham – see Frothingham, Nathaniel Langdon.

Brooks, Carolyn "Caddie" (Fellows) (1817-1862) Sister to John Foster Fellows. Caddie was living in her brother's household in 1850 in Chelsea, Massachusetts. Married Noah Brooks (1830-1903) on May 29, 1856. Caddie died in childbirth.

Brooks, Charlotte Gray (1800-1859) – see Everett, Charlotte Gray (Brooks)

Brooks, Noah (1830-1903) Journalist and editor who worked for newspapers in northern California, Newark and New York. He authored a major biography of Abraham Lincoln. Married Caroline Augusta Fellows (1817-1862) on May 29, 1856. After Caddie died in childbirth in 1862, Noah moved to California. He became editor of a San Francisco newspaper and correspondent for the *Sacramento Bee*.

Brown, Honorable John Bundy (1804-1881) Became wealthy in the sugar business in Portland, Maine. Established scholarships in the name of his son James (1836-1864) at Bowdoin College. One of the first men in Portland prominent in the railroad business.

Brown, James Olcott (1836-1864) Son of John Bundy Brown of Portland, Maine. Married Emily Kemble (Oliver) and had one child, Emily Matilda Brown (about 1863-1880) who died at the age of 17. James died of diphtheria. See Oliver, Emily Kemble for additional information.

Brown, Joseph Mansfield "Joe" (1832- 1915) One of Edward's chums from Harvard. Born in Boston. Graduated Harvard Class of 1853. In his junior year, with Dr. James M. Whitton of Yale Class of 1853, Joe organized the first intercollegiate contest in this country – the first boat race between Harvard and Yale. The Harvard crew, of which he was captain, was victorious. Settled in Detroit in the lumber business. At the outbreak of the war in 1862, he was commissioned a First Lieutenant of the U.S. (Michigan) Lancers. He married Mary Virginia Royston in 1866 and had three children: two died in infancy and the third, a son, died at the age of fourteen. Joe served in Kentucky as a Captain and as a Major in the famous 2nd Massachusetts Cavalry. He was a Brevetted Lieutenant Colonel and remained in the service until 1872. Towards the close of the war he was employed as Assistant Quartermaster on the staff of General O. Howard at Washington, D.C. while the General was organizing the Freedman's Bureau. Brown had almost exclusive charge of the troops in Washington, Arlington and the District of Columbia that were then referred to as the "colored" population. His position included settling disputes from southern slave owners seeking bounty as compensation for their "property."

Browne, Albert Gallatin (1835-1891) One of Edward's chums from Harvard. Born in Salem, Massachusetts. Fitted for College at the Latin Grammar School with Oliver Carlton, Master. Dismissed from Harvard with Edward. Returned to graduate. Entered Dane Law School in the fall of 1853. "It was during his second term in that institution that the memorable affair of the arrest and attempted rescue of the fugitive slave, Anthony Burns, occurred. He inherited from his father, an earnest abolitionist, ardent antislavery sentiments, which, with his naturally combative temperament and the enthusiasm of youth, combined to make him an active belligerent. Arrested on the evening of the attack on the Court House, May 26, 1854, during which an employee of the U.S. Marshal was shot. With others, he was brought before the Police Court on the charge of murder…but, the complaint was reduced to one of riot and he was admitted to bail on June 7. The Grand Jury found no indictment." Following law school and further studies at Heidelberg, he became a journalist and wrote articles for the *Atlantic Monthly* in 1859. He also served as a correspondent of the *Boston Daily Advertiser*. He became Governor Andrew's private military secretary and served him during the entire Civil War. This gave him the title of "Colonel."

Early in 1874 he moved to New York and became managing editor of the *New York Evening Post*. Married 1867 in New York to Mattie Griffith who sympathized with her husband for the antislavery cause and set free her many inherited slaves. No children.

C

Cabot, Harriet (Mrs.) (1812-) In 1850 the Cabot family in Lawrence, Massachusetts included: George age 38, Harriet age 36, Elizabeth age 13, Lydian age 11, Harriet age 6 and Sarah age 4. Edward mentions his sister Margie had been at the Cabots for nearly a month and that they lived close to the Storrows in Lawrence. In 1865 in Salem, Cabot family members lived on Chestnut Street: Joseph S. Cabot 65 (Bank President), Susan 43 and Elizabeth Howe 38. Joseph S. Cabot was the mayor of Salem 1845-1848.

Capen. Edward's sister's teacher. Lizzie was to board with the Capens in Lawrence the spring of 1850. No additional information found.

Carlton, Marcie Grace (1837-) A classmate of Lizzie's at Hamilton. Resided in Methuen, her father, Joseph Warren Carlton (1794-1855) was a magistrate and town officer of Methuen, a director of the Andover Bank, the Bay State Bank of Lawrence and President of the Spricket Falls Bank of Methuen. Her mother was Lucy Ann Mills (-1852). The Carltons had six daughters and one son.

Carlton, Edwin Bartlett (1832-1851) Edward's cousin. Eldest son of Oliver Carlton and Louisa Amelia (Bartlett). Died at sea in 1851. Edward mentions in his letter of January 26, 1852 he saw the notice in the *Indian Ocean Register*.

Carlton, Oliver (1801-1882) Teacher at the Latin School in Salem, attended by many of Edward's Harvard chums, including Albert Browne and Lizzie's brother Joseph (Joe). Mr. Carlton graduated Dartmouth College 1824 with honors. He married three times: first, to Margaretta Clagget in April 1828 at Haverhill, Massachusetts. She gave birth to a son who died in infancy and it appears she may have died the same year; second to Louisa Amelia Bartlett, Edward's aunt, on November 27, 1831 in Salem, Massachusetts, with whom he had five children; and third to Mary Smith, the daughter of Rev. David Smith, in Salem, Massachusetts on August 18, 1841. They had one child. A memoir of Oliver Carlton by Leverett Saltonstall, reads, "[He] descended from a line of ancestors representative of the admirable class of men who were the founders of New England. [They were] Puritan farmers, who had to earn their bread and support their large families by the severest toil, while they sang praises, and poured out their hearts to God in their homes, at their daily task in the churches which they built, having scarcely bread for themselves and their children. May their descendants never cease to regard those God fearing men with profound gratitude and veneration!"

Carlton, William Jarvis "Willie" (1835-1860) Edward's cousin. Son of Oliver and Louisa Amelia (Bartlett) Carlton. Married Eliza N. Ham of Danvers.

Chase, Theodore (1832-1894) Harvard Class of 1853. "Not being under the necessity of adopting a profession or engaging in business," he spent much of his time in Europe. "He had a large and extremely valuable musical library, but his enjoyment was impaired by deafness". Married in 1868 to Alice Bowdoin. No children.

Chauncey, Henry (1825-1863) Stock broker and member of the New York Stock Exchange. One of Edward's Uncle Edwin Bartlett's business partners. Uncle Edwin introduced Edward to Henry Chauncey, perhaps to procure further introduction to other business partners on the west coast. On November 19, 1847, the contract to carry the mail to California and the new territory of Oregon was assigned to William H. Aspinwall. On April 12, 1848, Aspinwall, with Gardiner G. Howland and Henry Chauncey, formed the Pacific Mail Steamship Company. They were granted a 10-year mail

subsidy of $199,000 per year on October 1, 1848. Henry married Emily Aspinwall Howland, daughter of Samuel Shaw Howland, who was a brother of Gardiner G. Howland. Henry was also a business partner with his brother-in-law, Joseph Alsop. Henry was in the West India Trade operated out of Valparaiso, Chile. He was the fourth grandson of Charles Chauncey, the second president of Harvard College.

Chisholm, Caroline (Jones) (1808-1877) Progressive 19th-century English humanitarian known mostly for her involvement with female immigrant welfare in Australia. She married Archibald Chisholm. They had eight children. In his novel *Bleak House* Charles Dickens is said to have based the character of Mrs. Jellyby on an amalgamation of three women of the period, including Caroline Chisholm. See Wikipedia for more information.

Choate, Rufus (1799-1859) Graduated Dartmouth 1819, valedictorian. Began a practice as a lawyer in South Danvers in 1823. Moved in 1828 to Salem to become a member of the Massachusetts State legislature and a State Senator. Elected as a Whig to the 22nd and 23rd Congresses 1831-1834 at which time he resigned and moved to Boston to fill Daniel Webster's vacated position of Senator from Massachusetts. Massachusetts Attorney General 1853-1854. Buried at Mount Auburn Cemetery in Cambridge, Massachusetts.

Claflin-Richards House in Wenham, Massachusetts - See Horton, Elizabeth Richards.

Clark, Edward (about 1825-) Servant in the Joseph Andrews family. Listed in the Massachusetts State census in 1855 as age 30.

Clinton, Alfred S. is thought to be a fictitious person. Edward asked Lizzie to address her letters to a "Alfred S. Clinton" while he was in Vermont visiting the Jarvis family in Weathersfield, Vermont.

Coletti, Filippo (1811-1894) An Italian baritone in Maretzek's Opera troop best known for his performances in Giuseppe Verdi's operas.

Cook, Captain Samuel (1769-1861) Wealthy master mariner. Married Sally Cheever (1779-1863) in Salem. Had three children. Samuel Cook bought land on August 24, 1801 and built the Cook-Oliver House at 142 Federal Street in Salem, Massachusetts. Tax returns show the house was built 1802-1803. Architect Samuel McIntire plans are now in the Essex Institute. The house is privately owned and still owner-occupied. The Cook-Oliver House is referred to as "The American Castle" as Found in the Flawlessly Perfect Colonial Mansion (*Boston Evening Transcript*, April 1, 1916.) "Through one of these doorways can be seen a glimpse of the parlor with its splendid mantel and French scenic wall-paper, brought home by Captain Cook about 1820 on his return from one of his sea voyages. It is said that he bought the paper for the purpose of decorating the "best room" for the approaching marriage of his daughter, Sarah Elizabeth Cook (1801-1866) to General Henry Kemble Oliver in 1825.

Cutts, Edward Holyoke (1831-1887) Born in Portsmouth, New Hampshire, one of nine children of the Honorable Hampden Cutts (1805-1875) and Mary Pepperell Jarvis (1809-1879), Edward's Aunt, who was a daughter of the Honorable William Jarvis and Mary Pepperell (Sparhawk). Cutts was a descendent of Edward Holyoke, the President of Harvard College, 1737-1769. He commanded a military company at Richmond during the Civil War. Married with two daughters named Mary Sherwood and Lizzie Katherine. Died in Faribault, Minnesota.

D

Devereux, John Forrester (1835-1883) Edward's chum at Harvard. His father, Gen. George Humphrey Devereaux, (1809-1878) Harvard Class of 1829, studied law with Leverett Saltonstall. He was adjutant-general of the State (1848-1853). His mother was Charlotte Story Forrester (1811-1873) the niece of Judge Story. John studied at the Salem Latin School under Oliver Carlton before entering Harvard and, upon graduating in 1859, joined his father's law practice in the firm of Wiggins and Devereux. Served in the Massachusetts Volunteer militia 1861 and remained active until 1863, fighting in every Civil War battle except Antietam. In 1864, he was commissioned captain of the 6th U.S. Colored Troops and was mustered out September 1865. In 1870, he published a volume of poems entitled "Our Roll of Honor" as tributes to heroes of the war. Went west and tried farming in Nebraska and Kansas without success. Never married. Lived with his brother in Iowa. Died at age 48.

Dickens, Charles (1812-1870) English writer. Edward mentions reading Dickens' novel *Bleak House*, which was originally published in 20 monthly installments between March 1852 and September 1853. Dickens also wrote *David Copperfield* in 1850.

Dorsheimer, William Edward (1832-1888) Born in Lyons, New York. Attended Phillips' Andover Academy. Attended Harvard in 1849. Expelled with Edward. Studied law in Buffalo. Admitted to New York Bar 1854. In 1858, he printed two reviews in the *Atlantic Monthly*, criticizing Parton's lives of Jefferson and of Aaron Burr. Harvard granted Dorsheimer an honorary A.M. (Master of Arts) degree in 1859. In 1867, he was appointed U.S. District Attorney for Northern District of New York. Served as a Major on Fremont's staff in Missouri during the Civil War. Elected Lt. Governor of New York 1874-1880. Served as a Democrat to the Forty-eighth Congress 1883-1885. Died while visiting Savannah, Georgia.

Dow, Catherine Williams "Katy" (Downing) (1836-1930) A daughter of Thomas (1800-1859) and Nancy (Brown) Downing. Married Josiah Dow (1838-1925) on Dec. 26, 1860 in Salem, Massachusetts.

Downing, Thomas (1800-1859) Born in Salem to Thomas and Catherine (Williams) Downing. Married Oct. 30, 1823 to Nancy Brown. Three known children, including Edward and Lizzie's friend Katy Downing. Thomas' occupation was listed as "dry goods" in the 1850 U.S. Federal Census. Wealthy businessman in dry goods business. Despondent over trouble in regard to block of houses he was building, he hung himself in the entryway of the Unitarian (First) Church, Salem in Jan. 1859. Gilbert Newhall and Thomas W. Downing, his son, were executors of his will.

E

Edward (Clark) A servant to General Joseph Andrews in Salem. Edward Tenney mentions that "Edward" will take care of the dog he, Edward Tenney, sent to Salem.

Emerson, Jacob (1829-1907) Visited Edward in Methuen with Margaret Phillips, December 7, 1853. Married Josephine Davis in 1861, Methuen, MA. Had four children. Listed in 1855 Methuen, Massachusetts Census as age 26, clerk.

Emerson, Ralph Waldo (1803-1882) Transcendentalist poet, philosopher and essayist. Born in Boston, MA, son of William and Ruth (Haskins) Emerson. His father was a clergyman. Unitarian minister 1826. Harvard University, Harvard Divinity School and Boston Public Latin School. He had four children with his second wife Lydia Jackson. One of his best known essays is "Self-Reliance." Of the Fugitive Slave Law of 1850, he said "I will not obey it, by God." Henry David Thoreau was his protégé and Walt Whitman his contemporary.

Emmerton, Carolyn Elizabeth (Osgood) "Carrie" (1828-1864) First cousin to Edward's stepmother Augusta Elizabeth Sprague and first cousin one-time removed to Lizzie. Oldest daughter of Nathaniel Ward Osgood and Mary Beckford (Archer). Married

Ephraim Augustus Emmerton on November 24, 1851. Had two sons: Frederic Augustus (1852-1928) and Nathaniel Osgood (1855-1855). Nathaniel died in infancy. Twelve years after her death, her sister Lucy married her husband.

Emmerton, Ephraim Augustus (1827-1901) Followed the sea for about 20 years beginning June 1843 at age 16, and after 1849 as a master mariner. During this time he made seven Zanzibar voyages, including visits to many, if not most, of the ports between the Cape of Good Hope and Bombay. He spent "275,000 miles at sea and never lost a topmast by stress of weather." Four times he brought guano from the Chinchas. Married on November 24, 1851 to Caroline Elizabeth Osgood "Carrie" (1828-1864), Lizzie's first cousin one-time removed. In 1855, he was an agent for Silsbees, Stone & Pickman at Manila. Had two sons: Frederic Augustus (1852-1928) and Nathaniel Osgood (1855-1855). On June 22, 1876, he married Carrie's younger sister, Lucy Derby Osgood (1835-1909). No children.

Emmerton, James Arthur (1834-1888) Born to James Emmerton and Mary Ann (Sage) was one of Edward's chums at Harvard. The 1850 U.S. Federal Census, Salem lists James as age 16. Graduated Harvard of 1853. In 1855, the Massachusetts Census shows James as a student, age 21. He became a physician and served in the 2nd Regiment Massachusetts Heavy Artillery, Union. 23rd Massachusetts Infantry Co. F, as a Corporal and Assistant Surgeon. James and Ephraim were brothers.

Emmerton, Lucy Derby (Osgood) (1835-1909) First cousin to Edward's stepmother Augusta Elizabeth Sprague and first cousin one-time removed to Lizzie. Youngest daughter of Nathaniel Ward Osgood and Mary Beckford (Archer). Married her sister's (Carolyn Elizabeth) widower, Ephraim Augustus Emmerton in 1876.

Everett, Charlotte Gray (Brooks) (1800-1859) Born to Hon. Peter Chardon Brooks (1767-1849) and Anna Nancy (Gorham) (1771-1830). Married the Honorable Edward Everett in 1822 and had six children. Her sister was Abigail Browne (Brooks) Adams.

Everett, Honorable Edward (1794-1865) Born in Boston. Entered Harvard at the age of 13. Graduated as valedictorian in 1811. Served as a U.S. Representative from Massachusetts for the 4th District 1825-35 and as Governor of Massachusetts 1836-40. Was U.S. Minister to Great Britain 1841-45, U.S. Secretary of State 1852-53 and a U.S. Senator from Massachusetts 1853-54. Ran as Constitutional Union candidate for Vice President of the United States in 1860. In 1822 married Charlotte Gray (Brooks), whose sister married Charles Francis Adams. Taught at Harvard and served as its president. He is best remembered as the featured orator at the dedication ceremony of the National Cemetery at Gettysburg in 1863, where he spoke for more than two hours immediately before President Abraham Lincoln delivered his famous, two minute Gettysburg Address. Everett was a Unitarian. Interred at Mt. Auburn Cemetery, Cambridge, Massachusetts.

F

Faneuil Hall. Built in 1742 by merchant Peter Faneuil, adjacent to the Quincy Market in Boston, Massachusetts, Faneuil Hall has served as an open forum meeting hall for more than 250 years. The meeting hall was the place where Americans first protested the Sugar Act and set down the doctrine of "no taxation without representation." Famous abolitionists Wendell Phillips, William Lloyd Garrison and Frederick Douglas spoke there. Edward mentions attending a Whig meeting at Faneuil Hall on November 7, 1951 to hear Rufus Choate and Judge Thomas.

Fellows, Carolyn "Caddie" (1817-1862) See Brooks, Carolyn "Caddie" (Fellows).

Fellows, Capt. Charles Oliver (1845-1924) Eldest son of John Foster Fellows and Mary Louisa (Sprague) Fellows, who was Lizzie's mother's sister and Edward's step-mother's sister. Charles served in 17th Massachusetts Infantry commanded by his father John Foster Fellows during Civil War.

Fellows, Edward A. (1848-1919) Youngest son of John Foster Fellows and Mary Louisa (Sprague) Fellows, who was a sister to Lizzie's mother and Edward's step-mother. Younger brother to Charles and Louisa and older brother to Elizabeth.

Fellows, Elizabeth (1853-1914) Youngest daughter of John Foster Fellows and Mary Louisa (Sprague) Fellows, who was a sister to Lizzie's mother and Edward's step-mother. Younger sister to Charles, Louisa and Edward Fellows. Living with her father 1880 at age 27

Fellows, Colonel John Foster (1815-1887) Married Mary Louisa (Sprague) Fellows, who was a sister to Lizzie's mother and Edward's step-mother. Had four children: Charles, Louisa, Edward and Elizabeth. Enlisted as a Lt. Col. in the 17th Infantry Regiment Massachusetts in 1861 and served until 1864, throughout the Civil War. At the end of 1864 he had been promoted to full Colonel. Buried at Harmony Grove Cemetery, Salem, Massachusetts.

Fellows, Louisa (1846-1894) Eldest daughter of John Foster Fellows and Mary Louisa (Sprague) Fellows, who was a sister to Lizzie's mother and Edward's step-mother. Younger sister to Charles and older sister to Edward and Elizabeth. Living with her father in 1880 at age 34. Married at age 39 to William P. Innis June 18, 1885 in Chelsea.

Fellows, Mary Louisa (Sprague) (1815-1875) Younger sister to Lizzie's mother and Edward's step-mother, Lizzie's aunt married Col. John Foster Fellows. Had four children: Charles, Louisa,

Edward, Elizabeth. Edward mentions his Aunts Mary (Fellows) and Margaret drove with him to Mrs. Bridges in Andover.

Felt, Catherine (Bartlett) (1795-1869) Edward's mother's sister. Seventh of 15 children born to the Honorable Bailey Bartlett and Peggy White. In 1847, married the Honorable John Meacham. No children. Later married Rev. Joseph Barlow Felt. No children. In 1870, she was age 60 living with two sisters in Haverhill: Margaret Longley age 70 and Abbey Kimball age 65.

Felt, Elizabeth (Curtis) (1764-1837 dates unconfirmed) Married John Felt (1764-1802) in 1785 in Marblehead, MA. Eight-children: John Jr. (1785-1805), died at sea. Never married. David (1787-1807), Joseph Barlow Felt (1789-1869) (first married Abigail Shaw, 2nd married Catherine (Bartlett) Meacham), Elizabeth Curtis (1792-1864), (married William Osgood in 1817), Jonathan (1794-1796), Robert (1796-1797), Hannah (1798-1799) and Susan Becket (1800-1877) married Alfred Dutch.

Felt, Elizabeth Curtis (1792-1864) See Osgood, Elizabeth Curtis (Felt)

Field, Capt. Horace B. (1818-1853) Born in New York. Graduated West Point 1840. Served in Florida War and the War with Mexico. Washed overboard during disaster of the *San Francisco*. Buried St. Andrews Cemetery, New Berlin, NY.

Fillmore, Millard (1800-1874) 13th President of the United States 1850-1853. Last Whig president. Signed Compromise Measure of 1850 which included the Fugitive Slave Act.

Fitzmaurice, Mary A. Born in Ireland about 1832. Servant in Tenney household in 1850.

Forrest, Edwin (1806-1872) An American actor with a reputation for being temperamental to the point of being abusive. His jealousy of the English actor William McCready resulted in the Astor Place Riot in 1849. In 1853 he played Macbeth, with a strong cast and fine scenery, at the Broadway Theatre for four weeks—an unprecedented run at that date—and at the end of this engagement he retired from the stage for several years.

Foster, Ruth Bradstreet (1831–1911) Born in Salem. Married Edwin O. Tufts in 1852 in Boston and had one son Walter Brownell. (b.1859). Resided in New York, listed in city directory 1891, 1894, 1910 and in 1911 as "widow" with son Walter Brownell Tufts (1859-1936). Died in New York.

Fremont, Sewall Lawrence (1816-) Born in Vermont. Graduated from West Point in 1841. Rescued by the *Kilby* following the wreck of the *San Francisco* with his wife and three children: Ellen Mae (1849-1856), Richard (1850-), Mary Lawrence (1852-1854). They had three more children: Sewall 1855, Mary E. 1856 and Francis M. 1859.

Fries, August (-) The Mendelssohn Quintette Club was founded in 1849 with August Fries (first violin), Gerloff (second violin), Eduard Lehmann (first viola, flute), Oscar Greiner (second viola) and Wulf Fries (cello), brother of August. August was a member for 23 years; later he was a member of the Beethoven Quintet Club. August also figured in the Music Fund Society and the Harvard Musical Association. The Mendelssohn Quintette Club (1849-1895), based in Boston, Massachusetts, was one of "the most active and most widely known chamber ensemble[s] in America" in the latter half of the 19th century. It toured throughout New England and beyond, including Georgia, California and Australia.

Frothingham, Octavius Brooks (1822-1895) Born in Boston to Rev. Nathaniel Langdon Frothingham (1793-1870), a prominent Unitarian preacher, and Ann Gorham (Brooks). (Through his mother's family he is related to Phillips Brooks (1835–1893), a contemporary of Edward and Lizzie who became an American Episcopal clergyman and briefly Bishop of Massachusetts, and is remembered as lyricist of the Christmas hymn "O Little Town of Bethlehem" and for introducing Helen Keller and Anne Sullivan to Christianity.) Octavius Graduated Harvard Class of 1843 and from the Divinity School in 1846. Married Caroline Martha Curtis (1825-1900) on March 23, 1847. Unitarian clergyman in 1850, at the age of 27. Lived next door to Joseph George Sprague, who was also related to the Frothinghams—Joseph George's great grand aunt Hulda Sprague married Jonathan Frothingham. Octavius was pastor of the North Unitarian Church of Salem 1847-1855. He broke with this congregation over the issue of slavery and became pastor of a new Unitarian society in Jersey City 1855-1860. Had two children, one died in infancy.

Frothingham, Jonathan (1733-1802) Married 1757 Hulda Sprague (1737-1799), the great grand aunt of Joseph George Sprague. Had seven children. Their son, Ebenezer Frothingham (1756-1841) and wife Joanna Langdon (1755-1841) had nine children, including the Rev. Nathaniel Langdon Frothingham (1793-1870), who was the father of Octavius Brooks Frothingham.

G

Garden Troop Theatre An opera company from the Tacon Theatre of Havana. Considered to be the finest company that had visited New York. Performed at Castle Garden for fifty cents admission, beginning early in July of 1850 and created a profound sensation. Maretzek engaged most of the artists, including the leads Steffanone and Tedesco; tenors Salvi and Bettini; and basses Coletti and Marini. He combined them with the best of his former company; Mme Bertucca, Signora Truffi and Benevantano.

Gillis, James Andrew (1829-) Lawyer with Phillips and Gillis with offices on Essex Street in Salem. Listed in the 1880 U.S. Federal

Census with his housekeepers. Gillis would have been four years older than his companion Corporal Lee, mentioned by Edward.

Godey's Lady's Book. Published in Philadelphia 1830-1878, Godey's was the most popular monthly magazine before the Civil War. Cost $3.00 a year. *The Saturday Evening Post* cost $2.00 a year. Godey's was said to contribute to the popularity of the Christmas tree in America. It was noted for the hand-tinted fashion plate in each issue, a pattern for a garment to be sewn at home and a sheet of music for piano. Contributors included Edgar Allan Poe, Nathaniel Hawthorne, Oliver Wendell Holmes, Washington Irving and others.

Gray, Aunt see Gray, Olive Frost (Bell) Edward mentions Aunt Gray as being at "Grandmother's," saying Aunt Gray thinks he and Lizzie are engaged. She wonders why she has not been invited to the wedding.

Gray, Olive Frost (Bell) (1787-) Born in Rockingham County, NH. Sister of Lizzie's grandmother Andrews. Married Gideon Gray, 2 Aug 1809 in Portsmouth, NH. They had two sons: James M. Gray (1814-1894) and Joseph L. Gray (1810-).James married Almira Hoyt (1813-) 30 Apr 1843. Both sons had adjoining farms in Barrington, Strafford, NH. Olive is listed with James' family in the 1850 US Federal census. Gideon had also been a farmer and probably died prior to 1850.

Green, Mrs. Edward mentions "seeing some tableaux at Mrs. Green's" in his letter of September 1853. There are possible connections to the Spragues. Unable to verify additional information.

H

Haliburton, Mrs. (1828-1898) Referred to as the "lovely widow of Portsmouth." Susan Hamilton (Peters) was born in New York.

She married James Pierrepont Haliburton (1824-1849) in 1846. She later married George Wallace Haven (1808-) in 1858. She died in Boston.

Harrod, Carolyn (aka Caroline) (1796-1893) – See Bartlett, Carolyn (Harrod)

Harrod, Joseph (1785-1875) Father of Carolyn Harrod, who married Edwin Bartlett. Edward enjoyed his visits with Joseph while staying with the Bartletts at Rockwood. Joseph was born in Haverhill, Massachusetts but lived in Bath, Maine and later Portland, Maine. He became a merchant in New Orleans. U.S. Federal Census for June 27, 1870 shows Joseph Harrod, age 85, in the town of Red Hook in Dutchess County, New York with a post office address in Annandale, New York with Caroline [Carolyn] Bartlett, age 61. Occupation: Deacon.

Hawkes, Dr. William H. (1846-1904) Teacher at Phillip's Academy in Andover. In 1870, when he was 24 years old, he resided as a boarder with Augusta Elizabeth (Sprague) Tenney where he met Laura "Lottie" Sprague Tenney. William and Laura were married in Methuen on October 25, 1887. The Reverend Charles Mitchell, Margaret Tenney's husband, performed the marriage ceremony.

Hayes, Catherine (1818-1861) Left an impoverished childhood in Ireland to become the most famous Irish singer in Europe. Came to America 1851. Gave concerts in New York, Boston, Toronto, Philadelphia, Washington, D.C. and 47 other cities and towns along the Mississippi and in the south. She met presidents and statesmen and her famous future husband, P.T. Barnum, Jenny Lind's former manager, who sponsored her travels to the "gold rush" in the San Francisco area in the 1850s.

Healy, Bridget (about 1830-) Servant in the home of Gen. Joseph Andrews, Salem. Listed as in the 1850 U.S. Federal Census as "age 27, born in Ireland. "Also listed with the Andrews in Salem

1855 as Bridget Haley, age given as 23. In 1865 Massachusetts State Census, listed with the family of Benjamin W. Stone on Chestnut Street, Salem, age 35 years. The Andrews had moved to Boston.

Hodges, Ellen Probably a teacher or aide at Miss Ward's School.

Holyoke, Dr. Edward Augustus (1796-1855) Physician to the Andrews family, attending Lizzie's mother at her death. Born Edward Augustus Holyoke Turner but at his grandfather's urging dropped the name Turner to carry on his mother's family name of Holyoke. Graduated Harvard Class of 1817. Descendant of Edward Holyoke, who was Harvard College President from 1737-1769. In 1826, married Maria Osgood (1802-1868) at North Andover. Had seven children.

Holyoke, Francis Epes "Frank" (1831-1856) Returned from Jamaica in ill health. He thought he would go back to Cambridge Scientific School as an assistant to Professor Horswood. Met with Edward at the Astor House in New York on November 29, 1853.

Holyoke, George Osgood (1833-) George was a freshman at Harvard when Edward Tenney was a senior. Graduated Harvard Class of 1856. Son of Dr. Edward Augustus Holyoke and Maria (Osgood) Holyoke. Married Jane Wildes (Blake) of Boston in 1861. Taught for a while in Louisville, Kentucky. Returned to Boston in 1858 and began business as a broker in tobacco. Then moved to New York and formed a co-partnership of Holyoke and Rogers continuing as commission merchants in tobacco.

Horton, Elizabeth Richards (1837-1928) Daughter of the Richards family who owned and occupied the Claflin-Richards house from the early 1800s until 1921. Her famous doll collection was donated in 1922 to the Wenham Museum as part of the collection of over 5,000 dolls permanently displayed in the Osgood Gallery of the Museum. Mrs. Horton sent her dolls all over the United States for displays to raise funds for different children's charities.

Howe, Joseph Sidney (1832-1923) Married Mary Augusta Tenney (1837-1905) in 1859 in Methuen. Had two children. Mary was Edward's sister. Joseph was a civil engineer and, for more than forty years, town clerk. He was the leading historian of the region and President of the Methuen Historical Society.

Howland, Edward (1832-1890) Born in South Carolina, a direct descendant of John Howland, a "Mayflower" passenger. In 1846, his parents moved to Boston. Harvard Class of 1853. Looked forward to a career in architecture, but found himself representing his father for seven years as a cotton broker in Memphis, New Orleans, Boston and elsewhere. Became a Bohemian journalist and died a member of a socialist community in Sinaloa, Mexico. Married Mrs. Marie Stephens Case in 1865, whom he had met in his travels. Loved fine books and literature and had an extensive collection from his travels to Amsterdam, Leipzig, Paris, Oxford and London. First lived in New York City. Eventually moved to a little farm near Hammonton, New Jersey. In New Jersey, the Howlands experimented with raising fruits and vegetables and became very active in the new agriculture Grange movement. The Howlands moved to Mexico, where he died in 1890. His literary collection was given to the Fairhope Public Library.

Howland, Emily Aspinwall (1833-1897) Daughter of Samuel Shaw Howland (1790-1853) and Joanna (Hone). Born Far Rockaway, Queens, New York. Her father was a brother of Gardiner G. Howland (1787-1851). Married Henry Charles Chauncey (1830-1915). Two children: Henry Chauncey (1856-1899) and Lucy Chauncey (1860-1945)

Howland, Gardiner Green (1787-1851) Edwin Bartlett's business partner in New York. An uncle to Wm. H. Aspinwall. Samuel

Shaw Howland was his brother, also engaged in the Pacific Steamship Mail Company. Their sister Susan Howland (1779-1852) married John Aspinwall (1774-1847) and their daughter Mary Rebecca Aspinwall (1809-1886) married Isaac Roosevelt (1790-1863) whose son James Roosevelt (1828-1900) was Franklin Delano Roosevelt's father.

Howland, Samuel Shaw (1790-1853) Edwin Bartlett's business partner in New York. Married Joanna Hone (1799-1848). Had seven children. Daughter, Emily Aspinwall (Howland) (1833-1897) married Henry Chauncey (1856-1899).

Howland, Susan (1779-1853) Sister to Gardiner G. Howland and Samuel S. Howland. Married John Aspinwall (1774-1847). Their daughter Mary Rebecca Aspinwall (1809-1886), sister of William Henry Aspinwall, married Isaac Roosevelt (1790-1863), whose son James Roosevelt (1828-1900) was Franklin Delano Roosevelt's father. Susan Howland is the great grandmother of Franklin Delano Roosevelt.

Hubbard, Anna and Philena. Edward went riding with "two Miss Hubbards from Boston" and Margie Phillips. There was a John Capen Hubbard in the Boston 1850 U.S. Federal Census, age 47, Ann (his wife) age 47, John C. age 23, Anna age 22 and Philena age 20. It is probable the Miss Hubbards were Anna and Philena.

Humphries, John Fictional character from Susan Warner's novel *Wide, Wide World* that Edward was told he resembled.

I

Irving, Washington (1783-1859) American author, essayist, biographer and historian. Best known for his short stories "The Legend of Sleepy Hollow" and "Rip Van Winkle." Served as Ambassador to Spain (1842-1846). An extensive biography and list of his works appears in Wikipedia. Irving acquired his famous home in Tarrytown, New York, "Sunnyside," in 1835. This is where he died of a heart attack at the age of 76.

J

James - see Ridley, James

Jameson, William Henry (1818-1887) Captain of the Josephine. Born in Saco, Maine. Married Mary E. Gilbert (1827-). Had seven children. Needs further research to determine correct William Henry Jameson. Died in Brooklyn, New York.

Jarvis, Anna Bailey (Bartlett) (1787-1869) Edward's mother's sister. She was the first of 15 children born to the Honorable Bailey Bartlett and Peggy White. Born in Haverhill. Married the Honorable William Jarvis, his second marriage, and had 10 children. Died in Weathersfield, Vermont.

Jarvis, Major Charles (1821-1863) Third child of the Hon. William Jarvis and Ann Bartlett, who was the oldest daughter of Hon. Bailey Bartlett. Born in Weathersfield, Vermont. Rising member of the bar of Windsor County, Vermont when he raised a company for the 9th Vermont Regiment of volunteers and lost his life in action near Newbern, North Carolina in 1863.

Jarvis, Dr. Charles (1748-1807) Edward's great uncle. Charles' nephew William C. Jarvis, Esq., of Pittsfield, Massachusetts wrote an unpublished biography of his uncle Dr. Jarvis.

Jarvis, Catherine Leonard "Kate" (1831-1916) Ninth child of the Honorable William Jarvis and Anna Bailey Bartlett. Married Col. Leavitt Hunt in 1860. Had six children.

Jarvis, Louisa Bailey (1835-1888) Tenth child of the Honorable William Jarvis and Anna Bailey Bartlett. Buried in Weathersfield

Bow Cemetery in Windsor, Vermont. Inscription: "Blessed are the pure in heart for they shall see God."

Jarvis, Hon. William (1770-1859) Edward's uncle. Only son of Dr. Charles Jarvis. Served under Presidents Thomas Jefferson and James Madison. Consul to Lisbon, Portugal. First married Mary Pepperill (also spelled Pepperell) (Sparhawk) (1781-1811) in 1808. Their grandfather Enoch Bartlett had three wives but William and Mary had different grandmothers. William and Mary had two daughters: Mary Pepperell Jarvis (1809-1879) and Elizabeth Bartlett Jarvis (1811-1854). Second, William married Anna Bailey (Bartlett) (1787-1869) in 1817. She was a sister of Edward's mother (as well as a cousin of his first wife). William and Anna had 10 children, losing one in infancy, one at age two and one son in the Civil War. Consul Jarvis was an affectionate father and known for providing elegant hospitality. Edward mentions visiting the two youngest Jarvis children, Catherine Leonard "Kate" Jarvis (born 1832) and Louisa Bailey Jarvis (born 1835). Lived in Weathersfield, Vermont and buried at Weathersfield Bow Cemetery.

Joe - see Andrews, Joseph Sprague

Judd, Col. Henry Bethel (1819-1892) Cadet at West Point 1835-1839. Fourteenth in a class of 41. Married to Elizabeth Cox (Bonneau) (1824-1899). Rescued from the *San Francisco* by the *Kilby* with the initial group of officers and troops.

J.W. - see Sprague, Joseph White

K

Kemble, Frances Anne "Fanny" (1809-1893) Father was the actor Charles Kemble and mother, Marie-Thérèse de Camp. Made her debut as Julia (while her father played Mercutio) in 1829 at the Covent Garden Theatre in London. Played most of the major female

Shakespeare parts and toured the U.S. with her father. Married the rich American Pierce Butler and retired from the stage, but found out that her husband was a slave owner owning plantations in Georgia with seven to eight hundred slaves. After years of quarrels and reconciliations, the marriage broke up in 1850. In 1847 she returned to the stage as Mrs. Butler, but smallpox had damaged her beauty and from that time onwards she gave lectures on Shakespeare. Fanny returned to England, wrote against slavery for the *London Times*, and finished her first novel at the age of 80. Actress, playwright and Unitarian.

Kimball, David Mather (1813-1857) Principal of Quaboag Seminary 1850-1851. Edward's teacher and Edward lived in his home as a boarder. Born in Leyden, New York to Reuel Kimball and Hannah Mather, a descendent of Cotton Mather of Boston. Graduated from Union College and lived in several locations throughout New England before settling in Warren. Married in 1842. Had three children. First wife died 1849 in Warren. Married Charlotte Lincoln (1821-) on May 18, 1851 while Edward was at Quaboag. Had three more children. Six years later, Mr. Kimball was run over by a cart and died from his injuries in Kingston, New Hampshire, leaving a widow and six children.

Kimball, Ann Marie (1804-1893) Edward saw Ann Marie, Martha and Carrie Bird, in Brooklyn on December 19, 1853. Ann Marie was the daughter of Nathaniel Kimball (1777-1821) and Sarah Knight (1779-1849).

Kimball, William (1842-) A stockbroker in New York in 1880. (United States Census 1880 William C. Kimball in household of Mary A. Kimball, New York, New York.

L

Laur - see Allen, Laura White (Sprague)

Laura - see Andrews, Laura

Lee, George Cabot (1830-1910) Brother of Rose Lee. Neighbors on Chestnut Street. A prominent banker with Lee, Higginson & Co. of Boston. He was in charge of the Union Safe Deposit Vaults. Married Caroline Watts Haskell. Daughter Alice Hathaway Lee (1861-1884) married Theodore Roosevelt who became the U.S. President.

Lee, Francis Henry (1836-) Brother of Rose Lee. Neighbors on Chestnut Street.

Lee, John Clarke (1804-1877) Married Harriet Paine Rose (1804-).

Lee, Rose Smith (1835-1903) One of the "Chestnut Street Ladies," One of 10 Lee children. Her father was a merchant and a banker who had lost both his parents before he was six years old. Raised by his great-grandmother in Salem. Harvard Class of 1823. Master's from Harvard in 1842. Director in many corporations, trustee of various funds, fellow and treasurer of the American Academy of Arts and Sciences. Prominent member of the Essex County Natural History Society. Chairman of the finance committee of the Essex Institute from the date of its organization until his death. Rose Lee's mother was born in Antigua, British West Indies. She was the granddaughter of Dr. William Paine of Worcester, Massachusetts. Rose Lee married Leverett Saltonstall from a very prominent Salem family. Had six children: Leverett (1855-1863, Richard (1859-1922), Rose Lee (1861-1891), Mary Elizabeth (1862-), Philip (1867-1919), Endicott (1872-1897)

Lee, Corporal William Paine (1833-1888) Born in Boston. Lieutenant in the Civil War. Later a banker with Lee, Danforth and Company of Boston. His father was a banker. His mother was the granddaughter of Dr. William Paine of Worcester, Massachusetts.

His sister was Rose Smith Lee, one of the young ladies Lizzie's age who lived on Chestnut Street.

Leland, Leonard Lorenzo (1833-1899) Chum of Edward's at Harvard but not the Class of 1853. U.S. Federal Census of 1850, lists Leonard, age 17, living with Joseph H. Coolidge family, Worcester, Massachusetts. Leonard was the son of Amasa Leland (1793-1842) and Martha Seaver (1797-1837). Buried at the Old Burying Ground Gardner, Worcester, Massachusetts.

Lind, Johanna Maria "Jenny" (1820-1887) A popular singer known as the Swedish Nightingale whose concerts in America were managed and heavily promoted by P. T Barnum. One of the most highly regarded singers of the 19th century, she was known for her performances in soprano roles in opera in Sweden and across Europe, and for an extraordinarily popular concert tour of America beginning in 1850. Member of the Royal Swedish Academy of Music from 1840. In 1850, Lind came to America and gave 93 large-scale concerts for Barnum and then continued to tour under her own management. She earned more than $350,000 from these concerts, donating the proceeds to charities, principally the endowment of free schools in Sweden. With her new husband, Otto Goldschmidt, she returned to Europe in 1852 where she had three children and gave occasional concerts over the next two decades, settling in England in 1855. From 1882, for some years, she was a professor of singing at the Royal College of Music in London.

Liz - see Tenney, Elizabeth

Lizzie - see Andrews, Elizabeth

Longley, Caroline (1826-1902) Daughter of Dr. Rufus Longley and Peggy Bartlett. Died in Orchard, Maine, Nov. 8, 1902, organic heart disease. Single.

Longley, Margaret "Peggy" (Bartlett) (1790-1880) Third of 15 children born to the Honorable Bailey Bartlett and Peggy White. Married Dr. Rufus Longley in 1819. Lived in Haverhill, Massachusetts. In 1870, she was living in Haverhill with sisters Abigail "Abbey" (Bartlett) Kimball, age 65, and Katherine "Kate" (Bartlett) Felt, age 60. Had four children: Margaret, William Rufus, Carolyn and James Henry.

Longley, Dr. Rufus (1788-1855) Married Margaret "Peggy" (Bartlett) (1790-1880) in 1819. Son of Joshua and Bridge (Melvin) Longley. Born in Shirley, Massachusetts on September 2, 1788. Descendant of William Longley, one of the first settlers of Groton. Entered Harvard College in the summer of 1804, but his class was the one principally concerned in the college rebellion which broke out in the spring of 1807, when many of the members were expelled, including Rufus Longley. Began the study of medicine under the instruction of Dr. Oliver Prescott, Jr. of Groton. Earned a degree of Bachelor of Medicine at Dartmouth Medical School Class of 1811. Established himself in practice in Haverhill, Massachusetts where he passed the remainder of his life. Had four children. Member of the Massachusetts Medical Society. Received an honorary MD degree from Harvard in 1850. His last professional visit was made only a few days before his death, which took place on March 12, 1855and, by coincidence, his first patient was also his last. His widow Peggy (Bartlett) died at Haverhill on January 6, 1880 at age 89 years, 4 months and 8 days.

Lottie - see Hawkes, Laura Sprague (Tenney)

Loeser, Lt. Col. Lucien (1818-1897) Born in Orwigsburg, PA. Died Mar 6, 1897 at Brooklyn, NY. No. 26 in class of 1842 West Point. Brought the first piece of gold discovered in California in 1848 to Washington DC. On board the *San Francisco*, rescued with his family on the bark *Kilby*. Transferred to the packet *Lucy Thompson* and taken to New York.

M

Macready, William Charles (1793-1873) English actor born London. Specialized in tragic roles. Performing *Macbeth* at the Astor Place Theatre when Edwin Forrest announced his performance in the same role. Resulting riot in 1849 at the Astor Place Theatre caused the death of 23 people and injured 100. Married first Catherine Frances Atkins (-1852). Of their numerous children, only one son and one daughter survived. Second marriage to Cecile Louise Frederica Spencer (1827-1908). Had one son.

"Maggie" or Margie - see Tenney, Margaret Bartlett

Maretzek, Max (1821-1897) Austrian impresario; born in Brünn, Moravia on June 28, 1821. Pupil of Seyfried in Vienna. Attended university in Vienna. Several years later, became connected with Italian opera in London. In 1848, began his career in New York as the leader of the orchestra at the Italian opera. Organized and managed the grand opera at the Astor Place Opera House, the Academy of Music and Pike's Opera House (now the Grand Opera House) (1849-1878). He occasionally made professional tours to other cities of the United States, to Mexico and to Cuba. In 1849, he brought the celebrated singer Mlle. Bertucca to America. She later became his wife. He died Pleasant Plains, New York on May 14, 1897.

Margo - see Soley, Margaret. Servant in Andrews household.

McKeever, Commodore Isaac (1793-1856) and Mrs. Mary Flower (Gamble) McKeever Dined with Edwin Bartlett, Edwin's wife Carolyn and Edward Tenney at Rockwood. Native of Pennsylvania, born 1793, Commodore McKeever was a U.S. Navy officer of the War of 1812. Entered the Navy as midshipman in 1809. Attained the rank of Lieutenant during the war with Great Britain. While commanding a gunboat on Lake Borgne, LA., in 1814, he was captured by the British forces that were advancing on New Orleans.

After the war, in 1830, he became Commander and in 1838 became Captain. In 1850, he was promoted to Commodore and commanded the Brazilian Squadron. Was afterwards in charge of the Norfolk, Virginia Navy Yard. Died in Norfolk, Virginia in 1856.

Mitchell, Charles Langdon (1845-1930) Married Margaret "Margie" Bartlett Tenney (1845-1905) 1871, Edward's half- sister. Ministered in New York, Pennsylvania, Missouri and Methuen, Massachusetts. Graduated Yale in 1866 and Andover Theological Seminary in 1870. Had four children: Eliza Caroline (1872-) and twin sister Augusta Sprague (1872-1872), Laura Tenney (1876-1894) and Chauncey Leeds (1878-1928).

Mowatt, Anna Cora (Ogden) (1819-1870) Author, playwright, public reader and actress born in Bordeaux, France. Cora was the tenth of a family of 17 children. Father was Samuel Gouveneur Ogden (1779-1860), an American merchant. Mother was Eliza (Lewis) (1785-1836), granddaughter of Francis Lewis who was a signer of the Declaration of Independence. The family returned to the United States in 1826. In 1834, she eloped with James Mowatt (1805-1851), a wealthy New York lawyer. In 1853, she married William Foushee Ritchie (-1868). She died near London, England on July 28, 1870. Buried beside her first husband, James Mowatt in Kensal Green Cemetery London.

Mussey, Delevan (1833-1892) Lizzie's second cousin. (Common ancestor was Dr. Joseph Osgood.) Son of Reuben Dimond Mussey, who had been a professor of medicine at Dartmouth, later at Ohio Medical College and at Miami Medical College. Graduated from Dartmouth in 1854. Young Mussey came from a long line of physicians but preferred to be a newspaperman, getting his start 'out west' in Cincinnati, Ohio. In 1861, he went with the Lincoln inaugural party to Washington, D.C. The war soon followed, and Mussey, commissioned a captain, became the mustering officer for the Army of the Cumberland. Captain Mussey volunteered to raise "colored" troops in spite of the widespread prejudice against the enlistment of Negroes and the scorn of his fellow officers. He believed that the Negro as a soldier could prove his ability and thus gain the respect of the nation. As the war progressed, the need of Negroes became urgent. Mussey mustered in large numbers, was made Colonel of the 100th Regiment of "colored" troops, and later given the rank of Brevet Brigadier General. At the close of the war he was ordered to Washington and arrived there the night of Good Friday, April 14, 1865. The city was ablaze with lights and people were celebrating the Union victory and the President was attending the theater. Then came the tragedy—Lincoln was shot and revelry gave way to anxiety. People crowded about the theater and surged against the house where Lincoln lay dying. The city was in turmoil. Troops were called out and all officers ordered to give their services wherever needed. Mussey was stopping at the Kirkwood House and Vice President Andrew Johnson was also staying at the Kirkwood, so Mussey devoted himself to the Vice President's needs. As a result, Mr. Johnson, upon going to the White House as President, took General Mussey along as military secretary. John Wilkes Booth was pursued and shot. Conspirators were arrested, tried and sentenced. General Mussey favored clemency for Mrs. Mary Elizabeth Jenkins Surratt, who was convicted of taking part in the conspiracy to assassinate President Abraham Lincoln. Johnson showed no signs of granting clemency and she was executed. This case aroused Mussey's interest in legal matters and several months later he left the White House and military service and took up the study of law." (Source: Fate Rides A Tortoise). He married Lucinda Sparrow (Barrett) (1830-1870). Had two children: Dela P. Mussey (1866-1942) and Susan Victoria B. Mussey (1869-1880) with Lucinda. She died from a postpartum infection. Second marriage was to Ellen (Spencer) (1850-1936) on June 14, 1871. Had two more children: Spencer Mussey (1872-1891) and William Hitz Mussey (1874-1939).

N

Nevins, Sr., David C. (1809-1881) Wealthy New England Industrialist. Owned the Pemberton Mill in Lawrence, Massachusetts. Namesake of the Nevins Memorial Library in Methuen, Massachusetts. Married Eliza Coffin (1817-1895), daughter of ship merchant Jared Coffin of Nantucket. First son David Jr. was born on July 30, 1839. In 1842, protective taxes began hurting the textile importing business and Nevins switched to manufacturing textiles. Second son Henry Coffin Nevins was born in 1843. In 1859, he purchased the Pemberton Mill. In 1864, he purchased the Methuen Cotton Company on the Spicket River. His wife and sons had the Nevins Memorial Library built as a memorial to him. Nevin's sons took over the manufacturing businesses and ran the textile mills, including India Bagging Company and Bengal Bagging Company in Salem, Massachusetts. David C. Nevins' surname, as well as that of fellow "Methuen city fathers" Edward F. Searles and Charles H. Tenney, appears in the name of the "Searles, Tenney, Nevins Historic District" established by the City of Methuen in 1992 to preserve the "distinctive architecture and rich character of one of Massachusetts' most unique neighborhoods." David Sr. and his wife Eliza are buried on the library grounds, under a statue titled the Angel of Life sculpted by George Moretti of New York. The bronze figure holds aloft a banner which reads "The pleasant memory of their worth," the last line from "The Living Lost," a William Cullen poem.

Nichols, William (1798-1861) Born at Brookfield, Massachusetts to Isaac and Abigail Nichols. In 1845, at age 47, married Lizzie's Aunt Margaret (Sprague). She was age 31. In the Methuen vital records of marriage, Mr. Nichols was referred to as a "widower of Dedham." He was a printer. Massachusetts State census for 1855 lists William and Margaret in the residence of Samuel Noyes in Cambridge, Massachusetts. William died in Cambridge.

Nichols, Margaret (Sprague) (1813-1860) Younger sister to Lizzie's mother and Edward's stepmother Augusta (Sprague) Tenney. The 1850 Federal census recorded Margaret as living in the Tenney household in Methuen, which is where she was living at the time of her marriage. Her youngest sister Augusta was married to John Tenney, Edward's father. Massachusetts State census for 1855 lists Margaret living with her husband William Nichols in the residence of Samuel Noyes in Cambridge, Massachusetts. She died in Cambridge at McClean Hospital for the Insane five years later at age 47.

O

Oliver, Emily Kemble aka Emily (Oliver) Brown and Emily (Oliver) Andrews (1835-1920) Born to Henry Kemble Oliver and Sarah Elizabeth Cook in Salem. Emily was the same age as Lizzie Andrews and Liz Tenney. Edward mentions Emily appeared for a visit with Mr. Briggs. Emily married first in 1860 to James Olcott Brown (1836-1864) of Portland, Maine. They had one child, Emily Matilda Brown (about 1863-1880). James died at age 28 of diphtheria. Their daughter died at age of 17. On May 13, 1874, at age 39, Emily married Brigadier General George Lippitt Andrews (1828-1920). They did not have children. Both are buried in Arlington National Cemetery, Washington, D.C. George Lippitt Andrews' first wife, Alice Potter is also buried at Arlington. George and Alice had a son named George A. Andrews (1850-1928) who graduated from West Point and, following a career in the military, was also buried at Arlington.

Oliver, Joseph Henry (1868-1927) Born in Salem on January 10, 1868 to Mary Elizabeth "Lizzie" (Andrews) and Samuel Cook Oliver. He held a variety of jobs, including being a clerk for American Express, a brakeman (1893), a traveling salesman (1900) and a truck driver for Railway Express (1920). Married Violet Monica Kinsella (1880-1959) and had two daughters, Cecilia G. Oliver

(1901-1904) and Lillian Oliver (1902-1990) who married Charles Carpenter (1897-1984). Joseph Henry divorced and married Ethel May Cox (1891-1959). They had one son, Herbert Wellington Oliver (1908-1949). Joseph and Ethel divorced and he died in Lynn, Massachusetts on May 23, 1927.

Oliver, Josephine Sprague "Posie" (1863–1867) Born in Salem on December 2, 1863 to Mary Elizabeth "Lizzie" (Andrews) and Samuel Cook Oliver. Died on August 24, 1867 of cholera infantum (intestinal flu) at three years and eight months of age. Buried in Beverly and was later moved to Harmony Grove Cemetery in Salem, Massachusetts.

Oliver, Dr. Henry Kemble (1829-1919) Born to Henry Kemble Oliver (1800-1885). Brother of Emily Kemble Oliver. He is the chum who called on Edward with Daniel Upton. Graduated Harvard Class of 1852 and Harvard Medical School in 1856. Became a surgeon and was among those who made early advances in germ theory. Established the Department of Hygiene at Harvard. In 1880, he gave up his practice to engage in cancer research and became a member of the Harvard Cancer Commission. Never married. Dr. Oliver provided for the education of his nephew, Thomas Edward Oliver, at Harvard. "Henry Kemble Oliver, famous surgeon of Boston, Massachusetts, who died last October, has left his entire fortune consisting of several thousands to Harvard University. The late Doctor Oliver is the uncle of Professor T. E. Oliver of the Department of Romance Languages [University of Illinois, Champagne-Urbana, Illinois]."

Oliver, Gen. Henry Kemble (1800-1885) Married Sarah Elizabeth Cook (1801-1866) on August 30, 1825. Had seven children: Samuel Cook (1826-1888), Sarah Elizabeth (1828-1883) married Joseph Porter Battles, Henry Kemble (1829-1919), Maria Kemble (1831-1872), Emily Kemble (1835-1920) married James Olcott Brown and George Lippett Andrews, Mary Evans (1838-1911) and Ellen Wendell (1842-1923) married Charles Gilbert Cheever.

Adjutant General of Massachusetts 1844-48. Superintendent of the Atlantic Cotton Mills in Lawrence 1848-1858. Member of Lawrence school board and superintendent of schools. State Board of Education. Mayor of Lawrence 1859. Treasurer of Massachusetts 1861-1866. 21st Mayor of Salem 1877-1880. Member of Salem Glee Club. President of Oratorio Society. Organist at various periods at St. Peter's in Barton Square and the North Churches and a member of the Handel and Haydn Society in Boston. Published the Oliver Collection of Sacred Music and a Te Deum in F. His melody 'Federal Street' appears in many collections of church music. 'Federal Street by Henry Kemble Oliver' appears eight times #30, 51, 241, 242, 246, 247, 487 and 488 in Services for Congregational Worship, American Unitarian Assoc., Boston, Massachusetts 1914.

Oliver, Mary Elizabeth (Andrews) Oliver - see Andrews, Mary Elizabeth "Lizzie"

Oliver, Mary Evans (1838-1911) Youngest daughter of Henry Kemble Oliver and Sarah Cook Oliver. She would have been 14 years old at the time Edward mentioned meeting her when she was presumably traveling with her older sister Emily. Married Charles Sadler. Had two children.

Oliver, Colonel Samuel Cook (1826-1888) Eldest son of General Henry Kemble Oliver. Born at home at 142 Federal Street in Salem, Massachusetts. (Source: Notebook of H.K.O. Phillips Library, Essex Institute, Salem, MA) He first married Sarah Elizabeth Crosby (1830-1858) in Lawrence, Massachusetts in 1853. One child, Sarah Elizabeth Cook Oliver (1857-1927). Second married Mary Elizabeth (Andrews) and had three children: Josephine Sprague (1863-1867), Joseph Henry (1868-1927) and Thomas Edward (1871-1946). In 1849, attended Harvard for a short time and then organized Company I Sixth Regiment Massachusetts Volunteer Militia in Lawrence and was its first Captain. At the outbreak of the Civil War, was appointed Lieutenant Colonel of the 14th Regiment Massachusetts Volunteers, which was changed to the 1st Massachusetts Heavy Artillery. He was stationed at Albany, one of the defenses of Washington, but desiring more active service, he resigned the 14th Regiment and joined the 35th Massachusetts as Captain where he participated in the battles of Smith Mountain and Antietam. At Antietam, the explosion of a shell close to him threw him against a stone wall and injured his spine, paralyzing the lower half of his body. The regiment was so near the rebels that when the Union soldiers, after exhausting their ammunition, announced the fact to their officers, the rebels heard them and were preparing to charge when the order was given to take ammunition from the bodies of the dead and wounded. Thus supplied, the men of the 35th Massachusetts kept up the fire until night. Although Oliver was severely wounded at the Battle of Antietam, he recovered enough to walk with crutches and returned to active service as Lieutenant Colonel with the 2nd Massachusetts. This regiment remained in service three months after Richmond was taken. After the war, Colonel Oliver became more and more disabled until he was nearly helpless. The family story has been told of how he had to eat standing up. For this purpose, the mantle over the fireplace in his home was made wider to accommodate his plate. At the Harvard Commencement of 1887, at the request of his former classmates, he received the degree of A.B. as one of the Class of 1849. He died after many years of "suffering cheerfully and bravely borne." Samuel Cook Oliver is buried in the Oliver Lot in the Broad Street Burying Ground, Salem, Massachusetts. His tombstone is decorated with a sword through the laurel wreath of victory.

Oliver, Sarah Elizabeth (Cook) (1801-1866) Daughter of Capt. Samuel Cook (1769-1861) and Sally Cheever (1779-1863). Married Henry Kemble Oliver in 1825 and lived in the historic "Cook-Oliver" house at 142 Federal Street in Salem, Massachusetts.

Oliver, Thomas Edward (1871-1946) Son of Colonel Samuel Cook Oliver and Mary Elizabeth "Lizzie" (Andrews). Married Elizabeth Reinhardt on June 9, 1904. Had three daughters: Elisabeth

Andrews (1905-1997), Martha Reinhardt (1907-1980) and Sarah Cheever (1913-1989) and adopted a son, John Lee (1911-1959). Thomas' uncle, Dr. Henry Kemble Oliver paid for his education at Harvard from which he graduated Class of 1893 magna cum laude. Received his A.M. and PhD from the University of Heidelberg, Germany. Married Elisabeth Reinhardt (1879-1963) in Cleveland, Ohio in 1904 where he held his first teaching position as Professor of Romance Languages at Western Reserve University. Professor of Romance Languages at the University of Illinois from 1903-1940 and acting head of the department 1928-1929. From August 1915 to May 1916, he served on the Commission for Relief in Belgium. Received a gold medal from the Belgian "Comite National de Secours et d'Alimentation" and a bronze medal from the Commission for Relief under Chairman Herbert C. Hoover. Professor Thomas E. Oliver's publications are listed in Who's Who in America: Vol.2, 1943-50. Clubs and societies included: Modern Language Assn of America, "Societe Amicale Gaston-Paris, Corda Fratres," Association of Cosmopolitan Clubs, The Players (University of Ill.). Travel included a sabbatical year, 1931-1932, in study and travel in Finland, Germany, France, Switzerland and Italy. Avocation was his interest in amateur dramatics, given by the Faculty Players Club of the University of Illinois. He was a Unitarian. (Thomas was the grandfather of Elisabeth Claire Johnson and great grandfather of PJ Watters, authors of The Courtship of Lizzie Andrews based on Edward's 62 letters Thomas discovered in his mother's attic in 1922.)

Osgood, Carolyn Elizabeth "Carrie," "Caddie" or "Caddy" – see Emmerton, Carolyn Elizabeth (Osgood)

Osgood, Elizabeth Curtis (Felt) (1792-1864) Married William Osgood (1785-1834) in 1817 in Salem. Had seven children: Abigail (1818-1880), William Henry (1821-1889), Joseph Barlow Felt (1823-1913) married Mary Jane Creamer, John Felt (1825-1892),

Ellen Punchard (1827-1875), Mary Shepard (1830-1904) married James B. Curwen, Susan Elizabeth (1833-1920).

Osgood, Dr. Joseph (1746-1812) Married Lucretia Ward (1748-1809) in 1770. Had 10 children, including Margaret Osgood, who had Elizabeth Maria Sprague, who had Lizzie Andrews.

Osgood, Lucy Derby (1836-1909)Youngest daughter of Nathaniel Ward Osgood and Mary Beckford Archer. Married her sister's (Caroline Elizabeth) widower, Ephraim Augustus Emmerton in 1876.

Osgood, Margaret (1778-before 1837) Born to Dr. Joseph Osgood (1746-1812) and Lucretia (Ward) (1748-1809). Married Hon. Joseph Sprague, Jr. (1739-1808). Had 11 children, seven lived past childhood, including: Edward (1808-1842), Lizzie's mother Elizabeth Maria (Sprague) (1809-1841) married Joseph Andrews, Lucretia Osgood (Sprague) (1812-1839) married Professor Thompson, Margaret (Sprague) (1813-1860) married William Nichols, Mary Louisa (Sprague) (1815-1875) married John Fellows, Laura White (1816-   ) married George Allen and Edward's stepmother Augusta Elizabeth (Sprague) (1819-1874) married John Tenney.

Osgood, Mary Beckford (1833-) Daughter of Mary Beckford (Archer) and Nathaniel Ward Osgood. Single in 1900 census, living with her sister Lucy (Osgood) Emmerton and her sister's husband Ephraim Augustus Emmerton. Emmerton's first wife was Caroline, the older sister of Mary and Lucy.

Osgood, Mary Beckford (Archer) (1800-after 1870) Lizzie's great aunt. Married in Salem in 1822 to Nathaniel Ward Osgood (1797-1863). Had four children: Joseph (1825-1877), Caroline Elizabeth (1828-1864), Mary Beckford (1832-) and Lucy Derby (1836-1909).

Osgood, Nathaniel Ward (1797-1863) Lizzie's grandfather. Brother to Margaret Osgood, who married Joseph Sprague, Jr. Nathaniel married Mary Beckford (Archer) (1800-1863) in 1822. Had four children.

Osgood, William (1785-1834) Ship Captain, Salem, Massachusetts. Married Elizabeth Curtis Felt (1792-1864) in Salem, Massachusetts on April 20, 1817. Had seven children. Lived in Salem.

P

Pacific Mail Steamship Company Founded April 18, 1848 by a group of New York City merchants, William H. Aspinwall, Edwin Bartlett, Henry Chauncey, Joseph Alsop, Gardiner G. Howland and Samuel S. Howland. These merchants had acquired the right to transport mail under contract from the United States Government from the Isthmus of Panama to California, awarded in 1847 to one Arnold Harris. The company initially believed it would be transporting agricultural goods from the West Coast but, just as operations began, gold was discovered in California, and business boomed. During the California Gold Rush in 1849, the company was a key mover of goods and people and played a key role in the growth of San Francisco, California.

Paine, Charles Jackson (1833-1916) American railroad executive, soldier, yachtsman and a general in the Union Army during the American Civil War. Served as Colonel of the 2nd Louisiana (USA) Infantry, one of the first Union "colored" units. Bachelor of Arts, Harvard Class of 1853, Master of Arts degree in 1856. The great-grandson of Declaration of Independence signer Robert Treat Paine. Married Julia Bryant (1847-1901) in 1867. Had seven children.

Panama Railroad Company. In 1848, William H. Aspinwall, senior partner in Howland and Aspinwall, obtained a railroad concession from New Granada. John L. Stephens (a lawyer), Henry

Chauncey (a banker) and other partners began construction in 1850. Stephens was a keen archeologist but died after contracting a fever at the site. An estimated 22,000 workers died of yellow fever and malaria during the construction of the railroad. Bodies were sold to medical schools all over the world and the proceeds maintained the hospital for the rest of the workers.

Parodi, Teresa aka Teresa Stolz (1827-after1878) Maretzek opened the season at Astor Place Opera House on October 4, 1850. On November 4, 1850 the great Italian soprano, Teresa Parodi, made her first appearance as the character Norma.

Peck, William Henry (1830-1892) Edward's Harvard chum. Born in Augusta, Georgia to Colonel Samuel Hopkins Peck and Sarah A.D. (Holmes). His father was from Connecticut and the seventh in descent from Deacon Paul Peck, who came from England in 1635 and settled in Hartford. Graduated Harvard Class of 1853. In 1854, became first assistant in the New Orleans Public Schools. Held positions at University of Louisiana, Masonic Female College in Georgia, Lavert College in Georgia. Combined a life of teaching, journalism and writing. Authored several novels. In 1854, married Mona Blake (Kenny). Had six children who survived him. Mona died in 1891. William died five months later in 1892.

Peirson, Dr. Abel (or Abiel) (1794-1853) Born in Biddeford, Maine. Graduated from Harvard Class of 1812. On April 18, 1819, married Harriet Lawrence. He died in a tragic train accident at Norwalk, Connecticut. The *Salem Gazette* mentions it as a remarkable fact in the family history of the late Dr. Peirson, that he and his four brothers, who were all sons his father had by his first wife, have died accidental deaths; viz: two were drowned, when quite young, in Saco River; a third was drowned at sea; a fourth was killed on board the ship *Putman* of Salem, while manfully defending the ship against the attack of the Malays; and now the last of the brothers has had his life sacrificed to the reckless conduct of railroad operators."

Peirson, Charles Lawrence (1834-1873) (also spelled Pierson). Born in Boston to Dr. Abel Peirson and Harriet Lawrence. Supervisor of a cotton mill in Fall River, Massachusetts. Peirson may have attended Harvard for a short time but there is no record of him graduating. He married Emily Russell (1844-1908) on Jan. 19, 1874. Charles' older brother Edward Brooks Peirson (1820-1874) married Catherine Saltonstall (1823-1852) in 1846 (no children).

Peirson, Edward Brooks (1820-1873) Older brother of Charles L. Peirson, son of Dr. Abel Peirson and Harriet Lawrence .Married Catherine Saltonstall (1823-1852) in 1846, Salem, MA. (no children).

Perry, Mrs. Anne Perry's mother who lived in Lawrence, Massachusetts.

Phillips, Margaret "Margie" (1835-1902) Daughter of Rev. John Charles and Harriet (Welch) Phillips of Methuen. Her father was the Pastor in Methuen. Margie may have gone to school with Lizzie Andrews in Hamilton. Edward later mentions time spent horseback riding with Margie and that she was "dreadfully bashful." Another connection with the Phillips is through Margie's brother Johnny Phillips, a later Harvard graduate who Edward visits in Andover. At age 22, Margie married Alfred B. Hall in Methuen in 1858.

Phillips, Rev. John Charles (1807-1878) Methuen minister born to the Honorable John Phillips (1770-1823) and Sarah (Walley) (1772-1845). His parents, the Hon John Phillips (1770-1823) was the son of William Phillips (1737-1772) and Margaret (Wendell) (1739-1823), descended from a notable lineage. The Hon. John Phillips graduated Harvard Class of 1788, was president of the Massachusetts State Senate and the first mayor of Boston. His mother Margaret was the eleventh and youngest child of the Hon. Jacob Wendell (1691-1761). John Charles graduated Harvard Class of 1826. Became Colonel of the Boston Regiment and one of the Governor's Council. Married Sarah Oliver (1696-1782), daughter of Dr. James Oliver of Cambridge and Mercy Bradstreet. Mercy was the daughter of Dr. Samuel and Mercy (Tyng) Bradstreet of Cambridge and granddaughter of Governor Simon Bradstreet by his first wife Anne Bradstreet. Anne was the daughter of Governor Thomas Dudley. John Charles and Sarah had seven children: Margaret Welch 1835; John Charles 1838; Emily Susan 1842; Harriet W. 1845; Merriam W. 1849; Anna Dunn 1850; Caroline Crowninshield 1852.

Phillips, Margaret "Margie" (1835-) Daughter of Rev. John Charles (1807-1878) and Harriet (Welch) Phillips (of Methuen. Edward mentions time horseback riding with Margie and that she was "dreadfully bashful". Another connection with the Phillips is through Margie's brother, Johnny Phillips, a later graduate of Harvard who Edward visits in Andover. At age 22, Margie married Alfred B. Hall in Methuen in 1858.

Pierson - see Peirson

Pollard, Catherine "Kate" (1830-) Probably Resided in Harvard, Worcester, Massachusetts in1850. Parents were Otis and Catherine Pollard. Resided in New York in 1852.

Putnam, Clara (1833-) Student at a boarding school, listed in the U.S. Federal Census with teachers and students in 1850 in Andover, Massachusetts. Became Mrs. Gadsen. (See reference in letter 20 to Poor Billy Y.)

Q - R

Ridley, James (1823-) Born in Ireland. Servant in the household of Joseph Andrews, Salem 1850, along with Bridget Healy, age 21, and Margaret Soley, age 30, both born in Ireland.

Riley, Esq., Theodore W. Agent in New York for Peruvian Guano. Business friend of Edwin Bartlett in New York. "The beautiful residence of Mr. Edwin Bartlett, near Tarrytown, exhibits strong evidence of the fertilizing power of guano upon the poor, unproductive hill sides of Westchester Co. That place, now so luxuriant was noted, a few years ago, as too poor to support grasshoppers. It was the poverty stricken joke of the neighborhood."

Roberts, Caroline Elizabeth (1835-1896) Born in Salem, daughter of Nehemiah Roberts (1800-1840) and Hannah Ward (Osborne) (1808-1888). Married Henry Clay Leach (1832-1906) on July 30, 1866 in Salem. Had four children. Edward had asked Lizzie to invite her to the Harvard commencement.

Rockwood (Rockwood Castle, Rockwood Estate) - Edwin Bartlett built this 200-acre estate overlooking the Hudson River at Tarrytown, New York. Sold to William Aspinwall for a fraction of its cost. In 1886, William Rockefeller (1841-1922), brother of John D. Rockefeller, purchased it from Aspinwall for $250,000. Accounts vary as to whether he demolished it and used the rock or made extensive renovations. In 1941-1942, John D. Rockefeller did demolish it and deeded the property to his son Laurance. In 1999, Laurance donated the land to the state as part of Rockefeller State Park Preserve. Only the foundation and a gatehouse remain (3.1 miles from Sleepy Hollow, New York).

S

Saltonstall, Leverett (1825-1895) Born in Salem. Married Rose S. Lee (1835-1903) in 1854. Lizzie's neighbor in Salem. Harvard Class of 1844. Master of Arts degree and Bachelor of Law Degree in 1847. Collector of Customs for the Port of Boston by the appointment of President Cleveland in 1885-1890. Board of Overseers of Harvard College. Resident member of the New England Historic Genealogical Society from 1856 until his death. Wrote "Ancestry and Descendants of Sir Richard Saltonstall." His son Richard saw that the book was printed. Had six children. Died in Newton, Massachusetts. His father, also named Leverett Saltonstall (1783-1845) was the mayor of Salem 1836-1837.

Santos, John Henry "Johnny" (1835-) Chum and friend of Charlie Peirson. John Henry Santos was born in Salem to John A. and Maria (Monarch). Los Santos married January 29, 1831. (Johnny dropped the use of "Los" in his parent's name.) The Los Santos also had a daughter named Josephine Augusta on February 13, 1831.

Sargent, George Henry (1828-after1912) Son of Joseph Denny Sargent and Mindwell (Jones). Entered Harvard as a freshman in 1849, remaining there until November 1851. In 1852, he entered Harvard Law School, rooming with his old chum Howe. In 1853, he formed a partnership with his brothers in their hardware business. The business grew to the manufacture of hardware by "Sargent and Co." at New Haven, Connecticut. His degree was given in 1895 by the pressing request of his classmates. Married Sarah C. Shaw in 1855. Had two sons and a daughter. Both sons were lost in a yachting accident between New Haven and Nantucket in August of 1883. The name of the yacht was "Mystery."

Sargent, Mrs. Edward's reference to Mrs. Sargent is presumed to be to the mother of George Henry Sargent, Edward's classmate at Harvard who also attended the Unitarian Church in NY.

Satterlee, Brevet Brigadier General Richard Sherwood (1796-1880) Born in Fairfield, NY to Major William Satterlee and Hannah Sherwood. Major Satterlee was an officer of Connecticut troops during Revolutionary War. General Satterlee married Mary S. (Hunt) (1806-1883), sister of a Michigan Supreme Court Justice.

Sedgwick, Miss (1833-1897) Edward's reference to Miss Sedgwick suggests that she must have been a school mate at Quaboag. All that is known of her from the letters is that she sent a generous valentine from New York to Edward. Possibly Grace Ashburner Sedgwick born 5 Mar 1833 in Lenox, Berkshire County, MA, married Charles Astor Bristed, 20 Aug 1867. Died 9 Feb 1897 in Paris.

Smith, Caroline (Sprague) "Carolyn" or "Cousin Carrie" or "Caddie" (1827-1879) Daughter of Joseph E. Stearns (Sprague) and Sarah Leonard Bartlett, and sister of J.W. Married the Reverend Charles Smith, Jr. and had three children: Edwin, Charles and Caroline.

Sontag, Henriette (1806-1854) German operatic soprano of international renown, appearing in New York in 1852 with Alboni and met with positive acclaim. Previously premiered in Beethoven's Ninth Symphony and Missa Solemnis. In 1828, she married Count Rossi. Stricken with cholera and died at the age of 48.

Sparks, Jared (1789-1866) Historian, writer, editor, educator, Unitarian Minister and President of Harvard. After graduating from Harvard, Sparks worked as a teacher and editor before becoming minister of the First Independent Church in Baltimore in 1819. While serving as minister, he continued writing and editing, including founding the Unitarian Miscellany and Christian Monitor in 1821. From 1821 until 1823, he served as Chaplain for the U.S. House of Representatives. Retiring from the ministry in 1823, Sparks returned to Boston, where he bought and edited The *North American Review*, founded The *American Almanac and Repository of Useful Knowledge,* and published books on George Washington and Benjamin Franklin. He became McLean Professor of History at Harvard in 1839 and was President of Harvard University 1849-1853, during Edward's attendance. He regretted having to suspend Edward from Harvard and encouraged him to return. Married Frances Ann (Allen) (-1835) and second Mary Crowninshield (Silsbee) (1809-1887).

Sprague, Augusta Elizabeth (1819-1874) – see Tenney, Augusta Elizabeth (Sprague)

Sprague, Caroline "Caddie" - see Caroline Smith. Lived in Warren.

Sprague, Elizabeth (Bartlett) (1789-1817) Married Lizzie's uncle, Joseph E. (Stearns) Sprague in 1808. She was the second child of the Honorable Bailey Bartlett and Peggy White; the second oldest of 15 siblings. She had five children (only one survived childhood) and she died shortly after childbirth at age 28.

Sprague, Elizabeth Maria (1809-1841) Lizzie's mother. Daughter of Joseph Sprague, Jr. (1771-1833) and Margaret Osgood (1778-bef 1837). Married Gen. Joseph A. Andrews (1808-1869). Had three children: Joseph (1833-1861), Mary Elizabeth (1835-1922) and Laura (1837-1893). Died following an illness contracted on a trip to Missouri. Her sister, Lucretia Osgood (Sprague) Thompson (1812-1839) had died of consumption and Elizabeth went to Missouri to bring her sister's infant daughter Lucretia Thompson back to Salem to raise with her own family.

Sprague, Harriet Leonard (1822-1884) Daughter of Sarah Leonard (Bartlett) Sprague (2nd wife of Joseph E. Sprague). Joseph White "JW" Sprague's sister. Married Seth Hall Terry (1818-1884) in 1855. Had three children: Walter Clarke (1858-1860), Seth Sprague (1862-aft 1912) and Grace Bartlett (1864-).

Sprague, Joseph E. (Stearns) (1782-1852) Son of Dr. William Stearns and Sarah White. Legally changed his name from Joseph E. Stearns to Joseph E. Sprague at age 19. Graduated Harvard Class of 1804. Studied law with the Honorable William Prescott, of Salem. Intimate friend of Judge Story, a very influential leader of the Democratic party in Massachusetts and a friend and correspondent of John Quincy Adams. U.S. Deputy Marshall under President Jefferson. Postmaster of Salem 1815-1829. Representative three years in the Massachusetts State Legislature. Massachusetts State Senator. Member of the Governor's Council. In 1830, he succeeded his father-in-law, the Honorable Bailey Bartlett, as High Sheriff of Essex County until November 1851. In 1808, married Elizabeth (Bartlett) (1789-1817), daughter of the Honorable Bailey Bartlett and Peggy White. Had five children and died in childbirth after the fifth child. Only their second child, Elisa Bartlett Sprague (1810-1894) survived childhood. She married Maltby Strong, but had no children. In 1819, Joseph married Elizabeth's sister, Sarah Leonard Bartlett. Had four children. Three lived to adulthood, married and had children.

Sprague, Joseph George (1787-1852) Son of Ebenezer Sprague (1760-1856) and Molly Cross (1763-1790). Married Priscilla Gould. (1790-1864). One child, Caroline Augusta (1828-1855) married John Samuel Draper (1816-1864) and had three children. Joseph and Priscilla adopted Lucretia Thompson (1839-1906), infant daughter of Prof. John Thompson and Lucretia Osgood Sprague (1812-1839) after Lizzie's mother died. (Lizzie's mother became ill and died following a trip to retrieve baby Lucretia after baby Lucretia's mother died. Baby Lucretia's mother, also named Lucretia, was a sister to Lizzie's mother and Edward's step mother). Joseph and Priscilla lived in Salem where Joseph was a bank cashier. Joseph was a neighbor and relative of Octavius Frothingham. Lucretia married Amos Blanchard (1831-1908).

Sprague, Joseph White (1831-1900) Referred to as "JW" in this book. Edward's cousin. Graduated Harvard Class of 1852. Son of Joseph E. (Stearns) Sprague and his second wife Sarah. Joseph W. Sprague was a brother to Carrie Smith and Harriet S. Terry. Occupation was civil engineer. Became President of the Ohio Falls Car Co. at Jeffersonville, Indiana. In 1860, resided in Rochester, New York with Maltby Strong, Elisa Strong and Joseph W. Strong. In 1880, U.S. Federal Census listed JW as a boarder and mining superintendent in Nevada City, California. In 1899, he applied for a passport, listing his residence as Louisville, Kentucky and his occupation as retired manufacturer. Never married.

Sprague, Joseph, Jr. (1771-1833) Lizzie and Edward's grandfather. Harvard Class of 1792. Merchant in Salem. In 1801, married Mary Osgood (1778-bef 1837). Had three sons and eight daughters, including Lizzie's mother (Elizabeth Maria) and Edward's stepmother (Augusta Elizabeth).

Sprague, Major Joseph (1739-1808) Lizzie's great grandfather. Married Sarah White. Had two children: Sarah White Sprague (1764-1844) who married Dr. William Stearns and Joseph Sprague, Jr. (1771-1833) who married Margaret Osgood.

Sprague, Louisa Amelia (Bartlett) (1809-1840) One of 11 daughters of the Honorable Bailey Bartlett of Haverhill and Peggy White. She married Oliver Carlton (1801-1882), as his second wife, on November 27, 1831 in Salem. They had five children. Lived in Salem.

Sprague, Lucretia (Thompson) (1839-1906) Daughter of John Thompson and Lucretia (Sprague). Born in Marion, Missouri. After baby Lucretia's mother died, Lizzie's mother went to Missouri to bring her sister's daughter back to Salem in 1841 to raise her, but was met with her own untimely death, so Lucretia was adopted by Joseph George Sprague and his wife, Priscilla (Gould). Lucretia married Amos Blanchard, Jr.(1831-1908) in Lowell, Massachusetts on November 8, 1865. She was 26 and he was 34. She died of pneumonia on September 13, 1906 in Conway, New Hampshire.

Sprague, Margaret (1813-1860) see Nichols, Margaret (Sprague).

Sprague, Sarah Leonard (Bartlett) (1793-1864) Fifth of 15 children of the Honorable Bailey Bartlett and Peggy White. Second wife of Lizzie's uncle Joseph E. (Stearns) Sprague. Had four children: Harriet Leonard (married Seth Hall Terry); William Jarvis (died as infant); Carolyn Louisa "Carrie" (married Rev. Charles Smith); and Joseph White (referred to as "J.W." in *The Courtship of Lizzie Andrews*). Sarah's sister Eliza was Joseph's first wife. Joseph married Sarah after her sister Eliza died. Marrying a sister of a deceased wife was not uncommon at the time. Lived in Salem. In 1855, Sarah and her daughter Harriet were living with Oliver Carlton's family. Her sister Louisa Amelia was married to Oliver Carlton.

Stearns, Carolyn Sprague (1798-1852) Sister to Joseph E. (Stearns) Sprague. Never married.

Stearns, Joseph E. (1782-1852) - see Sprague, Joseph E.

Stearns, Sarah White (1792-1876) Daughter of Dr. William Stearns (1754-1819) and Sarah White Sprague (1764-1844).

Stearns, Dr. William (1754-1819) Graduated Harvard Class of 1776. Studied medicine with Dr. Joshua Brackett of Portsmouth, NH and commenced practice of medicine with Dr. Hall Jackson of Marblehead. He soon relinquished the practice of medicine and, after qualifying himself under the instruction of a chemist in Boston, commenced the business of apothecary and grocer in Salem. Married Sarah White Sprague (1764-1844) 1781. Had 10 children.

Stevens, (Mrs.) Abial. Possibly Abial Stevens in Methuen (1840 U.S. Federal Census) or Abiel Stevens in Andover (1850 U.S. Federal Census.) In 1860 U.S. Federal Census, Abial Stevens of Lawrence was listed as age 70, hat manufacturer living with his wife Abigail age 67, son Frank age 23, clerk. Civil War Draft registration for Abial Stevens states age on July 1, 1861 as 41 and residence as Lawrence, Massachusetts.

Storrow, Charles Storer, Sr. (1809-1904) Edward was to dine at the Storrows in Lawrence. Born in Montreal, Canada. Charles attended private school until 1824, since his father was a Boston merchant who moved his business to Paris, France in 1818. Returned to attend Harvard and graduated in the Class of 1829. Became a civil engineer with Boston & Lowell Railroad in 1832 and engineered its first train on May 27, 1835. Married Lydia Jackson 1836. Had seven children. Was Chief engineer and agent of the Essex Company in 1845. The Essex Company developed the water power at Bodwell's Falls on the Merrimack River 12 miles downriver from Lowell. Storrow designed the dam, supervised its construction, planned and laid out the streets of the new community called Lawrence and built several of the mills. Elected first mayor of Lawrence in 1853.

Storrow, Charles, Jr. (1841-1927) In 1859, Charles was expelled from Harvard (his sophomore year) for participation in a college brawl. His parents sent him to Stockbridge under the care of a clergyman. He returned to Harvard briefly, leaving again to voyage to India and China where he was shipwrecked in the Straits of Malacca. He then returned to raise his own company of the 44th Massachusetts Volunteer Infantry and served as its captain in the Civil War. In 1866 he married Martha Robinson Cabot, the daughter of the Lt. Colonel of the 44th Regiment. He next ventured into the oil business and eventually formed a cotton brokerage.

Stowe, Harriet Elisabeth (Beecher) (1811-1896) Born in Litchfield, CT to the Rev. Lyman Beecher (1775-1863) and Roxanna (Foote) Beecher (1775-1816). She was the sixth of eleven children. All seven sons became ministers. Her mother died when she was five. Harriet married Calvin Stowe in 1832. Had seven children. Stowe wrote for fifty-one years. In late 1850, she hid a fugitive slave in her home despite the penalties imposed by the Fugitive Slave Act. *Uncle Tom's Cabin* was her bestselling work which appeared in two volumes in 1852.

T

Taylor, Maj. George (1816-1853) Washed overboard from *The San Francisco* on the voyage to California. Graduated from West Point in 1837. Taught at the academy. Artilleryman, served in the second Seminole War and fought in the Mexican War. Drowned in the wreck of the steamship *San Francisco* which was transporting his regiment to California. His wife was also swept from the deck. Monument at Old Smithville Cemetery, Southport, North Carolina.

Tenney, Augusta Elizabeth (Sprague) (1819-1874) Edward's stepmother and Lizzie's aunt. Younger sister to Lizzie's mother Elizabeth Maria Sprague (1809-1841). Born in Salem. Second wife of John Tenney (Edward's father). Lived in Methuen. Had four children: Margaret (1845-1905) m. Rev. Charles Langdon Mitchell (1845-1905); John (1847-1905) m. Emily Morgan and second Cordelia Marvin; Laura (1849-1922) m. William Hawkes; Augusta (1852-1905) m. Prof. David Young Comstock. After John's death Augusta moved to Andover and ran a boarding house. She died in Andover, Massachusetts.

Tenney, Augusta Sprague (1852-1905) Fourth child of John Tenney and his second wife, Augusta Elizabeth (Sprague). Married Professor David Young Comstock in 1877. Resided in Andover in 1880 and, in 1900, St. Johnsbury, VT. Had one daughter who married John Bridgman.

Tenney, Edward Jarvis "Ned" (1833-1853) Second child of John Tenney and his first wife, Mary Augusta Bartlett. Born in Methuen. Edward's mother died in August 1837. Beginning at age 16 between the years 1850 and 1853, Edward wrote 62 letters to Mary Elizabeth "Lizzie" Andrews, his third cousin. Graduated Harvard Class of 1853, although he was suspended from Harvard, which was duly noted in the class notes. After graduating, at the age of 20,

Edward embarked on a voyage as a clerk aboard the steamship *San Francisco* bound for Valparaiso, Chile and California. His plan was to seek his fortune and return to Massachusetts to marry Lizzie. His was the first death of a member of the Harvard Class of 1853.

Tenney, Elizabeth Sprague "Liz" (1835-1895) Edward's sister. Third child of John Tenney and his first wife Mary Augusta Bartlett. Attended school in Lawrence. Liz never married and lived to be 60.

Tenney, John Elisha (1799-1853) Edward's father. Graduated from Dartmouth in 1824. Attorney and County Commissioner of Essex County. Served as a Representative and a Senator of the Massachusetts State legislature and was a member of the executive council. Married Mary Augusta Bartlett in 1830. Had four children: Margaret (1831-1839), Edward (1833-1853), Elizabeth (1835-1895) and Mary (1837-1905). Married second wife Augusta Elizabeth Sprague in 1844. Had four children: Margaret (1845-1905), John (1847-1905), Laura (1849-1922) and Augusta (1852-1905).

Tenney, John "Johnny" (1847-1905) Second child of John Tenney and his second wife Augusta Elizabeth (Sprague). Johnny was educated at Andover Academy and went to sea at the age of 14. Returned to the U.S. in 1864 and spent some time in the U.S. Navy. Married Emelie Letitia Morgan (1844-1884) in 1873. Had two children, John Tenney, Jr. and Ruth Morgan Tenney. After Emelie died Johnny married Cornelia Augusta Marvin (1864-1951) in 1890. One child: Eleanor (1892-1972) married Frederick Webster Cook (1883-1958). In 1870, Johnny entered the insurance business. In 1900, he lived with his family in Philadelphia and worked in the insurance industry as Manager of the Royal Fire Insurance Company of Liverpool, England, with offices in Philadelphia.

Tenney, Laura Sprague "Lottie" (1849-1922) Third child of John Tenney and his second wife Augusta Elizabeth (Sprague).

Married Dr. William H. Hawkes. Lived in Washington, DC. Died in Plainfield, New Jersey. No known children.

Tenney, Margaret Bartlett (1831-1839) First child of John Tenney and his first wife, Mary Augusta (Bartlett). Margaret was born and died in Methuen, Massachusetts at the age of eight.

Tenney, Margaret Bartlett "Margie" or "Maggie" (1845-1905) First child of John Tenney and his second wife Augusta Elizabeth Sprague. Married the Reverend Charles Langdon Mitchell in 1871 who ministered in New York, Pennsylvania, Missouri and Methuen, Massachusetts. He graduated from Yale and the Andover Theological Seminary. They had four children.

Tenney, Mary Augusta (Bartlett) (1804-1837) Edward's mother. Twelfth child born in Haverhill, Massachusetts to the Honorable Bailey Bartlett and Peggy White. Married John Tenney in 1830 and had four children: Margaret (1831-1839); Edward (1833-1853); Lizzie "Liz" in the story (1835-1895); and Mary (1837-1905). Lived in Methuen. Died the same month she gave birth to her fourth child, Mary Augusta Tenney.

Tenney, Mary Augusta (1837-1905) Fourth child of John Tenney and Mary Augusta Bartlett. Married the Honorable Joseph Sidney Howe in 1859. Had two children. Lived in Methuen.

Terry, Seth Hall (1818-1884) Married Harriet Leonard Sprague (1822-1884), daughter of Joseph E. Stearns and Sarah Leonard (Bartlett). Seth Hall Terry graduated from Union College NY in 1838. He was a lawyer in Troy, NY and Rochester, NY. They had three children: Walter Clark Terry (1858-1860), Seth Sprague Terry (1862-1932) and Grace Bartlett Terry (1864-).

Thillon, Anna (1819-1903) Born in London. An operatic singing sensation in the United States, based in San Francisco and then

New York. The English soprano studied with Bordogni, Tadolini and Claude Thomas Thillon, conductor of the Havre Philharmonic Society whom she later married. Favorite of Auber and created the role of Catarina in his "Les Diamants de la Couronne." Made rare appearances in the Jullien concerts 1855-1858.

Thompson, Mary L. (1835-) One of the "Chestnut Street" ladies who lived right next door to Lizzie Andrews. Her father was James W. Thompson, a clergyman. She had five younger siblings in 1850. The Thompsons were living in Roxbury, Massachusetts in 1870.

Truffi, Teresa (1825-) Opera singer. Married May 5, 1850 to Testo Benedetto, opera singer, age 33.

Tufts, Edwin O. (1823-1885) Born in Alstead, NH. Married Ruth Bradstreet (Foster) on Nov. 20, 1852 in Boston. Son of Walter Tufts and Almira (Towne). In 1870, census listed Tufts residing in Boston, dry goods merchant, age 47 wife with Ruth B. age 38 and son Walter B. age 11.

U

Unitarianism grew out of the congregationally independent churches, which Puritan New England had required. These churches initially followed Calvinistic doctrines, offering no religious choice to their parishioners, but shifted over time lessening the strict doctrines of original sin and predestination. The Puritan revival of the mid-1700s stressed eternal bondage to sin. People who opposed this doctrine, believing in "free human will" and the loving benevolence of God, came to call themselves Unitarians. By 1800, the First Church of Salem had split into four different churches, three of them Unitarian and one of them Congregational. Members of these different churches would become leaders of many social initiatives and reforms in the ensuing decades.

Upham, Charles Wentworth, Jr. (1834-1864) Attended Oliver Carlton's school in Salem. Graduated Harvard Class of 1852. In 1850,

U.S. Federal Census listed Charles as age 20 living with William H. Whittemore's family in Cambridge. He graduated from Dane Law School. Admitted to the Essex Bar. Set up a law practice in Salem but went abroad until 1857. When he returned, he went to Buffalo. Admitted to the New York Bar in 1857 and by 1859 was a partner of the Honorable S.G. Haven and Samuel Dorsheimer. Married Mr. Haven's daughter, Mary (1840-), on June 22, 1859 in Buffalo, Erie, New York. No children. Died at the age of 30 in Buffalo, New York.

Upham, Charles Wentworth, Sr. (1802-1875) Born in Saint John, New Brunswick. U.S. Representative from Massachusetts. Member and president of the Massachusetts Legislature. Seventh Mayor of Salem in 1852. Twice a member of the Massachusetts State House of Representatives. On March 29, 1826, Upham married Ann Susan Holmes, sister of Dr. Oliver Wendell Holmes. Fifteen children all born in Salem, Massachusetts. Only four lived to adulthood, including Charles Wentworth Upham, Jr. Died Salem, Massachusetts.

Upton, Daniel of Salem. Cannot conclusively confirm which Daniel Upton in the 1850 U.S. Federal Census is the one referenced in Edward's letters. First we find: Daniel, age 17, clerk, son of Benjamin Upton, Salem, Ward 1; Daniel, age 15, clerk, son of Benjamin Upton, Salem, ward 2. Secondly we find: Daniel Upton, Edward Upton and Francis Upton, children of Benjamin and Eliza Upton, all baptized May 7, 1839 (C.R.4) C.R. 4 East Church. This was the family in Ward 2, Salem. Edward mentions Daniel Upton several times: Daniel came to Salem with Henry Oliver; Daniel attended rehearsal of Musical Fund in Boston with Whittredges, Daniel went to Cambridge for a football game and Daniel writes to Edward to come to Dr. Holyoke's.

V – W

Van Voast, James (1827-1915) Born New York. Graduated West Point 1852. Survived wreck of the *San Francisco*. Rescued on the *Three Bells*. Brigadier General in 1904. Died in Cincinnati at age 88.

Walker, Judith (1826-1914) Lizzie's stepmother. Born in Maine. Married General Joseph Andrews, his second wife, on Jan. 15, 1857. Had three sons. Left a widow in 1869. The 1870 U.S. Federal Census, Boston, lists Clement age 12, Horace age 10 and Joseph age 7, all attending school. Lizzie lived with her father, stepmother and three half-brothers until she married in 1862, the year her third stepbrother was born. Judith had always taken an active part in various charitable organizations and was president of the South Friendly Society beginning in 1876. In 1886, president of the Woman's Auxiliary conference and, in 1889, president of the National Alliance of Unitarian and Other Liberal Christian Women.

Washington, Major John Marshall (1797-1853) Born in Virginia. Graduate of West Point 1817. Born in Fredericksburg, Virginia. Served as Governor of New Mexico 1848-1849. Assigned to lead troops from the 3rd Artillery Regiment to California. The steamer *San Francisco* ran into a storm and on Dec. 24, 1853 he was washed overboard, along with 181 soldiers, and drowned. Findagrave reports middle name 'Mcrae."

Watkins, Captain James Thomas (about 1810-1868) Captain of the steamship *San Francisco*. His father was a sea captain, also named Capt. James Watkins, and was lost at sea by shipwreck while returning to Baltimore from the West Indies. When his mother was dying she gave him and his sister Margaret to the care of her brother, Capt. Thomas Kennedy, formerly a shipmaster out of Baltimore. Capt. Watkins married Ellen Merriken in 1833 in Maryland. They had a son, James Thomas Watkins, born in 1839, and were living in San Francisco in 1860.

Webb, General James Watson (1802-1884) Army 1819-1827. Newspaperman for thirty years and diplomat. Publisher and Editor of the *New York Courier* (purchased the *New York Enquirer* in 1829). Webb had been indicted, convicted and sentenced to two years in Sing Sing Prison for acting as a second to Henry Clay in a duel with Tom Marshall. Governor William Seward pardoned him before he went behind bars. Married Laura Virginia Cram in 1849. Served for eight years as the minister to Brazil beginning in 1861.

Webb, Mrs. Stephen P. (1805-1895) Wife of former Salem Mayor Stephen P. Webb. Her name was Hannah Hunt Beckford (Robinson).

Webb, Stephen Palfrey (1804-1879) Born in Salem to Sarah (Putnam) and Stephen Palfrey Webb. Graduated Harvard Class of 1824. Studied law with Hon. John Glen King. Admitted to Essex County Bar. Law practice in Salem. Mayor of Salem 1842 through 1844. Sixth mayor of San Francisco 1854-1855. He was in San Francisco in 1853 and witnessed the violent mobs that ran through the city. Returned to Salem and became mayor of Salem 1860 through 1862. The 1860 U.S. Federal Census, Salem, Ward 3, lists Stephen P. Webb, age 55, occupation Mayor, living in a boarding house with Caroline B. 50, Caroline 16, Mary Fellows 28 and Caroline Fellows 11. Member Unitarian Church in Salem.

Webster, Daniel (1782-1852) Graduated Dartmouth in 1801. U.S. Statesman. Secretary of War under Presidents William Henry Harrison, John Tyler and Millard Fillmore. Served as the 14th and 19th Secretary of State. Served in House of Representatives for 10 years representing New Hampshire and in the Senate 19 years representing Massachusetts. Considered one of Senate's greatest orators. Member of the Senate's great triumvirate: Henry Clay, John C. Calhoun, Daniel Webster. Worked to preserve the Union in the years leading up to the Civil War. Supported the Compromise of 1850. Married twice: Grace (Fletcher) Webster (1781-1828), Abigail

(Eastman) Webster (1739-1816). Wikipedia lists 2nd wife: Caroline LeRoy Webster. Buried in Winslow Cemetery, Marshfield, Massachusetts. Cause of death: cerebral hemorrhage, (fall from horse).

Wheeler, David Everett (1805-1870) Son of John Brooks and Hannah (Hills), born in Grafton, Vermont. Preparatory studies were principally at Kimball Academy in Meriden, New Hampshire. After graduating, he passed one year at the Law School in Cambridge, Massachusetts and then moved to the city of New York where he studied with the Honorable Jonas Platt for two years. Admitted to the Bar in 1830. In 1844, elected a Representative to the State Legislature and a member of the Board of Education of the city of New York. Editor of two periodicals printed in New York City for four years. While a member of the Legislature, he was the author of a Report on the Quarantine Laws and, in 1851, of a Discourse before the Order of United Americans. Married on February 14, 1833 to Elizabeth Jarvis, daughter of the Honorable William Jarvis of Weathersfield, Vermont. Had five children, of whom Everett Pepperell and Mary Hannah, were living in 1852. Elizabeth died on July 27, 1848. David died on May 13, 1870 in New York City.

Whig Political Party. Consisted mostly of wealthy Southerners and eastern Industrialists who favored a national bank and strong national government. It split from the Democrats in 1832 and sent its candidate to the White House twice, once around 1851. Note: Major political parties of the time consisted of Republicans and Federalists. The Federalists were the more conservative party in 1792, compared to the more liberal views of the Republican Party of the time. Between 1872 and 1876, the Republican Party eventually became what we know today as the current Democratic Party. This was when Edward's Harvard chum William Dorsheimer went from being dismissed from Harvard to becoming a delegate to the Liberal Republican Convention in 1876.

White, Elisabeth (1742-1807) Lizzie's great grandmother married to Major Joseph Sprague (1739-1808).

Whittemore, Charles (1832-)

Whittemore, William H. (1834-1857) Born in Boston. The 1850 U.S. Federal Census, Cambridge, Massachusetts, lists William H. age 16, student, living with his parents Thomas Jefferson Whittemore age 52 and Susanna (Boardman) age 42. Also listed is Charles W. Upham age 20, student. Charles became a lawyer and was back at home in Salem in 1855. His father was Charles Wentworth Upham. In his senior year, William's eyesight began to fail. Died of consumption, age 23, at his father's home in Cambridge in 1857. Unmarried.

Whittredge, Mary C. (1835-) Edward mentions seeing the Whittredge ladies with Daniel Upton. The 1850 U.S. Federal Census, Salem Ward 4, lists Mary as age 15, with parents Thomas C. Whittredge and Susan L., along with her sister Susan, age 17, and brother Charles, age 8. (see Thomas C. Whittredge)

Whittredge, Susan L. (1833-) - see Thomas C. Whittredge.

Whittredge, Captain Thomas Cook (1799-1854) Sea captain. Harvard Class of 1818. Resided in Salem. Married Susan Louisa Mead in 1827. Had five daughters and a son.

Wilson, Davies (1830-1905) Edward's chum at Harvard. Eldest child of Israel and Caroline (Davies) Wilson of Cincinnati, Ohio. His youth involved considerable travel. Summers were spent in Warren County, Massachusetts at his grandfather's. He "kept school" at Lancaster, Massachusetts during his winter break from Harvard his senior year. In 1853, he was engaged in laying railway from Cincinnati to Cleveland. In 1855, he surveyed the proposed town of Manhattan, Kansas. In 1859, he was admitted to the bar. Held numerous offices in Kansas 1860-1862. In 1861, elected clerk of first Kansas State Senate. In 1862, member of the lower house. In 1863, Aid-de-camp on General Ewing's staff. In 1865 commissioned Captain in 3rd Brigade of Kansas State Militia. In 1871 married Mehitable Calef Coppenhagen and settled in Cincinnati. His estate presented to the City of Cincinnati was known as "Wilson Common" on Price Hill. He returned to Cambridge in his final years.

Wilson, Carrie (about 1835-) Sister of Edward's chum at Harvard, Davies Wilson.

Winder, Brig. General Charles Sidney (1829-1862) Born in Talbot County, MD. Graduated West Point in 1851. Survived the wreck of the *San Francisco* and was praised for "energy and courage". Rescued aboard the *Antarctic*. Confederate officer in the American Civil War. Killed at the Battle of Cedar Mountain on Aug. 9, 1862.

Wyse, Maj. Francis Octavius (1811-1893) Graduated from the United States Military Academy in 1837. Rescued aboard the *Three Bells* following disaster at sea of the *San Francisco*. His wife, Mary Elza (Pope) Wyse (1834-1925) and child were rescued by the *Lucy Thompson* or *Titan*.

X-Y-Z

Lizzie's Uncles, Aunts and Siblings

Joseph ANDREWS married
(1773-1824)

<u>**Daniel**</u>	<u>**Eliza**</u>	<u>John</u>	<u>Joseph</u>
(1798-1879)	(1800-1876)	(1801-1835)	(1803-1803)
*	*	*	*

Key

* = never married

m = married

Bold = living between 1850-1854

<u>Underline </u> = ANDREWS bloodline

CAPS = Family Name

For more information:

See **Who's Who in the Courtship of Lizzie Andrews**

in the ANDREWS Family

Mary Bell had seven children - one married
(1774-1856)

<u>Mary Jane</u>	**<u>Dolly Ann Watkins</u>**	<u>Joseph A.</u>
(1804-1829)	(1806-1877)	(1808-1869)
*	*	

m 1st

Elizabeth Maria Sprague
(1809-1841)

3 children

<u>Joseph Sprague</u>
(1833-1861)
*

<u>Mary Elizabeth "Lizzie"</u>
(1835-1922)

<u>Laura Josephine</u>
(1837-1893)

m 2nd
Judith Walker
1826-1914)

<u>Clement Walker</u>
(1858-1930)
*

<u>Horace Davis</u>
(1859-1910)
*

<u>Joseph L.</u>
(1862-1937)

Lizzie's and Edward's Uncles, Aunts and Cousins

Hon. Joseph SPRAGUE, Jr. married
(1771-1833)

Edward	Elizabeth Maria	Lucretia Osgood
(1808-1842)	(1809-1841)	(1812-1839)
*	m	m
	Joseph A. ANDREWS	John Thompson
	(1808-1869)	
		Lucretia
	Joe	(1839-1906)
	(1833-1861)	
	*	
	"Lizzie"	
	(1835-1922)	
	Laura	
	(1837-1893)	

Key

* = never married

m = married

Bold = living between 1850-1854

Underline = SPRAGUE bloodline

CAPS = Family Name

For more information:

See **Who's Who in the Courtship of Lizzie Andrews**

in the SPRAGUE Family

Margaret Osgood had eleven children - seven lived to adulthood
(1778 - bef. July 1837)

Margaret	**Mary Louisa**	**Laura White**	**Augusta Elizabeth**
(1813-1860)	(1815-1875)	(1816-after 1859)	(1819-1874)
m	m	m	m
William NICHOLS (1794-1861)	**John FELLOWS** (1815-1887)	**George ALLEN** (1813-1852)	**John TENNEY** (1799-1853)
	Charles (1845-1924)	**Mamie** (1851-1922)	**"Maggie"** (1845-1905)
	Louisa (1846-1894)	**"Frankie"** (1852-1853) *	**"Johnny"** (1847-1905)
	Edward (1848-1919) *		**"Lottie"** (1849-1922)
	Elizabeth (1853-1914) *		**Augusta** (1852-1905)

Edward's Uncles, Aunts and Cousins

<u>Hon. Bailey BARTLETT</u> married
(1750-1830)

<u>Anna Bailey</u>	<u>Eliza</u>	**<u>Margaret "Peggy"</u>**	<u>Harriett</u>
(1787-1869)	(1789-1817)	(1790-1880)	(1792-1820)
m	m	m	*
Hon. William JARVIS	**Joseph E. (Stearns) SPRAGUE**	**Dr. Rufus LONGLEY**	
(1770-1859)	(1782-1852)	(1788-1854)	
10 children	*5 children*	*4 children*	

<u>Mary</u>	**<u>Abigail Osgood</u>**	**<u>Charles Leonard</u>**	<u>Mary Augusta</u>
(1799-1802)	(1801-1894)	(1802-1883)	(1804-1837)
*	m	m	m
	Rev. Moses KIMBALL	**Harriet Dorothy (Plummer)**	**John Elisha TENNEY**
	(1799-1868)	(1805-1901)	(1799-1853)
		7 children	*4 children*

Key

* = never married

m = married

Bold = living between 1850-1854

<u>Underline</u> = BARTLETT bloodline

CAPS = Family Name

For more information:

See **Who's Who in the Courtship of Lizzie Andrews**

in the BARTLETT Family

Peggy Leonard (White) had 15 children
(1766-1831)

Sarah Leonard
(1793-1864)
m
Joseph E. (Stearns) SPRAGUE
(1782-1852)

4 children

Bailey
(1794-1886)
m
Caroline (Long)
(1803-1902)
2 children

Katherine
(1795-1787)
m
1st Hon. John MEACHAM
(1776-1848)

2nd **Joseph Barlow FELT**
(1789-1869)

Edwin
(1796-1867)
m
Caroline Eliza (Harrod)
(1809-1893)

Frederick Augustus
(1805-1805)
*

Francis
(1806-1848)
m
Caroline Cogswell (Kneeland)
(1815-1864)
1 child

Louisa Amelia
(1809-1840)
m
Oliver CARLTON
(1801-1882)
4 children

Edward's Uncles, Aunts and Cousins

<u>Schubael TENNEY</u> married
(1739-1823)

<u>Capt. Shubael</u>	Martha	Samuel	Isaac
(1769-1830)	(1771-1842)	(1773-1803)	(1776-1817)
m	m	*	m

Mary "Polly" (Jameson) (1776-1824)
3 children listed below

William PARKER (1773-1815)

1st Eliza Jameson

2nd Anna Mitchell (1782-1858)

<u>**John Elisha**</u>	<u>**Shubael**</u>
(1799-1853)	(1801-1870)
m	m

1st Mary Augusta (Bartlett)
(1804-1837)
4 children

<u>Margaret Bartlett</u> 1831-1839

<u>Edward Jarvis</u> 1833-1853

<u>Elizabeth "Liz" Sprague</u> 1835-1895

<u>Mary Augusta</u> 1837-1905

2nd **Augusta Elizabeth (Sprague)**
(1819-1874)
4 children

<u>Margaret Bartlett "Maggie"</u> 1845-1905

<u>John</u> 1847-1905

<u>Laura Sprague "Lottie"</u> 1849-1922

<u>Augusta Sprague</u> 1852-1905

1st **Mary Ann (Fullwood)**
(-1847)
5 children

<u>John Jameson</u> 1833-1833

<u>Charles Burnham</u> 1835-1861

<u>Mary Jane</u> 1837-1844

<u>John B.</u> 1839-1870

<u>Eugene Lison</u> 1841-

2nd Dorothea Louise (Woodruff)

in the TENNEY Family

Martha Noyes had 8 children
(1743-1840)

Capt. William	Catherine	Rebecca	Mary "Polly"
(1778-1846)	(1781-)	(1784-1797)	(1786-1882)
m	m	*	*
Mary (Titcomb)	Robert OBER		
(about 1784-1872)	(1785-1829)		

<u>Elizabeth Jameson</u>

(1807-1892)

m

John CLARK

(1804-1890)

3 children

Key

* = never married

m = married

Bold = living between 1850-1854

<u>Underline</u> = TENNEY bloodline

CAPS = Family Name

For more information:

See Who's Who in the Courtship of Lizzie Andrews

Acknowledgements

I could not have completed this book, and therefore this trilogy, without the support of several people. In particular, I am grateful to my book designer Barb Ries who, with the patience of a saint, spent countless hours with me arranging the copy in myriad complex layouts, and to Teri Mathis for her expert technical assistance.

I am grateful for the support and encouragement of my husband George, who endured hours and days without my attention as I toiled to complete book three. George refused to read any of the books until he could read all three in immediate succession. His response was delightful: "I knew you could write, but this is really good, honey!"

I could not have completed the copy without the encouragement and retreat to the deafening silence provided by Keith and Janet Johnson's secluded off-the-grid cabin near Colville.

I am so grateful for my mother who was on-call to research 'just one more person' and 'just one more event,' answering questions to ensure historical accuracy of the story. She is also the sole author of *Who's Who in the Courtship of Lizzie Andrews*, having conducted all the primary-source research contained in that section. At 89 years old, she doesn't miss a beat.

I am grateful to my reader friends Mary McCheyne, RC Fahlgren and fellow author Steven C. Schneider who provided feedback and suggestions as the story unfolded.

Thank you to other readers of the first two books for their encouraging comments, including my baby sister Cindy who called me in tears (of joy) one day saying, "I just finished reading a bootlegged copy of book three! Thank you for writing this! Now I know what happened to Posie! I have her locket with her hair."

Mom, you no longer need to sneak copies to family. We finished!

www.ingramcontent.com/pod-product-compliance
Lightning Source LLC
Chambersburg PA
CBHW060935120726

47910CB00002B/339